FIDDLER'S FERRY is the fifth novel in Iris Gower's six-book sequence about South Wales at the turn of the century. It is set in Sweyn's Eye (the old name for Swansea) just after World War I.

The story centres around the Llewelyn family whose livelihood largely depends on the ferry, run by Siona Llewelyn, the kindly yet rugged head of the family. The family is large but close knit, held together by their mother Emily — a hard-working woman made old before her time having borne seven sons now with child once again.

Into the centre of this web comes Nerys Beynon, seeking work and lodging. Discovering both in the Llewelyn household she finds her role as an employee gradually changing until she becomes the central force struggling to keep the family united after Emily's death. This becomes an almost impossible task as she finds herself the cause of family conflict.

To Rosie, whose vision and faith helped create six books out
of one small chapter.

FIDDLER'S FERRY

Iris Gower

CORGI BOOKS

FIDDLER'S FERRY
A CORGI BOOK   0 552   13315 9

Originally published in Great Britain by Century Hutchinson Ltd.

PRINTING HISTORY

Century Hutchinson edition published 1987
Corgi edition published 1988

This book is set in 10/11 Melior

Corgi Books are published by Transworld Publishers Ltd., 61-63 Uxbridge Road, Ealing, London W5 5SA, in Australia by Transworld Publishers (Australia) Pty. Ltd., 15-23 Helles Avenue, Moorebank, NSW 2170, and in New Zealand by Transworld Publishers (N.Z.) Ltd., Cnr. Moselle and Waipareira Avenues, Henderson, Auckland.

Made and printed in Great Britain by
Cox & Wyman Ltd, Reading

CHAPTER ONE

The river rushed and bounded towards the sea – dark water, deep and mysterious, chillingly silver where the light of the moon cut a pathway of brilliance. A lone tug forged upstream, lamplight shimmering briefly on the restless river before disappearing from sight.

Sweyn's Eye was a town asleep, the streets silent and empty, houses clothed in darkness. Even the sparks from the chimneys of the copper and lead works were subdued, as though paying tribute to the perfect summer night.

Nerys Beynon shivered; the tears dried on her cheeks and she stared at the light from the tug for as long as it cast a glow, for it was a last link with life before she was plunged into a silent world of darkness.

She descended the broad wooden steps that led her closer to the water which sucked and tore the weeds along the bank, and stared into the dark depths; it would be so easy to slip into the river, to feel the water cover her and take away her pain.

She stepped forward, her eyes downcast, her ears listening only to the call of the river. It would be good to be at peace, to feel no longer the bite of humiliation and the rejection that twisted and turned within her.

She moved further out from the bank, the coldness welcome now as heat encompassed her body. How could she continue to live now among the people who had witnessed her shame?

The river held her in a chill embrace, the undercurrents taking her away from the bank, downward in the

5

direction of the open sea. As the water washed over her head, it was like being in a green-grey world of coldness, with fronds of weed waving to her as though they were beckoning arms; she closed her eyes, resisting the urge to fight against the river and the darkness.

Her thoughts became muddled, her being seemed to fade – to become spirit-like and without substance. She was filled then with terror, her hands striking out desperately as she tried to grasp at the thin weeds which waved towards her in ghostly silence. She kicked against the pull of the current, hampered by her skirts and knowing in that moment that she wanted to live.

Suddenly through the darkness there was a light. It was drawing closer to her and in spite of her reeling senses, she heard the slap of wood against water, the creaking of planking above her head. She felt herself sink once more beneath the river, out of reach and out of sight. Her entire body was jolted as her long loose hair was caught in strong hands. She gasped with pain and then she was lifted roughly out of the river.

She took in great gulps of air, her lungs straining, her senses reeling. She saw through a haze the brightness of the star-filled sky, smelled the tangy scent of the sea and the pure joy of being alive filled her as she fell against the damp-smelling wood at the bottom of the craft and lay there helplessly.

Gentle arms lifted her; she was held close against a broad shoulder, her soaked and matted hair was pushed away from her face and a soft voice spoke to her; though she heard nothing of the words above her own harsh breathing, she clung gratefully to a strong neck – there was warmth here and kindness and she needed both.

She began to cry, silently at first and then unashamedly, her eyes closed as she remained clasped in a warm, strong embrace. When she was spent she fell into a silent lethargy, content to be held close and warm without questioning.

At last, she was set down and the boat moved

rhythmically towards the bank. She remained quiescent, not considering her fate but leaving everything to the oarsman who had rescued her from the river and thus made himself responsible for her.

When the boat gently bumped the broad wooden steps of the bank, she felt herself lifted and laid her head down on the broad shoulder once more with a sigh of weariness.

A small hut stood solid against the pale dawn sky and from within came the cheerful glow of a fire. The warmth of the hut surrounded her and she allowed herself to be set in a chair without demur for here, she sensed, was sanctuary.

The dark figure flickered into life as the light from the oil-lamp illuminated the hut. She sighed softly, her eyes meeting his and they stared at each other for a long moment in silence, she unable to speak of her gratitude to the big man who had taken her from the river.

Siona Llewelyn remained silent, passive, as though waiting for some sign from the large-eyed girl seated before him. He was a big, handsome man of middle years; his dark springy hair held traces of silver, but the eyes set deep in the weatherbeaten face were green like a stormy sea and gleamed with a love of life. Too much love of life, some said, for his wife Emily was big with child again and she a woman past her fortieth year. And, he told himself, he was a man who had no right to be feeling strange stirrings within him, a half understood longing for his lost youth.

Siona's life was the river; she brought in his daily bread and he loved her as though she was a secret mistress; she and his wife Emily had been all he'd ever needed. He had inherited the halfpenny ferry-boat which had been passed down through four generations, carrying passengers across the River Swan in all but the worst of weathers, and by siring seven sons had ensured that the boat would remain in Llewelyn hands for many years to come.

'Going into the river is not the answer, *merchi*,' Siona said, startling Nerys as she watched him stir up the fire before adding fresh logs. 'Running away never solved anything.'

She didn't answer, she could not for there was no excuse she could make. It seemed to her now that there was nothing so bad that it was worth the taking of her own life.

He looked into the fire and she watched the strong line of his shoulders with a feeling of reassurance; he was a good man, this one who had saved her life, she could talk to him.

'This was to have been my wedding day,' she said softly, and thought of the fine silk frock which had hung behind the door in her lodgings, waiting to be slipped over her head and to make her into a beautiful bride. 'But I was a fool ever to believe in sweet promises and softly spoken words of love.'

Siona seemed to look right into her, his green eyes glowing redly in the light from the fire. He seemed so wise, so strong that she felt suddenly foolish.

'So you were let down, *merchi*, and your pride hurt; that doesn't mean that a fine-looking young woman like you should give up on life.' He paused and shook his head at her. 'This man – whoever he was – can't be worth a light, for anyone who would turn his back on a lovely girl like you must be a half-wit!'

Nerys sank back in her chair, her breath suddenly short, the pain within her growing and spreading as she saw behind closed lids the tall, thin frame of Terrence Marsh, a sophisticated man who had played in almost every theatre in the land. He had stood before her, his handsome face alight, and begged her to be his wife. Had he been acting even then?

The wedding had been arranged with such haste that there had been whispers from the townsfolk and curious, searching glances at her waistline. She had been a little angry at first and then amused, for

Terrence was nothing if not a gentleman and had done little more than chastely kiss her cheek.

'He took my money,' she said, forcing the words from numb lips. 'All my life's savings; I have nothing left.' He was right, this big man standing before her; her pride was hurt more than anything, for if she was honest hadn't she seen Terrence as a last chance to escape spinsterhood, and hadn't the prospect of being a married woman seemed more attractive than actually being Terrence's wife?

Siona crouched suddenly before her, his big shoulders hunched forward, his eyes compassionate.

'You've got the manner of a spirited girl, a hard worker capable of making a living. I'm not wrong, am I?'

As Nerys looked into the green eyes, suddenly his approbation seemed very important to her. 'Hard work is no stranger to me. Since the time I left St Thomas's School, I've earned my own keep.'

She sighed, remembering Sutton's Drapery Store, the bits of cotton and velvet which clung to the wooden floor that needed to be swept every day, the smell of the bales of cloth and the sharp crunch of the scissors biting through new material.

It was there at the drapery store that she had met Mary Sutton – 'Big Mary' as she was affectionately called. Mary had employed Nerys to be nanny to her son and later, when she took the boy off to America, never forgetting her own poverty Mary had left Nerys with a nest-egg – insurance for the future, she called it. Well, thought Nerys wistfully, her nest-egg was gone now and so was her future.

'I've been such a gullible fool,' she said softly. 'How could I be so mistaken in a man? I should have seen he was simply after my money.'

'Now then, *merchi*,' Siona smiled. 'Don't be too hard on yourself; where feelings are concerned, we can all act the fool.' He moved away abruptly. 'And as

9

to marriage, you've got plenty of time yet – you're just a young bit of a thing.' He stared at her, his eyes level. 'You can find work again, can't you? Or have you let this man knock all the spirit out of you?'

Nerys sat up straighter and, becoming aware of the wetness of her clothes, held the cotton skirt away from her legs. Siona turned away and threw another log on to the flames.

'Look, I've got to get back to the ferry – it'll soon be time for the lead workers to go on the first shift. You take off those wet things and get them dried by the fire.' He moved to the door. 'I only use the hut to make myself cups of tea and such, to save going up to the house. No one will bother you here. You get some sleep and then when you've rested, think things over with a fresh mind, righto?' There was such warmth in his expression that Nerys felt tears burn her eyes.

'There, there, *merchi*.' He didn't touch her, but his smile was crooked and full of compassion and it was as though he had taken her in his arms and was holding her tenderly. She wanted to cling to his strength, if only for a moment, but he was moving away from her.

At the door he paused and smiled back at her. 'Now promise me you won't go making any more silly moves; the river is as busy as the *Stryd Fawr* now that it's getting light, so you'd be seen, mind.'

She swallowed hard. 'I'm over that foolishness now, and I'm very grateful to you for . . . for your help.'

'You've got friends in Sweyn's Eye, haven't you, *merchi*?' he said, quickly dismissing her gratitude. 'People who care about you?'

Nerys shook her head. 'There's no one of my very own. All my life I've been alone, my only friends the people I worked with or for. I have no family, that's what I thought Terrence would be . . .' Her voice trailed away into silence.

'Forget him!' He spoke firmly. 'That man was a

10

no-good, only the lowest toe-rag would take a girl's money and run, you're best off without him.' He smiled through his anger and his eyes were light and green as the sun through the sea.

Then she was alone in the warmth of the little hut, the sounds of the river outside a constant reminder of what she had tried to do. Quickly she took off her clothes and spread them out over the back of a chair, standing it near the fire so that steam began to rise like spirals of mist in the air.

She wrapped herself in a heavy woollen blanket and lay down on the makeshift bed in the corner. Suddenly feeling unutterably weary, she smiled ruefully to herself; being jilted and throwing herself into the river had knocked the stuffing out of her! As she closed her eyes, she thought of the man who had rescued her, Siona Llewelyn. He seemed so wise, so caring – what a pity Terrence Marsh had not been more like that. And strangely, the thought of the man who had robbed and humiliated her no longer hurt quite so much; Siona was right – she was better off alone.

Sunlight was streaming on to her face when she opened her eyes and Nerys sat up, seeing the outline of a figure against the brilliance.

'Siona?' she said softly and the man moved forward, something in his bearing hostile as he came into her line of vision.

'Sorry to disappoint you.' The voice was smooth, the Welshness flattened out into what was the voice of a preacher or a scholar.

Nerys sat up and held on to the blanket, her eyes becoming accustomed to the light as she stared up slowly in recognition.

'Howel, Howel Llewelyn,' she said softly. 'Don't you remember me? I'm Nerys Beynon, we were at St Thomas's School together?'

He thrust his hands into his pockets. 'How could I

ever forget? You were the cause of a bitter fist-fight between my brother Ceri and me, the only real fight we ever had!'

The picture flashed into her mind with the sudden surprising clarity of childhood memories. Howel, a tall boy even at thirteen years of age, pulling at the ribbon on her crisp white apron, tearing it with harsh fingers. She had begged him to stop, for she knew it would mean a sharp beating from her auntie who barely tolerated the orphaned child's presence beneath her roof.

Only when she dissolved into hot, bitter tears had Ceri Llewelyn stepped in. He was younger than his brother and much smaller, but his righteous indignation had lent him strength. He had struck out in fury and it was Howel who had backed off, holding a spotless handkerchief to his bleeding nose.

'That was a long time ago,' she said defensively and her colour rose as Howel smiled dryly.

'Yes, indeed, and now it seems you have entered my life again as paramour to my father.'

His meaning took several seconds to become clear and Nerys felt shock ripple through her, dismayed by the sudden knowledge that Siona was a married man with grown-up sons. Had she been foolish enough then to think he might care at all for the waif he'd pulled from the sea?

Then came anger at Howel's insulting assumption that she was warming Siona's bed.

'Still as nasty as ever,' she said smoothly. 'Never did think kindly of anyone, did you?'

He met her eyes and she looked away first, frightened by the intensity of his gaze.

'I think the evidence of my own eyes is enough proof of your virtue or lack of it,' he said in a deceptively soft voice. 'It isn't every day that I come upon a half-naked woman lying in my father's hut – "warming his bed", to use your own words.'

She turned her face away from him. 'There's no reason why I should explain myself to you,' she said in a low voice, 'but for the sake of Siona's good name I'll try.'

'Don't bother to think up any lies for my benefit,' he interrupted quickly. 'What my father does with his time is none of my business.' He smiled. 'I suppose I should congratulate the old man on his enthusiasm.'

Nerys stared at him icily. 'Well, I will say this: the old wolf has more guts than the young whelp!'

'What a charming turn of phrase!' Howel's sarcasm was like a blow, and Nerys fell back against the cushions and closed her eyes.

'Just go away,' she said in a low voice. 'I have nothing to say to you.' She faced the old stone of the wall, seeing the mellowness of the colours under the glow of the sun, concentrating on the changing patterns of light and shade and willing him to leave her alone.

'Where did you meet the old man?' Howel leaned over her and she hated the knowing smile on his face. He was a handsome man, she realized, a younger version of his father; yet his appearance lacked the compelling charm that Siona wore like a cloak.

'I met him out there, in the river,' she said fiercely. 'I was trying to drown myself — if you look at my clothes, you'll see that they are still wet. Now does that satisfy you?'

He sat down on the edge of the bed and the cocky smile had gone; he rubbed his hand through his thick hair and sighed heavily.

'I can only say I'm sorry.' He shook his head, his eyes searching hers with apparent concern.

She sat up, willing at once to be friends with this man who was so like Siona in many ways and yet somehow different.

'I need a job,' she said softly, 'and I need lodgings too.' She shrugged. 'I might as well tell you the truth.

13

I've made a fool of myself over a man, allowed him to dupe me and to rob me. Now I've nothing except what I stand up in.'

'Let me help you.' He put his hand into his pocket and took out a leather wallet, but Nerys shook her head.

'I can't accept money.' She stared at him curiously. He was so different now from the man who had stood and sneered at her, who a few minutes ago had been so willing to believe ill of her.

'Of course not.' He rose to his feet. 'Well, I'm going into town this morning, it's the opening of the Queen's Dock and I'm taking my pupils to see the new rolling bridge.' He smiled. 'And to watch the procession led by the King and Queen, of course. I shall have a word in as many ears as possible; there are bound to be plenty of influential people at the ceremony.'

'There's good of you.' Nerys stared down at her hands and bit her lip, wondering why he was being so kind. Perhaps, she thought charitably, he wanted to make amends for his earlier bad humour.

The door swung open and two young boys stood in the sunshine, staring at Nerys in surprise. Howel smiled as he caught them by the arm.

'These two hooligans are my brothers,' he said warmly. 'This is Tom and the one with jam on his face is William.'

'Our mam says we must see if you've got lost over by here – supposed to be fetching dad for his breakfast, you are.' William, the younger of the boys, stared up at his brother with wide eyes and then his gaze moved to Nerys.

'I think,' Howel glanced ruefully at Nerys, 'you'd better come over to the house and meet my mother, otherwise the story that these two might tell could land my father in a lot of trouble!'

Nerys glanced at her clothes and at once, Howel ushered the boys outside. 'Come on, you two, get off to the school yard; I'll follow in a minute.'

Nerys dressed quickly; there were only a few damp patches left on her skirt and blouse, but the garments were creased and stained with the sea water. She shrugged; there was nothing she could do about it.

The kitchen of the Ferry House was sunlit and warm and as Nerys followed Howel inside, she felt a sense of belonging – it was almost as though she had been there before. A gingham cloth fell neatly over the table and the curtains on the windows matched the covers on the plump cushions.

The woman standing before the fire was handsome, with high cheekbones and fine dark eyes. She was small of stature but somehow imposing, and beneath her spotless white apron was an unmistakable swelling.

'Mam,' Howel said softly, 'this is Nerys Beynon. Had an accident, she did, and dad rescued her from the river.'

Emily took charge at once. 'Good heavens, girl, your clothes are in a dreadful state! Come with me to the bedroom and we'll find you something to wear before you take a chill.' She smiled and her eyes seemed golden. 'I wasn't always this size – we should be able to fit you out all right and then it's a hot cup of tea for you and a bite to eat.' She turned to her son. 'There's nothing more to be done here; you go and see to your work, Howel.'

Nerys saw the door close behind Howel with a sense of relief. She was uneasy in his company, even though his attitude – after the initial reaction of hostility – had been kindly. She was grateful that she was asked no questions; she was in need and that was enough for Siona's wife.

The blouse Emily handed her was high-necked and old-fashioned but scented with lavender and spotlessly clean. 'This is the only skirt that will fit you,' Emily said. 'You have such a tiny waist, and to think I was like that once – a long time ago, mind!'

Nerys changed her clothes and Emily immediately took up the discarded blouse and skirt.

'These can go in with my wash,' she said. 'I have made a start, it being Monday and a lovely blowing day, but my boys do hold me up expecting a big breakfast before they go out.' She smiled proudly. 'Our Howel is a teacher, mind, over at St Thomas's; taking some of his class for an outing, he is today.'

As Nerys followed Emily back to the kitchen, she saw Siona enter the room, so big that his size filled the doorway. She smiled at him warmly and he put his head on one side as though studying her.

'Well, Nerys Beynon, my Emily's seen you all right then?'

'Aye, well, I couldn't leave her in those damp things,' Emily said. 'Catch a death of cold, she would.' She gestured to the table. 'Sit you both down and I'll get some bacon cooking – set you up right for the day, will a good breakfast!'

Hungry though she was, Nerys could scarcely swallow the food set before her. She was very much aware of Siona at her side; she felt the warmth of his smile and glanced up to see the light in his green eyes as he met her gaze.

'Howel's going to speak to a few people, see if he can't find you a position with one of the rich folk he mixes with.' There was pride in Siona's voice as he spoke of his son and Nerys wondered if her first impressions of Howel had been unfortunate. He seemed harsh and only too willing to condemn her, yet could she blame him? After all, he had found her lying naked in his father's hut, so what was he supposed to think?

'Why don't you and me follow our Howel down into town?' Siona leaned forward and smiled at Nerys. 'Big Eddie is just lying upstairs in bed; it's about time my second son pulled a bit of weight around here – he can take charge of the boat for an hour or two.'

'Good idea,' Emily put in. 'Come to think of it, Siona, you might see your niece down there among the toffs. Mali Llewelyn might have a job of sorts to offer Nerys.'

'Mali Richardson, she is now,' Siona said as he turned to Nerys. 'Married Sterling Richardson, copper boss; gone up in the world, she has, but not a snob, mind.'

Nerys smiled slowly. 'I know Mali slightly – a friend of Mary Sutton, she was. Came to the house sometimes and left her children with me in the nursery when I was looking after little Stephan Sutton.'

'Enough chatting, off with the two of you, then,' Emily said with mock severity. 'I've got work to do.'

'Righto.' Siona rose from his chair and grimaced at Nerys. 'When the boss speaks, it's time to move.'

It was strange to walk into the town beside Siona Llewelyn; it was almost as though she was seeing Sweyn's Eye for the first time and she sensed the excitement that seemed to crackle in the air. Cockle-women walked straight-backed, made graceful by the burden carried on proud heads; barefooted boys hurried along sun-warmed pavements towards the docks and mothers nursing babies in shawls eagerly left the darkness and poverty of dingy courts behind them.

'Seems everyone wants to see the procession,' Siona said. 'The Queen's Dock has been in use for more than a year, yet there's so much excitement about the official opening!'

He took Nerys's arm to cross the road just as the police band struck up a rousing if shaky version of 'Rule, Britannia'. The press of people on the cracked pavements cheered as the royal coach drew up to the docks entrance.

'Look at the lovely flowers,' Nerys said softly, aware that her brush with death had somehow made her more appreciative of life. Bright marigolds covered

17

the roof of the coach, spelling out the initials 'G.R.' with small flowers forming the shape of a crown. A riot of rambler roses covered the entire coach within which sat Queen Mary and at her side King George V of England.

'Lot of nonsense!' Siona said as shouts of 'God Bless Queen Mary!' rang out around them. 'Only people like us they are, after all.' Yet even as he spoke there was a smile of pride in his green eyes.

The Queen left the plush greenness of her seat and rose graciously, lifting her gloved hand to the crowd. She was tall and stately, graceful as she climbed on to the raised dais decorated with flags that fluttered in the breeze from the water. Ceremoniously, the Queen pressed a button and the rolling lift bridge moved with majestic slowness. The crowds pressed closer as with a blast of a siren, a tug steamed through the opening, leaving a crystal wake behind as it made a symbolic entrance into the dock. To her surprise, Nerys found herself cheering with the people and her eyes were moist with tears of pride.

'There's our Howel with his class of pupils,' Siona said, taking Nerys's arm. 'See how good he is with those children – a born teacher, isn't he?'

Nerys saw that Howel was engrossed in his pupils, who open-mouthed stared at King George as he waved his stick in the air. She warmed to Howel as he encouraged the boys to salute and the girls to curtsey. Like herself, he loved working with children, so surely that should make some sort of bond between them?

'Come on,' Siona said urgently. 'I can see my niece. *Duw*, Mali looks beautiful enough to eat.'

Nerys swallowed hard as Siona led her forward through the crowd. Mali Richardson was impeccably dressed in a cream silk dress covered by a lace jacket and she appeared unapproachable.

However, Siona obviously didn't share Nerys's

fears, for he strode up to Mali and took her into his arms in a bear-like hug.

'Uncle Siona, there's lovely to see you! Isn't this a splendid occasion, the King and Queen and Princess Mary actually opening the new dock?' Mali kissed his cheek, her eyes alight and in that moment, the family resemblance was striking.

Hanging back nervously, Nerys watched as Siona spoke urgently to his niece. She felt Mali's eyes upon her and took a deep breath before moving forward.

'Do you remember me?' she blurted out. 'It's been a long time – I'm Nerys Beynon and I worked for Mary Sutton, looking after her boy.'

'Of course I remember you!' Mali spoke warmly and Nerys wondered briefly exactly what Siona had said to his niece. 'I understand you're looking for a position? Well, I can offer you a job just while the children are on holidays, if that's any good.' She smiled. 'The little monsters come home at the weekend, which would give you a few days to settle in.'

Nerys felt Siona's hand on her arm in what she knew was a gesture of reassurance and she smiled up at him in gratitude. With his sound common sense, he had made her see that she had everything to live for.

'Thank you, Mrs Richardson,' she said humbly and Mali laughed, putting her gloved hand on Nerys's arm.

'*Duw*, call me Mali or you'll make me feel about a hundred years old, mind!' She leaned forward and kissed Siona's cheek. 'See you soon, uncle. We'd best be going; I can see Sterling waiting by the car for me.' She turned to Nerys, taking her arm. 'You might as well come along with me now – we're just about to go home.'

As she sat on the plush seat of the gleaming car,

Nerys felt that events were moving so swiftly that she was left breathless. She turned and, looking back, saw Siona standing beside Howel and both of them watching her departure with mixed expressions – two strong, handsome men.

She thought of Terrence and in that moment knew that she had never loved him, she had been fascinated, bewitched, but not in love.

Suddenly she felt afraid and tears burned her lids. She dragged her gaze away from the two men and looked ahead of her; she was making a new beginning and it seemed she must make it alone.

CHAPTER TWO

The swish of the river and the calling of the bargees were sounds so familiar to Emily Llewelyn that she had long ceased to hear them, but the noise of sirens blaring over the waters was an intrusion. She dried her hands on her apron and eased herself upright, pushing away from the ridge-bottomed zinc bath, weary of the smell of soda and the feel of soap going soft and awkward from constant rubbing against cotton sheets.

Slowly, she made her way towards the door, moving heavily now that her time was drawing near; her back ached and her legs were swollen to twice their normal size.

She was too old for motherhood. This was the time of life when she should be nursing grandchildren, talking with old friends of the days when watercress grew in streams, there were chestnut woods over at Llangafelach and the Foxhole road was simply a narrow track. But she had lost touch with her friends long ago and except for her family had time to spare for no one. The meeting with Nerys Beynon earlier this morning had disrupted her usual complacency, for she had sensed the girl might in some way be a threat.

On the ferry steps, Emily shaded her eyes from the sun, but it was pleasant to feel the warmth on her face. The summer had been a poor one and it was already the middle of July.

Her husband looked up from beside his boat with a

21

smile in his green eyes and she melted with warmth for him. How could she deny him his pleasures when she loved him so much? He was crouched on the steps with his big hands hanging loosely between his legs and it was rare to see him so, for the ferry demanded his attention day and night. Long hours Siona Llewelyn worked, for he needed to run the boat at times convenient to the workers at the White Rock. At six-thirty in the morning he would begin his day and put in thirteen and a half hours before he could sleep. But for all that, Siona thought himself a king compared with the men who smelted the lead for twenty-five shilling a week.

Eddie, the second eldest of the Llewelyn boys, had taken over the sculling of the boat just for today, but the living wasn't good enough for two men and more often than not Eddie worked on the coal round with Bertie-No-Legs.

Bertie had been maimed during the war and it was only Eddie's guts and tenacity which had brought him through the hell of the trenches back to the safety of Sweyn's Eye. Bertie never ceased to be grateful and so Eddie could have anything he asked for, even the hand of Bertie's younger daughter who would one day own the thriving coal business.

Bertie was a fine man and though badly disabled, sat atop his cart as proud as Punch calling, 'Coke and coal best Welsh!' in a raucous voice so that women and children came to him where he waited in the street. Managed the selling well, he did, but it was the bagging of the coal and the hoisting of the sacks on to the cart which had him beat – which was where Big Eddie Llewelyn came in to his own.

Emily looked down the steps to where her husband sat. 'What are the hooters blaring out again for? Isn't the royal visit over, then?' She rubbed the small of her back with her fingers, impatient with the pain, but the ache was with her most days now and she took it for granted.

Siona smiled and rose to his feet in an easy movement.

'The King and Queen are off to see the works — Baldwins first, then all the Richardsons' I suppose.' He smiled. '*Duw*, saw the King plain as day, I did, could have reached out and touched him. But the best part of it all for me was seeing Nerys Beynon riding away in Mali's grand car, the girl will be taken care of, at least for the present.'

He moved up the steps and laid an arm casually around Emily's shoulders, his face close to hers as he spoke coaxingly.

'How about a nice cup of tea for your old man, then? There's thirsty I get, sitting out by here. Perhaps we could have a bite of dinner too – it's long gone one 'o' clock, mind.'

Emily pushed at him with an anger that was not all pretence. He was unusually concerned with this girl, Nerys Beynon, and though Emily was not the jealous kind, she did feel a little perturbed. 'There's a cheek! Go and make your old tea yourself Siona, man. I've got washing to do; it's Monday, or have you forgotten?'

He sighed and rubbed his hand through his hair, which was thick and strong despite being streaked with white.

'All right, what if I give you a hand to hang the sheets on the line, then; would that soften your heart?'

Emily felt her throat constrict with tears. Siona was not a man given to pretty words, but in his own way he often showed how much he loved her.

'Get away with you, man, do you think I'm going to be shamed in public having my husband act like a laundry maid? I'll hang out the sheets myself as I always do, then perhaps we'll have a cup of tea and some cold ham.'

But by the time she had the sheets flapping cleanly in the breeze coming off the river, Siona was away again, answering a call from the Hafod bank, so Emily sat alone in the kitchen sipping her tea, eyes half closed as she savoured the silence.

23

It seemed hard that now the youngest of her sons was safely at school, she should be bringing another babba into the house. And yet her heart warmed as she imagined the child – a daughter this time surely, a girl to dress in pretty frocks with colourful bows in golden hair.

She would have a friend then, someone to confide in when the work got backbreaking. Another woman about the place would make such a difference. But that was only a dream; no doubt the new baby would be another boy and as loved as any of them, too.

'On your feet, Emily Llewelyn, this won't get the work done!' she told herself sternly. There was supper to be cooked for nine of them – a huge pot of potatoes to be boiled with some swede and a fresh green-leafed cabbage to go with it. She had baked the ham last night, for it sliced more economically when cold. She and Siona would have some of it with their dinner, as she had promised.

He was a good man who worked hard and she was grateful to him, but she would need to impress on him that there must be no more babies in the Ferry House – she was much too old for childbearing.

She worked silently in the sun-washed kitchen, happy to be alone in spite of her occasional wish for company. The Ferry House was her domain, where she ruled her husband and sons alike but with a good-natured tolerance of which her menfolk approved.

She sliced the ham and set several pieces on a plate ready for Siona when he returned. She covered it with a cloth and began to peel the potatoes.

'Emily, I'm back!' Siona entered the kitchen smelling of salt and fresh breezes. 'And look what I've got for you!' He held up a squawking pullet, his face triumphant. Emily sighed.

'Another customer who didn't have the fare.' She shook her head. 'When will you ever learn, Siona

24

Llewelyn?' Emily's heart sank; she hated the prospect of killing the terrified creature, of dipping the carcase into boiling water and of the endless task of pulling the feathers from the goose-pimpled flesh.

Siona read her well. 'Don't worry, I know you're not up to it, girl. I'll see to the bird, and won't a bit of chicken be a change for us, then?'

'Aye, I suppose so,' Emily admitted grudgingly. 'Now get the thing out of my clean kitchen and then you can have something to eat.'

When Siona returned, there was a streak of blood along his shirt, but Emily turned her eyes away quickly and was ashamed of her weakness. It was her condition, just as Siona had said, but then wasn't that just an excuse? She had never relished killing animals, not even skinning a rabbit, though she knew it was foolish of her for other women did such tasks every day without a qualm.

'I'm glad that little Beynon girl got herself a job,' Siona said, cutting a chunk of fresh bread raggedly from the loaf. 'Nice young thing, wasn't she?'

Emily eyed her husband shrewdly, being well aware of his interest in the fairer sex. 'Aye, nice and pretty, young enough to be your daughter and don't you forget it!'

'All right,' Siona feigned indignation. 'I was only commenting. There's sharp your tongue is, Emily my girl, and me always a loving husband to you.'

Before Emily could think of a sarcastic reply the door swung open, spilling sunlight on to the stone floor and dazzling her eyes.

'Come like yourselves my sons!' she said when her vision had cleared. 'Hector, did you remember to bring me milk?'

'Aye, Alex has got a jugful there.' He grinned and folded his tall thin frame into a chair. 'You don't think your lovely twin boys, working on their aunt's milk round, would forget their mam's needs, do you?'

'A preacher you should be, my boy,' Emily said dryly. 'Got the gift of the wagging tongue all right. Here, Alexander, let me take that and put it in the larder or it'll be sour before I can use it.' She took the jug of milk and picked out a blade of grass from the frothy whiteness.

'Here, mam.' Hector took a crumpled twist of greaseproof paper out of his pocket. 'Betty-the-milk sent you some butter – says you should look after yourself now, what with the babba coming and all.'

'Shut that mouth of yours, Hector,' Siona said sternly. 'You don't go discussing your mam's condition with anyone, righto?'

'Don't be soft, Siona,' Emily said as she laid a placating arm on her husband's shoulder. 'It's no secret that I'm expecting now, is it?'

'Well, that's as may be, but I won't have you discussed outside these four walls and that's final.'

Alexander, always the peacemaker, sat alongside his father. 'Dad, there's a couple of people waiting on the Hafod bank for the boat – shall I take it across for you?'

Siona's good humour returned as he caught his son's thin arm between his fingers.

'*Duw!* It takes a man with muscles to pull that old boat – not a sixteen-year-old boy, mind. Weighs a whole ton she does, and more when she's got her full complement of twenty people sitting in her.' He rose to his feet. 'But give you another year or so and you'll be strong like your dad – taller than me too, I dare say, but for now I'm the boss man round here and I don't want anyone forgetting it.'

Emily saw Alexander give his father a guarded look. There was no answering smile in his eyes as Siona let himself outside into the softness of the summer day.

There was a drowsing silence in the kitchen after Siona had gone. A bee droned against the window pane and the soft scent of roses filled the air.

'I think I'll go for a swim in the river, mam,' Hector said, peeling off his shirt and discarding it carelessly. 'Are you coming, Alex?'

'Aye, I'll be there in a minute, boyo. I just want a drink of dandelion pop first – go on ahead, you.'

Emily smiled at Alexander, holding out her hand to brush back his hair. He was the son who of them all was most like herself. He was silent, often lost in secret thoughts. He kept his own counsel, not speaking of his feelings, but Emily always sensed his moods. He was a dreamer, but with a broad streak of common sense that kept his feet on the ground. And yet his twin Hector with his charm of manner was closest to her heart if the truth be known.

'What's wrong? Out with it!' She leaned towards Alex, not touching him but her tone brooking no excuses. He looked down at her, a thin boy but with an air of knowing that sat quaintly on his youthful features.

'I'm worried about you, mam,' he said at last. 'Betty says you're too old to be having a babba, she thinks it's dangerous at your age.'

'There's soft!' Emily smiled though her eyes were filled with tears – they came easily to her these days, she thought wryly. 'Maybe it's so with a woman having her first child,' she said firmly, 'but it's not so long since I had Will, is it? He's only nine years of age, mind, and Tom just a bit older, so don't worry about your mam, my son.'

'But I do worry. Talked about all over the place you are, mind, from the *Stryd Fawr* up to Ram's Tor. Too old, folks are saying, and daddy should be ashamed coming to your bed at his age.'

Emily's features felt as though they had been set in ice, yet anger sent the sounds of winds rushing through her head.

'Be proud of your father, Alexander!' Her voice sounded strained. 'He owes no one a penny-piece,

27

works hard enough for his bread and butter and what he does with his own wife in the privacy of his bedroom is nobody's business – nobody's, do you understand?'

Alexander's young face flushed and he looked down at his hands as though they had suddenly changed shape and texture. He was frowning and Emily felt his pain and embarrassment as deeply as if the feelings were her own.

'Look, lovely,' she said more softly, putting her arm around his thin shoulders, 'this thing between a man and woman that's called love is very strange – it doesn't alter as we grow older, and for that you should be thankful.' But it seemed she was making no headway, for her son refused to meet her gaze.

'Wait you, boy,' she said more sharply, 'until you yourself are in love, and then you'll find it a painful experience, believe me!'

Alexander rose to his feet, his eyes were filled with sadness. 'I just don't want to lose you, mammy.' The soft, childhood name hung in the silence and after a moment, Emily caught Alexander in her arms and hugged him.

'You won't lose me, love! *Duw*, aren't I as strong as a horse? Now go on, get out in the sunshine and have a nice swim in the river with your brother, there's a good boy, and let me get on with my work.'

When she was alone, Emily sat in the kitchen staring at the tub with the water gone cold and a rim of grime forming along the sides and shivered. There had been something in Alexander's fear which found an echo within herself and suddenly she was afraid.

*　　*　　*

Howel Llewelyn was relieved to be free of the burden of responsibility for the school children who had been in his care for the best part of the day. St Thomas's

28

school grounds had never been a more welcome sight than when he returned the exuberant youngsters to the headmaster and bid them all a hasty farewell.

Glancing at his pocket watch, he frowned. He would be late for his business meeting if he didn't hurry and that wouldn't do at all; he needed to make a good impression on Mr Sterling Richardson if he was to be accepted as a shareholder in the copper company. He thought briefly of Nerys Beynon, his surprise at seeing her drive away in the Richardson car. All Siona's doing of course – dad didn't like to see anyone down and out.

But Howel had more important matters to think of and unconsciously he squared his shoulders as he anticipated his future. It was in the army during the war when he had first been introduced to the intricacies of the world of stocks and shares. He had become friends with a broker – an 'old' man by Howel's standards – who had talked to him in the long hours of the nights when together they had kept watch.

'Look at it this way, my boy,' he had been fond of saying in his fine English voice. 'Whenever there is the merest hint of anything being wrong with a company, the share prices will fall and then is the time to buy.'

He had puffed endlessly on a long-stemmed pipe, his eyes seeing not the muddy trenches but columns of figures. 'Sometimes you will come a cropper if matters are really bad, but most of the time any crisis will be overcome. Companies will pull themselves up by their bootstraps fighting for survival and then you make your killing, for you sell at a much inflated price – do you understand, my boy?'

Howel had come to have a genuine liking and respect for the old man. Gradually, his interest in finance had grown, and for the last few months of the war he had done nothing but study the stock market, drinking in every piece of information and advice offered. It had stood him in good stead for already he was quite wealthy.

His aptitude for making money had not gone unnoticed in Sweyn's Eye, where he had been invited to sit on various committees. He was fast becoming a distinguished figure on the political scene and he intended to go right to the top.

His father was sitting in the boat, eyes closed against the late afternoon sun, his weatherbeaten face strong-featured, handsome even, and Howel felt an ache of pride even as he kicked the planking with mock annoyance.

'Wake up there, Siona Llewelyn, you've got a passenger – or haven't you noticed!' Howel smiled as Siona opened one eye and stared balefully at him.

'*Daro!* Don't give a man the gut-ache with your impatience, boy; what's the rush anyway?'

Howel climbed expertly into the boat, balancing with the ease of long practice. He had grown up as a ferryman's son but because he was the eldest and had shown ability coupled with an eagerness for learning, he had been given the chance to 'better himself', as his parents called it, and had attended the grammar school up on the hill.

Howel recognized that it was mainly by his mother's energy and determination that he had become a teacher and his love and gratitude went deep, but he was not content; his education had been thorough and had highlighted the opportunities which were open to a man. And so with acumen and a little bit of money to invest in stocks and shares, he had well justified the privilege of being the only one of the Llewelyn boys to have a proper education. And this was the bone of contention that came always between him and his brother Ceri.

'I'm late for a meeting, that's what the rush is,' Howel said dryly, knowing his father would be aghast if he knew Howel's real plans. If Siona had one

30

overwhelming belief, it was that the rich were parasites on the backs of the working people.

'Going to see some pretty little bit of skirt more like,' Siona said, eyebrows raised enquiringly.

'Well, if that's so, then I have only my father to blame for my interest in "pretty bits of skirt", haven't I?' Howel smiled as his father sculled the boat with skill and strength, crossing the tidal river that was on the ebb. So low was the water that a man could walk across if he chose the right spot.

'Been in to see your mam yet – tell her all about the royal visitors, have you, boy?' Siona asked, directing the boat towards the Hafod bank with easy movements of his big wrists.

'No, I'll see her later at supper and tell her all about the visit of the King and Queen; that will keep her interested for a while, I'll bet a shilling!' Howel rose to his feet and leaped ashore, dodging out of the way of passengers waiting to board the ferry. 'See you later, dad,' he said and strode away up to the road.

When Howel was admitted to Sterling Richardson's plush office, he moved forward confidently, hand outstretched, and was pleased at the firmness with which it was gripped.

'Good to see you, Llewelyn. You missed the royal party, they've just left.' He paused and thrust a hand through his hair. 'Making quite a name for yourself in local politics, aren't you?' He seated himself behind a great mahogany desk. 'Indeed, I was surprised you were not on the reception committee down at the Queen's Dock this morning?'

Howel smiled. 'I was there all right, but in my role as a teacher, far more arduous than any social function I've yet attended.'

Sterling smiled. 'As the father of young children, I more than take your point. Now, let's get down to business, shall we?' He pushed some papers with columns of figures towards Howel. 'These show our

31

imports of ore and exports of copper, zinc and lead, as well as the recovery of smaller amounts of bullion.' He leaned back in his chair.

'Without sounding insulting, I must admit to being amazed at the amount of money you are prepared and indeed able to inject into the business.' He paused. 'You do realize that copper sales are falling, I suppose?'

Howel nodded absently, engrossed in the figures before him. 'Yes, but it's as I thought – steel and tinplate are commodities still very much needed and will be for some time, I suspect.' He looked up at Sterling with a glint of humour in his eyes. 'As for the money, I seem to have acquired a flare for choosing the shares that are on the way up and selling them at just the right time before prices fall.'

Sterling returned his smile. 'Then you will have to give me a guiding hand, because I'm not so fortunate!'

Howel felt triumph burn in his gut – he was in, he could tell by the way Sterling was looking him straight in the eye. It was a step up, and only a step, for Howel meant to do great things with his life. He had not been content with second-best ever, and he meant to rise to the top of the heap, be the biggest business man in the town. He would see that Sterling Richardson taught him all he knew about his business and then, he would move on.

'Have we a deal then?' he asked evenly and after a moment, Sterling rose to his feet and held out his hand.

'I'll have my lawyer draw up a contract as soon as possible,' he smiled. 'But feel free to come and go in the works just as you like, you're one of the team now.'

As Howel stepped outside into the summer sunshine, he breathed a long sigh of relief. He felt like making a more exuberant gesture of his triumph, flinging his arms skyward, punching at the air with his fists. Instead, he contented himself with kicking a stone into the fast flowing River Swan and watched as the ripples spread outwards, making great circles on the water.

CHAPTER THREE

Plas Rhianfa stood tall and gracious, a dark fortress silhouetted against the rosy glow of the dawn sky. The windows were open, appearing as half-closed eyes with lights showing from the lower stories where the servants were already at work.

Nerys Beynon sat up in bed, staring sleepily at the maid who was pouring water from an enamel jug that looked too big for her to handle into the rose-painted basin on the marble-topped wash-stand.

The girl slipped quietly away, closing the door behind her, and Nerys stretched her arms above her head, smelling the soft perfume of roses drifting into the room. She pushed back the satin-covered quilt which had once been blue but now was purpled with age and stood for a moment, staring around her. Her room was at the top of the house and plainly furnished, but it was a palace compared with the poor rooms she had been accustomed to renting in town.

Removing her crackling cotton nightgown, she began to wash, luxuriating in the hot water and the softness of the soap. Being poor, she had found, meant much more than going hungry; it had meant a lowering of standards, unwashed hair and grubby clothing. It had brought Nerys a devastating feeling of failure and shame.

She had been at *Plas Rhianfa* for little over two weeks and so far her duties had been light. Most mornings she read to the solemn-faced, beautifully spoken Richardson children and during the afternoons, took them to

Victoria Park or for a walk along the golden curve of the bay. It was a pleasant life, a reflection of her years spent with Mary Sutton, and Nerys was happier than she had been for some time.

She dressed quickly in a navy skirt and a fresh white blouse, relishing the feeling of cleanliness that embraced her. Then she took a last look around her before letting herself out into the dimness of the long corridor.

The nursery was a cheerful room with a small fire burning behind a metal guard. The furniture was good oak and the smell of pencils newly sharpened lent the room a scholarly air. It was here that Nerys would take her breakfast along with the children.

But before that she would have a little time to herself and Nerys decided to make the most of her leisure. She took a book from the shelf and seating herself in a comfortable chair, lost herself in stories of other days and distant lands.

Sighing with contentment as the clock on the wall chimed the hour, she enjoyed these peaceful moments before the work of the day began. As she tucked her feet beneath her, she savoured the feeling of warmth and security; of the future, she refused to think.

* * *

Mali Richardson took a piece of toast from the rack and speared a curl of butter with her knife; she was preoccupied with thoughts of Nerys Beynon, for the girl evoked echoes of Mali's own past. She had been very young when she met and fell in love with Sterling Richardson, the man who owned the copper sheds where Mali's father had worked as a ladler.

It had seemed an impossible match – a man of Sterling's standing in the community consorting with a girl from the lower orders. But their love was an irresistible cord which drew them together and they had married in the face of much opposition.

Mali supposed she had grown used to her comfortable way of living, but the coming of Nerys Beynon had reminded her vividly of the small stone-flagged cottage where she was born and where she had seen her mother weaken and die.

'Couldn't we keep Nerys on in some other capacity when the children return to school, Sterling? She's such a nice girl.' Mali spoke her thoughts aloud and Sterling smiled and leaned forward to kiss her cheek.

'You are an incurable romantic, Mali. You know as well as I do that there's nothing she could do here once the children are back at school. We have enough staff, indeed more than enough to keep *Plas Rhianfa* going.' He picked up his paper and stared at her over the top of the page. 'I'm afraid there might be economies to make – a cutting down on staff, in fact.'

Mali felt fear claw at her as she met her husband's eyes. 'Why, what's wrong?' She took a sip of her tea, telling herself to be calm, that things could not be so bad otherwise Sterling would not be so casual.

'The business is declining, Mali,' he said after a pause. 'The war gave us a temporary boost, but now the demand for copper is on the wane. What I need to do is to develop the lead and tinplate, invest in better furnaces, bring my works into line with the new places that are starting from scratch with the latest equipment.' He smiled reassuringly. 'It can be done but it needs money, Mali, and most of mine is already tied up in the business.'

'We are not on the verge of bankruptcy, are we?' Mali heard the tremble in her voice and hated herself for it. She, a copperman's daughter who had managed her father's house on a few shillings a week, had grown soft.

'Of course not!' Sterling said. 'Indeed, I've just taken on a new man, who has quite a lot of money to invest and what appears to be a gift for knowing the right shares to buy. That fact alone gives me confidence; he wouldn't put his cash into something he thought would fail.' He smiled teasingly. 'It might surprise you to know that the man is kin of yours, Howel Llewelyn from Foxhole.'

Mali felt a thrust of surprise. '*Duw*, where's any of my family got the money to put into a business, then? Mind, Howel was always bright, him being a teacher and all, but I didn't know he was that clever!'

'Well, to me he's an invaluable asset and so is his money.' Sterling smiled. 'I only hope we can keep him, he's the ambitious kind.'

'Aye, I suppose his mother encourages him. Emily is a fine woman. When I saw her last, she was looking very tired. Having a baby at her age can't be easy, yet she's so independent and won't allow anyone to do much for her.'

The door opened and Mali smiled as her children entered the room. David, her son, was growing up to be a fine boy; he had grave eyes which reminded Mali of her father and a firm mouth that was all Sterling.

Her daughter was a pretty girl with fine skin and a small frame and an abundance of thick dark hair; Jinny looked much as Mali herself had been at the same age.

'Come and kiss me before you go up for your breakfast,' Mali said, holding out her hand.

She ached with love for her children; they were so dear to her, so cherished. And yet Sterling balanced Mali's indulgence, making quite sure that his offspring learned independence.

Mali thought with a pang of pain and loss of the other child she had borne, the baby who had slipped away without ever having grasped at life. The experience had heightened her feelings for her son and daughter.

She held David to her for a moment; he thought

himself too manly for kisses, but she felt his hand rest briefly on her shoulder.

'Go on, get off to your breakfast the two of you,' she said quickly, 'and tell Nerys she can have the afternoon free as I shall be taking you into town to buy your school clothes for the new term. I think we might call and see my uncle Siona and his wife while we're out, too.'

When the door had closed behind the children, Mali bit her lip thoughtfully. 'I can at least try to find Nerys some other job where she can live in and have a roof over her head,' she said and Sterling glanced at her, shaking his head.

'That's up to you, but it's not really our responsibility, you know. We only took her on in the first place as a temporary measure.'

'I know.' Mali rose from her chair and placed her arms around Sterling's shoulders, resting her cheek against his. 'All the same, I can't just turf her out on to the street, can I?'

'No.' Sterling turned and pulled her on to his knee. 'Being you, I don't suppose you can. Have I ever told you that I love you very much?'

Mali felt a warmth enveloping her as her husband's lips touched hers. In over ten years of marriage, she had never ceased to be amazed that she should evoke such love from a fine man like Sterling. Oh, she knew their friends laughed, though kindly behind their backs, calling them a pair of love birds, but she grew and flourished in Sterling's love and felt she would never be whole without him.

'Enough of this,' Sterling said with mock severity as he put her away from him. 'I'll never get to work if I'm besieged at breakfast by a beautiful woman.' He rose and put down the paper that was crumpled now. 'But I do mean it: we cannot keep Nerys on when the children return to school – there simply isn't a job here for her.'

'All right, I do understand,' Mali said quickly, 'but let me choose the appropriate moment to tell her.' She smiled. 'Don't worry, I won't be weak; you can depend on me.'

'I do,' Sterling said as he kissed her lips in farewell. When he left the room, Mali poured herself more tea from the solid silver pot and watched the leaves spin around in her cup. She was unsettled, needing to take stock of her own life for she was living it in idle luxury, perhaps being a liability to her husband.

Her children would be going back to their boarding schools soon and then Mali would be left alone for the best part of the day and there would be nothing to fill her life except for the teas taken in the emporium in town or the round of polite entertaining which left her feeling drained and more alone than ever.

It seemed that now she was approaching her thirties, her origins had become more dear to her than ever before. Her only blood relations were the Llewelyns, Siona who owned the ferry-boat and his sons. She had not had a great deal to do with them, for her father had never spent much time with his younger cousin. Indeed, Davie had always said that Siona was a bit on the flighty side, always after the women. But now Mali felt the need to find part of her past, to reassure herself that she was a person in her own right. Suddenly, she realized how proud she was of Howel who still being a young man had made himself a small fortune, or at least enough to invest a substantial amount in Sterling's business.

She would most certainly take the children to visit the Ferry House that afternoon, she decided – it was time she began to forge stronger ties between her uncle's family and her own children. She felt invigorated suddenly, as though now she had a purpose. Whatever she did from now on, she was determined that she would find herself a useful occupation and not simply sit like a spoiled child in the luxury of her home.

It was later that afternoon when Mali took her children on the tram-car towards the centre of Sweyn's Eye. She still felt guilty at the thought of Nerys's happiness at having a free afternoon, for she had not found the courage to tell the girl that soon she would be out of work.

'Why haven't I seen my uncle Siona before, mother?' David asked in his precise voice and Mali gave him a wry smile.

'You have seen him before, but you were too young to remember and Siona isn't really your uncle,' she corrected. 'He was my father's cousin. It's my fault that you don't know him, I should have taken you to meet the family more often, but then it's difficult when you're away at school much of the time.'

She saw through the window of the tram-car the busy streets of the town, the big walled market where cockle-women came in from Penclawdd and sold their shell-fish and the black lava bread made from seaweed that was tasty and rich with iron.

She seemed to have lost her familiarity with it all and she was seeing the town with new eyes. Cocooned in her home away up on the hill, she had become out of touch with reality.

It was true she had suffered emotionally when Sterling had gone away to fight on the Somme, but even during the war she had gone short of nothing. Was that something to feel guilty about, she wondered, for there was a certain sense of unease within her. It was as though she had turned her back on all that represented her roots and was only just realizing it.

She alighted from the tram-car holding her daughter by the hand though David pulled away, his budding masculinity threatened. She smiled and allowed him to walk at her side, aware that he was fast growing up. But then, she had been only a few years older than he when she was keeping home for a sick mother and a hard-working father. And that was one aspect of her comfortable life that didn't trouble her – indeed, she was fiercely glad that her children would suffer no deprivations or hardships.

'There's the river, mother,' David said eagerly, 'and is that the ferry-boat?'

She heard the disappointment in his voice and as she stood on the bank she recognized that she had doubtless made a fairy tale of Siona and the boat for it was very ordinary, looking smaller than its twenty-foot length as it lay lifting and turning on the wash of the river.

'Yes, that's it, David, and you should see the way Siona handles her when the river is high and swollen. See that chain there lying in the river? Siona attaches it to the boat so that in winds and high tides the ferry won't be washed downstream.'

When she saw Siona Llewelyn standing beside his boat, he reminded Mali so much of her father that as his eyes, green and clear met hers, she felt a thrust of pain. She moved forward and then he saw and held out his arms. As she leaned against him, she recognized that he even had the same scent about him as Davie Llewelyn.

She kissed his cheek and, feeling the scrape of his unshaven chin, laughed happily. 'Seeing you in town on the day of the royal visit made me realize that I've not kept in touch as much as I should.'

'Don't worry, *cariad*, it's good to see you whenever you can spare the time. *Duw*, grown into a big boy has your son!' He smiled as David frowned in embarrassment at being talked about. 'Know that look anywhere, the boy's the image of his granddad.' Siona rubbed his chin.

'Come on then, into the boat with you and that

lovely little girl of yours and we'll go and see my Emily – there's pleased she'll be.'

Mali felt the boat move and rock beneath her feet and clutched at the seat, urging the children to sit down carefully. She saw with amusement that David's respect for the big man who sculled the boat across the river was growing by the minute and indeed she privately agreed with her son, for Siona was a big man in every way.

Mali saw very little of Emily Llewelyn for she was proud and solitary, scarcely ever leaving her home on the side of the water. Yet Mali's heart tugged with pity at the sight of Siona's wife, a woman old by most standards but large and heavy with child. And too, Mali felt a sense of renewed pain for since she had lost her baby she had harboured the so far unfulfilled hope of having another.

'Come inside,' Emily said formally. It was only a matter of weeks since they had met accidentally in the market, but Emily was looking much more weary than Mali remembered.

'There's lovely to see you looking so well!' she lied. They were not a family for open displays of affection and so Mali contented herself with placing a hand on Emily's shoulder.

The older woman seemed to relax a little, sensing genuine warmth, and her face softened into a smile.

The hours spent in the Ferry House were pleasant and when at last Mali rose to go, she smiled warmly at Emily. 'I shan't leave it so long between visits next time,' she said. 'I shall certainly be calling before the birth of the baby at any rate.'

'All right, Mali,' said Emily, resting a hand on her arm lightly. 'I know I've a sharp tongue at times, but I don't mean anything by it.' She paused in the doorway. 'You took Nerys Beynon on, then; that was good of you.'

'Yes, but I'll have to let her go soon. The children go

back to their boarding schools next week and there's not enough to keep me occupied, let alone Nerys.'

She waved goodbye and sighed as she led the children towards the town, reflecting that she had learned more about Emily in a few hours than she had thought possible, and what's more there was a common bond of understanding between them.

After that, Mali made a point of calling often at the Ferry House and before the children returned to their school allowed them one last visit. Jinny was quietly pleased, but David was more vociferous. Intent on making friends with the boys, he liked young Will enough but was very impressed by Tom, who was nearer his own age.

'Come along, mother, do hurry,' he said impatiently, 'or I shan't have any time to spend with Tom.'

Emily appeared pale as she came to the open door. 'Come on in with you, then,' she said a little sharply. 'Don't stand by here in front of all Siona's passengers, who are staring as though they've never seen a lady in a fine frock before.'

Mali became aware of the difference in her dress for the first time and noticed that Emily's spotless but patched apron and flannel skirt were too heavy for summer wear. Briefly she considered sending a few of her clothes down to the Ferry House, but dismissed the idea at once; Emily would be mortally offended at any suggestion of charity.

'There's a lovely girl you've got, Mali Llewelyn!' Emily's eyes were soft and her gaze rested on Mali's daughter, who was prettily dressed in white cotton sprigged with rosebuds. 'Love a little girl, I would.'

The kitchen was as clean as constant work could make it, but Mali saw now that the curtains were fading and the covers on the chairs beginning to wear – for all that it was a pleasant room with sunlight streaming in through the windows and the scent of honeysuckle perfuming the air.

'*Duw*, there's hot it is in by here!' Emily fanned herself with her apron. 'Got to keep a fire going for the cooking, see?'

'I haven't forgotten that much,' Mali said, smiling. 'Didn't I have to cook for my dad enough times?'

'Aye, I suppose I'm thinking of you as never done a hand's turn – you looking so fine and all,' Emily smiled. 'But right proud of you Siona is, mind, you turning out so well and marrying a fine husband.'

'May we go out to watch the boats, mother?' David put in quietly and Mali bit her lip uncertainly.

'Well, so long as you don't go too near the water – will it be all right, Emily?'

'You wait by here,' Emily said as she pushed herself upright with difficulty. 'I'll call my two youngest; they're always swimming in the river and will be company for the boy.'

She called loudly from outside the door and after a moment returned to her seat. 'They'll be here now in a tick,' she said to Mali. 'Like fish, they are, in the water all the time they're off from school.'

After a few moments, two dripping figures stood in the doorway: Tom of a similar age to David but smaller of stature, with his thin brown body streaming with water; and behind him and looking over his shoulder with large eyes, the younger boy, Will.

'Now, Tom, you take good care of the children – see they come to no harm and remember, they don't know the river like you do.'

Mali felt a slight sense of unease, but dismissed her misgivings impatiently. She was becoming over-possessive and foolish. Why, Emily's two youngest boys were not very old; indeed, like little men they were, swimming alone every day in the river.

The kitchen was quiet, the ticking of the clock soothing and Mali watched as Emily made a pot of tea, her heavy figure bent over the table and her thin hand resting on the pristine cloth. Mali remembered how the kitchen had been in her own home: the table of white wood scrubbed daily with soap, the stone floor that turned grey-blue in the morning light and the flagged yard where she and her father had stood over the dark shape of her mother's coffin. Mali shivered; she was being morbid, dredging up memories best forgotten.

Yet the memories were not all bad. There was the day she had met Sterling and known in her heart that she loved him even though she had spat words of venom at him. He was the copper boss's son and so was the one to blame, she felt, for all the ills which had befallen her family.

'You're far away girl – not worried about the children, are you?' Emily's words penetrated Mali's thoughts and she looked up, startled, to see the older woman handing her a cup of tea.

'There's rude of me!' Mali spoke quickly. 'I suppose seeing Siona and him looking so much like dad always reminded me of my past.'

'Tut, girl, looking back is an old woman's fancy and not for young ones like you! Your future is a good one, so don't dwell on the bad things in your life – it will only make you bitter, for what's done can't be mended, mind.'

'I know.' Mali sipped her tea and, putting down her cup, smiled at Emily. 'I wish I had come here more often over the past years,' she said quietly. 'I feel we should be good friends.'

'Aye,' Emily said softly, 'for all your fine clothes and the posh voice, I think you're one of us.' She moved towards the cool of the pantry. 'There's a bit of lardy cake here for the children, they'll be hungry when they—' Her words stopped abruptly as she bent over the table, clutching at her stomach.

'What is it?' Mali was on her feet at once, but Emily had already straightened and her lips were pressed together determinedly.

'Just a little pang, nothing to worry about, my babbas don't get born quick like some! Now don't worry,' she insisted, but she was suddenly pale, her mouth drawn.

She sliced the lardy cake and buttered it carefully, then covered the plate with a clean cloth. She managed a smile, but her brows were drawn together in a frown.

'You've started your labour, haven't you?' Mali asked quietly. 'Don't bother to lie, I can see it in your face.'

'*Duw*, so what? I could go all day and all night, see, girl. As I said, I don't have my babbas quickly.'

'I don't care what you say, I'm sending for the midwife. Mrs Benson will see to you.'

'*Duw*, don't bother yourself, I'll be all right. Go on home and I'll get myself prepared here; I'm used to it, remember?'

'I don't want to know any of that,' Mali said gently. 'I'm going to send for the midwife and then I'll help you to get ready.' She hurried outside and spoke quickly to Siona, who nodded his head in assent.

It seemed to Mali that she was tinglingly alive, feeling needed for the first time in years. She organized matters with calm efficiency, helping Emily to undress and – remembering the old days – placing a padding of papers beneath the clean sheet on the bed.

'Fancy you being so good at a time like this,' Emily said, breathing more easily as the pain receded. 'Got a lot of common sense you have, Mali Llewelyn.' She hissed a little, catching her swollen belly between her fingers and closing her eyes as though to shut herself off from the world for a moment. 'It won't be easy,' she gasped, 'me being old, but I'll do my best, see.'

Mali hurried downstairs and searched in the kitchen for a large bowl. She found one under the curtained sink alongside the soda and a worn scrubbing brush. The kettle was already full of water and she pushed it on to the flames, hearing it begin to sing as the water came to the boil. Memories came of her mam lying sick in childbed, the baby weak, dying . . . and mam, losing her will, slipping away from life.

Siona returned quickly and looked in through the door — eyes wide, brow furrowed. 'Mrs Benson's coming as soon as she can, be delayed she will though. Can you stay for a bit, Mali, girl?'

Mali nodded, her expression calm though her hands were shaking. 'Yes, I'll stay as long as I'm needed, of course.'

She nodded to Siona. 'Go on, you, keep the ferry running. I'll see to everything here.' She picked up the china tea-pot, feeling as though she was back once more in the small kitchen of her home in Copperman's Row. How far she had come since then, used to rich living now and more with a family to love and care for. Yet underneath, she had changed very little from the frightened, vulnerable girl she used to be.

'Here we are then, Emily!' She pushed the door open with her shoulder. 'I've brought you a nice cup of camomile tea, it will help the birth, but then I suppose you know that?'

Emily was perspiring, her mouth twisted with pain. Her eyes became anguished as a groan escaped from between her clenched teeth, though she uttered no complaint.

'You are not to worry. Mrs Benson's on her way and she'll see to everything; you know how experienced she is.' Mali was talking soothingly, though she was worried at the pallor of Emily's face. Perhaps it might be a good idea to send for Paul Soames; a doctor at hand would be reassuring.

'I'm going downstairs to see what's happening, but I'll be back before you know it.' Mali knew from her own experience of childbirth how frightening it was to be left alone.

As she entered the kitchen the door was flung open

and the youngest of the Llewelyn children hurried in, his face grimy and his eyes wide.

'Come on quick!' He tugged at Mali's arm. 'They're killing poor Davie, knocking spots off him they are.'

Mali felt a sickness rise within her. 'Who are you talking about, Will? Tell me slowly, now.'

'Some big boys down by the river there, hitting Davie for nothing they are, though my brother Tom is doing his best to get them off him, mind.'

Mali looked round her in anguish. How could she leave the house now, with Emily in such pain?

From the pathway came the sound of voices and Mali stopped on the threshold of the cottage, her heart thumping. David and Tom were striding along, arm in arm.

'Oh, David!' Mali didn't move, but her eyes were on her son's scratched and bruised face. She wanted to hug him to her, but knew this was not the moment for such a demonstration.

'We licked them all between us!' David spoke proudly and then as an afterthought, he turned and put his arm around his sister who was trailing behind him, her dress muddied and torn. 'No need to cry, it's all over now.'

Mali held herself in check. 'You'd best wash up, all of you, and keep quiet for Emily isn't feeling very well.'

'Her time has come, has it?' Tom said gravely, his smile fading. 'Shall I go for the midwife then?'

'No, it's all right, she's on her way. Now I'm going upstairs and I want the lot of you looking more respectable by the time I come back.'

Emily was lying against the pillows exhausted but calm. 'Pain's gone for the minute,' she said thankfully and made an effort to raise herself. 'Are the kids in trouble again?'

Mali smiled and shook her head. 'No, they've had a scrap, that's all, and I think David and Tom have become friends.' She sat down, not touching Emily for she felt instinctively that such familiarity would be unwelcome.

'I'm glad you're here,' Emily said as though reading her thoughts. 'A woman needs a friend around at a time like this. I sometimes wish I had had a girl, then I'd have company. But you'll stay with me, won't you?'

'You try to shift me!' Mali said quickly. The two women smiled and then Emily's face folded into lines of pain and her hand crept towards Mali imploringly.

'Hold on,' Mali said with a tremble in her voice. 'Grip tightly, that's the way; come on now, it won't be long, soon it'll be all over.' She said the words without thinking, soothing softly spoken words which seemed to help.

The door downstairs opened and there was the sound of a hearty female voice and then heavy footsteps on the stairs.

'Mrs Benson's come – you'll be all right now, Emily, she'll soon have that baby born.'

The nurse summed up the situation at a glance. '*Duw*, why you women wait so long to call me, I'll never know. See, girl,' she looked towards Mali, 'the head's on its way out, the child is ready to be born.'

She rolled up her sleeves and, pouring water in a jug, washed her arms and hands. 'You've done a good bit of the work, Emily Llewelyn. The worst is over – just push now with all your might!'

In just over half an hour, the birth was over and the sound of crying hung on the still air. Mali took a towel and dabbed at Emily's face, smiling reassuringly.

'Is my babba all right?' Emily asked fearfully. The nurse smiled and held up a small golden-haired infant. 'You know what, missis?' she said. 'Eight times lucky, you've got a little girl!'

Mali felt her throat constrict as Mrs Benson wrapped the baby in a sheet and placed her in Emily's arms.

'I can't believe it, I just can't believe it, she's so

beautiful!' Tears coursed down Emily's pallid face as she held the baby close. 'Oh, thank you, thank you, thank you.' Eyes closed, she whispered the words against a fuzz of golden hair.

Mali backed out of the room. There was nothing more she could do; she was no longer needed in the little house on the riverside.

CHAPTER FOUR

The foundry shimmered with heat, the flat-hearth furnaces agape like open mouths, belching forth fire and fumes and stink. Mounds of galena – sparkling lead ore – lay on the stone floor ready for the first roasting, shovelled on to the bed of fire by men who had no time to wipe the sweat from their brows.

Ceri Llewelyn was young and handsome, third son of ferryman Siona Llewelyn and out looking for a job. He pushed back his hair, feeling the heat encompass him as he followed the foreman across the foundry.

'Come into the office, Ceri, boyo, there's a bit of peace there from the noise and the stink – but not much, mind!' Gareth Owen grinned, revealing blackened teeth that gave him a grotesque appearance.

'Now, are you sure you want a job in by here, man?' He sat at a rickety desk and leaned back in his chair, thumbs thrust into the armholes of his waistcoat. 'Used to the waterways, you are, and the fishing – I thought the river was your life.'

'Well, the river is dad's life right enough,' Ceri said wryly, 'but there's not enough work for all of us – you see that, Gareth.'

'Aye, I know, boyo, but then with your dad owning his boat and your brother Howel a teacher and coming on in politics, won't this job be a bit of a come-down like.'

'I'm only worried about earning a living, Gareth. I'm sick of fishing in all weathers and then taking the catch to Murphy's fresh-fish shop in Market Street.

Plenty of places for Mr Murphy to buy his fish without waiting for my little offering!'

'Ah,' Gareth's eyes were shrewd. 'You've taken a shine to the girl, Katie Murphy as she was before she got married, haven't you? Not that I blame you, mind; lovely girl, she is!' He sighed. 'She's got that pale skin that goes with red hair and such eyes! Nice ways on her too, in spite of the tragedy of losing her man to the sea.' He looked up. 'And now you want to earn her respect – is that it?'

Ceri shrugged. 'The money selling fish is poor and the work is stinking,' he said as he held out cut and chapped hands. 'I hate the very touch of the fish and I can't stand the job any longer, for there's no money in it.'

'Not going to talk about your love life then, are you?' Gareth smiled. 'Well, it's a true enough saying that a wise head keeps a still tongue. All right then, you're a good worker, boyo, come from a respectable family and if you really want a job here, then I'll give you one. But start on the ground floor, you do, mind – no favouritism because Siona is a drinking pal of mine.'

'Favours I don't want,' Ceri said quickly, 'and my father doesn't even know I've come here.'

Gareth sighed. 'All right then, don't get your hair off! What about your mam? Have a fit, she will for hasn't she always maintained that the White Rock kills off men like flies?'

Ceri forced a smile, though this was one task that he would have to handle carefully, for informing mam about his new job was going to bring down a storm upon his head. Emily hated the works, as Gareth said; she thought that the men who handled the lead were tainted, passing the scourge of disorders down through the generations. And to an extent, Ceri was bound to agree; babies born to the lead workers were pale to the lips and grew old

51

before their time. But then, the job in the foundry would be only a temporary one. He meant to get on, just like his eldest brother.

There was a bitter taste in his mouth as he thought of Howel, for they were always at odds with each other. They had never been close. Even back into their childhood days they had fought bitterly over some girl or other – a proper fist-fight it had been and both of them receiving the sharp end of mam's tongue for it.

But favoured by Siona Howel had been, the only son sent to the grammar school to be a scholar and God help the rest of the family. Yet, strangely enough, it seemed that out of all the brothers only Ceri resented the attention heaped on Howel.

Big Eddie, the second eldest of the boys, was content enough helping dad on the boat or Bertie-No-Legs on the coal, while the twins Hector and Alexander were set for life running a milk round with old Betty up on Ram's Tor. But he was the only one of working age not to have a proper job, Ceri thought angrily.

'Start tomorrow if you're sure, then,' Gareth said, nodding his head, 'and I'll promise to teach you all I know about the lead and the silver too – if you put your back into it, that is.'

Ceri smiled in triumph. 'Don't worry about that, I never was afraid of hard work.'

As he left the foundry, he stopped and stared across to the Hafod side of the river to where his father was helping an old lady into the ferry-boat. There was a pain within him that dad had never seemed to understand him.

Eddie it was who would probably own the boat after Siona's working days were past for Howel wouldn't touch it. And he . . . well, he would have to fend for himself, Ceri thought bitterly. He had always felt strangely out of touch with all but the youngest of his brothers; perhaps he was cut out to be a loner, but the thing he would not be was a failure, so the seeds must be sown now for his future.

Inside the cottage on the river bank, his mother was sitting in a chair before the open doorway with the new baby in her arms. Ceri's heart softened; there was a warmth in him for Emily, who unlike Siona had never shown favour but loved her boys equally. He was happy for her now that she had the daughter she had always longed for.

'Hello, mam.' He crouched beside her and pulled back the shawl from the tiny baby face of his sister. 'Sian is looking better; there's more colour in her little cheeks today.'

Emily's pinched face lit up. 'Do you think so, son? Well, it must be so, for Mali has been here this morning and she said the same thing.' Emily smiled. 'The baby has taken a little more milk than usual and I think she's gaining weight, but she's such a delicate thing that I do worry about her.'

'Come on, mam!' Ceri said heartily. 'You are used to us boys, starvers the lot of us. A girl is different, I expect.'

'Aye,' Emily conceded, 'perhaps you're right, Ceri. I'm probably over-anxious about her because she's so little and I'm too old to give her sufficient milk.'

Ceri allowed himself to rest his hand on his mother's shoulder. 'What nonsense you talk sometimes, mam, too old indeed!' He moved away from her and opened the oven to release the succulent smell of roasting meat.

'*Duw*, there's never been such a cook as you, mind. Will you look at the crispy crackling on that piece of pork!'

'You can take the joint out of the oven for me now, Ceri, I should think it's about done.' Emily held her baby close as the girl began to cry softly. 'There, there, my lovely, you shall have something to eat as well – come on, now.' She fumbled with the buttons of her

53

blouse and Ceri turned away, struck with pity at the thinness of his mother's breast.

'You should eat more yourself, mind, mam,' he said, his throat thick. 'Build yourself up now that the baby is born.'

'I do all right, don't you worry, son. Come on now, shift the meat on to the table, let it cool in the breeze from the doorway and then perhaps you'll be a good boyo and slice it up for me for your dad will be in soon, starving as usual.'

Aye and dad mustn't be put out at all, Ceri thought to himself, feeling a flash of bitterness against the rugged, hearty man who was his father. The entire household must revolve around Siona; he had his way in everything, even in bed with mam who as she rightly said was too old for the business of babies.

'Aye, I'll cut the meat right enough,' he said in an even voice, 'and make sure you have the best pieces too.'

'You're a good son to me.' Emily's voice quivered a little and Ceri glanced at her quickly. She had not been right since the birth, but been given to black moods and tears in place of her usual practical good sense. How was he going to bring himself to tell her about the job? His stomach contracted, for he knew she would beg him to reconsider since her hatred of the lead was almost an obsession. Well, it would be left until after dinner was eaten and then he would find the right moment, for telling her was something that just had to be done.

Siona heaved himself in through the door, his big shoulders appearing to fill the room. He kicked off his muddy boots and watching him, Ceri bit his lip against the harsh words that he wanted to say. Didn't dad realize how hard mam worked keeping the kitchen clean? For once in his life, couldn't he think about someone else and leave his old boots outside on the pathway?

54

'Something smells good, Emily!' Siona rolled up his sleeves carefully, slowly, as he did everything, his movements irritating Ceri. 'I see you've baked a piece of pork for my dinner – very nice, but I would have preferred beef for a change.'

'Beef is more expensive than pork, Siona *cariad*,' Emily said softly, her eyes warm as they looked towards her husband, 'but I'll get us a bit of topside at the market tomorrow if you like.'

'Now, mam, you're not well enough to go traipsing about!' Ceri said quickly. 'If you want meat, then I will fetch it.'

'Aye, good enough too,' Siona broke in. 'Nothing much else to do is there, boy, but pull that fish-cart about the place!'

Ceri felt a pain throb through his temples, but he would not allow his father to provoke him. 'I've not done bad out of selling fish so far, dad,' he said reasonably, 'though I will admit it's not the best job in the world.'

'Aye, and you're not wrong there!' Siona laughed. 'Even our Will could do it if he were called upon. Boy's work, that is.'

Ceri took a deep breath, but held his tongue as his father rubbed his hands through his thick hair.

'Why don't you get a proper job?' Siona was unwilling to let the subject drop. 'Ashamed you should be, trundling a cart around like a rag-and-bone man!'

For a moment, Ceri was blind with anger. 'Well, I'm not selling fish any longer!' he exclaimed between clenched teeth. 'I've got me a man's job now, with a man's wage.'

'Righto, then, let's hear all about this wonderful job you've found yourself, shall we?' Siona leaned back in his chair and folded big arms across his chest. His gaze was sharp, lacking in warmth, and for a moment Ceri wondered at the conflict that was between them.

'I'm starting in the White Rock tomorrow. I've seen

55

the foreman and he's shown me around the place; it's all settled.'

'Oh *no*, not that, Ceri!' Emily's voice broke into the strained silence and Ceri realized suddenly how cruelly he had blurted out his news.

'It's all right, mam,' he said, going to her chair and touching her shoulder lightly. 'I shan't be a furnace-man for long, for I mean to work my way up, don't you worry.' In the clouds that oppressed his brain, he heard his father laugh.

'Oh, aye, after my mate Gareth's job as foreman, are you? Well, there's not a chance in hell of you getting far in the lead works – you don't know anything about smelting.'

'I'll learn.' Ceri's voice was charged with anger. 'And I'll learn fast. Why is it, dad, that you don't give me credit for any guts?'

'Not a row, please God, not a row,' Emily said and in her arms the baby began to wail. She rose to her feet. 'I forbid you to go into the lead works, Ceri,' she said, impressive in her self-control. 'You know that the lead brings death in the end to you and yours and what is your reward from the bosses, I ask you?' Her voice rose. 'A coffin in which you can be put beneath the earth!'

'Now hush, Emily,' Siona said, but his voice was not lacking compassion. 'There's many an old man comes out of the White Rock as fit as when he went in there as a boy.'

'You know as well as I do that men grow old before their time and die with the flux of their kidneys.' Emily's voice was fierce. 'There is poison in the lead, it taints the blood down through the generations and I'll not have my boy giving his life for a bit of profit for the owners.'

'Now calm down, mam,' Ceri said. 'Let's have our dinner, is it, before the rest of the boys come in.'

'I don't want any dinner and I'll not prepare it for

56

the rest of you – so see to your sons, Siona Llewelyn, or the lot of you can starve!'

After Emily had left the room, Ceri listened to the sound of her light footsteps on the stairs. His eyes reluctantly met those of his father and he saw a glint of pain before Siona looked away.

'I suppose I'd best put the spuds on again.' Siona moved to the hob and looked into the pot. 'I don't know if they're done or not.'

Ceri took the black lid from his father's hands. 'Go on, sit down and I'll see to it.' He knew that his father thought it a weakness to work in the house, but Ceri had always been the one to help Emily with the chores, enjoying the rare moments of closeness with her.

He sighed. It was growing dark and soon Howel would return home from school, if he wasn't off out to one of his committee meetings; then Eddie would lumber into the house, big and good-natured, wanting an enormous meal before taking his girl for a walk.

The twins would be quieter, tired from working the milk round and the long walk from Ram's Tor Farm into town. Even now they might have lit the lamp on the other side of the river and be waiting for their father to bring them home.

The two youngest boys were playing on the river bank – Ceri could hear the voices of Tom and Will calling in the evening air. Normally they would have had their food early and be ready in clean nightshirts for their beds, but lately Emily had been tired – and let the boys have too much freedom, so that they had become undisciplined and rowdy. It occurred to Ceri that mam should see a doctor and he glanced at Siona, who was sitting in his chair reading a paper. Should he speak up, or would it be better if he talked quietly to mam herself?

The door burst open and the two boys flung into the room, pushing and pulling and tearing at each other.

They were muddy and untidy and Siona looked at them from over the top of his paper as though surprised at their existence.

'For pity's sake, what's going on in this house?' he said in a loud voice. 'Can't a man have a bit of quiet to read the paper?'

Ceri was not angry any more, he felt strangely sad. 'I think, dad,' he said softly, 'that you'd best take our mam to see the doctor – needs looking at, she does, see.'

When Siona met his gaze there was naked fear in the green eyes, but he didn't speak. He rose from his chair, calmly laid down the paper and moved out of the kitchen and up the stairs. Ceri sighed with relief; it was said now, his fear was out in the open and it was up to others to sort matters out.

'Go and wash, boys!' he ordered loudly. 'Otherwise there'll be no dinner for you.' He sighed as he prodded the potatoes with a fork, telling himself to hold on to his temper and to cheer himself with the thought that tonight, he was being allowed to take Katie Murphy to the music hall for the first time. A feeling of warmth engulfed him and he smiled at his brothers as they returned to the table with hands superficially washed. 'Good that's better – now eat up your food and then I'll give you both a halfpenny to buy sweets.'

'Hey, Ceri,' Tom said quickly, 'we're not babbas, mind, to be coaxed with sweets – we're growing boys.'

'Aye, all right, have it your own way then.' Ceri moved away from the table, suddenly unable to eat. He would go to the room that he shared with the twins and get himself ready and for once, he would not be smelling of fish-scales! He smiled to himself in the darkness. Things were not so bad after all; he had a job now and if necessary he could pay a doctor to see to mam . . . and above all, he was the lucky man who was walking out with Katie Murphy!

* * *

Market Street was quiet in the drowsing summer evening; there was no music, for no one had come to take the place of Dai-End-House who used to sit outside his door and play his old accordion, drawing tears from the eyes of his listeners. Now Dai was dead and his house rang with the sound of children's voices.

In her room above Murphy's fresh-fish shop, Katie stood before her mirror, staring at her reflection. Her hair had dulled from red-gold to russet and she leaned forward, pulling back a curl above her ear and looking for grey strands.

She was no young girl any longer of course, the milestone of thirty years had come and gone but she still retained the smooth creamy skin of her youth and did not look her age. And now the fact that she had a young follower had raised her spirits considerably. She sat down on her bed, running her hands over the patchwork quilt, seeing before her eyes the image of her husband Mark and feeling suddenly guilty because he was dead and she was alive.

Never would she forget the stormy sea crossing from France, the rending of the ship against the rocks and the swell of the waves like an enormous tongue licking men from the sodden decks. She hadn't believed that her husband was drowned, not until she saw him laid out beside the other victims of the shipwreck. To add to her grief, she had miscarried Mark's child, so she was deprived of any link with him at all.

She rose abruptly – there was no point in reliving painful memories and she had carved a new life for herself, taking over the duties of the fish shop, filling her days with work and her evenings with a round of music halls and parties and men, but none of the relationships ever grew or blossomed.

And now she had agreed to go out with Ceri Llewelyn, the man who sometimes brought fish from the river to sell in the shop. He was younger than she was, but he was thoughtful and earnest and seemed very mature. In any event, since she did not intend any serious alliance with him, the age difference didn't matter at all.

She stood before the mirror and twisted her hair into a knot at the nape of her neck. It was not a very becoming style, being one which made her eyes seem over-large and her face thin, but she was too old now for letting her hair fall loose on her shoulders. Having discreetly coloured her lips with rouge and applied a little to her pale cheeks, she felt slightly better, but wasn't looking forward to the evening with any real enthusiasm.

She had arranged to meet Ceri at the corner of Market Street and Copperman's Row, away from the prying eyes of her family. Her private life was her own and she had no wish to be questioned about it. She left the house without a word to her mother and stepped into the coolness of the evening air with a sigh of relief. It was good to be away from the ever-present stink of fish and the nagging, however gentle, of her mother, who wanted only that she be happy but thought happiness was to be found in crowds of friends.

He was there before her, a tall man with a shock of dark hair. When he turned, there was a warmth in his smile which reached some deep recesses of her heart, so that she moved towards him and put her arm through his in a gesture of friendliness.

'Sure I hope I haven't kept you waiting,' Katie said lightly. 'When does the show start?'

'Don't worry, we've got plenty of time.' Ceri hugged her arm to his side and a warning bell rang in Katie's mind – she would have to tread carefully with this one, for she sensed he could be easily hurt.

'I hear that "The Great Samson", the strong man, is part of the show,' Katie said conversationally. 'And there's bound to be a magician and a singer, so it should be a good evening.'

'Aye, it should, but what makes it a good evening for me is that you're with me. Do you know how long it has taken me to pluck up the courage to ask you out?'

She shook her head, not meeting his eyes. 'Now don't go putting me on any pedestal now. I'm just a woman with many a flaw, so remember that much, won't you?'

'Nonsense!' He leaned towards her and for a moment she thought he meant to kiss her, but then he drew away. 'You are a very beautiful woman, even with your hair screwed behind your head like an old schoolmarm!'

She touched the knot of hair self-consciously, thinking that perhaps she should have made a little more effort. 'Sorry!' she said acidly. 'I'll try to do better next time.'

The Empire was crowded, people pushing in the dimness of the lowered lights as they tried to find a seat. The orchestra was tuning up in the pit, the scrape of the violin setting Katie's teeth on edge. Yet there was an excitement within her as she stared at the folds of the curtain that covered the stage – an anticipation of a magical evening, an escape from the ever-present pain of her life without Mark.

The performance was lively, beginning with the 'Marvellous Maltese', a short, swarthy man built in the Welsh-Iberian image rather than the Maltese, but juggling cleverly with a number of batons and balancing a large ball on the end of his chin.

Katie felt Ceri reach out for her hand and allowed her fingers to rest within his without making any overt gesture of reciprocation. Glancing at him covertly, she was surprised to find his appearance pleased her. His profile was strong, his mouth large and humorous and there was about him an air of someone who would protect and cherish. Perhaps it was about time she thought of settling down again, rather than flitting like a butterfly from one unmeaningful relationship to another.

Katie did not believe she could ever love again, not really *love*. She had been too deeply hurt, yet there was one part of her which longed for a home of her own and a baby to hold close to her breast. A child would be an extension of herself and perhaps her iciness would melt if she could feel tiny arms around her.

The strong man was a bit of a disappointment, doing all the usual tricks of bending bars around a huge neck and lifting his rather thin girl partner above his head.

'Not much of a strong man!' Ceri whispered, echoing her thoughts. 'My father could do better than that any day of the week.'

Katie silently agreed, for she had seen Siona Llewelyn sculling the ferry-boat across the River Swan. He was a bull of a man, with big arms and a gleam in his eyes that revealed his liking for the fair sex.

Somehow, Katie was not enjoying the show as much as she might, but usually her escorts took her to the public bar of the Bellevue in Nelson Street and plied her with gin before going on to the Empire. She normally laughed a lot during the evenings and sometimes even smoked an occasional cigarette, but with Ceri she felt the need to be more sensible – she could easily become fond of him. She drew herself up sharply, knowing she needed to think a great deal before committing herself to anything but the lightest of flirtations.

When at last, Ceri led her down the steps and out into the night air, Katie sighed deeply as she looked up at the clear stars, her spirits low. Ceri seemed to sense her mood, for he didn't speak but walked at her side in a silence that she found somehow comforting.

'You're a very nice young man.' She had said the words without thinking and Ceri stopped walking and manoeuvred her into a doorway, his hands on her shoulders. Katie sighed, hoping there was not going to be the usual silliness of having to repel unwelcome advances. But Ceri simply stood there, looking down at her.

'I won't try anything on, I promise. I'm not that callous and in any case, I have too much respect for you.' He looked down at her, his expression soft. 'And what's more, I know you're still grieving over the loss of your husband.' The words fell softly into the silence and suddenly Katie found herself in Ceri's arms, looking up at him and touching his cheek.

'How is it that you're so sensitive?' she asked in wonder. She put her head down against his shoulder and suddenly she was crying against his waistcoat. He simply held her, his chin against her hair, and after a while Katie moved out of his arms and took out a handkerchief, rubbing at her face and feeling foolish.

'Sure and isn't it daft of me to carry on like a child?' she said softly, unable to look him in the eye. Yet she felt a sense of relief grow within her, because with this man there was no need for pretence and for that she was grateful.

'I'll take you home.' Ceri caught her arm and together they walked towards Greenhill, unaware that the sky was clouding over and the stars were disappearing. It was not until the rain started to fall that they began to hurry, running uphill towards Copperman's Row, Katie holding on to her hat with both hands.

'Come in,' she said as they neared the house in Market Street. 'It's all right, the family will all be in bed by now and you won't be quizzed about your prospects or anything like that. I'll even make you a cup of tea if you're very good.'

The fire still burned in the grate and Katie stirred it up before pushing the kettle on to the flames. She threw down her hat and impatiently undid the knot of hair, unaware how young and lovely she looked to Ceri who was watching her every movement.

'Talking about prospects,' he said, 'I'm starting in the White Rock tomorrow. In the foundry I'll be, for a start anyway.'

Katie looked at him consideringly, her lips pursed. 'Well, it's not really any of my business, but are you sure that's where you want to work. I've heard some call it the graveyard.'

'Rubbish!' Ceri said quickly and from his tone, Katie deduced that he had had this argument already.

'Fine!' She smiled at him and held out a cup of tea, ''Tis none of my business – and as long as you are sure it's what you want?'

'I'm sure,' he said, drinking his tea quickly. 'I'd better be off, I suppose.' He rose to his feet and on an impulse, Katie went to him and cupped his face in her hands. She pressed her lips to his for only a brief moment and drew away before he could respond.

'Good night, Ceri, and be sure to look after yourself in work, won't you?' She opened the door and saw the rain was still washing down on the cobbled roadway outside.

'Shall I see you soon?' he asked, his voice steady but Katie knew he was nervous by the way he was twisting his cap in his hands.

'Sure you'll see me soon – come and knock on the door and ask for me any time, right now?' She watched his tall figure hurry away for a moment before closing the door on the rain.

She felt unsettled by the evening she had spent with Ceri and guilty that he was starting in the White Rock – knowing that somehow she had been responsible for his decision. Perhaps she'd be better off not seeing him for a while; she would go out with one of her old pals, have a drink and a laugh, treat life like a joke instead of getting serious about it.

And yet, as she turned down the gas-lights and made her way up to her room, she couldn't get the thought of Ceri Llewelyn out of her mind.

CHAPTER FIVE

The fields of Ram's Tor Farm were bathed in the golden glow of an early September morning as Betty-the-Milk rounded the headland from Oystermouth village. Behind her, she could hear her nephews Alex and Hector arguing – amiably enough, for the twins were good friends – about who should take the churns into the cowshed.

'Right then, boyo, let's both go,' Alex said, his voice carrying in the soft scented breeze. Betty smiled, for the argument was always resolved in the same way with both the young men manhandling the churns from the back of the cart on to the stone flags of the farmyard.

The door of the low, whitewashed house was opened and Catherine Lloyd stood smiling cheerfully, her son next to her. What a change in a woman, Betty mused, for once Catherine had carried the cares of the world on her young shoulders, saddled after the war with a crippled and embittered husband. And when she was widowed, she had continued working the farmlands bravely enough with Morgan Lloyd on hand to help. He had eventually married Catherine and that had been the making of the girl.

'Morning, Catherine,' Betty said, edging herself off the cart and smoothing down her crisp white apron. 'There's well you're looking, marriage and mother-hood seem to suit you; happy enough you've been these past few years, that's been clear enough for anyone to see.'

66

Catherine smiled and waved her hand. 'Come on in and have a nice cup of tea, Betty,' she said warmly. 'The twins can see to the milk, can't you, boyos?'

'Aye,' Hector said, pretending reluctance though his eyes – light blue like those of his brother – were warm. 'We'll want a sup of that dandelion pop when we've finished, mind,' he added, dodging the swinging sweeps of Betty's hand.

'*Duw*, getting too old for these early morning jaunts, I am.' Betty settled herself into the wooden armchair near the fire and took the cup of tea that Catherine had poured for her. 'Going to have to give the twins a bit more responsibility, I am.'

Catherine Lloyd sat opposite Betty with her son leaning shyly on her knee, quiet as he usually was in the presence of other people. She ruffled the golden curls so like his father's and smiled; Betty was right, marriage and motherhood had brought her great happiness.

'Aye, I think I'll try the boys out for a day or so – let them collect the milk alone and do the rounds, come to that; they're big enough and ugly enough not to need wet-nursing any longer.' Betty stretched her legs, easing the cramp of her muscles, feeling the money pouch jangle against her plump stomach. 'But would they be able to handle the finances, I wonder?' she said thoughtfully.

'Give them the chance to prove themselves, Betty,' Catherine said slowly. 'They are sensible young men and should do well for you.' She allowed her hand to rest on her son's shoulder and Betty smiled, watching the young woman react to her son as though she had never been without him. Motherhood must be a wonderful thing, though the nearest she would ever get to that state was in her kinship with Alex and Hector. No chick nor child did she have to account to, so why not give the Llewelyn boys the chance to run the round for a while? It could be that eventually they could all three come to a more permanent arrangement.

Hector, rapping his knuckles against the open doorway, entered the kitchen and stared longingly at the bottle of pop lying just inside the pantry door. Betty followed his gaze and smiled as Catherine nodded her head, indicating that the boy help himself.

Hector brought out two mugs and just as he finished pouring the fizzy liquid, Alexander appeared as though drawn by some invisible thread of thought. Betty had witnessed this phenomenon many times and ceased to be amazed by it, but Catherine was wide-eyed as Hector handed his brother the mug.

'Got a silent language, have those two,' Betty explained. 'I suppose it comes from being brought from the same womb at the same time. Surprised me at first, only small they were when they first came on the round but it was there even then.'

She watched as the boys squatted down in the sunlit doorway, resting, enjoying the peaceful moments before they needed to be away to the village, delivering milk from door to door. Hector had become quite adept at calling from the cart in a loud voice. 'Milko!' had become his favourite word, shouted with such gusto that casual customers were drawn outdoors. And Hector would serve a gill of milk with such a warm smile that the customers would be made to feel important.

Alexander was the silent one, but with a warmth in his eyes that drew Betty's regard. Oh, yes, an asset were the twins and no mistake.

'Well, this won't get the work done.' Betty rose to her feet and brushed down her apron, so well-starched that it crackled. 'I'll see you come morning, Catherine Lloyd, and perhaps you'll keep the brownest eggs for me – love 'em with a brown shell, I do.'

The dreaming sunshine of the morning lulled her as she walked along beside the now full cart, her hand resting on the bridle of the docile horse drooping between the traces. 'Get a move on, Sabre!' she urged the animal, grown old in her service and thin now, but still strong enough to climb the hills around Ram's Tor.

'Give poor Sabre a chance, Betty girl,' Hector said cheerfully. 'At least she's not half-asleep like some I could mention.'

'*Duw*, I swear you get more cheeky every passing day and you not yet seventeen. Think you're a man now, don't you? Well, perhaps in the next few days you can prove it.'

Alexander and Hector looked at Betty and then at each other and nodded slightly. Betty sighed. 'Aye, you know what I'm thinking before I do. Yes, I want you to try out the round, just the two of you, see how you handle the money side of things.' She paused and saw two pairs of blue eyes resting on her gravely.

'You know I'd trust you with my life, but some people have sense about money and some folks have none, so we'll just have to see where you two boys come into things, won't we?'

Hector smiled and patted Sabre's head. 'Been counting my dad's takings from the ferry-boat this past year or so. We know about money all right, Betty, so rest easy, you.'

They continued to walk downhill towards Oystermouth village in silence, the air balmy on a fine September day with the salt scent of the breeze carrying inwards from the sea. The houses on the front sparkled in the bright light and the roadway shimmered with unexpected heat. On the beaches, ketches lay drunkenly for the tide was on the ebb, leaving small boats stranded.

A lone figure, stark against the sunlight, was bent over a shovel digging for the lugworms that made circular shapes in the wet sand. Children laughed and screamed as they ran along the beach, released from school by the ringing of the bell. Overhead seagulls, always hungry, called mournfully into the sunlight.

Betty nodded and smiled to her usual customers, but her mind was racing. What if she allowed the twins to buy the round from her? Oh, they had no money, she didn't think that for a moment, but they could do all the work and pay her a little bit each month out of the profits. She watched Alex smile at Gladys Richards who hobbled to the door on her sticks with a large jug covered in a spotless cloth. A sad figure was Gladys, her husband and son lost to the sea and she becoming more and more crippled with the bone-ache.

'*Duw*, there's well you're looking, girl,' she said, for a white lie was sometimes kinder. 'Got any of that *teisen lap* baked? My boys are partial to a bit of plate cake, especially yours.'

'Aye, come on in and have a sit with me; the twins will manage without you for once and they can have some cake later on.'

Betty glanced at Hector, who nodded and led the horse away down the road, the milk churns clanking out a tune in the quiet morning air.

'Been up to Ram's Tor Farm as usual for my milk,' Betty said, making conversation, for Gladys was looking puffy round the eyes – a condition due no doubt to the bottle of spirits she kept on her mantelpiece for dulling the pain in her poor swollen legs. 'Seen Catherine and her little son – lovely boy and like a grandson to you, I dare say.'

Gladys smiled, her eyes alight. 'Oh, aye, my happiest times are spent up on the fields with that little boy. A lovely placid child he is, mind. Going up there later on I am, if these bad legs will take me. But come on, let's get that cake ready for when the boys return, shall we?'

*   *   *

Alexander patted the warm flank of the horse and stared at his brother, who was ladling out a jug of milk for one of the village girls; she simpered and fluttered dark eyelashes at him, so that some of the pearly liquid spilled to the cobbled roadway. Alexander felt the same sense of excitement that he knew was gripping his twin and he frowned, thinking it was about time they both found out what this loving of a woman was all about.

His manly urges had come upon him early and Alexander thought pensively that he must be more like his father than he had ever realized. That Siona Llewelyn, owner of the ferry-boat, liked a bit of skirt was no secret, except from mam of course – perhaps even Emily knew the truth, but kept a still tongue in her head.

'Come on, man, you can't stand there gazing at Sarah Matthews all day – got work to do, mind,' Alexander said softly.

Hector turned and winked. 'Jealous, are you, boy? Well, I don't think the girl can make up her mind which of us she likes best, which is one reason why she should come out with both of us, isn't it?'

Sarah giggled and blushed richly, tossing back long silky hair that swung like a dark cloud around the pale creamy skin of her neck.

'Go out with you two, there's a laugh! Wouldn't trust you boys from Sweyn's Eye further than I could throw you!' She twisted her ribbons between slim fingers. 'But if I can bring my friend Bella, then I'll come.'

'Righto, see you outside the Empire tonight and then we'll give you a fish-and-chip supper and ride home on the Mumbles train.'

Sarah giggled once more. 'There's rich you must be, Hector Llewelyn, splashing out your money like that. See you later – perhaps.'

She closed the door on Hector who turned and laughed, his teeth gleaming white against the sunburnt skin. He was a handsome devil, this brother of his, Alexander thought, which must mean that he himself was good-looking. As always, Hector reflected his own thoughts.

'A pair of handsome boyos like us should be experienced by now, know what it's like to have a woman, especially if we're to take over the round from Betty and become business men.'

He paused and bit his lip thoughtfully. 'Make plans in that direction, we must. We'll have to be sure to sell a variety of produce like cabbage and lettuce, expand on the round a bit. Get another cart – one each, see, and soon we'll be men of importance.'

Alexander allowed his brother to go on; Hector was always the talker, even though between the two of them oral communication was superfluous. He clucked his tongue to the horse, who was drooping in the heat. 'Don't worry, girl, there's a trough down the road a little way and you can have a drink then.' He turned to Hector and smiled; today just might prove to be a turning point in both their lives.

* * *

Catherine Lloyd had given her son his dinner and, seeing that he was sleepy, had tucked him up in his bed where he lay completely relaxed and so like Morgan that she smiled involuntarily. 'Aye, you're a handsome boy, all right,' she whispered.

But she couldn't stand around idle for too long, there was still a great deal of work to do before she could make the dinner for herself and her husband. There were the hens calling protestingly on their perches, waiting to be fed their mixture of greens and ground cockle-shells bound by damp bran. And the cows would be trailing along the winding pathway from the fallow top field to the barn ready for milking.

She could hear Morgan's new ill-tempered bull

bellowing in the enclosed field behind the house and smiled, remembering how in less fortunate times they had had to sell the Welsh Black bull he had been so proud of. But nowadays things were better, the crops had been good and the farm was flourishing. And now too she was released from working with Morgan in the fields, for he had hired men to help on the land. Denny-the-Stack and Joe Beaver had become loyal and good workers, easing the load considerably. But the way the farm was now thriving meant that in the near future, more hands would be needed in the fields.

The day was balmy, the sun high and the scent of honeysuckle drifted on the breeze carried from the hedge that bordered the land.

Catherine opened the door of the wire coop where boxes containing nests were raised on a shelf, away from draughts and foxes; the birds fluttered in alarm until the smell of the grits made them calm again.

She paused for a moment, lifting her head and listening for the sound of her son's voice, for she was always alert to his needs; but all was quiet from the farmhouse kitchen.

The hens fed, Catherine made her way to the barn where the cows were standing patiently waiting to be milked. The herd was smaller now, black and white Friesians having replaced most of the short-horns. Quickly Catherine worked, watching the milk drum into the pail, knowing that here was a good profit for the cattle were healthy and yielded plentifully. She smiled, thinking of Betty and the twins; it would be a loss when the old woman gave up her round, but then Betty must be weary of work for the bone-ache was beginning to distort her chubby fingers.

But Hector and Alexander Llewelyn were good boys – well, no longer boys perhaps, but young men though still beardless. Sometimes she thought that she preferred the more gregarious Hector, but then Alexander would say or do something kind and she would warm to him. She supposed that being twins they were so much alike as to be indistinguishable, which could not be easy for them. Anyway, she hoped they would make a success of the milk round for all their sakes.

She moved around the barn dealing with the animals, carrying pails of milk to tip into the tall conical churns. It always gave her a feeling of satisfaction to see the churns become full of the foaming pearly milk, scattered here and there with bits of grass.

'Good girls,' she said softly as she left the barn. 'There's good girls, aren't you, then?'

When she returned to the house, John was awake. He stood staring at her, rubbing his eyes sleepily.

'Have you been quiet for mammy to work, John, my love?' She hugged him to her for a moment and then, moving away, tumbled potatoes into a bowl.

'Mammy will play with you in a minute, boy, but there's a bit more work to be done yet.' She bent over the potatoes, peeling them rapidly, some for the meal and some to be cooked for pig-swill. Catherine was proud of her animals and her pigs provided the best bacon in the district. She had got rid of the black wild boar which had stared at her with baleful eyes, replacing him with an amiable male which took to the female on sight.

Catherine shuddered, remembering the old sow she had been forced to have destroyed. The animal had injured itself on the wire fencing and had to be put to the knife. Catherine could still recall the creature's almost human squealing.

Swiftly, she put the potatoes on to boil and then turned to take her son on to her knee. 'There, mammy can play for a while now.'

Lovingly she smiled into her child's face, hugging him close. Hearing the sounds of the old cottage around her, the creaking of the boards, the ticking of

74

the clock, the falling of coals in the black-leaded grate, she was content.

* * *

Hector was standing before the mirror in the parlour, slicking down his thick unruly hair. Behind him, he heard a low laugh and grimaced at his double mirror image, for his twin was standing behind him.

'Don't want to look like something the river's chucked up, do we?' Hector said defensively. 'Anyway, you're looking clean and tidy yourself – just by way of a change.'

'What's the betting that I get Sarah's friend, who is doubtless as plain as sin?' Alexander said in his slow, almost lazy way. 'Can't see any girl being as pretty as Sarah.'

'Don't look on the black side, boyo!' Hector eyed his brother thoughtfully. 'I'll have Bella if it will make you feel any better. Anyway, you don't look at the mantelpiece when you're poking the fire now, do you?' He knew that his brother disliked crudeness, but Hector couldn't resist baiting his twin and seeing the fire flare into the blue eyes.

'I'm not rising to it, not this time,' Alexander said and Hector sighed. There were disadvantages to having a brother who knew your thoughts before you did yourself.

'Come on, then, let's get down to the Empire. Once we're across the river, it's not much of a walk.'

'Perhaps they won't even come,' Alexander said glumly as he followed his brother to the door.

'Who won't come – and where are you boys off to?' Emily stood in the passageway with the baby in her arms, challenging her sons. Hector put his hands on her shoulders and leaned towards her confidingly, but her eyes never left his face.

'We're meeting some girls,' Alexander said before

75

his twin could make up some story or other. 'No harm in that, mam – only human we are, mind, and like to get out and have a good time.' He paused and smiled down at his mother reassuringly. 'No harm will come to us and it's not often we get a night off, is it?'

Emily's stern expression relaxed. 'There's a lot of truth in that, my sons,' she said slowly, 'but no drinking and no smoking Woodbines, mind.'

When the door had closed behind them, Hector let out a long breath. '*Duw!* I thought mam was going to send us to bed like a pair of little boys! Wouldn't put it past her, mind!'

Alexander made his way silently towards the pole where the lamp was hanging. He lit it and watched as the wick caught alight before he replaced it. From the other side of the water, Siona would see the light and know he had a passenger, though he wouldn't be too pleased to see it was only his sons who needed sculling across the river.

But it was Big Eddie who brought the boat in towards the broad steps. He whistled through his teeth when he saw the twins.

'*Duw!*' He stared at them with a smile in his eyes as first Hector and then Alexander climbed into the boat. 'Going out tom-catting, aren't you? There's a pair of lucky swine! Come with you, I would, but our dad's gone for a drink in the Rising Sun and I'm stuck with this here ferry-boat.'

'Thank God for that.' Hector said but he was smiling, his shoulders tilted, feeling his brother's approbation and revelling in it. Hector was a little disappointed it was not his father sculling the boat, for Siona did not yet see the twins as men and he would have loved a chance to change his father's mind about that.

'Do I know the lucky girls then?' Eddie pursued the subject and Alexander simply hunched his shoulders and peered into the murky waters. It was left to Hector to reply.

76

'No, you wouldn't know them – from Oystermouth village they are, see? Taking them to the Empire, we are.'

'Then you're going to have the pleasure of walking the girls home along the sand dunes – crafty pair of boyos, aren't you?' Eddie grinned. 'I presume you're going to get a bit of romancing in, otherwise it's not worth the price of the entrance into the Empire, is it?'

Hector shrugged, for once at a loss for words. He didn't really know how to set about 'romancing' as Eddie called it. Girls were such strange creatures, full of giggles and screams, with silky hair tied in ribbons and neat ankles peeping from under their skirts. But he was sure he would enjoy exploring the subject with the help of Sarah, who seemed more experienced in these things than he was. At least, that was the impression she always gave him whenever he stopped to flirt with her.

It seemed an age before the ferry-boat bumped the shore at the other side of the river. A cold wind was whipping the water and ruffling Hector's carefully combed-down hair. He climbed on to the bank and thrust his hands into his pockets, jingling the shillings against each other as he tried to appear indifferent to Eddie's huge wink.

'Don't let any harm befall our Hector,' Eddie said, his eyes gleaming with amusement. 'He's such an impulsive fool, and anyway our mam would be furious if her favourite boy got hurt.'

Alexander eyed his brother with a level gaze and after a moment Eddie, discomfited, pushed the boat away from the bank.

'Don't take any notice of Eddie,' Hector said cheerfully. 'Only jealous because we're off out and he's stuck with the ferry.' His spirits rose as he walked down the road from the Haford towards the town. Sarah would come, he felt confident of it; he had seen the look in her eyes more than once, that look which told him she was interested. Perhaps he should buy her some sweets or a couple of Fry's chocolate bars, but then would such a gesture seem foolish?

Hector was not over-fond of the Empire; the juggling acts and the endless round of magicians performing the same old tricks wearied him. He would have preferred a good old music hall show, or even the darkness and warmth of the new cinema with the magic of Western cowboys shooting it out on the range, or the excitement of a train hold-up brought to vivid life before his eyes. Still, he would be with Sarah, seated next to her – and for all that he had offered to take the unknown Bella off his brother's hands, he knew it would be Sarah he would end up with.

His heartbeat quickened as he neared the ornate façade of the theatre and he glanced at Alexander, knowing his brother felt the same sense of anticipation. They smiled at each other and moved forward through the crowds thronging the pavement, eyes searching eagerly.

Hector felt his arm grasped and then Sarah was looking up at him, her lips parted, her teeth pearly. 'There's late you are, Hector, thought you weren't coming I did!' She turned to the girl standing in the background. 'Come on, Bella, don't be shy; there's no harm in Alexander, he's the quiet one. It's *this* boyo that needs watching!'

Hector glanced at Bella, a sweet-looking girl with soft blonde hair and pink cheeks. She was an innocent, without the provocative sensuousness that Sarah possessed. Alexander would be well suited, he thought wryly, and glancing at his brother was rewarded with a slight nod.

'Come on, then,' he said as he moved forward. 'No queuing for the "gods" for us, we'll have a good seat in the stalls.' He led the way as though he was filled with confidence, but only he and his twin brother knew that it was all an act.

78

They were seated only four rows from the front and the sound of the band tuning up grated on Hector's ears, but Sarah's fingers reached out and caught his and he smiled down at her.

When the lights were lowered, she leaned towards him and she smelled of honey and roses. He rested his cheek against her hair for a moment and she turned her face up towards him, her eyes promising unimaginable delights.

There was such a confusion of feelings stirring in him that Hector felt every act which appeared on the boards was possessed of some special magical quality. Even the foolish comic had him laughing and applauding and at his side, Sarah pressed her soft breast against his arm.

For once Hector didn't notice his brother. What Alexander chose to do was his own business, but later when they left the theatre he would be on his own.

Sarah's hand brushed his knee and he sat up straighter in his seat. He felt as though every muscle in his body had tightened to breaking point. He had experienced the usual longings and torments of puberty, of course, but nothing like this elation which held him in its grip, burning in his gut and sending a fire through his loins.

He couldn't wait to be outside in the coolness of the summer evening. His hand still clung to Sarah's, and he cared nothing for looking silly.

'I'm taking Bella to buy her some baked potatoes.' Alexander, in his usual knowing way, understood Hector's need to be alone with Sarah. 'See you later, righto?'

Hector made no reply, there was no need. 'Come on, Sarah, let's walk along the beach in the moonlight, *cariad*.'

She looked up at him, her neck arched backwards reminding him of an elegant swan. 'There's nice to hear you call me "love".' Her voice was soft, her eyes alight.

The sea was bathed with a soft silver glow and the sand was almost white in the moonlight. It was soft beneath the feet, still retaining the heat of the sun and on an impulse, Hector stopped and pulled off his boots. Sarah smiled up at him, her hair tumbling free of its ribbons.

'I know, let's paddle in the sea!' Laughing, she ran to the water's edge and paused with her hand to her lips. 'Oh, look how the white foam glows in the moonlight, Hector – isn't it lovely?'

'Lovely,' he said, taking her slim body in his arms and feeling her heart begin to pound against his. 'I must have you, Sarah – you know that, don't you?' He didn't wait for her reply! 'Are you frightened, Sarah?'

She leaned her head against his chest. 'Yes,' she said in a muffled voice, 'but I can't help myself. I've loved you and wanted you for so long, mind.'

He led her up the beach to where the hillocks of sand threw out dark shadows. There they sat down together and then he was searching for her mouth. It was very soft, much softer than he had expected. Her arms clung to him, holding him, pressing him closer.

Her body was firm and sweet and when he touched her naked breast a sensation of joy sped through him.

'Sarah!' he said thickly and she put a finger against his lips, leaning back in his arms waiting, quiescent, wanting him. His thoughts dissolved into pure beams of light that spun around his brain. He told himself to be careful of the silk beneath him, but the urge to plunge and take was so great that he lost himself until his own moans penetrated the cloud in his brain.

'Sarah, my lovely, have I hurt you?' he whispered hoarsely. She took his face in her hands and kissed his mouth. 'We are in love, my own sweet boyo, and love can't hurt – can it?' Her voice trembled and he held her close, tender now, smoothing back the tangled hair from her hot face.

'I'll take care of you always, Sarah. You are my girl

now, mind, and no one else must even look at you or I'll kill them!'

Hector felt the power of possession run like a rich wine through his blood. He was a man, he had proved it and this lovely girl in his arms had made him so — for that he would always be grateful.

He thought briefly about Alexander and then forgot his brother as the closeness of Sarah's naked body to his skin aroused him once more. This time he would be tender, would think of Sarah's needs, for he wanted her to know the same joy as he did.

He stroked her breasts, the flat of her stomach, her thighs, knowing instinctively how to please her. She closed her eyes, arching towards him, and with a feeling of heady power he went to her once more, longing to taste the sweet wine of love.

CHAPTER SIX

The cobbled roadway was wet and grey in the early morning dew. The scent of roses hung achingly sweet on the riverside air and the sky overhead was shifting from indigo to blue. It was going to be another fine September day.

Ceri climbed into the ferry-boat, nodding uncommunicatively to his father, neither expecting nor receiving any sign of interest for Siona seemed preoccupied with the scull, pulling from it a lump of glossy seaweed and examining it, his face turned away. Ceri sighed. It seemed to him that the bond between father and son should be inbuilt, a part of nature, so why did Siona always seem a million miles away from him.

The boat was filling up with lead workers. They seemed a people apart, pale of skin and almost universally thin with rotten teeth and sparse colourless hair showing from beneath jutting cap-peaks. Ceri felt a momentary qualm – was he doing the right thing working at the White Rock? Would the lead taint his blood as mammy had insisted, a taint that was passed on from one generation to the next? But then he did not intend to work the lead for very long; he would rise up in the business – be a manager perhaps – for his ambition had grown, along with the desire that ached in his loins as well as his heart for Katie Murphy.

His blood sang at the thought of her. He had taken her out several times now and she was warm and seemed to care for him, but she kept him always at a distance. But he understood that she had been hurt, as tainted with the pain of loss as the workers at the White Rock were with the effects of the lead – but hers was a sickness that he was determined to cure.

The ferry bumped the bank with Siona deftly throwing a rope over the post. Ceri rose to his feet, used to the swaying of the boat beneath his feet, but some of the workers were not so fortunate.

'*Daro!* There's a witch of a ride this is to take every morning, for the river always manages to turn my belly inside out.'

The lad was young, fresh out from school and Ceri knew him by sight for he fetched the ore to the furnace mouth.

'Steady on there, Reggie, or you'll be over the side and into the water.' Ceri grasped the back of the boy's shirt and hauled him upright, pity gripping him at the thinness of Reggie's frame for the rib-cage showed through sparse flesh. '*Duw*, there's nothing of you there, you should eat more, boyo.' The words were spoken without thinking and Reggie's young face grew red, for pride was something to be held close. 'I'm all right, Ceri Llewelyn, don't you worry about me.' But the boy's eyes were suddenly moist.

The heat of the furnaces was an almost physical blow. Ceri shrugged off his shirt and tied his sweat-cloth around the strong column of his throat. He glanced down at his arms with pride, for he had filled out since starting work in the White Rock; his arms were strong now, his back broader. Nevertheless he sighed; to his father he would always be a weakling and he felt Siona's indifference to be unjustified, for Ceri had always done his best to earn a living, however humble.

He began to work, pushing the unpleasant thought to the back of his mind; the White Rock bosses did not pay men to stand around philosophizing. He nodded towards his mate and Kenny – an old hand at the job –

lifted a finger indicating he was ready. Ceri felt suddenly exhilarated, knowing there was sweat and pain in the job but also satisfaction.

The charge was dropped into the furnace and with a rumbling sound the ore spread over the upper part of the bed of coke. All the side doors as well as the fire door were open and dust spread like grey fingers so that Ceri could taste it bitter on his lips.

Ceri wiped the sweat from his face, taking the brown glass bottle of dandelion beer which Kenny passed him. Kenny was a tall man not given to much talking, but Ceri found that he could work well with him; he was reliable and conscious of safety procedures in a way that some of the younger men were not. But then Kenny had a family to care for and could not afford to take chances. In silence they worked side by side as the clock on the wall ticked away the time unnoticed.

'Keep the damper well down, Ceri,' Kenny said tersely, 'and close the doors.'

Ceri obeyed the abrupt directions, for Kenny was the best lead smelter in the works and knew how to bring the purest lead from the ore. He kept the fire well made up, for heat was now essential. Soon the lead began to trickle from the furnace, shimmering grey and silver.

'I'll give it some rabbling,' Ceri said loudly and waited for Kenny's nod of assent before he opened one of the doors to the blast of the heat. He raked at the molten lead, drawing off the slag and allowing the lead to flow more freely. His belly gnawed at him, for it was a long time since he had eaten, but there was a great deal of work to be done before he could stop for food.

He brushed back his hair and into his mind came the picture of Katie. Thinking of her pale skin and soft red hair, a warmth enveloped him, pouring from his heart into his gut. He saw Kenny glance at him with a glimmer of a smile on his morose face.

'Now, Ceri boyo – no time for dreaming of women, is it? Get rabbling or we'll be here all day!'

Ceri smiled as he opened another of the furnace doors, stopped in his tracks for a moment by the blast of heat. He rabbled with vigour, well aware of the amusement in Kenny's eyes. 'It's all right for you, man, got a wife to bed whenever you please – there are others not so fortunate, mind.'

'Your turn will come and when it does, remember a woman isn't like a furnace to be rabbled that way,' Kenny grinned. 'Oh, no, you must approach a woman softly.'

It was quite a speech for the usually taciturn Kenny and Ceri winked at him. 'So it's an expert in more ways than one you are, man?' He smiled. 'Well, I suppose you've got to be and you fathering five children and I'll remember your words, if ever I get the chance to put them into practice, that is.'

As he stared into the mouth of the furnace, the red flames leaping from the molten metal reminded him of the lights in Katie's hair.

*   *   *

Katie had been busy all morning in the shop. Her hands were raw from handling the fish and she was weary of standing talking to gossiping neighbours who seemed intent on prying into her business. It was as though the whole of Market Street was waiting to see the outcome of her relationship with Ceri Llewelyn, and that was something upon which she had not made up her own mind yet.

She liked him and liked being with him, for he had a fine sense of humour and, what was more, he treated her with the utmost respect. He took her out to shows in town and for picnics in the park and all the time she was aware of his love for her growing round her, salving her wounds.

Mammy had the meal on the table and as Katie went into the back room and sank into a chair, she folded her hands over her thin stomach in a manner that marked disapproval.

'Now, Katie, my girl, when are you going to be serious with that young man of yours? Getting old, sure you are, and your chances less every day. Saints be praised for bringing the Llewelyn boy to our house, I say.'

'Don't start, mammy, I'm so tired.' Katie leaned back in her chair, having no appetite for the bowl of soup steaming on the table. Mammy seemed to have no sense of the appropriate; she provided hot winter food on a fine day, and was quite capable of serving cold potatoes when the snow froze hard on the pavements.

'A nice way to be talking to your mammy!' Mrs Murphy banged the tea-pot on to the white cloth and golden globules of moisture fell like tears from under the brown china lid. 'You take heed of what I say now, or you'll end up your days a lonely spinster woman.'

How could Katie even begin to explain that the hurt of losing Mark had not yet left her? She had loved him so much and they had been married such a short time. It was only natural that she should wake in the darkness of the night and reach out for him, wasn't it? In her dreams he was whole, restored to her as he had been in the vigour of his youth and health. Never did he appear as the sea-battered broken man she had seen laid out in death.

She drank her tea, glad of the warmth against her aching throat. Grief was something that did not bear parading before others, for they soon wearied of it.

'I know, I'll bring in the bath and put water on to boil for you to have a lovely soak. You'll be smelling like a blossom, sure enough, by the time I've finished with you, for I've brought some rose-water for you.'

Katie glanced up quickly, realizing her mammy was not so impervious to her feelings after all. 'That's very kind, mammy, sure it's good of you to go to the trouble.'

A bath would be heaven! She could rub herself free

of the smell of the fish, she would wash her hair and sprinkle on some of the rose-water and then she would go out with Ceri Llewelyn and be glad of his company.

She watched her mother busy herself with the zinc bath, placing it before the kitchen fire, pouring the kettle which sent water drumming against the ridged bottom, gushing steam into the room.

'I'll make sure the boys nor your daddy comes in, so take your time, Katie girl.'

On an impulse, Katie hugged her mother and almost shyly, kissed her lined cheek. 'You're good to me, mammy, and I'm not always very grateful,' she said softly.

'Jesus, Mary and Joseph! If a mammy can't look after her only daughter, then she's not much of a woman!' Embarrassed, Mrs Murphy bustled out of the room and closed the door and for a moment, Katie stood with tears in her eyes as she stared into the bath water.

It was good to ease her aching limbs into the hot water. The bath was too small for stretching out, but Katie was used to folding her legs, allowing the water to cover most of her body. The rose-water scented the room and Katie sighed in contentment, closing her eyes, not wanting to think, just to feel the almost sensuous sensation of the water lapping against her breasts. It seemed that whatever her mind and heart told her, her need to be loved was not dead.

Later, in her room, she dressed carefully in a softly sprigged muslin frock with a dropped waistline that fell gently around her hips. She twisted her hair into an unfashionable plait that nevertheless was becoming and then rubbed a little rouge into her pale cheeks.

Katie was aware that to mammy such practices were a sign of decadence, for in her opinion only women of the lowest kind resorted to paint and powder. She smiled at her reflection, knowing that her skin was still good, unlined and pure but so pale that she needed artificial colour to bring her to life.

Suddenly she was glad that she had agreed to go out with Ceri. This was a day of such softness and such ripeness, an Indian summer day that was clear and breathless and so beautiful that it hurt deep within her, bringing longings that she did not even fully understand.

And above all, it was a day to be shared . . .

But it would be evening before Ceri would come to Market Street to call for her and in the meantime, with the fish shop thankfully closed for the afternoon, Katie was at a loose end.

She left the house determined to be outdoors in the sunshine and yet with no idea where she might go. She walked down Green Hill and into the town and the street shimmered with the heat of the sun. Moving through the maze of houses and leaving the huddled streets behind her, she emerged on to the long golden crescent of the beach. The sea gently rolled inwards, blue beneath a cloudless sky, and Katie breathed the salt air and felt her throat constrict. For it was this sea which had taken Mark from her, not soft and gentle as it was now but raging in the wind.

'Forget all that!' Her own voice startled her and she glanced around, fearful of being overheard, but the bay was empty of people and she was alone with the calling seagulls.

She strolled along the sands and then left the beach at the slip and made her way through the flat, grassy grounds of Victoria Park. The floral clock was ablaze with colour against the ground, blooms carefully and cleverly worked together to form numerals and the long pointing hands at the centre. She sighed, feeling alone, the gorgeous sunshine only serving to highlight her solitude.

Self-pity was such a negative attitude, she told herself sternly, and with more purpose she began to walk towards the villas which sat upon the hillside facing the sea, deciding that she would go visiting.

Mali Richardson would always welcome her and even though Katie was diffident about intruding on Mali's home life, she felt compelled to walk on up the sloping ground. If she didn't talk to someone, then she would go out of her head.

Outside the gracious gates of *Plas Rhianfa*, she paused, seeing the rich spread of the grasslands around the big house and the tall oaks standing on the boundary – such a far cry from Copperman's Row, where Mali had been born. And yet she was the same sweet girl she had always been. Encouraged by her thoughts, Katie went towards the door and knocked, biting her lip as she waited for some response.

The girl who stood on the step had fine dark hair and large eyes and seemed vaguely familiar.

'It's Nerys Beynon, isn't it? You used to look after Big Mary's little boy?' Katie warmed to the smile in Nerys's eyes as she stood back for her to enter, for she had braced herself to confront a cold, disapproving maidservant.

'That's right and now I'm nanny to Mali's children, for the time being anyway. And you're Katie Murphy from the fresh-fish shop – I'd know that red-gold hair anywhere!'

Mali herself appeared from the drawing room, her green eyes alight with pleasure. 'Come in, Katie, there's lovely to see you!'

It gave Katie a sense of calm and solace to sit in the airy, graceful room with fine oil paintings hanging on the walls and glossy plants rising from glowing china jardinières. This was an environment with which she was totally unfamiliar but with Mali seated opposite her, leaning forward eagerly waiting for her to speak, she felt warmed and comforted.

'Sure, I hope I'm not intruding,' she said softly and was rewarded by a quirk of Mali's lips.

'There's formal and grand you've become, Katie Murphy. It's me, Mali, you're talking to – remember?'

Katie returned her smile. 'Sure, I know it is and you not changed a bit by all this.' She gestured around the room, hearing the loud ticking of the grandfather clock on the wall and seeing the softness of the curtains billowing in the breeze.

'I suppose it's nicer to meet up here than in the shop with the cold-eyed fishes staring at us!' Mali smiled. 'Though I've not been into the shop for a while because I've got a job up at Tawe Lodge – looking after unmarried mothers, I am.'

'Sure, that sounds like a fine thing to be doing,' Katie said warmly. 'It seems to have made you happy, for you're looking more at ease than of late.'

'Oh, I love the work,' Mali said, 'and the sense of purpose it gives me.' She leaned forward. 'But I mustn't be selfish and talk about myself. Come on, you're worried about something, so out with it!'

Katie sighed, for Mali always could read her mind. 'It's Ceri Llewelyn – I don't know if I'm being fair to him.' She brushed back a strand of hair that was coming loose from the plait. 'He's a fine man and treats me very well and I think he's beginning to fall in love with me.'

'Well, I will say this,' Mali spoke warmly, 'my kinsman has a lot of good sense and an eye for a beautiful woman, so what's wrong with that?'

Katie shook her head. 'If only folks would let us alone! There's mammy trying to push me into Ceri's arms and the neighbours in Market Street for ever watching us, and I just don't want to be rushed.'

She saw Mali rise and pull at the tasselled silk cord that hung above the mantelshelf, knowing the gesture was as much to give Mali time to think as to summon the maid.

It was Nerys who entered the room, a broad smile on her face as she balanced a silver tray on her arm.

'There's a good girl,' Mali said, taking the tray from her. 'You anticipated my needs, I see. Go and get another cup and then you can come and chat to us.'

When the door closed behind the girl, Katie looked

towards Mali, knowing that she would speak wisely for she was not only kind-hearted but also possessed of an abundance of sound common sense.

'Just let Ceri know how you feel,' she advised at last. 'Tell him truthfully, just as you've told me. And, if you've said it once, say it again and again so that he knows just where he stands.'

Katie nodded, 'Yes, I'll do that.' She looked up quickly. 'You don't think it's wrong of me, then, to go out with him? I feel sometimes as if I'm just using him.'

Mali rested her hand lightly on Katie's shoulder in a gesture of affection. 'Don't we all use each other in some way or another – and there's nothing wrong in that so long as we give something at the same time.' She laughed a little self-consciously. 'Forgive the homespun philosophy, won't you, *cariad*?'

The door opened and Nerys entered the room, her eyes alight with laughter. '*Duw*, that boy of yours should go on the stage, Mali – there's an actor he is! Been strutting about the playroom spouting something from William Shakespeare and all in that fine English voice of his.'

Katie felt a pang of pain for she had lost her child, the baby slipping from her in a nightmare of agony and terror. Would she never forget the way that she had been robbed of her one link with Mark? She took the fine bone china cup Mali held out to her, telling herself sternly to stop feeling sorry for herself, that it did no good to re-live painful memories.

'There's well you're looking, Katie.' Nerys's voice broke into Katie's reverie. 'So pretty and young, it's no wonder you've got callers beating a path to your door!'

So even Nerys Beynon had heard that she was walking out with Ceri! Katie felt a momentary sense of anger which quickly dissolved, for it was not the girl's fault. She forced a smile.

'Well, sure you're looking fine yourself, Nerys – are

you courting yet?' Katie wanted to turn the conversation to anything but her own affairs, but in that she was unsuccessful.

'Haven't found the right man,' Nerys smiled ruefully, 'but I must say I envy you. Ceri Llewelyn is a lovely looking boyo. Gone to work in the White Rock then – and I don't think his mam likes that one little bit. Always afeared of the lead, was Mrs Llewelyn, says it taints the blood, mind.'

Katie forced a smile, guilt gnawing at her, for even this move to the lead works was because of her and she knew it. Ceri was putting money by him, planning for their future together, and Katie was not yet ready to face that prospect.

She studied Nerys – the girl was lovely, her skin glowing, her dark hair shining and curling round her face. She was a little thin, perhaps, but then she carried it well, her head held at a proud angle on slim shoulders. It was strange she had not yet married and had children of her own – too busy with other folks' lives, Katie supposed, though such vicarious family life would not do for her.

The thought trickled into her mind, spreading outwards like ripples in a pond – wouldn't that be exactly what was before her if she didn't marry Ceri? She would be sitting on the sidelines of life, watching other people have children and in due course grandchildren, and she would for ever be alone. She was no longer a young girl and as mammy had said, her chances would become fewer and already her span of childbearing was nearing its end.

She looked into Mali's eyes and saw understanding there and on an impulse held out her hand, gripping Mali's slender fingers.

'You've made up your mind, then?' Mali said softly and Katie took a deep breath.

'Yes, I've made up my mind.' She rose to her feet. 'I'd best be going now. I want to comb out my hair and change my frock and, oh, all sorts of things!' She moved towards the doorway, looking back over her shoulder at Nerys who had crystallized her thoughts for her.

'Good luck to you, Nerys, and I'm sure you'll be courting soon!' She felt Mali's arm around her waist as she moved through the large hallway towards the door.

'I'm not going to ask you anything,' Mali said. 'There's no real need, is there? I can see by the look on your face what you intend to do.' She kissed Katie's cheek. 'I know you'll be happy, *cariad*, no one deserves it more than you do.'

Katie felt the warmth of the sun on her shoulders as she left the towering gates of *Plas Rhianfa* behind her, feeling at peace with herself for the first time in months. She still wasn't sure how much she cared for Ceri, but she knew that she would strive with all her being to make him a good wife. She would bear his children and care for him, warm his hearth and not demur at warming his bed too; she would make him happy and perhaps in doing so might find a little happiness herself.

She decided not to take a tram, for the walk home would eat into the time that spread out endlessly before her. Having made up her mind, she was impatient to be with Ceri now and to tell him of her decision.

The scent of honeysuckle was in the air as Katie made her way down the hill. Below, the sea was a blue mirror reflecting sky and sunlight. As the narrow streets of the town came into view she breathed deeply, knowing only love for the ugly, stricken place where she had been born. She mingled with the cockle-sellers as they carried baskets of shell-fish on finely poised heads and heard the raucous calling of the market traders as they shouted out the excellence of their wares.

Moving towards the eastern part of the town where Green Hill lay spread on the hillside like a spider's web of narrow courts and tall houses, the scents changed from those of flowers to the sulphurous odour of the works which straddled the banks of the River Swan. Used as she was to the smell and sounds of the streets where she lived, Katie wrinkled up her nose as a gust of sparks and fumes rose from one of the stacks that soared up into the sky like a blackened monster.

Where would she live with Ceri Llewelyn, she wondered with a pang of unease. She and Mark had made their home in a small cottage on the slopes of Kilvey Hill; they had been there for such a short time, yet she had grown to love the view of the docks and the sea spreading outwards towards Ram's Tor and the Mumbles.

Her mother's eyebrows rose as Katie entered the kitchen, dim after the sun outside, and she became aware that her hair had slipped loose from its ribbons and was lying untidily around her shoulders. She sank into a chair and closed her eyes, giving herself a moment to recollect her thoughts. Hearing the rattle of tea-cups and the hissing of the water running into the pot, she warmed to her mother who wanted only the best for her.

She opened her eyes. 'I'm going to marry him!' She had said it out loud now, which seemed to make her decision a reality. 'I've made up my mind at last, mammy. I hope you're pleased.'

'You do right, girl, believe me; you're too fine to waste the rest of your life being alone. And sure, don't I want grandchildren and me sons showing no signs of marrying?' She smiled. 'Here, girl, take your tea. I'm going to put a drop of gin in mine for a lifter, I'm that excited!'

Katie smiled to herself. Any occasion was an excuse for mammy to put gin in her tea, indeed if there wasn't an excuse, Mrs Murphy would never be slow in inventing one!

'Will you iron my best frock for me, mammy?' Katie asked softly. 'I want to do something with this hair of mine.'

Mrs Murphy immediately fetched the flat-irons from the floor of the pantry and placed them both on the hob to warm. Then she made her way upstairs and Katie could hear her moving about in the bedroom, excited as a child, pleased to be involved in her daughter's life once more.

Returning to the kitchen, Mrs Murphy threw a blanket over the edge of the scrubbed table and placed the soft blue dress carefully in position. If there was one thing she prided herself on it was her laundry, for no one in Market Street could show a cleaner line of washing or more neatly ironed piece of linen.

Katie sat brushing out her hair, watching her mother frown in concentration as she bent over her task. There was a feeling of tremulous happiness growing within her as she thought of her meeting with Ceri.

She would no longer hold him at arm's length, she should and would be eternally grateful to him for loving her.

Later, as she left the house in Market Street and made her way down the hill towards the Hafod, she felt confident that her decision was the right one. The bluish twilight dimmed the river to a soft grey and the lights of the tugs were reflected in the swiftly flowing water.

Ceri was late and Katie stood impatiently on the river bank, wondering if she should catch the ferry across the water and go to his home. But no, she could not intrude; it would be a sorry thing if his mother were to think her forward. So she waited . . . waited until the darkness fell and the moon silvered the river, but he did not come. At last, she turned and made her way back home to Green Hill.

* * *

The temperature in the furnaces had risen to six-hundred degrees and Ceri, wiping his face with his sweat-rag, knew that the roasting was taking longer than usual.

He watched as Kenny raised the damper fully. There was the sound of boiling and the hissing of steam and at last the lead began to flow freely.

'Get a shovelful and a half of slaked lime in there, Ceri,' Kenny said sternly. 'On the tap-hole side, man, move it!'

Ceri quickly threw in the lime and rabbled it with the long-handled rake, mixing it with the molten lead.

'I'll break loose the bits of metal that have stuck to the sides of the furnace, Ceri, man.' Kenny took up a paddle and leaned forward, shielding his face with one arm.

'*Duw*, it's as hot as hell by here, man. Push in the rabble on your side and try to free the solidified metal, Ceri, then let it fall back into the rest of the stuff.'

Intent as he was on the job, Ceri realized that now he must be late for his meeting with Katie.'Damn the furnace!' he said under his breath and rabbled the harder, taking out his anger on the metal which fell hissing into the molten lead.

Kenny passed a can of tea to Ceri and he drank it thirstily. 'Good thing I've got a wife who'll bring my snap in, boyo.' He held out a cheese sandwich. 'Got any plans for yourself in that department, have you?'

Ceri grimaced wryly. 'I might have if I can get out of this hell-hole on time!' He sank back on to his haunches and finished the food in silence, wondering what Katie would be thinking about him not turning up. Would she hurry away in a huff and never forgive him, or would she perhaps worry a little in case there had been an accident.

Later, as the tap-hole was opened and the lead flowed into the pot, he was too busy to think of anything but the work before him. He skimmed the lead with a perforated flat-iron shovel and then threw coal slack on to it, working the slack well in. Lastly, Ceri raked out the grey slag from the furnace on to the iron plate on the floor. The damper was still up, the furnace being prepared for the next charge; the whole process was about to begin once more.

CHAPTER SEVEN

The town was bathed in a soft morning glow, the mist rising from the river promising another fine September day. The shops in the *Stryd Fawr* were opening the doors, owners placing a variety of wares on display. A baker's van chugged along the cobbled street, crusty loaves emanating a mouth-watering smell, and Nerys Beynon remembered with fear the time when Terrence had taken off with her money and she had learned what it was like to be hungry.

She shook away her thoughts and concentrated on her task of seeking another job, for her duties at *Plas Rhianfa* were light – so light that she knew the time for the parting of the ways was drawing near.

The Richardson children had returned to their boarding schools several weeks earlier and since then Nerys had been given numerous inconsequential tasks: mending the linen sheets, clearing out the toy cupboards, even polishing the nursery furniture. But the pretence that there was work for her at *Plas Rhianfa* was wearing thin and even the warm-hearted Mali Richardson could not keep up the fiction for much longer.

Nerys made her way to the Emporium which had once been owned by Mary Sutton. Here she had been happy, sure of her position, knowing that Mary needed her as much as a friend as a nurse for the children, and sometimes as a helper on the linen counter.

The Emporium had changed hands yet again,

bought by a mysterious faceless consortium. Nerys walked timidly in through the doors, not knowing what to expect.

'Can I help you, madam?' The voice was smooth, the Welsh intonations purposely ironed out into flat vowel sounds. The young woman smiled patronizingly at Nerys, as though she was confronting an inferior being, and Nerys stiffened, clenching her hands to her sides and telling herself to be calm.

'I'm looking for some responsible person, someone in charge.' The words came out coolly, almost like an insult, and the young woman's fair eyelashes moved rapidly – the only sign that she was agitated.

'Well, my dear, you have found what you're looking for. I *am* a responsible person and I assure you that I *am* in charge.'

Nerys stepped back a pace. She needed a job, but not so badly that she would lower her pride and ask anything of this hoity-toity woman who stood with white hands clasped together as though about to bestow a benediction on those less fortunate than herself.

'It doesn't matter.' Nerys lifted her head. 'I shall take my business elsewhere.' The words were fine and brave, but they would not earn her one single farthing and as she stood outside, breathing in the soft morning air, she cursed herself for being a stiff-necked fool.

Once more she thought fondly of Mary, who for all her wealth had never treated her as anything other than an equal. Mary had known better than most what it was like to live in poverty, having risen above her poor beginnings to become one of the most influential women in Sweyn's Eye. But those days were past, Nerys reminded herself; Mary had left the country long ago to live in America.

In the twisting cobbled roadway of Wind Street, Nerys paused outside the windows of Taylors, the grocery shop. From the interior came the rich scent of ground coffee and the sound of the grinder which sent small puffs of dust on to the counter. Inside, Nerys looked around her; the shop was long, going right back into the building with shelves full of stock. The bacon counter was on the right and large rounds of butter were being cut and paddled into squares by a white-overalled young woman.

Nerys smiled diffidently, moving forward and holding her head high. 'Is the owner of the shop about?' she asked, mustering a cheerful voice and smiling calmly as though her heart was not beating at twice its normal speed. The woman, hard-faced, looked at her with an unblinking stare.

'No, Mr Taylor is out on business,' the woman replied. 'What do you want here?' She sounded suspicious, her lip curling in disdain, and before Nerys could reply she had launched into an attack.

'If it's a job you're wanting, there isn't one!' She leaned forward, her work-roughened hands pressed against the wooden counter. 'If there was, you wouldn't have a look-in, see. Got two sisters and four brothers out of work, I have – don't you think they'd be told first off if there was anything going by here?'

Nerys left the shop, her head high as she moved along the streets, staring into windows as though somehow a position needing to be filled would come out and meet her.

She *must* find a job, she was determined on it – anything so that she could go to Mali and give her notice graciously without waiting for the inevitable, painful moment when she would be told she must leave.

Suddenly the door of the Flint Mill was flung open and the stench of stale beer and sawdust was pungent on the soft air as a powdered young woman – wearing a fox fur around her shoulders in spite of the sunshine – stormed out on to the pavement.

'Keep your job, Bulla Johns! Rosa does not need to

steal money from any man's till! Anyway, worked me to death you did, all drudgery and no fun. Well, I'm cut out for better things than slaving from sunrise to sunset for an ungrateful oaf!' She swept past Nerys without a sideways glance and in a mist of heavy perfume stalked away down the street.

Nerys looked at the big, dark-haired man standing in the doorway. His arms were folded across his great chest and around his broad waist was a striped apron. Her throat was dry with sudden hope, so dry that for a moment she coughed and was quite unable to speak.

'I'm looking for a job,' she said quickly. 'And I can bring a reference from Mrs Richardson, wife of the copper boss, mind.'

The man regarded her in surprise for what seemed an eternity, then he nodded slowly and, taking her arm, drew her inside the darkness of the public bar.

'Right then, miss, we'll give you a trial, provided you can supply that reference. Go into my kitchen and make me a bit of dinner – we'll say that's your first job, shall we?' He pushed her past the men at the bar, one of whom whistled through his teeth.

'Sweet piece of meat you've got there, Bulla – not the usual sort though, is she? The customers here will eat her for breakfast.'

'Watch your mouth!' he said sharply, then turned and smiled at Nerys. 'Take no notice of those ruffians.' He led her into a surprisingly neat kitchen where the brasses round the fireplace glowed as though lovingly polished and the curtains on the windows were clean and bright.

'Need a housekeeper, I do. A widower I am, see, with three young daughters to care for.' He spoke almost in a whisper and Nerys felt pity for the big man wash over her.

'Are you used to children then?' He didn't wait for a reply, but hurried on. 'Well, you look respectable

101

enough, but you'd need to help out in the bar sometimes, mind.' He looked down at his hands. 'Not nice
work for a lady like you, but there it is.'

'We'll see what happens,' said Nerys, feeling her
confidence grow. 'And yes, I'm well used to children,
don't worry about that. For now I'll just cook your
dinner, so you leave me to find my way round the
kitchen and we'll be all right.'

He returned to the bar while Nerys, hearing the
coarse laughter of the men, closed her mind to it.
Bulla Johns seemed honest enough and he was willing
to give her a job; that was all that mattered.

She glanced round her. The building was small and
probably boasted few bedrooms, the paintwork
though clean was dour and unattractive, but if she
succeeded in convincing Bulla that she would be
invaluable in the house, then she could make alter-
ations. In the meantime, it would do well enough.

Of course her way of life would be entirely different
here, for she had never worked in a public bar, but she
could learn and she would face that problem when
she came to it. And she would hate leaving Mali
Llewelyn too and the comfortable room which had
become home to her, but she had no choice.

She wondered briefly where Bulla Johns's daughters were, but imagined they must be so young as to be
at school.

There was a shoulder of ham in the wooden safe
and Nerys sliced several pieces from it, placing them
in a large pan over the fire. The meal would be
ordinary enough – a few eggs and slices of fried bread
to go with the ham – but it was the best she could do at
such short notice.

As the ham sizzled in the pan, she looked around
her curiously. She opened a cupboard and found a
pile of clean clothes facing her; it seemed that Bulla
kept a good home, which was very reassuring. Yet
Nerys couldn't help comparing the small rooms with

the large, airy nursery at *Plas Rhianfa* – but she would adapt, she would simply have to, she told herself.

By the time Bulla had closed up the public bar, the meal was ready to serve. The ham was succulent, the rind crisp and flavoured by cloves. The eggs were white, firm on the top but with the yolk ready to spurt forth at the cut of a knife-blade.

'That looks good indeed, *merchi*.' Bulla sat down before the table, his big legs spread, his hands already gripping the shining cutlery. He ate daintily for such a big man, his eyes never once looking up from his plate. Even when Nerys handed him a cup of tea, he merely nodded uncommunicatively. He seemed to enjoy the meal – he certainly left nothing of the food she had prepared – but it was only when he had drained his cup and set it back on its saucer that he turned to her.

'That was lovely, fair play – you'll do for me. What's your name, *merchi*? I think you'd better tell me a bit about yourself; I need to trust any woman employed on these premises, see.'

'I'm Nerys Beynon, been working for Mrs Richardson up on the hill, and she'd give me a reference, I'm sure,' Nerys said quickly. 'Before that, I worked for Mary Sutton both in her home and sometimes on the counter at her Emporium. I'm honest and a hard worker, don't you worry about that.' She stared at him as he leaned back in his chair. 'It's true I've never worked in a public bar, but I'll do my best so long as the men keep a respectful tongue in their heads whilst I'm around.'

Bulla stared at her for a moment in silence. 'Well, there's no harm in giving you a chance and there's one thing certain – you couldn't do worse than that trollop Rosa. Took her here in all good faith, I did – she was reformed, see – but couldn't wait to get her hand in the till and then pop off after time with any of the customers who had some spare money in his pocket.'

'When shall I start?' Nerys asked quietly, choosing to ignore his remarks and feeling homesick already for *Plas Rhianfa* and Mali and the children. 'I'll have to give notice to Mrs Richardson, of course, though I'm sure she'll let me go straight away.'

Bulla rose to his feet. 'Start as soon as you can, *merchi*, for I need the glasses washed and the tables polished now, this minute, see?'

Nerys moved quickly towards the door. 'I'll do that before I go up to *Plas Rhianfa* and then I'll come back this evening with my things, if that's all right.'

In the public bar, the light fell dimly through the windows; empty glasses stood on the small round tables and ranged along the bar like a platoon of soldiers. She rolled up her sleeves, for there was a great deal of work to do and she was feeling tired already.

As she fetched water from the kettle and poured it into the sink, Bulla watched her approvingly.

'Well, I'll say this, you don't have to be shown every damn thing! Pardon my language, Nerys Beynon. I'm off into the parlour now for a sleep before I open up again here.' He unfastened a key from the chain on his belt. 'When you return, you let yourself in. Your room is the one in the front; I'll make sure it's clean, but there's nothing fancy here, mind.'

'Fancy you can keep, clean will do me.' Nerys smiled for the first time and Bulla, after a moment, nodded approvingly.

'It will be a change not to have a grumbling woman round my coat-tails. Nothing suited that Rosa – used to better things, so she said, but her chucked out of her place for not paying rent, mind. Come down in the world she has, or so she kept telling me. Go you now and let me rest.' He yawned hugely, revealing strong white teeth framed by his enormous beard and Nerys shivered – for a moment he looked like a rabid animal.

Out in the warmth of the street, she wondered if she

had done the right thing in committing herself to work for Bulla Johns, since she was not used to the life in a public bar selling beer to rowdy menfolk. Yet had she any choice? She comforted herself with the thought of Bulla's three daughters, sure he would need to keep a respectable house if there were innocent young girls to think of.

Slowly she made her way back to *Plas Rhianfa*, taking her time as she ignored the noisy jostling tram and strolled at a leisurely pace up the hill. The sun was hot on her shoulders and she sighed softly as she breathed in the scent of the late roses which sprang at random, splashing delicate pink through the green thickness of the hedgerows.

Tears clung to her eyelashes as the big house came into sight, familiar and comforting, though to feel homesickness for the place was foolish because she had been there only a matter of weeks, she told herself sternly. She would teach herself not to miss the dreamy calm of the nursery, the happy voices of the Richardson children and most of all, Mali's company.

After all, she would have new children to care for, the three little girls who were Bulla Johns's daughters. She was lucky, too, that she would have a roof over her head and honest shillings to put in her pocket.

Mali was sitting in the garden, her embroidery frame idle on her lap. She waved as she saw Nerys, but there were signs of tension around her eyes which Nerys was quick to see. She moved forward purposefully, knowing there was no turning back for Mali was about to tell her it was time she must leave.

She smiled as she settled herself into a chair and held up her hand, preventing Mali from saying anything.

'There's glad I am to see you out here, I want to talk to you.' She paused and Mali leaned back in her chair, waiting.

'It's like this,' Nerys rushed out the words, 'I've

found myself a job in the town, so can you give me a reference and let me go straight away?'

Mali took a deep breath, her clear green eyes knowing as they rested on Nerys's flushed face.

'You've been searching for a job this morning, haven't you? Now I don't want you to be hasty and take just anything. I won't have you working the lead, for a start.'

Nerys shook her head, swallowing the pain in her throat. 'It's nothing like that. Really now, Mali, it's right up my street – caring for three little girls for a widower man in town.' She picked at a grass stalk, thrusting the spiky sweetness into her mouth and giving herself time to think.

'He's a clean man and keeps a good house for the little girls, but it must be hard with him having to work and all.' She omitted to mention that Bulla Johns kept the Flint Mill in the Strand.

Mali leaned forward, resting her hand on Nerys's shoulder. 'Are you sure this man can be trusted?'

Nerys glanced up, smiling. 'I think so; he's been very respectful to me, I must say, and in the evenings his girls will be there as company for me. I can't see anything can be wrong in that, can you?'

Mali, as always, was shrewd. 'I don't know that that's the problem. I haven't met this man, what's his name?'

'Mr Johns. He lives in the town, his girls are at school in the daytime and I've said I'll go back tonight so as to be there to take care of them.'

Mali chewed her lip thoughtfully. 'I wonder if I should ask Sterling if he knows anything about Mr Johns. Where does he live exactly?'

'There's no need to worry about me, mind,' Nerys said quickly. 'Haven't I been taking care of myself for a long time now?'

Mali stared at her for a moment and then smiled.'You're right, of course, and I'm sure you can take good care of yourself. But I will say this: you can come to me at any time, for *Plas Rhianfa* is open house and you must promise you'll remember that.'

'I promise.' Nerys swallowed hard. 'Now I'd best go and pack my bag, or I'll be given the sack before I've even started the job.' She paused, knowing that she must give voice to her thoughts. 'But there's grateful I am to you, Mali. You've given me your friendship, just as Mary did, and I'll never forget your kindness.'

Which was one reason why she was taking a job down at the Flint Mill, Nerys thought wryly; it was partly to spare Mali the necessity of having to tell her to go. She had heard her pleading softly with her husband to keep Nerys on for just a little longer, and had also heard Sterling reply that there was not the money for doing kindnesses, not any longer. Times were hard, so it seemed, and according to Sterling Richardson were set to become harder.

In her room adjoining the nursery, Nerys looked round her longingly. How she loved the view from the window of the softly rolling seas and the far-off Devon coastline! And the room itself, though sparsely furnished, had been her home. The purple silk quilt was soft and warm, the jug and basin on the marble-topped dressing table brightly decorated with sprays of roses that blended with the soft pink paint on the walls. It would be hard to live in the dour and darkly painted rooms of the Flint Mill after this.

She would miss the Richardson children too, but somehow she had become inured to partings after saying farewell to Stephan Sutton whom she had tended since babyhood. And she would have the three as yet unknown children of Bulla Johns to fill the gap, she reminded herself.

It did not take Nerys long to pack her bag, for her possessions were few. She held her patched topcoat over her arm and stood for a moment in the dreaming silence of the day, listening to the hum of the bees and the whisper of the graceful fountain that played in the fine gardens below her window. But she could not prolong the moment indefinitely and, taking a deep breath, she stepped out into the passageway and moved down the richly carpeted stairs to the hallway.

At the sound of her footsteps, Mali came out of the drawing room and clasped her hands. 'Are you sure you'll be all right? Don't you want a little more time to think about all this?' she asked breathlessly, and Nerys smiled to find herself in the position of being reassuring.

'I'm not going to Australia, mind, only down near the Strand in Sweyn's Eye.' Her words were brave, but in spite of herself Nerys shivered.

'There's some wages coming to you and I'll make sure you get them.' Mali was following her to the door, fussing over her like a mother hen and Nerys was touched. 'And mind what I said, come back up by here if you're dissatisfied with your new job.' Mali was slipping into the Welsh idiom and Nerys couldn't help but smile.

'Don't worry!' She leaned forward on an impulse and kissed Mali's cheek. 'I'm a big girl now and used to working for a living!'

She moved away down the long, gracious drive, hardly seeing the sun-dappled roadway or the great gates bearing the Richardson crest of three lions rampant – which always stood open to visitors. This part of her life was behind her; she had a new career and must put her heart and soul into making it successful.

Nerys took the tram, climbing aboard and settling herself on the hard seat, staring unseeingly out of the window. It was one thing to utter brave words, but quite another to know that now she must put them into practice. The tram rocketed downwards into the heart of the town and when it shuddered to a stop, she stepped out into the cooling evening sunshine.

Staring around her as though dazed, Nerys tried to get her bearings. Her coat, so inadequate in winter, hung heavily over her arm and her bag felt as though it was weighed down with pieces of lead. As she moved along the Strand, hearing the mournful hoot of the tugs in the dock as the mist obscured the water, she felt alone and very vulnerable, unsure of the wisdom of putting her future in the hands of the unknown Bulla Johns. But she could not turn back – what was there to go back to? She had no roots. Orphaned as a child, she had been brought up by a reluctant aunt and since then had lived in a variety of homes, always other people's. Her happiest times had been those spent with Mary Sutton, caring for young Stephan; she had had stability then and a sense of purpose in life. She had felt she belonged, but Mary's husband Brandon had decided to return home to America, taking his family with him and Nerys had been alone once more.

She straightened her back and walked more resolutely towards the door of the Flint Mill. There was nothing to be served by being fearful and indecisive; she had taken on a job of work, honest work, and she would just have to do the best she could with it.

CHAPTER EIGHT

The Sunday autumn glow that fell over the sea and hillside of Mumbles Head reflected the warmth of emotion which grew and burgeoned within Hector Llewelyn. He sat in the hollow of the hillside with Sarah nestled in the crook of his arm and a feeling of well-being softened his young features into a smile.

'You're a lovely girl, mind,' he said softly, his lips against her hair. She turned to look up at him and there was a coquettish smile in her green-flecked eyes.

'Well, fancy you coming over all romantic then, Hector, and you only wanting one thing. I'm not daft, remember!'

He kissed her warm, full lips, knowing that she teased him. He wanted her always; she only had to lay a hand on his arm, to touch his cheek or just look at him and his need for her was like a fever. But there was more than that; there was a sweetness, a real true love in him for Sarah. Perhaps it was only that she was his first conquest, the girl who had made him into a man. At least that was what the quiet Alexander – his twin and the being closer to him than anyone until Sarah – told him, but Hector felt his gut melt whenever he held her. He wanted to set up house with her, to have her near him constantly; he could scarcely bear the time spent on the round, for his days of flirting with all the women were over and he had eyes only for Sarah now.

Alex called him all sorts of a fool, insisting that the business needed building up, especially now Auntie

Betty had made up her mind to enlist them as partners in the round. She had called them into her neat little house at the edge of Oystermouth village and sat them down in her best parlour, looking strangely small and defenceless without the bundle of shawls and the black hat she usually wore.

'You are men now,' she told them. Her voice had been brisk and matter-of-fact, but her eyes had flickered over them almost nervously. 'And I mean to treat you as such. I want you to take over the round and pay me a percentage of the takings every week.' She had paused, staring first at Hector and then at Alexander. 'What if we divide the takings three ways, a third for each of us – is that fair?'

'But we'll be doing all the work!' It was Hector who had raised the protest and Betty smiled, her arms folded across her chest.

'I know that, man, but didn't I build up the business and isn't it my horse and cart, not to mention milkchurns, that you'll be using?'

Hector had considered in silence for a moment and then looked at Alex, who had nodded imperceptibly.

'Aye, I suppose that's fair enough, but when I've saved up enough money I shall expect to buy you out. I think that's fair, too.'

'Agreed.' Betty had held out a small, capable hand and after a moment Alexander had taken it, shaking it gravely without a trace of a smile on his face, though Hector knew his brother was longing to laugh at the strangeness of the moment. Then it was his turn to shake hands with Betty, gripping her fingers tightly, knowing that his aunt had given him and his twin a good start in life, a better start than was given to many of the young boys who had attended St Thomas's School and for that he was grateful.

'You're very quiet all of a sudden.' Sarah's fingers traced a line around his mouth. 'Not gone off me already, have you, Hector?'

He leaned forward and kissed her, feeling her tongue dart against his lips, probing, rousing, so that he drew her closer, never ceasing to be moved by the litheness of her body as it moulded itself against his. Laughing, she pushed him away.

'Behave yourself, Hector Llewelyn!' She knelt beside him, her face flushed, her eyes sparkling, and he knew she was proud of the power in her to awaken him to a ready response. '*Duw*, you'd have us making love out by here in the broad daylight, so you would – no shame, you!'

'I'd make love to you any time anywhere and you know it, you witch!' He lay back against the coarse grass and put his hands behind his head, staring up at the sky.

'What about marrying me, though! I suppose that's a different kettle of fish.' Sarah pouted prettily at him, but her eyes were suddenly anxious. She looked down at her hands and they were trembling and suddenly, Hector was uneasy. He took her hand and smoothed it with his thumb.

'What is it, Sarah? There's something worrying you, so come on – you can tell me, can't you?'

Her eyes avoided his and she bit her lip, twisting her ribbons around her finger with her free hand, unable to look at him. He couldn't understand her sudden change of mood.

'I think I'm having your baby, Hector Llewelyn!' Suddenly she began to cry, tears running down her cheeks as her mouth puckered in a childlike expression which made her seem entirely vulnerable. It knotted his gut with pain.

'You won't want me now. I'll be a burden, I know I will.' She put her hands over her face as though to hide from him and he reached out and drew her to him, love melting him inside. She crouched against him, her arms clinging. 'I don't want to end up in Tawe Lodge. They cut your hair and put you into check pinnies and parade you round the yard for everyone to see your shame.'

'Don't be so soft, as if I'd let you go to the work-house!' He kissed her tenderly, a feeling of strength growing within him, a determination that he, Hector Llewelyn, was going to take charge of this girl's life and make everything right for her.

'We shall be married as soon as you like, my lovely, I want you with me for always, don't you know that?' He smoothed back her hair and drew her hands from her cheeks, kissing the tears that tasted salt on his lips. 'Let's start looking for somewhere to live straight away, shall we?' He drew her down towards him, touched by the glow that illuminated her eyes.

'Oh Hector, do you mean it, *cariad*? Will you buy me a wedding ring and take me to church all proper then?'

'Haven't I said so?' His voice was calm, but there was a pride in him that took his breath away. He had fathered a child; it was growing there inside Sarah's small frame and it was a son, he knew that with a certainty that was unshakeable.

'I'll make the arrangements straight away and we'll be married in the Methodist church in Oystermouth as soon as the banns are called. In the meantime, we can be looking for a nice little home for us.'

Sarah, unaware that tears still clung to her cheeks, stared at him. She was nothing if not practical, even in her moment of triumph.

'We shall have to rent a house just for now, until you've made enough money for us to buy our own little place.' She frowned. 'Couldn't you ask Betty-the-Milk? She's bound to know someone who rents out houses, her being rich and all.'

Hector drew Sarah into his arms and cuddled her close and she felt small and defenceless, the mother of his son. The thought poured like wine through his blood. His love for her was overwhelming and he

113

kissed her with such tenderness that she clung to him, a child yet now a woman.

'Come on, then – we'll go to see Betty straight away. No point in sitting around the hillside doing nothing, is there?' He laughed and kissed her mouth once more, unable to keep away from her. He was impatient to set events in motion, he wanted his own hearth and a home ready and fit for when his boy was born.

Sarah held him still for a moment, reaching up slim young arms to encircle his neck. As he felt her sweet weight against him, the roundness of her breast, the curve of her hip, he was a man grown ten feet tall.

'You do love me, Hector, don't you?' she asked, her eyes liquid with emotion. 'You're not just marrying me because you've got me into trouble, are you?'

He wanted to swing her around in an arc, to lift her high above his head, to throw back his head and laugh with exultation. He had laid with her, become one flesh with her and now she was going to have his child and he was filled with joy.

But he merely cupped her face with his hands, kissed her soft mouth tenderly and then led her down the hill towards the village.

'When will you call the banns, Hector?' Sarah's voice was small and uncertain and he squeezed her hand gently, offering her reassurance, unable to explain the welter of emotion she had aroused in him.

'I shall take you to see Betty. We'll ask her about a house and then go to the church and make all the arrangements. There now will that suit you, Miss Fusspot?'

'You're laughing at me, Hector!' Sarah chided, but there was a smile on her lips for she knew that he was proud that he was to be a father. She nestled close to his side and they walked together down the grassy slopes towards the village.

Betty stared at Hector with a direct, unnerving gaze as he stood beside Sarah in the small, neat parlour.

The grandfather clock chimed the hour, the tones echoing in the silent hallway and Betty sighed softly.

'There's no point in me telling you that your actions are ill-timed, is there, boy?' She sat down slowly. 'But I hope this marriage is not going to affect the milk round; need all your powers of attention to make a go of it, you will, mind. There's always a bit of a dropping off in sales when a new person takes over a business – you should know that, Hector Llewelyn.'

But her words left him undaunted. He could do anything, achieve just what he wanted and gradually, as he spoke persuasively to Betty, her sternness melted. 'So you see,' he concluded, 'I'll have even more reason to make the round a success, won't I Betty? I'll have a son to look out for.'

She nodded her head several times, the tension easing from her features.

'Well, in the circumstances where we find ourselves now, I think I've got some very good news for you – very good indeed.'

Hector looked at her, the hairs on the back of his neck rising, feeling in his bones that she was about to offer him some prize. He tensed, waiting to hear what she would say next and his mouth was dry with anticipation.

'Alun-the-Shop is retiring, going to live with his sons up in Cardiff; sold all his fixtures and fittings, he has, but is willing to rent out the premises. He leaves behind him a good trade in milk and butter and such, going to waste down at West Cross.' She paused, enjoying his reaction. 'Now there's a house going empty for you and what a big round you'd have if you two boys took over from lazy old Alun-the-Shop. Plenty of room for improvement there, mind.'

Hector stared at her for a long moment, his mind exploring the possibilities not only of extending the round but of having somewhere for Sarah and himself to live.

West Cross was several miles from Oystermouth, but well-populated, and the prospect of enlarging the present round most certainly presented an opportunity not to be missed.

'But won't he want some money for the goodwill at least?' Hector asked and Betty shook her head.

'Not him – can't be bothered, see. Never was much of a business man, that Alun. Content to have a fair rent he'll be. Now, let's see to the round we've got already and see how you two boys are handling it, right? I've had one complaint that you're a bit slow, mind.'

Hector forced himself to pay attention to the matter in hand. He pored over the books with Betty, arguing amiably with her about the customers' needs, but at the same time was tinglingly aware of the challenge she had held out to him. It was only when Sarah coughed apologetically that he realized the time was passing and the fine sun of the day was dwindling into twilight.

'So you must get up to Ram's Tor a bit earlier in the morning, mind,' Betty concluded, rising to her feet. 'Catherine Lloyd milks those cows of hers at crack of dawn most days, so there's no excuse for you to be idle half the morning!'

Her words were harshly spoken but Hector knew her, knew she wanted him to succeed, longed to see the twins improve the business which had been her life's work.

She saw them to the door and stood there in the long shadows of the passageway, a small figure and yet always imposing. 'And I shall write to Alun-the-Shop, never fear. You'll have a home there, I'm sure of it.'

When the door had closed and Hector was leading Sarah away from the house, she looked up at him appealingly.

'Do you think we'll be lucky enough to have a little

place of our own, *cariad*?' she asked as she leaned against him under the shelter of his arm.

'We'll see, my lovely girl, we'll see.' But plans for the house they would share must take second place to the vista spread before him now, the vision of himself and Alexander as men of big business – perhaps in time employing others to do the donkey-work for them. It had been a good day when Betty-the-Milk had taken them under her wing.

That night in the bedroom high up in the attic of the house on the ferry, Hector spoke in whispers to his twin, telling him about Betty's proposition, careful not to wake the two young ones who lay curled up beneath the patchwork quilt unaware of the candle flickering on the table. Alex looked at him, seeming to catch fire from Hector's enthusiasm, for his eyes held a strange light.

'We can do it, together we can do it, Alex,' Hector said fiercely. Alexander was silent for a long time as he leaned back against the wall, his hair falling darkly across his forehead. As always, he knew Hector's innermost thoughts and did not even have to ask why his brother was visiting Betty-the-Milk on a Sunday.

'It's Sarah,' Hector said slowly, replying to an unspoken question with a wide smile on his face. 'She's going to have my son!'

'Yes.' Alexander tipped back his head, his expression difficult to read in the flickering light from the candle, but Hector leaned forward and rested a hand on his shoulder.

'It will make no difference to me and you, Alex. We're more than brothers, we're part of the same piece of fruit – each of us only half an apple without the other. We'll never be split asunder, don't you worry on that score, boyo.'

When there was no response, Hector took his brother's hand, holding it firmly. 'What is it, Alex, boyo? You're disturbed, I can feel it.'

But Alexander simply leaned forward and hugged him close. 'I'm always near, mind!' This brother of his wasn't much for giving speeches, Hector mused, but it was clear that Alex was pledging his allegiance to him in whatever he wanted to do.

'Better get to sleep, then,' Hector said, shrugging off his braces. 'Got to make an early start in the morning. Seems that some old bugger has been complaining we're too late with the deliveries, so Betty told me to buck up a bit, see.'

But for a long time Hector lay awake, listening to the gentle snoring of the two young ones, Tom and Will, thinking about his future and knowing with a strange sense of unease that Alexander also lay awake in the darkness beside him.

In the days that followed, Hector worked on the round as he had never worked before. He found that his old charm had returned and was an invaluable asset, for housewives tired of indifferent husbands enjoyed a bit of teasing and flirting. And then on Saturday, after the usual round had been completed, Hector and Alexander loaded the cart once more with milk and butter and round, muslin-wrapped cheeses and began the long walk from Ram's Tor Farm through the villages of Oystermouth and Southend into the new territory of West Cross.

'Milko!' Hector's voice was strong and clear and he was rewarded by the sight of curtains twitching away from shining windows.

'One customer we want, Alex, that's all,' he muttered, 'and the rest will follow like sheep.'

He saw a woman appear on her doorstep – her skirt longer than was fashionable, a Welsh shawl wrapped around herself and her sleeping infant – and Hector smiled slowly, his eyes warm.

'Morning, miss, is your mam home? Does she want any milk, butter or cheese? Go on and ask her.'

The woman smiled hugely. 'I'm the mam of this

house, there's soft you are!' But she dimpled and giggled and came forward to look into the cart.

'Give me a couple of gills of milk, there's a love. Hang on and I'll get something to put it in.'

She hurried into the house and reappeared a few moments later holding a jug aloft. Soon, as Hector had predicted, other women came out of their houses, clamouring around the cart, anxious to save themselves the long walk to the farm for supplies.

'We'll be around three times a week,' Hector promised, though he wondered how he and his twin would find enough hours in the day. 'Any special order and we'll deliver, right?'

The woman with the baby in the shawl moved forward importantly, for it was she who had discovered the new source of provisions. 'How about potatoes, can you bring some round for me when you come next? It would save me getting out, see, for my little boy's got the croup.'

'You ask, we'll deliver,' Hector said firmly, and as he looked down at the swiftly emptying cart a feeling of triumph warmed him.

'I think we've got them, Alex!' He clicked his tongue and the horse moved forward easily now, the empty cart no burden. 'I think we're going to be big business men in no time at all! It's not only our Howel who's got brains and drive – we'll show the lot of them, you'll see, Alex.'

Hector slept well that night and rose before the sun. He hurried down the stairs into the kitchen, where Emily was kneeling on the floor before the ashes of the fire. The baby was wrapped in a shawl held against her thin breast as with one hand she raked out the dead ashes. She looked up at her son with dark-circled eyes.

'I knew last night I should have riddled the fire and set it for this morning – knew I'd be sorry going to bed and leaving it but *duw*, there's tired I was, son.'

A pain caught Hector as he lifted his mother and set her into a chair. 'As I'm up early, I'll do that, mam; it won't take me a minute.'

There was anger in his heart as he fetched the wood. Emily had borne seven sons and now, late in life, a daughter, and still she was expected to see to the chores alone. How remiss they had all been – himself most of all, for he knew Emily and was closest to her.

Perhaps it was his love of Sarah and the knowledge that she was carrying his child which made him more intuitive, more considerate of his mother, but whatever the reason for his new flush of conscience he was determined that he would put things right, would organize his brothers into helping mam more.

Alexander appeared as silent as a shadow and took the baby from his mother's arms. 'Sit by there, mam, rest a minute. You look worn out.' He stared down almost in awe of the baby girl as she lay asleep, her soft lashes resting against her marble cheeks.

Hector smiled as he watched his twin, knowing something of the tenderness his brother was feeling for, as always, an invisible cord linked them. A warmth engulfed him as he imagined his own child lying in his brother's arms; he knew the boy would be like Alexander's own, part of him just as surely as if he had fathered the baby. The thought was pure and yet, Hector smiled to himself, might almost be incestuous to an outsider. But he and Alexander were more than brothers, each unable to function properly without the other.

'Come on, boy, we'd better get to work.' Hector stood back from the fire which was now well ablaze and gazed at the cheerful flames in satisfaction. Soon, very soon, he would be sitting at his own hearth with his wife and son at his side. He took a piece of cheese and cut several slices of bread from yesterday's loaf. Suddenly his news would not wait a moment longer.

'Mam,' he took her hands, 'I have something to tell

120

you and I hope you are going to be glad for me. I'm going to be married.'

Emily looked at him blankly, almost as though he was speaking in a foreign tongue.

'It's Sarah, mam. She's carrying my son and we will be wed as soon as we can.'

Emily drew back from him, her eyes wide. 'But you're a boy still, a *bachgen bach*; one of my babies. How can you think of marrying?'

This was not the reaction that Hector had hoped for. He had anticipated reluctance on his mother's part to accept that he wanted to leave home, but not this horror that darkened her eyes.

'It's all right, mam,' he spoke reassuringly, realizing that she was not yet over the birth of the little girl; at least, that's what the doctor had said. 'I'm a man now with my own business and old enough to father a child, so old enough to take the responsibility. Isn't that what you'd want?'

'Oh no, boy, not yet. I don't want you to go away from me. I can't lose you – you're my son, close to my heart, the one who always understands what I feel and think before I do myself.' She put her arms around his shoulders, her head heavy against his neck. 'Please don't say any more, not now, Hector; for I can't agree to you marrying yet – you're so young, so very young.'

He felt her tears dampen his collar and pain filled him. He loved his mother, yet he had his own life to consider, his future and that of Sarah and their son.

'All right, mam, don't worry! I won't say any more about it. You have some breakfast now and stop crying, there's a good girl.'

The door to the stairway opened and Siona entered the kitchen, his hair tangled over his forehead giving him an air of youthfulness. Father and son stared at each other over Emily's bent head.

'Been upsetting your mammy, is it, boy?' Siona

asked sternly, doing up his trews with quick movements of his fingers as though venting his anger on the buttons. 'What is it now? Better tell me, for I mean to know.' He held his belt lightly now between his fingers in unspoken threat and though he seldom beat them, both the twins had known the ferocity of their father's anger and dreaded it.

Hector moved away from his mother and faced his father unflinchingly. 'I've told mam about me and Sarah; she's having my son and we are going to be married!'

Siona was silent for a moment and then, to Hector's surprise, threw back his head to reveal the strong column of his throat as he laughed.

'There's a boy after my own heart!' Siona sat at ease now on the rocking-chair, drawing on his socks. 'What's the matter with you Emily? Why the tears? Your son has only done what comes naturally to a man. Good for you, boyo, but remember that you don't have to enter into marriage, mind. If a girl gives in willing like, then the consequences are her worry, righto?'

'I want to marry Sarah,' Hector said at once, irritated and at the same time warmed by his father's approbation. 'She's a pretty girl from a good family and she'll make me a fine wife.'

Emily dried her tears on the corner of her apron. 'I don't know,' she said heavily. 'One son gone to the lead works and now Hector getting married; it's all happening too fast for me and it frightens me.'

Hector laid his hand on his mother's shoulder, indicating with a jerk of his head that Alexander open the door. 'Now don't go worrying before you know all the ins and outs, mam. We'll talk more tonight.'

Once he was outside, with the tang of the river in his nostrils and the breeze lifting the hair from his hot forehead, Hector breathed a sigh of relief. 'Come on, let's get up to Ram's Tor Farm early and get our stocks in. I'd rather face a day's work than mam's tears,' he said softly.

CHAPTER NINE

The autumn day was hazy with warmth, the long line of the River Swan covered in snaking mists. Alex sat up in bed and stared out of the window, wondering at the cold chills that gripped him. He knew he had had a bad dream, but all that remained of it was the sensation of horror as quickly he pushed back the bedclothes and began to get ready for work.

He was the first one downstairs and soon set a light to the fire, watching the sticks crackle and burn, slowly setting light to the coal. At least he would have saved mam one job, he thought with satisfaction.

Having filled the heavy black kettle, he put it on to the hob and then sat in a chair biting his lips worriedly. He felt strange and uneasy, but doubtless he was still half in his dream. A hot cup of tea would set him up.

His mother must have heard him moving about, for she entered the kitchen and pushed back her greying hair. 'Little Sian is still asleep,' she said quietly. 'I'll leave her be for a while, it'll give me a chance to get something done here.'

She stared into the flames of the fire gratefully. 'Thank you, *cariad*; there's good of you to bother.'

'Don't be silly, mam, it's the least I can do.' Alex rested his hand on his mother's thin shoulder for a moment. 'Sit down for a minute while I make us both a nice brew.'

They sat in companionable silence and Alex was rewarded by seeing some of the tension ease from his mother's face. She had grown visibly older since the birth of the baby and she was much too thin. Yet the doctor who had come to examine her did not seem to think there was anything seriously wrong.

'Now don't go working too hard, mam,' Alex said. 'There's nothing that can't wait, so take a day off, right?'

Emily smiled. '*Duw*, there's green you are! Who do you think is going to bake the bread and wash the dishes then? The housework won't do itself, mind.'

'I know that, but you should be taking things a bit easier, mam. We must get someone in to help you – there's enough of us earning, after all.'

'Tut! I don't want no other woman messing around in my kitchen, boyo. It wouldn't feel right. Now don't you worry about me – strong as a horse I am and don't you forget it.'

Hector came into the kitchen rubbing his eyes sleepily. He yawned and rubbed a hand through his hair and felt the pot to see if it was still hot.

'I could drink the sea dry this morning,' he said, winking at Alex. 'This falling in love lark, takes it out of you, mind.'

'Hush that sort of talk,' Emily said, but her eyes were warm as they rested on her son. Alex accepted without rancour that there was a special sort of affinity between his mother and his twin and he smiled as he saw them together now, Emily reaching out a tentative hand to straighten Hector's collar. 'Still can't believe you are going to be married, mind,' she said softly. 'Naughty you are to go getting a girl into trouble!'

'Don't go on now, mam,' Hector said, pinching her cheek. 'I'm a big boy now and you can't send me up to bed without any supper!' He cut a slice of bread from the loaf and spread it thickly with butter.

'Come on,' Alex said good-humouredly. 'I thought we were setting off early this morning – that was the idea, wasn't it?'

Later, as the twins caught the tram to Oystermouth

village, sitting together on the wooden seats in silence, Hector glanced at his brother. Alex was unusually silent, his good humour seemingly evaporating the further away they went from home. He was ill at ease, even morose, and he looked pale and worried.

The tram jerked to a halt and Hector saw his brother rise to his feet almost reluctantly and follow him out into the beginning of a sunny autumn day.

At Betty's house, Hector moved around to the back and led the horse from the stable, then quietly harnessed the animal between the shafts of the cart.

'I expect Betty-the-Milk is still asleep, and good luck to her!' Hector said in a low voice, but Alexander didn't respond. He merely rested his hand on the animal's mane and looked glumly at his shoes.

'What's wrong?' Hector asked as he guided the horse out on to the curving roadway that led to Ram's Tor Farm. 'You look as if you've lost a shilling and found a farthing.'

'I don't know.' Alexander glanced up at his brother, his eyes dark, his expression troubled. 'I've just got this feeling that something's going wrong, I can't explain it.'

For once Hector was not in tune with his twin. He felt good as the sunlight, brightening now, fell upon his shoulders and warmed him. The clip-clop of the horse's hooves against the road was like music, for everything was good with Hector's life.

'Tempting fate, mind,' Alex said and Hector grinned, knowing his brother had read his mind.

'Well, I'm in love and I've fine prospects, so what else could I want?' He justified his mood of optimism in a cheerful way, believing that Alex's ill humour was the result of the discussion about his marriage which had taken place earlier in Ferry House.

It hurt Hector to see mam worried and unhappy too, yet the affection she had shown him by her touch had more than made up for her reluctance to accept that he was a man now and about to be married.

The rutted pathway leading to the farm was warm and fragrant with the scent of ripe blackberries as Hector paused, glancing down to see where the sea ran gently against the small patch of sand far below. He pushed open the gate which led to a short cut across the field and breathed deeply of the sea-salted air.

Alexander moved ahead of him, glancing from side to side with head held high, senses alert as though fearing danger. What on earth was wrong with his twin?

'Alex?' Even as the name formed on Hector's lips, he too felt the creeping of his scalp, the tingling of his senses, the fear which had transferred itself to him.

He heard the bellowing of the bull then and looked up, dragging at the reins of the horse as the creature reared in fright. But the animal would not be held and galloped like a mad thing, dragging the cart over the rutted land so that the pails leaped and clanked as though with a life of their own.

'Get back, Alex!' he cried as his brother stood transfixed. The bull snorted, eyes red-rimmed and malevolent, hooves pawing the dusty ground. 'Get back towards the gate!' But Alexander seemed incapable of movement.

Hector's mouth was dry and his legs felt as though they were being dragged into thick wet mud. He moved towards his twin in agonizingly slow motion, as though in the grip of some terrible nightmare. The bull was charging, head down, hooves drumming against the earth.

It was like the pictures Hector had seen on gaudy posters of the bull fight, but now there was no matador – just the enraged animal pounding mercilessly towards Alexander.

Hector was suddenly spurred into action and

leaped forward, waving his arms, shouting loudly, hoping to turn the animal aside. The nostrils quivered. The red eyes rolled. The horns were almost touching the ground. Hector heard a cry and simultaneously felt a blow in his groin. The sky was whirling round his head; he saw the sea, the land, the sky in swift kaleidoscope. Then he heard Alexander scream, felt his twin nearby . . . and at the same time pain tore through his guts.

'Take care of Sarah and my son.' He may have said the words, he may only have thought them, but he knew Alex would understand. He fell heavily to the earth and the nostrils were above him, the horns lifting, tossing him as though he was nothing but a rag doll. And then there was only a merciful blackness.

It took Morgan Lloyd and two of his farm-hands all their combined strength to distract the maddened bull from further savaging its victim. The earth was red with blood as Alexander – eyes anguished – mourned in a stark silence over the torn body of Hector Llewelyn, his twin.

CHAPTER TEN

The day, which had been crisp and yet sunny in the early hours, had turned overcast, with grey clouds rolling across the skies above Kilvey Hill. The water of the docks became dimpled as a heavy rain began to fall and the sea rolled inwards towards the open arms of the pier with windswept vigour, the waves noisy and ferocious as they attacked the crescent-shaped beach.

In the school of St Thomas the pupils were restless – a feeling which communicated itself to Howel Llewelyn as he wrote on the blackboard, the chalk gritty beneath his nails. There were days when he hated teaching and longed to be away from the class-room – and never more so than now when he revelled in the certain knowledge that his ambitions were being realized.

But he had not had it easy. Howel had gradually made his way up through the ranks of the Liberal Party, at first simply tolerated by the more affluent members – shipowners, landlords and the like – until slowly but surely he had made himself indispensable. He had sat on committees, enduring the boredom of speeches made by men who had no new ideas but simply liked the sound of their own voices. He had been tutored in diplomacy by the situations in which he found himself. Wooed by opposing sides, he had risen to the position of councillor, knowing that his goal was to enter parliament where perhaps he might be able to help the poorer people of Sweyn's Eye.

His knack of making money on the stock market had been a fine asset and had put more than one of his fellow councillors on to a quick killing, making up portfolios for them as if it was a talent he had been born with instead of learned on the battlefields of France. And now that he was allied with the illustrious Mr Sterling Richardson, he was openly accepted. Oh, yes, his future was secure and a warm glow drove away the irritations of the classroom just for a moment.

'Sir, please sir, shall I get out the sacks?' The boy looking up at him was small in stature, his face thin, his eyes circled darkly. He was one of the children receiving free school meals; these consisted of a tiny portion of porridge and a slice of bread and margarine for breakfast, and a lunch of Irish stew – so thin that the bottom of the dish could clearly be seen through it – served with a piece of dry bread. Howel burned with anger at the plight of his pupils.

'Shall I get the sacks out then, sir? It's time to go home, see,' the boy repeated and Howel's face relaxed into a smile.

'Aye, go on then. I suppose it is raining pretty hard.' He watched as the barefoot child opened the cupboard and dragged forth a variety of potato sacks, much washed, which served as substitute overcoats for the poorest of the class. The sack would be worn, cloak-like around the head and shoulders and later, washed and dried, would be returned to the school.

Sometimes he felt sickened knowing that there was so much that should be done for the inhabitants of the town in which he had always lived so comfortably. It was true that at home on the river bank there had been no luxuries, but there had always been good stout boots and plenty of food to put in the bellies of the sons Siona Llewelyn sired so effortlessly. But then, Howel reasoned, his father had always made a respectable living out of the boat and had worked all the hours God gave – give him credit where credit was due.

The children had gone, their noisy voices fading into silence, and it was good to sit in the now peaceful classroom, gathering his thoughts. Teaching was much more difficult than anyone at home gave him credit for. Siona, though proud of his son's education, thought the job 'cissy'. And yet he had been surprised at first at the salary Howel commanded, then dismissed it good-humouredly as 'money for old rope'.

Howel rose to his feet – he might as well get off home. He pushed the sheaf of ink-blotched essays into his case, deciding to mark them later if he could find somewhere to sit in comparative peace.

The worst of the storm was over and the rain fell in light droplets now, hardly noticeable to Howel as he strode down the hill towards the river bank. His thoughts were of his future as Member of Parliament and as a shareholder in the Richardson empire. Granted that empire was not so splendid as it had once been, but perhaps his coming would change all that, Howel thought exultantly. He was new blood and would bring in new ideas, for imagination was not something he lacked.

As soon as he reached the cottage, he knew something was badly wrong. The door was firmly shut, as were the windows, the drawn curtains giving a blank appearance to the building. A gaggle of women with shawls covering their heads stood outside, talking in low tones.

The light was beaming from the Hafod side of the river – a signal that the ferry was needed – but the boat stood empty, bumping ceaselessly against the broad steps.

'Not enough left of him to warrant a coffin – a waste of good pine, it was, so they say!' A woman's voice, quickly hushed, penetrated Howel's consciousness as, hurrying now, he covered the last few steps towards his home.

Emily was sitting in her chair, hugging the baby to her breast. Her eyes were bright as though she had a fever and at her side crouched Alexander, his face hidden in his hands. Siona was bending his great height over the fire, making a pot of tea, which in itself was enough to indicate that something dire had happened.

'What is it?' Howel moved into the room, knowing that his voice was edged with fear. 'Mam, what's happened?'

Emily looked up at him as though she scarcely recognized him. When he took her hand, it was cold and clammy as he held it to his face.

'He's gone, my *bachgen bach* is gone and I can't even see him to say goodbye, see.' She didn't cry; perhaps it would have been better if she had broken into floods of tears, but she simply stared sightlessly at him.

'It's Hector,' Siona spoke quietly, his blue eyes dark. 'Gored by the bull up on Ram's Tor Farm – your brother's dead!'

Howel sank into a chair, the full horror of the remark he had heard outside turning him sick to his stomach. 'Christ!'

'Don't blaspheme, boy.' Siona handed round cups of tea without saucers and Emily rose automatically to fetch them from the pantry, carefully placing each one beneath a cup as though it was the most important task in the world.

Alexander did not move and Howel's being ached for him. He must have seen it happen, witnessed the terrible death of his twin who was more like the other side of the same coin than a brother. Alexander was too passive, too silent; it was clear that he was badly shocked and Howel felt it imperative to try to rouse some response from him.

'Alex, tell me about it,' Howel said in his best classroom voice. This had some effect, for the twin

131

looked up at him, red marks running down both cheeks where he had been resting them in his hands.

'I can't, Howel,' he said flatly. 'I just want to put it out of my mind.

Howel went to him, drawing him to his feet, surprised to realize that Alexander was now as tall as he was. 'It will sink into your mind, into the dark recesses where it will fester and make you sick – you *must* talk about it,' he said urgently. He was aware of Emily rising and taking the baby upstairs, fumbling with the buttons on her blouse. He understood her need to be away from the scene that was about to take place.

'Leave the boy be,' Siona said, but Howel ignored him. He meant well, but even after fathering eight children he knew nothing about young minds. Siona was essentially a man of action, not thoughts.

'Tell me, Alex, come on out with it!' Howel shook him slightly and Alex's face dissolved into a mask of pain and despair.

'He did it to save me.' The words were so low that Howel strained to hear them. 'The bull was after me, see, and I just stood there like a fool watching the animal pounding towards me. Breathing fire he was, his eyes red and evil. I'll never forget those eyes – the devil was in him, for he meant to kill me.' Alex gave a ragged, shuddering sigh.

'Then Hector was in front of me, between me and the bull, see, and he was thrown high up in the air on those terrible bloody horns. His last thought was for Sarah, he was trying to make me understand that I must look after her and then he crashed on to the ground.

'Even then the bull wasn't finished; he stamped and gored and tore at Hector, not even feeling me beating at him with my fists. By the time Morgan Lloyd came, it was too late.' Alexander suddenly looked up. 'Then Morgan sent for an undertaker, said he'd see to everything, and they got a good pine coffin with shining brass handles on it and took our Hector,' he shuddered, 'what was left of him, down to the Methodist Church.'

Then he began to cry, silently at first with the tears coursing down his cheeks. The sobs that were dragged from him shook his entire body and then he was keening like a baby.

Siona came forward unhesitatingly and took Alexander in his arms, rocking him to and fro, talking softly to him. 'That's right, you cry it all out, boyo, you'll feel better then.' The words were meaningless, for Alexander would never forget his twin and his terrible death, but the gesture of love, and comfort from Siona was deeply moving and Howel felt tears burn his eyes.

Howel pushed the kettle on the fire once more, thinking that mam would need some hot tea for hers had grown cold, untasted in the cup. When he went upstairs to the bedroom, she was crooning over the baby as the tiny girl suckled at her breast. There was a wan, faraway look in Emily's eyes which alarmed him and he knelt beside her, touching her cheek lightly.

'Mam, are you all right?' he asked, and she looked at him carefully as if remembering his face.

'God gives and then he takes away,' she said reasonably. 'I wanted a girl child and I've had to pay with the life of my lovely Hector. I thought I was being too lucky.'

'No, mam, it's not like that at all. Hector had an accident – it isn't anything to do with you having the baby.'

'It is, of course it is,' Emily said as though she was cross with a stupid child. 'It's my fault – too old to be lying with your dad enjoying the sins of the flesh, I am, and this is a punishment on me for my wickedness.'

Howel felt afraid, for this was not the first time he

had seen his mother behaving oddly. He knew that Ceri had drawn Siona's attention to mam's uneasy state of mind and his father had eventually sought medical advice. But the doctor who had come to look at her had little time for the lower orders. He had dismissed Emily's condition as the natural result of childbirth, the debilitating nature of which he was constantly confronted with, he had informed them. He had been pompously patronizing, a far cry from old Bryn Thomas or even Doctor Soames – still called the 'new' doctor after years of working in Sweyn's Eye – and he left the inhabitants of the Ferry House no wiser than they were before he came.

After the visit and the medication, which consisted only of an iron tonic, Emily had seemed a little improved. She had been more cheerful and tackled her household tasks with something like her old energy; but now she looked dreadfully ill, the shock of Hector's death had obviously been too much for her.

She was clasping the baby so tightly that the little girl began to cry. Emily looked down at her and suddenly thrust her into Howel's arms. 'Take her, Howel. I shouldn't have been so wicked as to ask for a girl – I've killed my boy, my lovely Hector, and I shall never forgive myself.'

Howel stared down at the infant in dismay. The child was so tiny; how could she be cared for if Emily was rejecting her? The baby was not robust to begin with and Emily's thin breasts doubtless contained little nourishment. Howel sighed. He who could command a class-full of children, make himself a councillor, work his way on to the board of the Richardson Copper Company was at a loss when it came to looking after an infant.

'You get into bed, mam,' he said, forcing a note of reassurance into his voice. 'I'll take the baby downstairs and put her in the crib; she'll be all right.'

Siona looked at him askance when he entered the kitchen with the baby gripped awkwardly in his arms.

'Mam's not well.' Howel said and Alex, who was sitting at the table, looked up at him anxiously. 'It's the shock,' Howel continued. 'She's naturally taking it very badly. We shall need to get a woman in to look after the baby, dad – you'll have to see to that.' He stared round him. 'Push the crib over by here, Alex. Put the covers right so that I can lay the baby down.'

'I'll take her.' Alexander was surprisingly good with the child, handling her tiny form as though he was used to the task – and he probably was, Howel mused. The twins had always been close to mam and Alex was thoughtful enough to help in the house.

'I'll go and fetch Doctor Soames for mam,' Howel said to Siona, who was standing as though stunned near the door. 'Alex, can you cope by here? And when Eddie and Ceri come home, I think it will be up to you to break the news the best way you can.'

'I'm all right,' Alex said hoarsely, and Howel rested his hand on his brother's shoulder.

'That's a good man,' he said gently. He moved to the door and paused for a moment to look back into the small kitchen which had always been a haven, a place of warmth and comfort, but now everything was frighteningly different. Suddenly his ambitious way of life seemed shallow and unreal.

'I won't be long,' he said and closed the door behind him with a snap of finality.

It was the talk of Sweyn's Eye, and all the men in the public bar of the Flint Mill were full of the gruesome details of how a young man had been gored to death by a wild bull up on the fields of Ram's Tor Farm. And the bull, a valuable animal, was subsequently shot by its owner, Morgan Lloyd.

Nerys Beynon was trying not to listen, for it pained her to know that grief had come to the people of the Ferry House. She concentrated on washing glasses in the tepid water which could scarcely be called clean; her back was aching and her feet felt on fire. She had never realized that working in a bar could be so hard and gruelling.

Apart from the hard work, there were the constant unwelcome attentions of the customers, some of whom seemed to think she was a woman off the streets to be pinched and mauled whenever the mood took them. So far, she had managed to extricate herself from embarrassing situations without too much aggravation, for she did not want to lose her job or the roof over her head.

The work of caring for Bulla Johns's children was far more suited to her taste, and the time she spent with the girls was passed in a feeling of happiness and a sense of belonging. The girls were sweet-natured and always happy and they were clean, sensible children who made as little work in the way of mending and washing as they could. If only she didn't have to spend any time in the public bar, she would have been passably happy, Nerys thought.

'Fetch a drink over by here, *merchi*!' Bulla called loudly and Nerys looked up at him sharply, for Bulla – usually so moderate in his drinking – was downing glass after glass of the rich brown ale. He was now becoming maudlin, reminded by the tragedy of Hector Llewelyn of the death of his own dear wife.

'Never so much as looked at another woman in all these years,' he said on a loud belch of wind. 'Been a model father to my babbas, I have, as the good Nerys will testify – won't you, *merchi*?' He smiled fatuously. 'Admires me, does Nerys!'

She was uneasy; it was a difficult situation in which she found herself and slowly she nodded her head in agreement.

'Yes, you are a good father, indeed.' She could agree with that much anyway. Bulla leaned over and took the glass from Nerys's hand. 'Been a perfect gentleman I have . . . until now, that is.'

136

He grasped Nerys's wrist and drew her closer. 'I'd make an honest woman of you any day, *cariad*,' he said, his voice ringing with fervour.

There was a loud roar of laughter from the other men at his table as they looked at Nerys with fresh interest. 'Been warming your boss's bed, have you, girl?' one of them said, leaning over and pinching her breast playfully.

'No, I have not!' Nerys said through gritted teeth. 'And I'll thank you to keep your hands to yourself!'

'You must be a dishonest woman for Bulla to want to make you into an honest one – now doesn't that make sense? Go on, Bulla, show the wench who's lord and master of the Flint Mill, if you dare!'

Bulla drew Nerys down on to his knee and thrust his hand into the bodice of her blouse, tearing away the small pearl buttons in his haste. Nerys pushed at him frantically, tears of anger and humiliation blurring her vision.

The more she struggled, the more excited Bulla became. He pressed his mouth against hers and she gagged at the smell of ale on his breath. She tried to push him away, to slap out at his face, but he was past any sense now and – urged on by the roar of the men around him – he swept the glasses from the table and laid her down on the beer-damp surface.

A sense of disbelief washed over Nerys as she felt her skirt being pushed aside and her legs exposed to the leering gaze of the men who crowded round the table urging Bulla on.

'Go on, man, give it to her – let the little flossie learn her place!'

'Bulla, don't be silly, let me up – this is no way to treat me. Haven't I been good to your girls?' She tried to appeal to his better nature. 'Let me go and we'll say no more about any of this.' Even as she said the words, she knew that once she was free, Bulla Johns wouldn't see her for dust. She would leave the Flint behind her for ever, for how could she trust the man now that she had seen him in drink?

He grunted and pushed her skirts higher, tearing at her underwear, his fingers scoring her skin. She tried to twist over on to her stomach but one big hand came down heavily on her breast, expelling the air from her lungs so that she felt she couldn't breathe. God! She was going to be raped right here in the bar-room with no one lifting a hand to save her!

'Help me, please help me!' she entreated, twisting her head and trying to find a compassionate face amongst her tormentors.

'No one can't help you, not now!' Bulla said as he began to open his buttons. 'A man has natural urges, like, and I haven't had a woman for such a long time see, *merchi*,' he continued, slurring his words, 'not since . . .' His voice trailed away into silence.

A big man had moved forward, pushing his way through the crowd. Grasping Bulla's shirt-front, he finished the sentence for him.

'Not since you got drunk once too often and drove your wife into running away, Bulla Johns! Well, there'll be no more of this ill-treatment of innocent young women, do you understand me?'

A sense of shock washed over Nerys as she struggled to her feet and wrapped her torn blouse around her bruised breasts. Her arms ached from straining against Bulla's attack. She stared at him with horrified eyes; he had been so kind, so considerate an employer and suddenly he had turned into a monster, a wife-beater.

Through the mists of fear clouding her brain, she became aware that her rescuer was Siona Llewelyn, who now grasped her arm and drew her towards the door.

'Come on, get your things, Nerys Beynon. I'm taking you out of here and informing the constable of all that's gone on too.' Before he had finished speaking, the bar had miraculously emptied, the customers of the Flint Mill wanting no truck with the law.

'Who are you to interfere?' Bulla said belligerently, his eyes gleaming through puffed lids.

'I'm Siona Llewelyn, as well you know, and if you don't shut your big mouth then I shall have to shut it for you!'

Nerys screamed as Bulla lunged forward, his arms flaying. One fist caught Siona's eye and immediately it puffed up. With a roar of rage, Siona threw himself at the man and knocked him cold with a blow to the chin.

Nerys pulled at Siona's arms. 'Come on, let's get out of here,' she pleaded. 'I don't want any more trouble.'

He looked at the man lying prone on the ground and rubbed at his face wryly. 'There won't be any more trouble, righto? Go fetch your things now and we'll get back to the house.'

Nerys didn't question him further. She hurried up the stairs and into her room, where she threw her clothes into her bag and picked up her worn coat. Except that she would miss the girls, she wouldn't be sorry to leave here. She could only be grateful that Bulla's daughters were staying with their aunt and had not witnessed the disgusting behaviour of their father.

Hurrying downstairs again, she allowed Siona to take her bag from her trembling fingers. She sighed heavily and breathed in the fresh smell of rain on grass and flowers, grateful to have escaped so lightly from Bulla's clutches. How fortunate she had been that he had not come to her room in the dark of night and forced himself on her. Too much ale was his problem, clearly.

'What will Emily say?' Nerys spoke softly and almost immediately remembered that a tragedy had taken place, one of Siona's sons had been killed. She looked at Siona with sympathy.

His shoulders seemed to sag. 'You know there's been a death in the family, *merchi* – one of my twin boys, killed he was by the bull up on Ram's Tor. I expect you heard all about it.'

Nerys drew in a sharp breath. She had heard the men in the public bar talking about the accident, but Bulla Johns's attack had put it right out of her mind. She stopped walking and laid her hand on Siona's arm, concerned to see that his eye was closed and turning purple.

'There's sorry I am!' The words were inadequate, but Siona sensed her sincerity and squeezed her fingers.

'It's a terrible thing, and turning my poor Emily's mind queer, like. I've been into town and seen my niece Mali, asked her help with finding a woman to look after the baby.' He frowned. 'Passing the Flint Mill I was when I heard the commotion and all that palaver with Bulla Johns happened.' He smiled, but his face showed signs of strain. 'Lucky for you I came along.'

'Well, Siona, couldn't I look after the baby?' she said breathlessly. She waited for his reply not daring to hope, and then he smiled at her.

'*Duw*, that's the best idea yet. Why didn't I think of it?'

The wash of the river soothed Nerys as she settled herself into the boat and drew her torn skirt over her knees. There were passengers waiting, but not one showed signs of impatience; it seemed that everyone had heard of the tragedy which had befallen the Llewelyn household. Condolences were offered and accepted but no one was impolite enough to mention Siona's black eye.

Siona sculled the boat with ease, his big arms moving the craft swiftly through the strong currents of the River Swan. Nerys looked at him with genuine affection, for he had never shown her anything except kindness and sympathy and a willingness to help. As he caught her gaze and nodded to her encouragingly, she became aware for the first time of the curious stares being directed at her. She lifted a hand to her tangled hair and felt the breeze from the water disturb the torn edges of her blouse.

Quickly, she drew her coat around her shoulders and turned her face away, staring across the water to the Foxhole side of the river where the squat white Ferry House stood, smoke billowing from the chimney.

She wondered what her life would be like beneath the grey slate roof of the building on the river's edge. It was almost inevitable that her presence would be resented by some of the Llewelyn boys, but then she was there at Siona's request to do an honest job of caring for the new baby. It was a job she would do to the best of her ability, a job she must keep for she was running out of alternatives.

The boat gently bumped against the quayside and the passengers filed silently on to the bank. An air of gloom seemed to fill the very air as Nerys took Siona's hand and clambered ashore.

'Come on, *merchi*, let's go inside and I'll get you settled. I think it best if you have a bed in with Emily for the time being, and I'll doss down in the kitchen. It will be a bit cramped, but then I don't expect you'll mind that, will you, Nerys Beynon?'

'I won't mind anything so long as I've got a decent household to live in and where I'll be needed to do some honest-to-God work.'

'You'll work all right, don't you worry about that!' Siona said heavily. 'There will be so many mouths to feed that you won't know whether you should do a bowl of potatoes or a sack-full! Come on then, let's go inside.'

In spite of his words, Siona's pace didn't quicken and Nerys realized that it was an ordeal for him to face the solid facts of what had happened to his family. And so it was she who pushed open the kitchen door and led the way inside, coming face to face with Howel Llewelyn and at his side the doctor.

'Oh, dad, there you are.' Howel ignored her after one quick glance at her dishevelled state. 'The doctor's just been again to see mam and he's given her something to quieten her.'

Paul Soames thrust his hands into his pockets. 'I can't say how sorry I am to hear of your son's recent death, Mr Llewelyn,' he said in a strong, compassionate voice. 'The tragedy has obviously affected your wife badly, but I do feel that her problem started a while before all this and the accident has just served to precipitate a kind of nervous disorder.'

'What does that mean?' Siona went and stood before the fire, his hands resting on his hips. He was tense and uneasy as he waited for the doctor to continue.

'It means that your wife's state of mind is abnormal; it is a temporary condition, I hope, but she will need to be watched very carefully. She could do harm to herself or to someone else through sheer negligence.'

Siona sighed and shook his head. '*Duw!* There's an awful state of affairs! What else can go wrong then?'

'I've left some powders,' Dr Soames said kindly. 'Give her one before nightfall so that she sleeps; that's still the best cure for many of mankind's ailments. Have you anyone to help you with the baby?'

Siona nodded towards Nerys. 'Aye, there's a girl who has looked after many babies round these parts — do for me, she will.'

'But is she qualified?' It was Howel who spoke, his voice breaking roughly into the silence and Siona looked at him with eyebrows raised.

'I said she'll do for me.' His voice was hard, brooking no argument, and Howel's eyes did not waver as they ran over Nerys's dishevelled appearance.

Paul Soames smiled and inclined his head. 'I can

vouch for Nerys; her care of young Stephan Sutton was beyond reproach.'

She smiled at him gratefully, stepping aside as the doctor made for the door. 'You will have to keep your eyes peeled,' he addressed Nerys. 'If Mrs Llewelyn shows any change in her behaviour, any aggression towards the child or towards herself, then send for me at once.'

Siona went outside and stood talking to the doctor for a moment while Nerys, her bones aching, sank into a chair. Howel came and stood beside her, resting his hands on the snowy cloth as he stared into her face.

'There was a brawl,' she said quickly, defensively. 'Your father came to my rescue, for Bulla Johns was maddened by drink. And there will need to be some decision made about Bulla Johns's three daughters – he's not fit to keep them, you see.'

'All I know is that father has come home with a bruised face,' Howel said slowly. 'Well, I'll make my feelings plain so that even you will understand. Nerys Beynon, in my book you are nothing but trouble.'

CHAPTER ELEVEN

Market Street was filled with lights, lanterns that flickered as they dangled from wires stretched between the houses. A fire had been lit and it crackled and blazed, acrid smoke burning the eyes, for it was November now and the weather was turning chill.

The fiddler from the Ferry Boat Inn sat ensconced on a chair, his bow tucked beneath a bony chin, gaunt cheeks sucked in as he whistled along with the tune. Mog-the-Fiddle was well-known in the district, so much part of the fabric of the place that it came to be called after him. He played an Irish tune as befitted the occasion, for the betrothal of Katie Murphy to Ceri Llewelyn was being celebrated. And a celebration was not before time too, for there had been enough of grief at the Llewelyn household, and although Emily still mourned her lost son Hector, the twin who had been closest to her heart, she seemed resigned now and filled with acceptance.

Detaching herself from a group of laughing friends, Katie saw that Emily sat alone, her arms hanging listlessly at her sides as though she was at a loss without her baby daughter to nurse. Sian was safely at home in the capable hands of Nerys Beynon and there were those who said the girl was taking Emily's place in the home in more ways than one, for Siona appeared enamoured of her. He seemed like a new man, taking to wearing dashing colourful waistcoats and silk scarves, his green eyes merry, his tone jovial, but Katie treated the gossip with the scepticism it deserved.

'Are you all right?' Katie asked as she sat beside Emily, a little intimidated by her air of reserve; even now her cheek was turned slightly away, her shoulders tense. She inclined her head and for a moment Katie thought she would not answer but then, in almost a whisper, Emily spoke.

'Don't go giving life to babbas, girl, but stay sensible and whole.' She looked up then and there was such pain in her eyes that she seemed almost crazed. 'You bring a child into this world and then it is taken cruelly from you and there isn't anything you can do. Not all your grieving, nor all the loving you've lavished so willingly can bring back the dead.'

Katie took a deep breath and leaned forward to hold Emily's hand, expecting at any moment to be repulsed. 'Sure I know all that, for didn't I lose my husband to the sea and slip my baby through the shock?'

She was surprised to hear herself speak about something which until now had been sacrosanct – a part of her life pushed away into the nightmare corners of her mind where no one was allowed to visit. She felt Emily's fingers curl into hers and the woman looked at her, really *looked* for the first time.

'Ah, yes, Katie Murphy, you say rightly that you've suffered too, but you have more courage than me for I can't bear it.' Her eyes were bright. 'There's not a day passes but I think of my son Hector dying so horribly, and it's like a wound that won't heal. Nothing, not even Alexander's pain or Ceri's foolishness at working the lead – or even Nerys Beynon taking the attention of my Siona – none of it seems to matter any more.'

Katie was alarmed. Certainly she knew the anguish of loss and had pictured many times the way Mark had died, battered by the sea, beaten against the rocks so that he was crushed and bloodied. She had been almost driven out of her mind with grief but she was sure she had never appeared almost demented as Emily did in that moment.

'Look, come nearer to the fire; you're cold.' But as soon as she spoke, Katie felt Emily withdraw her hand and once more turn away; it seemed there was no way to reach her now and Katie rose to her feet, determined to find Ceri and send him to his mother.

Ceri was laughing, his head held in a way that was becoming familiar to Katie, and she stood for a moment watching him, remembering her chagrin and surprise the night he had failed to meet her. She had made up her mind to accept him, to allow him to court her and then when she stood alone waiting in vain for him to come, she had realized that she did care for him more than she had been willing to admit even to herself.

She had made her way back home feeling betrayed and bereft, thinking only that he had changed his mind and abandoned his pursuit of her. The thought had left her feeling empty and alone and she had cursed herself for a fool. So when he came to her the next day, explained how there had been a delay at work and he had been unable to get away, she had smiled and taken his hand.

'Never mind, you're here now and that's what counts.' The words had been spoken softly, intimately, and he had read in her eyes the feeling she could not express in words.

And so they were betrothed now, promised to each other before their families and friends. Yet as Katie stood a little apart from Ceri, she wondered if she could ever give him the depths of love she had given Mark.

'Hello, sister-in-law!' A strong voice spoke behind her and startled, Katie spun round.

'Oh, Howel, you frightened me!' She smiled and put her hands on his shoulders, kissing his cheek. She liked Howel – his keen eye, his sometimes sharp tongue and even sharper mind.

'I'm not surprised; you were a million miles away,' he said gently. 'I was half afraid to speak.'

'Well, to be sure I'm glad you did!' She tucked her hand into his arm, 'Come on, let's walk a little; I'd like to talk to you.'

When they were on the outskirts of the crowd, away from the sound of the music, Katie paused and looked up at Howel. 'This might not be the right moment to speak, but I can't help it. I'm worried about your mother.' There, the words were spoken and she sighed softly.

'I know you are, and rightly so – I'm worried too.' He moved away from her and thrust his hands into his pockets. 'She seems to have no real will to live.' He glanced down at Katie. 'It seems her sickness began some time ago, perhaps with the birth of the baby, perhaps even before that, but since Hector's death she has become morbid and withdrawn, almost a different woman from the one who used to bustle about the house knocking us all into shape. I'll admit it, I don't know what to do.'

'Has she seen the doctor?' Katie asked and then shook her head at her own stupidity. 'Of course she has, what am I thinking about?'

'Aye, Paul Soames is very good, but there's not much he can do. It's my mother's mind that's affected, you see; it's her will to live that's lacking. And things have been worse since that woman's been there, damn her!'

Katie was surprised at the anger in Howel's voice. She failed to understand who he meant for a moment and then remembered that Nerys was living at the Ferry House, helping with the baby.

'You're surely not talking about Nerys Beynon, are you?' she asked and Howel kicked moodily at a stone.

'Oh, yes, she's the little mother where the baby is concerned – and her making eyes at my father at the same time. She knows which side her bread is buttered, all right.'

Katie moved forward, resting her hand on Howel's arm. 'Look, I don't know what's happened but I'm sure you're wrong about Nerys – she's a nice girl sure enough. If she says she cares for the baby, then so she does, for she's honest as the day is long.'

Howel took a deep breath. 'I'm sure you mean well by defending her, but to me she's always meant trouble. When we were kids, she caused a fight between Ceri and me and we seem to have been at each other's throats ever since. All right,' he held up his hand, 'I know I must sound harsh, but she's trouble I tell you. Look at the way dad came home on the day he brought her there – bruised, he was, his eye puffed and swollen through fighting over her!'

Katie shook her head. 'Well, don't go getting all hot under the collar. Forget your problems now – sure and isn't this supposed to be a day for fun and laughter, and all of us going round with long faces as though at a wake? Come back to the warmth and the music and have a drink of ale.'

She watched as Howel moved towards the beer barrel set out on the pavement and bit her lip anxiously. He was a forceful man and if he had taken against Nerys Beynon, then her life at the Ferry House would not be easy. Sternly, she told herself to mind her own business; there was nothing she could do about the situation, not right at this moment anyway, so she would take her own advice and enjoy the festivities. Yet a cloud had passed over her party and she could not help but feel a little sad. There was so much pain in the world and she must grasp at happiness with both hands, for in her experience it did not last long.

'There's a sorrowful look from a girl who's just become betrothed – sure you'd think the devil was snapping at your heels!' Mrs Murphy slipped her arm around Katie's waist and hugged her in an uncharacteristic display of emotion. 'You've done the right thing, girl. Believe me, sure there's nothing to be gained by living your life as an old maid now, is there?'

Katie smiled warmly. 'I'm just sorry for Emily Llewelyn, that's all – grieving sure she is, and who can blame her?'

'Well now, other folks' problems are their own and not yours. You must enjoy yourself, for who sorrowed with you when you lost your husband, girl, I ask you that? Jesus, Mary and Joseph – will you never learn to look out for yourself, child?'

'I've forgotten it already, mammy, honest!' Katie lifted her hands in mock resignation. 'I'm going to find my Ceri and have him dance a jig with me – there now, will that do you?'

Katie left her mother laughing and pushed her way towards the crowd of people where Ceri was standing talking to Howel. She hoped the brothers were not arguing, for they both looked intense.

'You mean to tell me you've bought shares in the White Rock?' Ceri's voice was bristling with anger. 'Kept that quiet, didn't you? God, man, you're going over to the other side with a vengeance, aren't you?'

'It's not a case of going over to the other side,' Howel said shortly. 'I just don't want to be a schoolteacher all my life.'

'Oh, well, some of us would have given our right hand to have your education, boyo, and not grumbled at the fine job and good wages you bring in. Be living in a grand house soon, I shouldn't wonder, and forgetting the sacrifice mam and dad made to put you through the grammar school.'

'I'm forgetting nothing!' Howell's tone was short. 'I shall pay back my dues, don't you worry about that.'

'Right then, how about starting now and getting our mam proper treatment for her sickness?' Ceri was shorter than Howel, but he faced up to him with fists bunched and quickly Katie moved between the brothers.

149

'Sure, aren't you the fine ones then, quarrelling on my party day! Don't you dare make a fuss now, Ceri Llewelyn, and as for you, Howel, I think you should go on home – you're nothing but a skeleton at the feast, upsetting everyone you put your tongue to!'

Katie clung to Ceri's arm, the urge to protect growing strong within her. She felt his hand grasp hers and then she was smiling up into his face, slipping her arms around his neck, drawing him away from his brother.

'I promised mammy we'd do a jig, so come on now, no backing out, right? Fiddler, start playing and I'll bring you a lovely shiny shilling, so I will!'

The music was fast, beating like a pulse within Katie's veins as she swung Ceri around and showed him a few dance steps, lifting her skirts high. Joining in the spirit of the moment, he copied her and someone in the crowd began a rhythmic clapping. The music moved faster; Katie felt her hair sweep free as the pins scattered to the ground and she laughed, flirting with Ceri, her eyes sending him messages.

'You are asking for it, my girl!' he whispered as he leaned towards her, 'and by God, if I can get you on my own I'll show you what I'm made of!'

'Talk is easy, Ceri, man!' Katie smiled up at him. 'But when the party is over and my folks have gone to bed, I'll come down and let you in – see if you live up to your promises.'

He caught her waist and swung her round and the clapping of the crowd became more rapid. 'Hey, give us a chance!' Katie called breathlessly. 'I'm not as young as I was, remember!'

'Go on, girl, you can do it!' Tom Murphy leaned out from the press of people, his ginger eyebrows raised in merriment. 'Don't let a daughter of mine be beat by a Welshman!'

Ceri spun her round until her skirts rose above her knees and at last she fell against him, breathless and laughing. He held her close, his mouth hovering above hers. 'You look like a wanton there with your hair tangled and your eyes bright and I love you so much that it hurts.' He kissed her briefly and then led her to the chair that Mog-the-Fiddler promptly vacated.

'Keep your shilling, Katie Murphy,' the old man said, laughing. 'For 'tis a long time since I saw such dancing; takes me back to the good auld days in Ireland, sure it does!'

Katie held her hand to her heart and took deep gasping breaths of air. 'Sure, and don't I owe you the money for the wonderful way that bow of yours tickled the strings of the fiddle! Take the shilling with all my thanks. Ceri, dig your hand in your pocket, man, and pay up gladly, too!'

Tom Murphy clapped her on the shoulder. 'What a daughter I've got – sure and aren't you made from the very earth of Ireland? 'Tis proud of you I am, Katie, girl!'

'Less of the praise and give us some of your ale, daddy.' Katie held out her hand and took the mug from her father, sipping gratefully at the cool liquid which shone amber in the lights from the lanterns. 'You've done me proud,' she said softly, giving him back his ale. 'I shan't forget it, ever.'

'Well, and don't you deserve a bit of happiness at last? He's a good man, Katie, a fine man and don't you go selling him short, do you hear?'

'I hear, daddy, don't you worry. Oh look, Ceri's mam is pulling on her shawl. Siona Llewelyn's come to fetch her home, so I'd best say goodbye to her.'

Emily smiled vaguely as Katie took her hand. Her lips, pale and edged with blue, spoke words of farewell which had no answering echo of warmth in her eyes. Behind her stood her husband, tall and imposing, dressed in leather trews and a colourful waistcoat with a scarf knotted around the strong column of his throat. If it was true that he was enamoured of Nerys Beynon, then the girl had a formidable task before her in resisting a man like Siona Llewelyn!

As though at a given signal, the neighbours began drifting away back to their homes. The moon was a huge glowing orb in an unusually clear sky, the air cool with only an occasional spitting of sparks from the copper works to disturb the quiet of the night.

Katie clung on to Ceri's arm, smiling up at him while above them the lanterns – doused now – creaked to and fro in the soft breeze drifting across from the canal.

'Well, Ceri Llewelyn, we've made our promises before our folks and our neighbours, so there's no drawing back now, to be sure.'

He cupped her face in his hands and his eyes were dark. 'I don't want to draw back, my lovely girl, what about you?'

'I want to be with you, Ceri, that's all I know.' She put her head on his shoulder, wishing for the flame of love that did not come when he held her close. But desire was there, the need to be possessed by a man. 'Let's walk a little, wait for mammy and daddy to go to their bed and then, Ceri, we shall be together.'

He held her hand as they strolled away from the narrow courts of Green Hill. On the banks of the River Swan, he took her in his arms and held her close, kissing her hair tenderly.

'I'm a lucky man, Katie Murphy, do you know that?' He held her away from him and smiled down into her eyes. 'All I want is for us to be married, settled in our own home with you at the fireside waiting for me to come in from work of an evening.'

'That's not very ambitious of you, Ceri,' Katie said lightly. 'I thought your belly was on fire for you to make something of your life, and I don't want to be the one to hold you back.'

'Having you will make me more determined,' Ceri

declared, his voice vibrant. 'I am learning the ways of the lead and the silver and when I know enough, I shall move out of the White Rock.' His tone hardened as he went on. 'Especially now that my brother is part of the management of the place. It would be intolerable working under Howel, believe me.'

Katie sighed. 'Ideally brothers should get on well with each other, but I know from my own that it doesn't always work that way. Never mind all that, this is our night so let's enjoy what's left of it, shall we?' She moved away from him, smiling wickedly. 'Though you'll have to be out of my bed early before daddy wakes; he's the old-fashioned sort.'

When Katie opened the door of the house in Market Street, all was quiet except for the creaking of the boards and the ticking of the clock in the kitchen. She took Ceri's hand and led him upstairs to her room and though she was smiling at him in the slant of moonlight from the windows, she was fearful of giving herself to another man after so long. In her heart she still belonged to Mark, but she had to overcome that notion if she was ever to live a normal life again.

She took off her frock and, still wearing her petticoat, slipped into the coldness of her bed. When he took her in his arms, she turned her face into his naked shoulder. 'I'm frightened,' she whispered.

He stroked her arms and her neck and kissed her mouth gently. He was in no hurry and she relaxed against him, grateful for his sensitivity. Tentatively, she raised her arms to embrace him and his body was hard and firm against her.

She closed her eyes, her mouth warming to his kisses, and as his hands pushed aside her petticoat to linger on her breasts she sighed deeply.

'My sweet girl,' he whispered. 'I love you so much I could die of it.' He came to her gently and they became one flesh moving in the rhythms of the earth and sea. Desire wild and free flared through her as she

153

arched herself towards him, clinging to the silk of his back and feeling his tongue dart across her nipples. He was young and vital, he wanted and loved her and her response to him was one of gratitude and thankfulness, for he made her feel alive.

Colours of the rainbow kaleidoscoped within her as she moaned softly, feeling the sweet wine of release. Passion was not dead in her, she was a woman lying with a man who loved her and for the moment that was enough.

CHAPTER TWELVE

The moon shafted silver through the kitchen window as Nerys bent over the fire, rekindling the dying coals. She had been unable to sleep, lying wide-eyed on the hide couch, the blankets slipping from her as she tossed and turned in her efforts to find comfort.

Usually she shared Emily's room, on hand to tend the baby if she woke, though Sian was a good, placid child and scarcely ever roused Nerys during the hours of the night.

Tonight, however, the routine arrangements were changed because Emily was disturbed. She had returned from the betrothal party of her son Ceri in tears and had clung to her husband, wanting Siona to stay with her; to keep away the nightmares that haunted her restless sleep. So Nerys had had no choice but to make up a bed on the horsehair couch in the parlour; but at last she had given up the struggle to find sleep in despair, knowing that she would have no rest, and had crept into the kitchen anticipating a hot cup of tea.

The fire was almost out, the ashes grey in the black-leaded grate, but with some paper and kindling and a little patience flames were soon rising cheerfully, illuminating the shadow-filled kitchen.

Nerys tensed, lifting her head to listen. She was sure there had been a sound at the door and now she turned, lifting the iron poker, her heart beating swiftly. The door creaked open and a tall figure stood in the shadows; Nerys, her mouth dry, moved forward raising the poker threateningly.

155

'Hey, don't go crowning me with that! It's Ceri — don't be afraid, I'm not a villain out on the prowl!'

'*Duw!* You gave me a fright, boyo.' Nerys sank into the rocking-chair, the poker hanging from her nerveless fingers. 'I don't know what I would have done if you were a thief, I'm sure!'

He crouched before the fire holding his hands to the small blaze, and there was a look of happiness about him which touched Nerys deeply.

'Your mam would give you the sharp edge of her tongue if she saw you come home in the early hours of the morning, mind,' she whispered, her eyes full of merriment. Ceri grimaced at her and aimed a playful slap at her hand.

'Well, you're not going to tell her, are you?' he said softly. 'Never took you for a tale-bearer, mind. See too much, you do, Nerys Beynon!'

Nerys touched his shoulder. 'I can see only that you are very happy and I envy you, Ceri Llewelyn, for I don't think I was meant to find love. *Duw*, here I am getting to be an old maid! Looking after other people's children and with none of my own to hold in my arms — it's not fair, is it?'

Ceri looked at her in the firelight and smiled widely. 'You're just a young thing yet, and pretty too; plenty of time to meet the right man.' He pushed the kettle on to the fire and rose, moving about the dimly-lit kitchen on sure feet, finding the tea-cups and setting them out with quick deft movements of his hands.

'What's it like to be in love, Ceri?' Nerys asked wistfully. 'I think I've only ever known the love of children and sweet though that is it can't match the passion and pain which must exist between a man and his woman.'

'Oh, passion there is all right.' Ceri stood before the fire, his head raised so that the shadows played on his face and gave him a noble mien. 'And pain too when things don't go right, but the joy outweighs the pain, girl, and it's all worth it – well worth it, believe me!'

Nerys watched as he made the tea and poured it steaming into the cups; she felt tired and with a restless longing, but for what she did not know. She tried to imagine herself in a man's arms, kissing, caressing . . . but all she had experienced was the harsh fingers of Bulla Johns tearing at her and that was something she would sooner forget.

'When will you be married?' Nerys leaned forward to where Ceri was now seated on the mat before the fire. He was handsome and young and very sweet, but he would never send her pulses racing. Was she lacking in womanly desires, was there some element omitted from her being which made her different and destined to be alone for ever?

'Oh, I want to be married just as soon as Katie will have me, for every minute spent away from her is wasted time. I can't wait for the day to pass so that I can see her again, watch her smile, hear that soft Irish voice of hers.' He laughed. 'You see, I'm besotted, a lost cause, putty in my woman's hands!' He leaned back against the wall and drank deeply of his tea.

'And yet I'm ambitious too,' Ceri continued. 'I don't want to work the lead for ever. I'll learn all I can and then make the most of my knowledge to move away from the White Rock.'

He looked at Nerys. 'I'll tell you something now that I haven't told another living soul, not even Katie.' He smiled. 'I want to work the silver, forge it into beautiful ornaments. I've seen it flash, turn from a dull grey-brown substance to pure shimmering silver and it becomes a pool of shining metal – you wouldn't believe how lovely it is. Beauty in the lead works sounds unbelievable, doesn't it?'

The sound of creaking floorboards overhead startled Nerys. She looked questioningly at Ceri and he rose to his feet, placing his cup on the table cautiously. The door to the stairway opened and Siona moved into the room, his eyes taking in every detail of the situation.

'What's this then?' he asked curtly and Nerys, frightened by his tone of voice, realized she was wearing only her stiff cotton nightgown with a woollen shawl thrown around her shoulders.

'I came in rather late, or should I say early?' Ceri said softly. 'Stayed with Katie for a long time after the party I did, see?' He sighed. 'My mouth was as dry as anything and I wanted a drink of tea, so Nerys joined me. Want to make something of that, dad?' The words, though gently spoken, were both a rebuke and a challenge and after a moment Siona nodded.

'Aye, I see, boy. Thought some tomfoolery was going on under my roof for a minute, but I admit I was mistaken.'

Nerys rose to her feet, suddenly angry. 'That doesn't say much for me, does it, Siona Llewelyn?' she said in a low voice. 'I'm not a flossie, I'll have you know, and if you can't trust me to be alone with your boys then I'd better leave first thing in the morning, for it's alone with one or the other of them I'm going to be much of the time!'

'All right, let's calm down now. I said I was wrong, didn't I, and I'll get back off to bed. There's work for me in less than an hour, see.' He left the room without another word and Ceri stood with eyebrows raised, staring at Nerys in surprise.

'Duw, I never did see dad back down like that before – you must have some sort of hold over the old man!' He moved towards the door. 'He's right though, there's work before long and I'd better try to get a bit of shut-eye while I can. Good night and thanks for listening. You're a very nice girl, Nerys, and I'll thump anyone who says any different!'

In the silence of the kitchen, Nerys stared into the fire knowing there was little point in trying to sleep. She might as well begin the work of the day, for the thought of the lumpy horsehair couch held little attraction.

She moved silently into the parlour where her clothes were laid out over a chair, shivering as she dressed in the coldness of the front room that looked out over the swiftly flowing river. On the other side of the bank, the lantern waved red-gold like a glow-worm in the darkness. It seemed that somebody wanted the boat and Siona not yet ready for work.

There were clothes to be washed, which was always a huge task, so Nerys boiled up the kettle again and again, taking what seemed an endless time to fill the ridge-bottomed bath. The soda stung her hands as she swished it through the water and she winced, wondering a little at her patience with the job which offered unstinting hard work and very little money – yet she had come to love living at the Ferry House, it was her home now.

She washed the baby's clothes first, for they were comparatively easy – the small gowns and vests and bodices taking only a matter of minutes to rinse through. She set them in a pile ready to be rinsed under the cold tap and then tackled her own clothes along with Emily's.

The men's clothes were more difficult, ranging from Howel's fairly clean shirts to Ceri's which were grimy and gritty with dust. Lastly she set about washing the trousers; they needed a great deal of soaping and rubbing against the brass-ridged scrubbing board, and she winced as the hard tough material wore away the skin at the cuticles of her fingers.

It seemed no time at all before Siona was in the kitchen looking for his breakfast and Nerys, staring at the splashes of dampness on the kitchen floor, shook her head in despair.

'If I stop now, the water will go cold and I'll never

finish the washing by the time the baby wakes,' she said edgily. Siona merely smiled and opened the door of the larder, helping himself to bread and cheese.

'It's all right, girl, I'm not a child to be waited on, mind. You get on with that and when it's done I'll help you hang the clothes out on the line – there, how's that?' He was being conciliatory, making up for his suspicions of her, and Nerys was grateful to him; she was bone-weary already and the day scarcely begun. Never in any of her jobs had she been called upon to do so much work. No wonder Emily was weakly and sick – it was all too much for one woman to cope with.

The breeze blowing in from the sea was brisk without any hint of rain and Nerys sighed in relief. At least the washing would dry outdoors instead of being hung on the line in the kitchen, dampening the air that was heavy with the smell of soda.

She watched as Siona put the clothes over the line inexpertly but willingly, and smiled at him warmly. He came to her and rested his arm around her shoulders.

'You're a good girl, Nerys. I know we all put too much work on you, but don't think of leaving us, will you, for there's a right mess we'd be in without you. I'll do my best to get someone to help you, righto?'

She was surprised and pleased, for it was as though Siona had read her mind and was ensuring that she would stay in the Ferry House.

'Well, help I could do with,' she said quietly. 'For to tell the truth, Siona, I sometimes feel I can't manage all this.' She waved her hand around the small kitchen and Siona brushed back his hair with a quick, almost nervous movement.

'Well now, I'll empty the bath now and swill it out and hang it on the back door. Then tonight I'll speak with the boys, tell them they must all do a bit in the house until we get more help. It will be all right, you'll see.'

Howel entered the kitchen doing up his tie, his quick

glance at Siona revealing his surprise that his father was bothering himself with the task of taking out the bath-tub.

'You never did that for mam,' he said evenly, though his eyes were cold as they rested on Nerys.

'No, and perhaps I should have,' Siona retorted, 'and what's more, if you and the rest of the boys had been any help around the place perhaps your mam wouldn't be so sickly now!' He rubbed his hand through his hair. 'I'm off to work anyway – we're not all privileged teachers, mind!'

Nerys ignored the men as she quickly placed some rashers of bacon in the big pan and thrust it over the edge of the flames. Breakfast time was usually a nightmare, with the younger boys arguing and Big Eddie grumbling goodnaturedly that he never got enough to eat. And this morning was no exception as Nerys hurried about the kitchen, placing plates of food on the table and seeing the men of the Llewelyn family disappearing one by one, until she was left alone with only the taciturn Howel for company.

As usual, he paid her very little attention, but when she began to prepare a tray for Emily, he took it from her. 'Have something yourself, you look worn out.' He spoke tersely but she glanced at him quickly, grateful that he had noticed her fatigue.

'I am tired,' she said slowly. 'We'll have to sort out something about the washing – send some of it out to the bagwash or get a woman in – for I can't do it all and that I'll admit readily.'

 'I'll see to it, don't worry.' He pushed open the door to the stairway with his elbow. 'And by the way, I've dealt with Bulla Johns. His children are to remain with their aunt, so they will be safe.'

Nerys sat down with a sigh and sipped at a cup of hot fresh tea, pleased that Howel had taken the trouble to see to the Johns girls. He was a man of his word in spite of his sometimes abrasive attitude.

She looked gloomily at the greasy plates which littered the table. If this was what being a wife meant – the constant, unending work, without reward – she had missed nothing by remaining single, she decided.

When Howel returned to the kitchen, there was an easing of the indifference with which he usually treated her. 'My mother is feeling a little better today. She's getting up soon and I think it might be a good idea for her to get out a bit. What about the pair of you going into town to do some shopping?' He rolled up his sleeves and began to carry the dishes to the stone sink.

Nerys felt distinctly uneasy at the unexpected softening in his manner. 'Well, there's nothing stopping us going out if Emily feels up to it. I can wrap the baby in the Welsh shawl, which will leave my hands free to carry the bags.'

'Good.' Howel washed the dishes quickly, using the water from the kettle, and Nerys straightened her aching back, thankful to have at least one task done for her.

He cleared the table, shook out the cloth and put it away in the drawer.

'I'll just build up the fire before I leave,' he said, almost smiling. 'And I'll see that the boys do more around the place. I heard dad talking to you about it and he's quite right; we must take our share of some of the load.' He sat back on his heels in front of the fire. 'After all, we're nothing to you but a job of work and slavery was abolished a long time ago!'

Nerys didn't know quite how to take his remarks. Was Howel being sarcastic, or was he genuinely taking an interest in her welfare?

'Well, there's considerate of you.' She couldn't bring herself to say his name; he was aloof from her and almost a stranger, not like his brothers who offered her warmth and friendship.

'Not consideration really,' he spoke slowly. 'I'm just being practical. Mam needs help and you seem to get

162

on well with the family; you work hard enough, we could do worse.'

'Oh, thank you!' There was more than a hint of sarcasm in her own voice as she lifted her brows, staring at Howel with anger beginning to burn inside her. 'Hard work it *is* too, with you men eating like pigs and walking in dirty, muddy shoes all over the kitchen floor. Like children you are, the lot of you. It's only Siona who shows any real consideration.'

'Oh, yes, my father.' Howel said the words softly, with some hidden meaning that Nerys failed to understand. And yet she sensed an implied criticism.

'Yes, your father – and good to you boys he is, working all hours of the day and night and still not with too much manly pride to help a bit in the house. If it wasn't for him and your poor sick mam, I'd walk out now and leave you all to fend for yourselves.'

'And where would you go?' Howel rose to his feet, staring at her with undisguised scorn. 'Back to the Flint Mill to be pawed by the customers – or would you fancy a spell in the workhouse? Don't you dare to threaten me,' he continued. 'I know you were happy enough to come here with my father and be given a roof over your head. And I've seen you both making sheep's eyes at each other – do you think I'm stupid?'

'I was glad to work here and earn an honest wage, I'll admit it readily, but that doesn't make me a slut. I'm an honest woman with no slur on my character and I'll thank you to remember that.'

He smiled slowly. 'You are just angry because I've touched on the truth. Getting a bit beyond girlhood now, aren't you? Jilted by the one man who promised you marriage and perhaps thinking it's about time you took a lover before it was too late.' He paused. 'Well, you might appeal to the old man but it's a certainty you haven't got what it takes to catch a young one.'

Nerys took a deep breath, telling herself not to rise to the bait. Howel Llewelyn had touched her on the raw by reminding her of the fiasco of her wedding day, but she would not give him the satisfaction of seeing her pain. 'I'll not do another hand's turn for you,' she said calmly. 'I shan't cook or wash for you or make your bed, I'll simply ignore you.'

She moved away towards the stair, hearing his low laughter with a feeling of frustrated anger. Was there nothing she could do to hurt him? But wait a minute, perhaps there was; he seemed to be obsessed by the thought that she was chasing his father well then let him go on thinking it, let the thought be a thorn in his flesh for she would enjoy taunting him.

Emily was dressed in her usual haphazard fashion, wearing an ill-fitting blouse and a loose skirt that hung untidily at the hem, but she smiled as Nerys entered the room.

'Howel says we're to go out today, is the sun shining?' Emily spoke in a strange almost childlike way and Nerys went to the window, staring out into the dull November day.

'It's not too bad but you must put on a warm coat, Emily, and a pair of stout shoes, mind. I'll see to little Sian.'

The baby was unusually pale but she gurgled with laughter as Nerys lifted her from the crib.

'Come on, babba, let me change you and make you comfortable, then,' Nerys said softly. The child was thin, too thin, but then Emily's milk was scant and had little nourishment in it. Perhaps, Nerys thought, it might be as well to give the baby some cow's milk; she would talk to Emily about it later, for now there was enough to do to get them all to the shops.

Emily was bright-eyed, her voice thin and high-pitched; her cheeks were flushed, although there was a blue line around her mouth. She stared into the shops in the *Stryd Fawr* as though she had never seen them before, seeming unaware of the baby held in Nerys's arms and taking little notice even when the child cried hungrily.

Nerys was concerned as she followed Emily into the Emporium, wondering what on earth she could do with the restless baby in her arms. She rocked the child, patting her thin spine, talking softly but to no avail.

'Emily, we must go home,' she said at last, but Emily was busy lifting a bolt of blue silk and staring at its shimmering surface with childlike wonder.

Beginning to feel distraught, Nerys looked around for someone, anyone who might help her. The shop assistant with a disdainful look on her face was staring, doubtless wondering why she couldn't quieten the crying baby. 'Emily, Sian is hungry and we must catch a tram home,' she insisted, but Emily looked at her with eyes grown dull.

'I don't want to go home,' she said. 'I'm losing my mind, do you know that, girl? Losing my mind.' She began to cry, wailing along with her baby, and Nerys bit her lip in agitation.

'Will you fetch a doctor?' she appealed to the saleswoman, who was moving forward with a frown of disapproval on her face.

'I most certainly will not!' she said. 'That woman is drunk, you can see it a mile off!'

Nerys caught Emily's arm and drew her out into the street. 'Hush now, everything is going to be all right. Come on, we'll go to see Doctor Soames; he doesn't live very far away. See, there's Canal Street, just around the corner.'

Emily was still crying as Nerys hammered on the door of the doctor's house. It seemed that the well of her tears was everlasting, as they brimmed from her eyes and ran unchecked down her cheeks, dripping from her chin on to the collar of her coat.

'Hush now, Emily, the doctor will be able to help,' Nerys said edgily. She knocked again, rapping hard on the wooden panelling which could have been improved by a coat of paint. At last, to her relief, there was the sound of footsteps in the hallway.

'I'm sorry to trouble you like this, Doctor Soames, but I didn't know where else to turn. Can we come in, please?'

He nodded, taking the child from her arms and leading the way into his room. It smelled of leather and wintergreen oil and in the corner stood an old skeleton which seemed to leer at Nerys as she sank into a chair.

The doctor she knew well, for he had visited Mary Sutton's house many times – and always with a kind word for Nerys, even though she was simply nanny to young Stephan Sutton. To her surprise, he set the baby on the long high couch and examined the child, holding up his hand when Nerys would have pointed out it was Emily she was concerned about.

But Emily had stopped crying and was watching Paul Soames intently, her eyes clear and lucid so that Nerys wondered if she had imagined the vagueness she had seen there.

Paul's face was grave as he covered the baby's small frame and wrapped the child in her shawl.

Emily spoke, her voice falling hard and clear into the silence. 'It's the tuberculosis, isn't it, doctor? I've known it for some time, but I didn't want to face up to it.'

'I'm afraid you may be right, Emily, but with care and good nursing – why, who knows what might happen?'

'She'll die,' Emily said simply. 'I saw it happen to my mam and my sister too – you don't get better from that tuberculosis.'

Nerys sank back in her chair, overwhelmed by the horror of what she was hearing. It was no wonder Emily was acting strangely, her mind struggling to get away from reality. She took a deep breath, knowing she had to get them all back to the house on the banks of the River Swan.

'Thank you for your trouble, doctor,' Emily said in

166

a soft voice, not seeing the irony of thanking Paul Soames for passing a virtual death sentence on her child.

'Now don't despair,' the doctor said as he led the way along the darkly-painted passageway to the door. 'Give the child plenty of milk and fresh air and remember, miracles do sometimes happen.'

'Not in my family, doctor,' said Emily in a voice completely devoid of self-pity. She held her head high as she stepped out into the street and looked at the baby lying silent now in Nerys's arms, as though seeing Sian for the first time.

'Poor little babba,' she said. 'What good will all the milk and fresh air in the world do you?'

She followed as Nerys led the way towards the tram-stop and waited in silent patience, her hands folded across her stomach. In spite of everything, she seemed clear in the head, her eyes unmisted, her lips set firmly in her pale face. Nerys glanced at her from time to time, trying to read her mood, but she was effectively shut out by Emily's silent dignity.

In the jolting tram, Emily took the baby from Nerys and held her close. Sian began to cry again and, unconcerned about the other passengers, Emily put the child to her thin breast, her hard gaze defying anyone to disapprove.

It was a relief when the banks of the river came into sight and Nerys caught Emily's arm, helping her to her feet. 'You'll be all right now. You'll have Siona at your side and he'll look after you,' Nerys said gently, but Emily shook her head.

'Nothing anyone can do, good girl; not even Siona can change what's happened to my little babba.'

The house was empty and cold as Nerys pushed open the door. 'Sit you down, Emily, and hold little Sian while I build up the fire.' She shrugged off her coat and knelt before the grate pushing thin sticks into the coals, coaxing the flames into life. It took only a few minutes to bring the fire roaring up the chimney and with a sigh of satisfaction, she washed her hands free of the clinging coal-dust.

'I'll light the lamps and close the curtains and it will seem more cosy in by here,' she said, attempting to speak cheerfully, but Emily didn't even look up. She was staring into the face of her child as though memorizing every detail of the baby's appearance.

Life had not been kind to Emily Llewelyn of late. She had lost one of her sons, her twin boy Hector who had been like a pulse within her own body. She had borne a child, a longed-for daughter, only to face almost at once the prospect of losing her. And she had grown old over the past weeks, her once indomitable spirit fading as she watched her husband Siona fancy the girl Nerys who had come to take her place in the Ferry House.

'Emily?' Nerys saw with concern that the older woman's eyes were misted, as though her thoughts took her far away from the small kitchen. 'Emily, look, I've made you a nice hot cup of tea. Come on, drink it, it will take away the chill.'

Nerys poured a measure of pearly milk from the big enamel jug into a saucepan and held it over the flames. 'See, I'll feed little Sian some of this milk, it will do her good,' she said, but Emily did not seem to hear.

'The boys should be in bed by now; they must be playing by the river bank. You'd best go and call them, girl,' Emily said, her voice sounding matter-of-fact as though there was nothing in the world to trouble her.

'Go on, I'll see to Sian,' she added and, after a moment's hesitation, Nerys left the house. It was growing dark now and Emily was quite right – the boys should be indoors.

'Will! Tom!' she called into the dimness. 'Come on, time to come in!' She moved further along the bank. 'Boys! Come here at once!' She heard the sound of running feet and, to her relief, the two young boys emerged from the gloom hearty and full of high spirits.

'Our Will hit me!' Tom declared indignantly. 'I ought to give him a good pasting, and I will too if he tries it on again!'

'Don't quarrel, you two. Your mam isn't feeling well, so be quiet, will you?'

'I'm starving,' Will said, looking up at Nerys through a shock of dark hair. 'What's for tea?'

Nerys felt an immediate sense of contrition. The children should have had food hours ago, but then she couldn't do everything at once.

'Look, there's our Howel!' Will ran towards his brother and caught his hand. 'I'm starving, Howel, I haven't had anything to eat since dinner-time.'

Howel's eyes rested briefly on Nerys. 'Well, that's not good enough, is it, boyo? Never mind, I'll come and give you a good plate of bacon and eggs – how will that suit?'

Nerys bit her lip. Somehow she had been put in the wrong and her own sense of guilt held her silent.

'Been too busy to feed the boys, I take it?' he said, unwilling to let the matter drop.

'Your mam isn't well ... there's bad news,' she stumbled over the words. 'We went to the doctor in town, he said that the baby has probably got the tuberculosis. I'm sorry, there's no other way to say it.'

He hissed through his teeth and for a moment, Nerys felt sorry for him. She almost reached out and took his hand, but he had the same manner as his mother: the way of turning his shoulders which excluded other people.

'We'd better get home, then.' He strode forward quickly, holding Will by the hand.

At Nerys's side, Tom caught her arm. 'Is our baby going to die like Hector did?' He was trying to be manly, but his voice shook and Nerys grasped his hand tightly.

'Not if I have anything to do with it!' She followed

close on Howel's heels, entering the little house behind him.

'Mam!' He was calling up the stairs, his voice anxious, then he ran quickly up to the landing and called again into the silence.

Nerys felt a crawling of fear down her spine as Howel returned to the kitchen and shook his head at the unspoken question in her eyes.

'Go, Tom, and call dad,' Howel said. 'Tell him to come home urgently.' He turned to Nerys. 'What was she doing when you left her?'

Nerys moved to the fire, where the pan of milk stood cold and congealing on the hob. 'She seemed calm, in full possession of her senses. You don't think she'd do anything silly, do you?' Her voice rose and Howel gave her a quick look.

'Now don't go all hysterical on me, for Christ's sake!' He went to the door and peered into the gloom. 'Eddie, thank God you've come home! Our mam's gone out, heaven knows where, but we must search for her.'

Eddie, big and slow-moving, looked into the kitchen as though disbelieving his brother's words. 'But where could she go? It's too dark to see your hand in front of your face.'

Howel sighed heavily. 'You know how she's been lately, don't you – not herself at all – and today she's had bad news about the baby. Oh, God, I'd better look down by the river.' He glanced at Nerys. 'You stay here, wait to see if she comes home. We'll go and search – come on, Eddie.'

In the silence of the kitchen, Nerys stared into the flames of the fire, a feeling of dread beginning to grow within her. Emily was missing and Nerys felt that she was to blame.

She put her head into her hands and closed her eyes, telling herself that the Llewelyn boys would find their mother and bring her from the darkness, but somehow she knew the hope to be a false one.

CHAPTER THIRTEEN

The darkness lent an air of calm to the hills of Ram's Tor and the silver light of the moon set pools of brilliance in the grass. Alexander looked at the silent girl at his side, his heart heavy as he saw the clouding of Sarah's features and the air of despair that sat strangely upon her young shoulders.

He eased his own shoulders in an effort to relax. It had been a long hard day. Working the milk round alone was difficult enough, but the pain of the customers' sympathy reminding him constantly of the death of his twin had worn him down.

He had brought Sarah to the hill-top to be alone with her, to tell her his plans, yet now that the moment had come his tongue was silent in his head, refusing to form the words that were somehow a betrayal. He would only be doing what Hector wanted, his brain told him that, but his body said something different for he coveted his dead brother's woman.

'Sarah, there's something I have to say to you.' He coughed over the words and she looked at him, becoming aware of his presence, leaning against his arm as her breath mingled sweetly with his own.

'I know, *cariad*. We must marry and be together and try to give comfort to each other. Don't look so surprised, Alex; you are not the only one to have feelings that need no explanation, mind.'

He took her hands. 'I know it's right that I give Hector's baby the name of Llewelyn, but Sarah – I feel I'm cheating him out of his life.'

Sarah took his face between her hands. 'Look, we both loved him, will always love him, but he's gone and we can't bring him back whatever we do. He wanted us to be together, you know that he did, so kiss me and hold me and let us wash away our unhappiness so that we can make a new life for ourselves.'

She kissed him on the lips, a warm womanly kiss, and passion flared through him as for a moment his arms tightened around her. Then he released her, shame turning his blood to water.

'We must be married soon,' Sarah said, laying her head on his shoulder. 'The banns were called for Hector and me and there's only a small difference in name – that won't matter will it?'

'I don't think so, girl.' Alex brushed her hair away from her face. Even as she spoke of their forthcoming marriage, he could hear the tears in her voice.

'The baby will look like Hector, a fine boy.' Sarah glanced up at him, her profile young and vulnerable, her skin pure silk in the moonlight. 'And of course, he will look like you too. You will love him, won't you, Alex?'

Alex drew her into the warmth of his arms. 'How could I not love him? He will be flesh of my flesh, blood of my blood and Sarah . . . Perhaps I shouldn't tell you this, but I love you with all my being. I think I loved you from the first moment I ever saw you, but you were for Hector, I knew that.'

She began to cry, great gulping sobs so that her body shook against him. His body melted as he rocked her, closing his eyes against the rush of protective love which burgeoned within him. He would live for Sarah and he would gladly die for her, but he could not forget that it was his brother's death which had given her to him.

The horror of it had never left him. He could still smell the stink of the bull and the sickening smell of

172

blood. He heard in his nightmares the pounding of hooves, saw great curved horns gouge and tear – and sometimes it was he who died and not Hector.

But now he forced those thoughts away into the dark recesses of his mind, turning his attention to practicalities.

'Stop crying now and let me tell you my plans,' he said softly, and held her close as she would have moved to look at him. 'The shop in West Cross is pretty run down and needs a lot of work, but I'll knock it into shape, don't you worry. We'll have a good home and a fine business, you'll see.'

'Oh, Alex, I hope we can make a success of it. I feel so confused and so frightened. I wish to God I wasn't having this baby!'

'No, don't say that, *merchi*, for it's all we'll have of my brother.' He kissed her gently on the cheek that was turned away from him.

'Yes, but the child will be a constant reminder to you that I was your brother's girl first. Can you live with that knowledge, Alex? It's not going to be easy, mind.'

Easy . . . nothing in life would ever be easy again, for half of him was lying beneath the ground in *Dan y Graig* Cemetery. The hopes and plans he had shared so enthusiastically with Hector, the dreams of fortunes made and of successful lives led as business men were dust now, for the thought of accomplishment without his twin to share in the glory took the edge off the prospect.

'You've gone very quiet, Alex. Not thinking of backing out, are you? Though I'll understand if it's all too much for you, of course.'

She was a proud woman, was this Sarah, and he smiled as he looked down into her eyes that were dark and mysterious, lit at the edges by the moonlight.

'Backing out – are you mad, Sarah? I'd never be such a fool.' He hugged her, keeping passion at bay, for the moment was not right for making love.

173

'I'd best take you back home, *merchi*, your mam will be worried about you.'

'Worried about me. There's a soft thing to say, Alex, and her down at the public bar every night with my dad. Thinks I'm grown-up enough now to look after myself, she does, mind.'

He drew her to her feet and she shivered a little in the cold breeze blowing in off the sea far below. 'I haven't told them about the baby yet,' she sighed, 'though I don't think mam and dad would notice if I walked out of the house tomorrow, if the truth be known.'

Alex hugged her to his side. 'Well, don't worry, I'll deal with everything and soon we'll be in a house of our very own, I promise you.' He chewed his lips as he led Sarah away from the cliff-top and on to the road winding down into the village, where the lamps threw soft pools of warm light on the ketches lying drunkenly on the sea-front.

He would use some of the profit from the business to do up the premises above the shop, he decided. It was not a course he would have chosen, for he needed capital badly, but in the circumstances it was the only thing he could do.

Contrary to Sarah's expectations, her mother was at home and she stared up coldly at her daughter as she entered the dimly-lit and heavily furnished room.

'Well, you're a fine one!' Her voice was harsh, though her lips quivered a little and it was obvious she had been drinking heavily. 'To think that strangers – *strangers*, mind – have to tell me my own daughter is getting married! For shame on you, Sarah; how dare you call the banns without speaking to me and your father first?' She rose and pulled off the basin-shaped hat she was wearing; it seemed she had just returned from the public bar of the Antelope Hotel alone – no doubt she'd quarrelled with dad again, Sarah thought wearily as her mother's voice ran on.

'It's a good thing Charlie didn't come back with me –

took his belt off to you, he would, and no blame attached to him either. Forbid this marriage, he will, I'm warning you!'

Sarah sighed heavily but remained silent and it was Alex who moved forward, holding out his hand politely. 'I'm Alexander Llewelyn. I'm sure you must have seen me doing the milk round in the village.'

'I'm not shaking hands with you! Nothing but a young boy – not old enough to shave yet, I dare say. No, there'll be no more nonsense about marriage, you're both too young.'

Alex stared at the woman, feeling slightly sorry for her. Her face was pale under a coating of powder and her eyes filled with tears. 'But we must be married; Sarah is going to have a baby, you see.'

The words fell into a silence and Sarah's mother sank on to a chair, staring down at her hands. 'It's all my fault, see. Not here with her half the time – but I can't stay in, can I, and leave my Charlie to go to the public among all those flossies on his own?'

'Mam, mam!' Sarah put her arms around her mother's shoulders. 'Look, don't blame anyone but me. I knew what I was doing and I was in love. I couldn't help myself, any more than you can help being jealous of our dad.'

'I'm *not* jealous!' her mother denied hotly and then her shoulders slumped. 'Yes, of course I am. I can't bear to see the girls playing up to him. Handsome devil he is, see, and younger than me – but don't you go repeating that, mind. Got to keep up with these flossies, I have, otherwise they'd be whispering temptation in Charlie's willing ears.'

'Well, there's no need for you to worry about us,' Alex said. 'Sarah and me will be married and then we'll go and live in our own little place and you'll have the house to yourself.'

His words struck a chord and Mrs Matthews looked at him with fresh interest. 'Know how to get round people, don't you, boyo – good salesman you must be, finding out a person's weak spots like. Well, you'd best take the girl out of here tonight then, for if her dad comes back he'll leather her for sure.'

'Mam!' Sarah's voice was filled with shame and indignation, but Alex took her arm and drew her to him.

'Look love, come home with me – it's for the best. You can sleep in with mam and Nerys and the baby for now, and it won't be long before I do up the old shop, I promise.'

Sarah looked uncertainly at her mother, who turned away and stared into the grey dusty grate without speaking. They remained for a long moment, unmoving, then abruptly Sarah moved towards the door.

'I'll fetch my things; it won't take long, for I haven't got very much!' Her reproachful words were ignored by her mother who remained seated, unblinking, as though disassociating herself from the proceedings.

He would see Sarah had a good home, Alex told himself fiercely, even if it took every penny he had. He would work night and day to make a success of the business. For the present Sarah could serve in the shop, at least until the baby came. Later on he would have to think of employing someone to help sell the butter and cheese that he intended to produce.

Oh, yes, he would make a success of his life, for he was suddenly and upliftingly determined on it. Hector's son would have all the advantages that it was possible to provide. See how a good education had served Howel, for instance. His older brother was a teacher, dabbled in stocks and shares, made himself a personality in the town by his work on the council. The baby would have all that and more.

Sarah returned to the room clutching a small cloth bag in her hand. Her lip was trembling, for she was leaving the only home she had ever known. Alex saw her look to her mother for some sign of affection, a warmth, a regretful farewell, but there was no response from the woman who sat as though turned into stone before the empty fireplace.

'Come on.' Alex took the bag from Sarah. It was pitifully light and his throat constricted. He would make up to her for all that was lacking in her life; she would be loved as no woman was ever loved and he would work his fingers to the bone to make her comfortable and happy.

'I can't believe it,' she shivered as they moved out into the street. 'I can't understand my mother just letting me go like this – hasn't she *any* feelings for me at all?'

'I think it's those feelings she has to hide,' Alex said gently. 'She wants to save you from a hiding, and she can't show any emotion or she'll break down altogether.'

'I'd like to think you're right,' Sarah said in a small voice, 'but it's only dad she thinks of really. I've always known ever since I was little that I took second place.'

'Well, not any longer.' Alex hugged her arm to his side and smiled down at her. 'From now on you'll be Mrs Alex Llewelyn, wife of Sweyn's Eye's most up-and-coming business man, and then everyone will look up to you.'

Sarah laughed softly into the darkness. 'You're good for me, Alex, you make life seem so funny. I do love you.'

Alex felt warmth envelop him as he led Sarah along the Strand towards the ferry-boat. He wondered what his father would say when he saw that his son was bringing Sarah home. He could hardly turn her out into the night – neither would the thought enter his head, for Siona was always a fair and kindly man. But for all that, it would be crowded in the little house that was already full of men. Alex shrugged the thought aside, for the situation was merely a temporary one.

'*Duw*, it's cold down by the river-side, boyo!' Sarah

177

drew closer to him as the breeze from the river lifted the hair from her face. 'I'm glad we're not to live here for always – afraid of the water, I am, mind.'

'Nothing to be afraid of in the River Swan so long as you know and respect her moods, *cariad*,' Alex said softly, '*Duw*, where's the boat? I thought dad would be sitting by here waiting for the public bars to close. Pay well do the customers when they're full of ale – and not like dad to miss the opportunity.'

He took the lamp from its post and swung it to and fro, trying to see across the river through the darkness and the night-time mist that obscured his view of the Ferry House.

'I'm cold, Alex.' Sarah moved closer to him, creeping into his arms like a mouse, her face upturned and pale, her eyes shadowed. Love for her twisted within him as he held her close, encircling her with his own coat so that they were like one person.

He felt restless, uneasy. Something must be wrong at home for Siona to be away from his post for so long.

'I think we'd better go down river and cross on the bridge,' he said at last and Sarah sighed in resignation.

'Aye, all right love, though all I want to do is to crawl into bed and sleep. This baby's changed me, mind. Full of fun and keen for adventure I was once, but now I'm like a bird longing to make a nest – there's soft, aren't I, Alex?'

He took off his coat and put it around her, taking her hand and leading her downstream as though she was a child.

'No, not soft, it's a perfectly natural reaction, girl.' He smiled to himself in the darkness – here he was talking like an expert, and him scarcely knowing anything about womanhood!

Sarah slipped a little on the grassy bank that was dampened by the mist and he held her close for a moment, feeling her heart beating against his rapidly and knowing her fear as though it was his own.

'The water won't hurt you, love, for I shan't let anything hurt you ever. Come on, it's not far and we'll soon be home sitting by a warm fire – with a nice hot cup of tea in our hands before we're in the door two minutes, if I know mam!' But even as he spoke the words, a feeling of dread gripped him. He told himself not to be stupid, that he was still very much affected by Hector's death and inclined to the miseries from time to time. And yet, as he led Sarah along the river bank towards the bridge, he had the heavy unbearable feeling that yet another tragedy had befallen the Llewelyn family.

*   *   *

Emily had remained for a long time in the small, sparsely furnished bedroom she had shared for so many years with Siona, though now it was Nerys who was her constant companion. She stared down into the face of her tiny daughter who had just been given a death sentence. It was all very well for the doctor to be filled with false optimism and to talk about 'fresh air and plenty of milk', but no one ever recovered from the tuberculosis and so what hope did a tiny baby have?

Emily longed to cry but her throat was constricted, her eyes burning with the tears that would not fall.

Her life had dissolved into a meaningless maze of pain as fate dealt her one blow after another. Now it was enough, time to call an end to her suffering. She could no longer think of her living sons; they had Nerys and turned to her more and more often, as though aware that their mother was locked into her own world of grief. As for Siona, well . . . the sparkle in Siona's eyes was no longer for his wife.

Carefully Emily dressed Sian in her fine cotton christening robe. She fastened the buttons with shaking fingers and then adjusted the small rose-trimmed

179

bonnet over her baby's sparse hair. 'You shan't go alone, my little love,' she said softly, kissing the pale cheek.

The shawl was white and delicate, knitted at a time when Emily was happy and well; it held memories, good memories, and she hugged the baby to her in a moment of pain. Then she rose and wound a sheet around her body, encircling the baby and binding Sian securely to her. 'We don't want you drifting away from me, do we, my lovely?'

She heard Nerys's voice from far away calling the two boys, and knew that she must go now while the house was empty. Hurrying light-footed down the stairs, she paused only to push the pan of milk to the back of the hob and then went out from the kitchen into the coldness of the misty air. She moved downstream, away from the house and the people who waited for Siona to take them across the river to the Hafod bank, for there must be no witnesses.

Her feet sank into the mud as she walked towards a crop of bushes – she wanted no last-minute hitches, no nosy neighbours spoiling her plans.

'We'll be all right, *cariad*,' she said softly to the baby who stirred in her arms, eyes wide in a small, pale face. 'We'll go together, me and you, for I don't want to watch you dying, coughing up your life's blood before my very eyes.'

The child smiled, eyes bright and intelligent, and Emily bit her lip as she hugged Sian to her. 'Here we are, then. Soon we'll be out of it all and there'll be no suffering for either of us, my darling girl.'

She waded into the water, feeling the coldness with a sense of shock. Sian began to cry as the water covered her, mouth open like a bird in distress. Emily closed her eyes and moved deeper into the river, the water now like arms caressing her, comforting her and taking away her pain. She felt herself struggle as the coldness covered her face but told herself to be calm, that soon it would all be over.

Sian seemed to sag, heavy as though in sleep, and Emily allowed herself to drift with the current, her thoughts becoming blurred. She thought of Siona briefly and of her youngest boys, but nothing mattered . . . nothing except that she and Sian would soon be at rest.

* * *

Alexander's footsteps quickened as he drew nearer to the Ferry House. He heard Sarah panting behind him but he couldn't wait for her; she would just have to understand how imperative it was for him to find out what was wrong.

In the kitchen all seemed normal. A pan of milk stood on the hob and the table was set for supper with the spotless white cloth and the bread cut into slices as though the meal was about to begin.

'Mam!' he called, but his voice echoed in the emptiness. Tom's head appeared round the door and behind him was Will, both boys looking pale and anxious.

'Dad and the older boys are out looking for mam,' Will said in a small, anxious voice. 'Nerys is upstairs; I think she's been crying.'

Alex knew then that mam was gone from his life for ever. He slumped in a chair and looked up with dull eyes as Sarah came into the kitchen, her face flushed, her voice breathless when she spoke.

'What on earth's the matter?' she asked and Alex shook his head, unable to speak. It was Will who answered her question.

'Our mam's missing, and the baby too. Dad's gone looking for her, says he won't come back without her.' The boy was trying to be brave, but his mouth quivered and Alex held him close for a moment.

'Go and get Nerys, there's a good boy,' he said softly and Will pounded upstairs, eager to be of help. Alex heard slow, heavy footsteps on the stairs and then Nerys entered the room, her eyes red with weeping.

'Come on and sit down, girl.' Alex took charge. 'Sarah, I think we could all do with a cup of tea, love. Now, Nerys, tell me exactly what has happened here?'

Nerys rubbed at her face with her handkerchief. 'Your mam's been gone hours, must have slipped out of the house when I was looking for Will and Tom. I blame myself, I knew she was acting strange-like and I should have stayed with her.

'But she urged me to go – worried about the boys she was, see, had nothing to eat since dinner and it was turning dark and all . . . oh, I don't know!' She put her head in her hands and Alex felt strangely removed from the little scene; it was as though he was a bird fluttering above, watching the acting out of a play. He knew the answer before he asked the question.

'Mam had had bad news about the baby, hadn't she, Nerys?' He felt chilled, as though the heart had gone out of him, as she nodded.

'Aye, took Emily and the baby to see Doctor Soames, I did. He examined little Sian and said that she had the tuberculosis. I think Emily knew it already, for calm she was then, as though her tears had all been shed.'

'She'll have gone into the river with the baby.' His voice fell soft and defeated into the silence of the kitchen. He felt Sarah come to him, put gentle arms around him, but he was beyond comfort as he fell back into his chair and closed his eyes against the tears burning his lids.

CHAPTER FOURTEEN

The River Swan rushed down towards the sea, following the ageless pattern of the tides. The pale pink of dawn was lightening the sky, washing the water with redness. Siona Llewelyn shivered as he picked his way through the harsh stunted bush on the eastern bank, knowing exactly where he was going. He knew the river in all her moods and understood where she would deposit her dead.

Siona walked alone, wanting the silence for he felt guilt burn in his belly. He had tried to be a good husband, loving Emily and wanting her always. But she had grown tired, wearied by the bearing of children and turning her back on him at night – afraid, he knew, of becoming again with child and her too old for the pain of it.

His days had become drab, his nights long hours of frustration when he tried to keep his passions still, respecting Emily's feelings. But his own feelings were of some importance and he had felt himself become like a eunuch, a dried-out old man with no sap left in him.

But then Nerys Beynon had come into his life and his blood quickened whenever he thought of how he had rescued her from Bulla Johns. She was on the point of being violated, thrust down on the table of the public bar at the Flint Mill. He had seen her fine legs, firm with the flesh of youth, had observed the whiteness of her thighs – all taken in at a glance before rage had made him tear at her attacker. It had been a pleasure and a satisfaction to take the trembling girl to his own home and install her at his fireside; from that moment, it seemed that Nerys Beynon was in his very pulse.

But he had done nothing wrong, he told himself quickly. He admired a fine turn of ankle and a slim young waist, but not a finger had he laid on Nerys. Yet Emily with her blasted feminine intuition had seen through him as through a pane of glass in a window.

His feet slipped a little in the mud and he paused, wiping the sweat from his brow as he contemplated the pain his wife must have been feeling. She was an old woman by most standards, her hair turning grey, her hands roughened and red from too much housework.

And of late, life had dealt her some cruel blows. But the strange vagueness which had been only occasional before the death of her son had become more pronounced; her eyes had become deeply shadowed, her hands trembling.

The latest and most devastating tragedy to strike at the root of Emily's life was the sickness of her daughter. The girl child she had longed for had been tainted, just like the lead workers Emily was so fearful of, and Siona felt in his heart that it was the knowledge of the baby's sickness which had been the final straw, pushing his wife over the edge of sanity.

He parted the crackling undergrowth, fear heavy within him, pausing as he caught sight of what looked like a bundle of rags lying amongst the weeds. He drew in a deep sighing breath, closing his eyes and hearing around him the familiar sounds of the river that he loved. Then he moved forward, eyes wide now, fearful of what he would find.

He saw it then . . . her hair, waving to and fro like fronds of dark grass, moved in ceaseless motion by the restless waters.

His breath caught in his throat and he remained

motionless for a long moment, postponing the pain of reality. Then, taking a deep breath, he went towards the edge of the river.

The baby was still bound to Emily's thin breast. The water had not damaged mother or child, for the river must have thrown them out immediately after they had drowned. Siona knelt on the bank, head bent, eyes burning.

'There, there, *cariad*, you will never be hurt again.' He wished he could cry, for tears would relieve the pain in his big chest, but he was a man and not given to weeping. He stared down at Emily; she looked like a china doll, the baby bound to her and turned face inwards as though seeking to suckle the meagre breast. He did not know how long he remained on the bank, but when he rose he felt like an old man, as though his life had drained away along with Emily's.

Siona took hold of himself then and lifted his wife and child in his arms. He would see that they were buried alongside Hector in the cemetery at *Dan y Graig* and then, somehow, he would make what he could of his life.

*   *   *

Howel stood in the classroom staring out into the greyness of the day. Around him his pupils stirred — there was the sound of pen scraping against paper, a cough, a scuffing of feet against the wooden floor — but Howel was so used to the classroom sounds that he had long ceased to be aware of them.

He prided himself that he was a good teacher and more, that he took a real interest in the children he taught. He saw a poet's soul in one boy, the oratory of a preacher in another and in spite of the poverty in which some of them lived, his aim had always been to give them as good a start as was possible. But soon he would be leaving St Thomas's School behind him and he chewed his lip thoughtfully, a little worried that he had not chosen his latest shares wisely. But then he had had much on his mind.

The rain was beating against the windows, running downwards like tears and reminding Howel of the ceremony at his mother's graveside. Emily Llewelyn had been laid to rest almost a month ago, and her going had left a great gap in the life of the Llewelyn family.

Siona was working harder than usual, manning the ferry-boat almost all hours of the day and night. Big Eddie had moved out, marrying in haste and setting up house with the daughter of Bertie-No-Legs for, he said, they had been courting long enough.

Howel himself would be leaving home at the first opportunity, for he found that without the presence of his mother there was little to draw him back to the Ferry House. In any case, he was determined to buy himself a big property on the western slopes of the hillside outside Sweyn's Eye; to live in an area more fitting to his rising fortunes.

The school bell rang loud and harsh, intruding into his thoughts. The children immediately began to bang desk-lids and pick up books, eager to be free from the classroom.

'Anyone wanting sacks to put around their shoulders go to the cupboard *quietly now*, and don't forget to return them tomorrow.'

He sat on one of the desks and watched the children push and press against the school gates. Many of them were barefoot, sending up small splashes of water which muddied young ankles, but they were unaware of their poverty – accepting, as children did, what the adult world dealt out to them. How many, he wondered, would ever shake off the shackles of their birthright?

Impatiently, he rose to his feet. It was time he was going home; he was becoming sentimental, like a maudlin old man in his cups.

In the yard, he waved his hand in farewell to his colleagues. The headmaster responded by raising his stick slightly and Howel knew that the man disapproved of him heartily.

Howel Llewelyn was an upstart, born of poor parents and coming into his school to teach subversion to the children and make them discontent with their 'rightful place' in life. But all Howel had tried to do was to show the children that there might be better things around the corner, to give them some hope.

He moved outside and paused before his gleaming car, watching in amusement as the headmaster passed by with head bent, determined not to acknowledge this evidence of wealth so blatantly displayed. Howel started the Austin and deftly drove away from the school gates and downhill towards Foxhole. Tonight, he decided, he would tell Siona that he was going to leave home as soon as he could find a suitable house. It was not a task he relished, for he was aware that his contribution to the housekeeping funds was considerable and in fact helped to pay Mona, the young girl who had been employed to help Nerys Beynon with the chores.

Anger burned within him at this thought. His own mother had been expected to handle the work alone as well as bring up her children, but Nerys – a younger, stronger woman – must be given help! There was no justice in life. And yet he had to admit that Nerys had been looking pale and tired and it was obvious she could not cope single-handed.

He drew the car to a halt on the gravel roadway beside the house and pulled on the brake. Then he heard the sound of voices and his two younger brothers raced up behind him breathless, cheeks red, hair tangled and sticking up on end.

'*Duw*, you look like two chimney-sweeps there, boyos,' he said softly, thinking that these two – grave-faced Tom and the boisterous Will – he would

187

miss when he left home. He had considered taking them with him, or even offering to pay for their education, but he doubted that his father would even give the matter a passing thought. A proud man was Siona, even if sometimes his pride was more than a little misplaced.

'We nearly raced you home,' Tom said, puffing a little. 'Us running and you in your posh car and all!'

'Get away with you – could have had a lift from school if you weren't so damned pig-headed, the two of you.'

Tom looked offended. 'Be teased something awful by the boys if we came home in a car, man,' he said reasonably.

'Aye, I suppose you're right. It's the call of the wild: kill anything that's different.'

'Oh, you and your big ideas, Howel. I don't know what you're talking about half the time.' Tom pulled at Will's arm. 'Come on, let's do a bit of fishing then before tea, is it?' The two boys disappeared and with a smile, Howel climbed from the car and made his way inside the house.

Nerys glanced up from the grate where she was busy stirring a large pot that hung over the flames. He grimaced.

'Don't you know how to cook anything else besides confounded *cawl*?' he asked irritably.

'Soup is good for you, mind,' Nerys said in a voice which informed him clearly that she had no intention of entering into a debate on the issue.

He sighed and, sinking into a chair, took a newspaper from his pocket. He noticed that Nerys was still looking tired, that her eyes were shadowed and she was very thin. But then no one had asked her to work at the Ferry House; she could leave at any moment that she chose.

As she leaned over him, reaching for the cloth from the sideboard drawer, he inhaled the soft clean soap scent of her. He looked up at the same moment when she looked down, and their eyes met and held.

A piece of her dark hair escaped from its pin and fell soft against the whiteness of her neck. She appeared suddenly very young and vulnerable, and in that moment he felt both pity for her and an unmistakable desire to take her in his arms.

'Have you ever had a lover, Nerys?' he asked almost in a whisper and her eyes became large. He read in her expression that she was frightened, though she had not moved physically away from him. 'Not still virginal, surely?' He smiled as a blush rose from her shoulders to her hairline.

He was so near to her breasts that he could have moved forward and touched the crispness of her blouse with his lips. She must have seen his glance, for she jerked backwards as though stung.

Her apparent indifference to him irritated him and he leaned back in his chair, determined to provoke her. 'Being untouched at your age is surely evidence of a flaw in you?' He spoke mildly, reasonably. 'Left on the shelf as you are, I expect you'd be grateful for any man's attention.'

'Not yours!' she said flatly and he smiled, knowing he had touched her on the raw. 'I would rather die an old maid than have anything at all to do with *you*!'

'You very probably will die an old maid,' he said agreeably, 'for I can't see any full-blooded young man wanting a woman past her youth.'

She stood staring at him for a long moment and then, to his surprise, she smiled. 'You are very unhappy and uncertain of yourself, aren't you?' It was she who spoke tauntingly now. 'Only the inadequate person finds satisfaction in striking out at others.'

He rose to his feet and threw down the newspaper and her smile told him that she knew she had triumphed. Anger began to burn within him – he would have Nerys Beynon eating out of his hand before he left the Ferry House and then she would see where her homespun philosophies got her.

He sat down at the table just as his father came in through the door. Nerys smiled warmly and pulled out a chair for Siona – treating him as though he was some wealthy Eastern potentate, thought Howel angrily.

'Thank you, girl,' Siona rested his hand on Nerys's shoulder for a moment and instead of drawing away, she leaned a little towards him, a flower warming to the sun. She was ready for the plucking all right, Howel mused – and by God! he was the one who would do it!

Later, he left the house dressed in his good suit and crisp clean laundered shirt which crackled with starch and gleamed from the attentions of the blue-bag. He had been invited to supper at the house of Sterling Richardson, a rare crossing of the barriers between working man and the bosses.

But then Sterling was no ordinary owner. He was well-known for his liberal views, for hadn't he married Mali, a girl from the lower orders?

And yet for all that, Howel felt a sense of satisfaction as he guided the car through the streets of Sweyn's Eye, negotiating the busy roads of the town, heading out towards the fine villas high up on the hill. There they sat, graceful and elegant, buildings with many windows which gleamed like eyes staring out to sea. Soon, he promised, he would own one of the properties himself.

Lights shone from the large carved open doorway on to the drive as Howel drew the Austin to a halt. He pulled on the brake and alighted easily, wondering a little at the tinge of apprehension which tightened his throat. He held his head high; he might be the son of a working man, but he had made his own way in life and owed not one penny piece in debts – which was more than could be said for Sterling Richardson, who until Howel had stepped in seemed to live his life on a constant precipice.

A dimpled maid in dark frock and gleaming apron smiled up at him and Howel returned her smile, immediately feeling more assured. He was not unaware that he possessed an attraction for the opposite sex, but he had never considered himself a handsome man; his jaw was too square, his hair too thick to comply with the smooth appearance of the dapper men who looked out from the newspaper advertisements.

'Ah, Howel, come inside, my wife is anxious to see you again.' Sterling held out his hand in a genuine gesture of warmth and Howel felt liking for the man begin to grow. But he cautioned himself not to become too involved; Sterling was only a stepping stone and soon, hopefully, he and his troubled copper works would be left behind.

Mali Richardson was kin and she too had the dark hair of the Llewelyn's. Howel smiled at her, taking her small hand in his, surprised when she reached up and kissed him.

'There's sorry I was to hear of all your troubles.' She spoke softly, still with the hint of the Welsh intonation in her voice. 'I would have come to the funeral but I was nursing my little girl through the scarlet fever and thought it best to stay indoors until the danger of spreading the sickness was over.'

Howel had intended to murmur some polite platitudes but Mali's open generous smile and the eyes so green as though they had been washed by the sea disarmed him.

'I hope all is well with your daughter and that she's made a full recovery by now.' He said and meant it.

Sterling ushered him into the drawing room. 'Howel, I'd like you to meet my cousin Jennifer, she's come from Cornwall to live with us and is hoping to make friends in Sweyn's Eye.'

Howel took the girl's hand, she was young and attractive, her smile spirited and he liked her on sight. He wondered if there was an ulterior motive in the introduction but his fears were dispelled by Sterling's next words.

'Jenny's only been here a month and already she has half the young men in the town running after her.'

'Nonsense!' Jenny said swiftly, 'I'm simply a novelty, no one takes me seriously.' She spoke with a firm, well-modulated voice and Howel liked her frankness.

'I'm sure you're wrong,' Sterling persisted, 'I think you underestimate yourself.'

Howel sat beside Jenny at supper and covertly he glanced round the long dining room. The furniture was huge and highly polished, the china wafer thin and beautifully decorated.

The silver held the Richardson initials on the handles and Howel, in spite of himself, felt overawed by the grandeur.

'You're very quiet Mr Llewelyn.' Jenny took a forkful of meat and neatly popped it into her mouth and he admired her poise.

'Make the most of it,' he said, raising an eyebrow. 'I'm a teacher by profession and so usually I'm talking too much!'

Her arms and throat gleamed pink in the candlelight; her hair shimmered, smelling clean and rose-scented. She was a lovely, intelligent woman and certainly seemed to be more than a little interested in him. He became aware that Sterling was talking about him.

'Howel is far too modest – not only is he a damn fine teacher but he's a virtual wizard on the stock market. You should see the portfolio he set up for me – and with all the companies coming up trumps. It must be a gift, for I don't know how he does it.'

Jenny's eyes widened. 'Goodness, you must be

clever. I've never understood all the coming and going myself. What does it all mean?'

'It's not as complicated as it seems,' Howel explained. 'There are brokers who act on behalf of their clients and jobbers who are simply traders. You could always go up to London and sit in the visitors' gallery of the Stock Exchange if you wanted to.'

Jenny smiled at him, fluttering her eyelashes a little, and Howel realized with a stab of surprise that she was flirting with him. 'Perhaps you could take me one day and give me some guidance. I'd love to speculate some of my small capital.'

Howel inclined his head in assent, registering the fact that Jenny did not have a great fortune. Finding her frankness refreshing and her obvious admiration flattering, he smiled at her warmly and she responded by leaning closer to him.

Coffee was served in fine bone china cups and Jenny sipped hers with a gentle arching of the neck. She was a graceful, lovely girl at least five years younger than he was, and he could not imagine her being burdened with bringing up children or worn out with back-breaking work. She was privileged, cushioned by circumstances, and would retain her looks into a graceful old age.

She became aware of his scrutiny and smiled up at him through slanting blue eyes heavily fringed with long golden lashes. She was a coquette, well used to leading men astray, and the thought made his pulses race.

He had been too long without a woman, he told himself sternly. Indeed, there had never been any-thing but the lightest of entanglements in his life. He was far too wary to be tied down at an early age, as happened so often with men from poorer homes. It was as though they rushed from one fireside to another, taking on the burden of wife and children before they were ready to fend for themselves.

His own brother was a case in point, he thought. Alex was nothing but a green boy, planning to marry silly, pregnant Sarah in an effort to make up for the misdeeds of his twin. Yet, strangely, Howel found himself admiring Alex.

And now, enjoying Jenny's attentions, Howel felt he had been celibate for long enough.

Perhaps it had been the earlier closeness to Nerys Beynon which had stirred him, the soft soap scent of her, the way her dark hair fell against the alabaster of her neck. But whatever the reason he was restless, wanting a woman in his arms, and he leaned towards Jenny feeling that she would match his advances with some of her own.

Her eyes were knowing, which in a woman of his own class would have put her in the category of a harlot, but the gentry had a different set of values – or so he had been told – and perhaps he was about to find out the truth for himself.

'You are a very attractive man.' Jenny leaned away so that she was hidden from every eye but his own and mouthed the words at him. 'How about a walk in the garden?'

'Would you like to take the air, Jenny?' he asked rather abruptly and cursed himself for a tactless fool. But she saved the situation by rising at once to her feet and fanning her face with her hands.

'I would like nothing better, it is so hot in here. I think Wales must have a more moderate climate than Cornwall.'

'I take leave to doubt that,' Sterling said, but his look of amusement revealed his shrewd summing-up of the situation.

'Put on something warm, mind,' Mali advised. 'There's brave you are, Jenny,' she added, smiling, her green eyes full of merriment, 'to go out alone with a boy from the Llewelyn family! I mean, real tom-cats they are, mind, the lot of them.'

'My kinswoman exaggerates,' Howel said, consciously copying the rather genteel speech of the Richardsons.

Outside the sky was star-studded, a silver moon cast a cold light over the hills and through the trees, and a sly wind was whipping up from the sea.

'Alone at last,' Howel said mockingly. 'Now what?' He stopped walking and put his arm around Jenny's waist. She placed her slim arms around his neck, the thick fur cape slipping from her shoulders as she pinched his cheeks with her fingers.

'If you don't know, then I'm not going to tell you!' She tilted back her head and her white throat was an invitation. He kissed the pulse in her neck and she pressed herself closer, her hips against his. She was wanton in her desires, but some instinct told Howel that she was a tease. He released her abruptly and caught her wrist in a tight grasp.

'I think I should warn you not to play with me,' he said softly. 'I'm no gentleman, remember, and Mali was not joking when she called the Llewelyn men tom-cats!'

'Oh dear, what have I got on my hands then?' she asked mockingly. He drew her close and kissed her gently, his tongue probing, his hands moving subtly to her breast. He heard her draw a ragged breath as he pressed her against the rough bark of a tree and then he had her gown from her shoulders and he was kissing, teasing the soft proudness of her.

'Don't!' She spoke faintly and, enjoying himself immensely, he continued to rouse her until she was panting in his arms. Even then, he knew that she would protest if he attempted to cross the last hurdle. When he stepped away from her, she appeared drugged with emotion, her eyes misty and her breathing uneven.

'I think it would take more than you to satisfy a man like me,' he said gently as though with regret, surprised to know he meant it. Immediately she came into his arms again, but he held her away. 'No, poor little Jenny, I need a full-blown woman, you see – one who would fly with me to the moon if I were to ask it.'

She stared at him perplexed and then he began to laugh. The sound rose through his throat and fell musically on the quiet air and Jenny, standing back, aimed a blow at his face. He caught her wrist easily and, still laughing, drew her towards the lighted doorway of the house.

Inside, Mali looked up at them both, her eyebrows raised. 'It sounds as though you two have been having fun,' she said dryly, not unaware of Jenny's tangled hair and flushed face.

'Oh, yes indeed,' Howel said easily. 'I find Jenny most amusing. I hope I may call again and enjoy her company further.'

He turned away from the anger in her eyes, knowing that he had roused her interest as well as her passions. She was a spoiled madam, one to whom men bowed and scraped, but she might as well learn right from the start that Howel would be subject to no one.

As he took his leave, he kissed first Mali's hand and then Jenny's, and winked slowly as Jenny snatched her fingers away. Then he climbed into his car and drove along the tree-lined drive without looking back.

It was a soft night, a silent mystical kind of night with the moon racing through the clouds. Yet even as he remembered Jenny's body against his, the feel of her breast beneath his hand, it was Nerys Beynon he wanted to hold and touch, for she had a natural reserve that presented a challenge . . . and Howel had always loved a challenge.

It was the next day that the blow fell, when shares in which Howel had invested heavily plummeted and he found that he was practically penniless. He searched the papers, studied his books and knew that for once in his life, he had made a mistake. That was a sharp lesson and one he would not forget in a hurry.

He had skimped his research, paid too little attention to his work – and now he was suffering for the lapse.

He went to see Sterling in his office and stood before the big desk feeling uncomfortable and weary.

'I've taken a beating, I'm afraid,' he said. 'Those McDonalds shares – I've made a mistake and I've no one to blame but myself.'

Sterling frowned. 'I'm sure you'll make good your losses, Howel,' he said encouragingly. 'Even you are allowed to be wrong from time to time, you know, it's not a crime.'

Howel smiled ruefully. 'No, but I've left myself flat broke – took a chance for once instead of hedging my bets. I suppose I could sell my car, start small again.'

Sterling rose to his feet. 'No need for that, you've helped me out of a mess in the past and now it's my turn to help you. Pick out some shares – the very best ones you can find – and I'll put up the business as collateral.'

Standing in the plush office, hearing the sounds of the copper works that had been in the Richardson family for generations, Howel suddenly felt humble. Here was the man he had thought of as a stepping stone offering to risk all he had.

'I won't let you down,' Howel said gruffly and Sterling reached over to shake his hand.

'I know you won't,' he said softly.

CHAPTER FIFTEEN

The silver flashed and dazzled, glowing in the saucer-shaped melting dish as though imbued with a life of its own. At one side of the furnace, Kenny was sweating, his thin arms straining as he rabbled the coals vigorously.

Ceri rubbed his sweat cloth over his face with little effect. The melting point of silver was much higher than that of lead, with the result that the furnaces burned more fiercely. He sighed heavily, feeling bone-weary. There was no doubt about it – the combination of hard graft along with the late nights he was keeping was sapping his energy.

He took up his ladle – wielding the implement with its six-foot-long handle more expertly now that he had become practised – and dipped it into the shimmering metal, making a sea of effervescence before discharging the silver into a waiting pot.

Deliberately, he spilled some of the dregs on to the floor where the coldness solidified the silver into small shards. These he dropped into his pocket, knowing that should he be discovered he would face instant dismissal. But the love of working the silver had grown in him. He had fashioned brooches intricately twisted into patterns, working over a fire in the shed at the back of the house, raising the heat with a pair of old bellows.

The craft was a hard and difficult one but the resulting ornaments – long globular earrings and silver rings lovingly polished and shaped, bearing the wearer's name – were a joy to him. If only he had the money, he would go to Mr Sterling Richardson and ask to buy some of the silver openly and set up as a silversmith, but his wages went mainly to saving for his wedding to Katie Murphy. Yet through his happiness ran a thread of pain, for mam would not be there to see him married to his lovely girl.

The thought of his bride-to-be brought a smile back to his lips. She was like a summer sky, light and fair one minute and glowering with shadowed clouds the next, and he loved her to distraction. It would not be long now before they would be able to afford to rent a house, and then there would be no bar to their marriage.

'Hey, there's silent you are today, boyo,' Kenny said breathlessly. 'Is everything all right – not quarrelled with that lovely girl of yours, have you?'

Ceri bent calmly and slipped more shards of silver into his pocket. '*Duw*, nothing like that, man – I'm not soft in the head, mind! No, quarrelling with Katie would be like cutting off my right hand.'

Kenny knocked bits of encrusted cinders from his rabble before standing it against the wall. 'Another thing, you don't want to let Gareth Owen catch you putting your hand into your pocket so often, mind – he might just get suspicious!'

Ceri raised his eyebrows. 'Suspicious, of me, never!' He smiled innocently and Kenny lifted his fingers in a lewd gesture.

'Only giving you a word of warning, boyo. Seen men kicked on the arse and out of the door for much less than you've done by here.' He smiled wickedly. 'Nice little ring for my missus would be just the ticket for her birthday, don't you think so?'

Ceri nodded thoughtfully. 'Aye, that might just do the trick, but an accomplice that makes you, mind.'

'Do it indeed? *Duw*, there's a long word for eight o'clock in the morning then! But an accomplice I'll be if it will keep the wife sweet.'

Ceri smiled knowingly. 'Not found out about that little Irish barmaid at the Dublin, has she?'

Kenny looked offended. 'I don't know what you mean, boyo – soul of discretion, me, and a loving husband and father, mind.'

'But not above taking a piece of sugar plum when you can,' Ceri laughed. 'I don't blame you, man; life's hard enough, God knows, and you must grasp your joys with both hands. In any case, you'll be too old for that sort of thing in another year or two, won't you?'

Kenny aimed a piece of cinder and Ceri easily dodged out of the way. Kenny shrugged, took up his enamel tea-can and drank from it thirstily.

'*Duw*, this lot in by here is for fools, not men; wish I could get out of the lead works, mind.'

'Aye, well, it's not for me for much longer,' Ceri said decisively. 'I want to have better than this, and I'll get it anyway I can even if it means robbing Mr Richardson of some of his profit.'

'Hush!' Kenny shook his head warningly. 'I can hear a voice and a posh one at that.'

Ceri looked towards the door just as Sterling Richardson came into sight. Beside him hurried Gareth Owen, anxious as always to please.

'Oh, Ceri, boy, the boss wants a word with you.' Gareth all but bobbed a curtsey before retreating to a discreet distance.

Sterling Richardson was not smiling, but there seemed to be a glint of humour in his eyes as he held out his hand, palm upwards, to reveal a gleaming ornament.

'Yours, I presume?' he said and Ceri stared at him defiantly, even in his discomfort knowing that the boss was a fair man, a brave man who had fought well in the war and even now was little older than Ceri himself.

'There's little point in denying it,' he said evenly. 'Yes, I made the brooch. Stole a little bit of your profit into the bargain, I expect, but I love to feel the silver coming into shape under my hands.' He didn't know why he was revealing himself to the boss, who would doubtless give him the order of the boot whatever he said, yet there was something essentially likeable about Sterling Richardson and Ceri did not want to appear a mere sneak-thief in his eyes.

'Well, I'd like you to come to my office when your shift's finished,' Sterling said, no hint of his intentions in either his voice or his expression.

He moved away from Ceri then and had a word with the rest of the men, speaking pleasantly and asking pertinent questions, even stopping to ask young Reggie about his mam before leaving the foundry.

'*Jesu*! You're for it now, boyo!' Kenny said in awe. 'And you having the barefaced cheek to stand there with a pocket full of the boss's silver and tell him you enjoy working it!' He wiped his face with his sweat rag. 'I don't know where you get your courage, but I wish I had some of it.'

Ceri laughed. 'Oh, well, I didn't want to stay here much longer anyway, did I?' He picked up his ladle and examined it thoughtfully. 'I suppose it's easy to have courage when there's nothing to lose.'

They set to work once more in silence and Ceri practised in his mind the words he would use to tell Katie that he no longer had a job. She would be worried, of course – women were always bothered by a man being out of work – but he would soon find himself something else, something better, he was determined on it. But for now he was still working with the silver and he'd better keep his mind on the job, for the molten metal could burn and scar despite its beauty.

'Right then, Kenny,' he said loudly. 'Let's get this silver moving, shall we?'

Later, as he stood in the long, carpeted corridor outside the boss's room, his pocket was still full of the shards of silver he had picked up that morning. If he was going out, he might as well take something with him, he reasoned.

The door opened and Sterling Richardson was beckoning him inside the pleasant, airy office.

'Sit down, Ceri – and you can stop looking so worried, for I'm not going to dismiss you.'

Ceri felt his eyebrows rise. 'No?' The word came out short and hard. 'Why not? You can't keep me on here now, can you?' The boss had always been fair and in many cases kind, but Ceri's instinct to distrust the rich was inbuilt; they were almost always self-seeking and arrogant, taking from the land without giving anything back.

Sterling held the brooch in his hand, twisting it so that the light shone from it. He did not answer at once, but examined the ornament consideringly.

'It is true that I want you to leave the White Rock,' he said, 'but only so that you can set up a workshop of your own. You have a rare talent, Ceri, and I want you to use it for our mutual benefit.'

Ceri moved to the edge of his chair, fascinated in spite of himself by what the boss was saying. 'What could you possibly get out of it?' he asked, frowning.

'I shall fund your workshop and supply you with small quantities of silver. In return you can let me organize the selling of the jewellery, perhaps in London where higher prices can be charged.'

'Sounds fine to me,' Ceri smiled. 'Make the shop one with living premises and I'll work day and night to make the business pay!'

'It's a bargain.' Sterling rose to his feet and leaned forward and Ceri was somewhat embarrassed to find himself shaking hands with his boss.

He moved towards the door, but Sterling halted him with a word. 'Wait.' He came from behind the desk and held out his hand. 'As you're not yet officially in business, I think it advisable that you return the silver you have accumulated this morning.'

He smiled as Ceri sheepishly complied. 'You see, I might just as well spend a little money setting you up and hope for some return, as to let you work illicitly at my expense!' He laughed. 'Go on, give in your week's notice to Gareth Owen and I'll make sure there are suitable premises ready for you to move into as soon as possible.'

Ceri could scarcely believe the way his life had changed in a few short minutes. What power a man like Sterling Richardson held in his hands! Money certainly talked, all right, and Ceri was determined to make it shout out loudly for him.

Kenny was waiting anxiously for his return, leaning on the long handle of his ladle, expecting the worst. 'Did the boss give you a dressing-down, then, boyo?' he asked.

'Aye, I've got the order of the boot all right,' Ceri said slowly, but he was unable to keep the smile from his face. 'I'm going to have my own shop, Kenny. Mr Richardson likes my work enough to set me up to work the silver all legitimate-like, so I'll be my own boss.'

'You lucky sod!' Kenny said, but he was smiling. 'Well, don't forget your first order is a ring for my wife, mind!'

'I won't forget, don't you worry. I've some silver in the house and I'll see to it that you have a gift for your wife – indeed, I'll give it priority.'

He spoke to Gareth Owen, giving in his notice with such a carefree manner that the foreman was not quite sure what to make of the situation.

'What's up with you, boyo?' he asked at last. 'Lost a farthing and found a shilling, have you?'

'You could say that,' Ceri smiled. 'I've landed on my feet; going into business on my own, I am, and can't wait for my week's notice to be worked.'

Gareth looked morosely at him for a long moment in

silence. 'I suppose that brother of yours has got something to do with all this, Howel being the boss's blue-eyed boy and making him all that money on the stock market and all. Nice to have powerful friends, isn't it, boyo?'

Ceri forced down his feelings of anger and frustration. Why did Gareth have to take the edge off his joy, demeaning Ceri's talent and putting down his good fortune to Howel's influence?

'It's nothing at all to do with my brother.' Ceri spoke with a deceptive calm. 'Doesn't it cross even your mind that it could be more to do with my ability to make something lovely out of the silver?'

'Oh, I didn't mean anything, boyo,' Gareth said quickly. 'I'm sure Mr Richardson is too much of a business man to be doing any favours – sorry I spoke.'

Ceri turned away. His elation had vanished and he found himself wondering if Howel's position in the firm had indeed influenced the boss's decision to set him up in business. It was not a palatable conclusion, and Ceri pushed it to the back of his mind; yet for the rest of the shift, he felt the irritation burn within him whenever he remembered Gareth's words.

However, being with Katie would ease away his pain and frustrations. Even now he couldn't really believe that she meant to marry him. He had lain with her, held her beauty close in his arms and tasted of her sweetness, yet still he knew in his heart that he did not possess the inner core of her being.

As he left the works behind him and stared up into the unusual clarity of the sky of early spring, with stars shining down as though in a blessing, his spirits sank low, for he must go home to the house on the river bank and feel the loneliness of the place without mam's vibrant presence.

It was true that Nerys did her best; certainly she

worked hard enough, baking and cleaning from morning till night, but she was not a replacement for Emily
and never could be.

An owl hooted in the distance and the wash of the
river intruded on Ceri's thoughts. When he saw the
ferry-boat bumping gently against the steps and the
big bulky figure of his father seated in the stern, he felt
a momentary pity for Siona Llewelyn, a man alone.

'*Nos da*, dad. It's me, Ceri; got away from work first I
did. There'll be a boat-load behind me in a minute or
two.' He rested his hand on Siona's broad shoulder
and then settled himself on the damp wooden seat.

'I'm finishing up at the White Rock next week, dad –
starting up on my own I am, mind, as silversmith.' He
still wanted his father's approbation, even as he had
when he was a boy. There was silence and he plunged
on as though towards a precipice. 'Mr Richardson
likes my work, see, and is going to set me up in a shop
of my own. I'll be made, dad, and out of the works just
like our mam wanted.' He held his breath waiting for a
word, a crumb of praise, but Siona's next words
plunged him into despair.

'Oh, there's good then, boyo. Our Howel arranged
that, did he?' Siona took the scull in his hands,
turning without waiting for a reply to greet the strag-
gling line of lead workers.

'Now watch yourself, Dicko Miles. Don't go dropping your bottle of whisky over the side of the boat
again, righto, for I'm not fishing for it at low tide!'

Ceri sighed deeply. Why did he do it, why ask for
hurt and frustration? He must accept that in Siona's
eyes he counted for nothing. Then anger began to burn
deep inside him; he *would* be a success, even if it
killed him.

He slumped against the side of the boat, smelling
the scents of the river, hearing the soft plop of fish
among the weeds, feeling the slap of the water against
the sides of the boat . . . turning his mind to anything

but his father's reaction, for the taste of disappointment was bitter in his mouth.

*   *   *

Katie smoothed down the skirt of her pale blue frock, tied the sash of deeper blue around her waist and stared at her reflection in the mirror. Her hair was unfashionably long, curling in an almost childlike way around her face. The colour had faded a little from the bright red-gold of her youth, but still retained a warmth and was what her mother chose to call an 'amber sheen'.

She moved restlessly towards the window of her bedroom and stared out into the darkness. The town had faded into a mistiness of indigo shapes against an inky skyline. Katie sighed. Soon, any moment now, Ceri would be coming to see her. Then why did her heart not lift at the thought of him?

He was handsome, a sensuous man, and she could not deny that he filled all her needs in that direction. He was perceptive and sensitive too, but why did she find it necessary to keep making a catalogue of his virtues to herself? Was it to mitigate the knowledge that she didn't really love him?

Nevertheless she was to marry him, and she would make him a good and faithful wife. She made a wry face into the darkness of the window pane. Faithful. How easy it would be to keep that promise – hadn't she had enough of men to last her a lifetime? And within her was a longing that needed to be filled, a longing she recognized as the urge for motherhood.

She had conceived of a child with her husband Mark, only to have the storm and the sea rob her of the unborn infant. Now, as she grew older, she knew the pain of empty arms.

Ceri came from a large family and he would want children as much as she did, she was certain of it. She sighed; there was so little time left and soon she would be too old for motherhood. It was true that many women kept adding to their families as the years advanced, and even Ceri's own mother had given birth while in her forties. But the event had hastened Emily's unsoundness of mind, Katie thought with a shiver.

Impatiently, she moved towards the door, telling herself she was becoming morbid, introspective in a way that did little good. She hurried downstairs to join her mammy, who sat alone in the kitchen drinking her favourite tipple of gin.

'Sure 'tis quiet in here, where are the boys gone?' Katie drew a chair closer to the fire and sat down carefully, intent on keeping the creases from her frock.

'Gone out with your dad – still after the fish, they are, or so they say.' Mrs Murphy smiled widely. 'Though I'm sure your dad's got them boys drinking ale with him down at the Dublin. Sits the youngest one outside with a glass in his hand, so I've heard, but what harm does it do? And it keeps them out from under my feet!'

She glanced at Katie. 'Waiting for Ceri are you, then? Sure he works hard enough down at the White Rock, can't fault the man on that score.' Her eyes were shrewed. 'So why aren't you blooming with the light of love, Katie?'

'Mammy!' Katie said quickly, feeling the colour rise to her cheeks. 'I'm too old for all of that – I'm no young bride, remember.'

'Aye, I remember all right,' Mrs Murphy said softly, 'and I know you need a man to care for you and love you, but sure I'd like to see the shine back in those eyes of yours, I must confess.'

'I'm content, mammy, and that means a lot to me after all I've been through. Ceri's a good man, he loves me and we laugh together a lot – and he's quite a catch with those fine looks of his, wouldn't you say?'

'Sure he's a good catch, and so long as you know your own mind then it's not up to me to interfere. There! That must be him knocking on the door for you now – go on, what are you waiting for?'

Ceri's eyes were full of warmth and as Katie opened the door wide, he took her in his arms and swung her off her feet. She clung to him breathlessly, knowing that part of his charm was that he made her feel young and fresh once more.

'Great news, my lovely girl!' He set her down and raised his cap to Mrs Murphy, who was leaning forward in her chair, her eyes wide with curiosity. 'Oh, good evening – sorry to barge in like this!'

'Come on in, boyo, have a drop of the water of life with me and let us all share your good news.'

'Mammy,' Katie said reprovingly, 'you are a nosey one, sure enough. Don't you say anything, Ceri – you keep your good news for my ears alone.' She laughed and touched his cheek with soft fingers, then relented. 'Oh, all right, let me old mammy hear, then, if it's so important to her.'

Ceri stood with his arm around Katie's waist. 'I won't say no to a drop of gin, Mrs Murphy, seeing that this is something of a celebration, like.'

'Oh, Ceri, don't keep me in suspense!' Katie said, laughing, but she led him to a chair and waited while her mother rose slowly to her feet and fetched another glass from the dresser.

Mrs Murphy brought a generous measure of spirits to where Ceri sat; then she subsided into her chair, her eyes wide and expectant. She coughed a little over her own drink and then gestured impatiently for Ceri to begin.

'Well, I've been fired from the White Rock!' he said, and Katie stared up at him in disbelief, his cheerful smile denying the seriousness of what he was saying.

She knew he needed a job in order for them to be married, so why was he so happy? A tremor shook her

– was he regretting their betrothal already? Had he seen through her and somehow knew that she had not given him her love?

'*But*,' he paused for effect and looked down at Katie with such warmth in his eyes that she knew he cared for her as deeply as ever. 'But, Mr Sterling Richardson, copper boss, is going to set me up in business.'

Katie felt her heart lift. Ceri was really leaving the lead works and what was more, moving on to something better.

'Well, come on, what business is he setting you up in? Don't be such a beast, Ceri, but tell me!' Katie tugged on his arm and he bent forward to kiss her lips lightly.

'Somehow he found out that I was pinching silver from the foundry,' he said and Katie sighed. He meant to tell the story in his own way and would not be rushed.

'So you were caught stealing – why weren't you out, then, with a boot up your backside?' she demanded.

Mrs Murphy clucked in disapproval. 'Katie! Sure, aren't you talking like a fish-woman now? You watch your tongue, young lady.' Apparently she needed the consolation of drink, for she poured herself another liberal measure of gin and gulped at it thirstily, her eyes wide as she watched Ceri brace himself to continue.

'I'm going to work the silver, make brooches and rings and ornaments just as I've been doing for weeks, only now it will be legitimate.' He hugged Katie to him. 'I'll be a real silversmith with the proper equipment instead of working my . . .' he paused for thought ' . . . instead of wearing myself out handling the bellows, trying to build up the heat on an old fire.'

'It sounds too good to be true,' Katie said, leaning back in Ceri's arms. Looking up into his face, so young and so full of enthusiasm, she felt a million years older than him.

'There's a thing to say now!' Ceri pretended indignation. 'Me being made into a silk purse and you so scornful of the miracle – for shame on you, Katie Murphy.'

'Sure I'm not scornful,' she protested. 'I'm just sceptical of bosses suddenly being so good – what is he getting out of it, I wonder?'

'Well, he'll be managing the selling side of it – at first,' Ceri said slowly. 'But he's too big a man to concern himself for long over such a small industry. Curious he is, I expect; wants to see what sort of a bloomer I'll make of it all, I dare say.'

'No.' Katie shook her head. 'Mr Richardson is not like that at all. Fair play now, he probably likes the idea of being a patron of the arts – you know what these rich men are when it comes to ideals.'

'Ideals?' Ceri said dryly. 'My brother Howel is the one to talk about ideals. He pontificates like a preacher about the poor and needy, but he can't wait to leave them all behind and become one of the wealthy.'

Katie shook her head and tried unsuccessfully to conceal a smile. 'Look who's talking! Now, come on, Ceri – you want to be rich just as much as Howel does, otherwise why are you going into business at all?' She hugged his arm to her. 'Now forget your grumpiness with your brother. Howel can't be all bad, so take that look off your face – sure it's enough to turn the milk sour!'

Mrs Murphy clutched her gin bottle protectively and smiled with a rare flash of humour. 'Well, and who cares about the milk just so long as this beautiful drink don't go sour on me!'

Katie raised her eyebrows. 'Mammy, you're incorrigible. Sure 'tis a wonder your liver don't turn to alcohol inside you, the amount of gin you pour down your throat.'

'Does you good, sure enough,' Mrs Murphy said,

smiling, 'and if it don't, then 'tis too late for me to mend my ways now. Been drinking this stuff since you were a baby on my breast, so I have!'

Katie became aware that Ceri was trying to attract her attention, so she picked up her coat and bent to kiss her mother's cheek. 'Shan't be long, mammy, sure I'll be home early.'

'Aye and fiddles can fart!' Mrs Murphy said as she sank back into her chair, but she was smiling. Her daughter was going to settle at last, and with a boy who had a bit of go about him. 'Don't be late, now, for I'll be waiting up for you.'

Outside, Katie leaned against Ceri and laughed. 'What are we going to do with her? She'll never change – you know that, don't you?

'Well, who would want her to?' Ceri drew her away from the tall narrow houses of Market Street and along Copperman's Row towards the banks of the canal. He held her hand lightly, stopping beneath the arch of one of the bridges and drawing her close to him.

'I haven't told you the best bit of news yet.' He kissed her lips and Katie responded to him warmly, liking the scent and taste of him.

'What's that?' She stood on tiptoe, pressing herself close to his young strong body and feeling his arms close around her protectively.

'There'll be a shop for me to work in, but there'll be premises too – somewhere for us to live. You know what this means, don't you, Katie? We can be married as soon as we like!'

He took her face in his hands and looked down into her eyes, but in the darkness she knew he would not read the naked fear which she was sure she could not hide. She had wanted to marry Ceri – and still did, for she longed to hold a child in her arms and suckle her very own baby at her breast. Yet the thumping of her heart was loud in her ears as a small, protesting voice whispered, 'Not yet'.

CHAPTER SIXTEEN

Light March winds blew flurries of foam along the surface of the River Swan, driving foam-tipped waves along the banks, churning up mud, drawing unwary insects to a watery grave. It was a day for chaining the ferry-boat, for doing the washing, for picking the riot of daffodils in the garden . . . for March had come in like a lion.

Inside the Ferry House Nerys put out the lamps, for daylight was trickling through the windows. She stacked cleaned and dried dishes into the cupboard and then, with a sympathetic glance towards the young girl bent over the washtub, pushed the big black kettle on to the fire.

'Come on, Mona, have a bit of a rest. You've been working there since early this morning and now it's half-past eight; you deserve a cup of tea.'

The girl straightened her thin spine and rubbed her soapy hands against her already wet apron.

'*Duw*, I won't say no, missis – fair worn out, I am.' Mona was little more than a child, tall but with little flesh on her jutting bones. She was not pretty by any standards, but she had fine eyes and an open smile. Eldest of a large family, she needed to work to support the younger children, for her mother enjoyed being sickly and took every excuse to lie in her bed all day.

Nerys pushed the mens' trews into the tub and topped up the swiftly cooling water from the kettle. She saw Mona glance at her and smiled reassuringly.

'I'm not taking over your job, don't worry! I've

enough to do as it is, but I just thought I'd give you a bit of a hand.' This was an understatement, since the trousers of coarse tweed were the most difficult items of washing and both of them knew it.

'There's good you are, Nerys Beynon – and you not owing me nothing.' Mona sipped her tea, her eyes wide as they looked at Nerys over the brim. 'I wish you could be my sister – never had no sisters, only brothers.'

'Well, I've got no family at all,' Nerys said softly, 'so I don't see why we can't be like kin to each other.'

Mona smiled in response and her features were transformed from plainness into sudden beauty.

Nerys scrubbed furiously at the trousers, her eyes misted not by the heat rising from the tub but by her own tears. She was suddenly reminded that she was safe and secure here in the little house on the river bank; she owed Siona Llewelyn a great debt of gratitude and she would never forget it.

Mona put down her cup just as Nerys finished wringing out the last pair of trousers.

'I'll leave the younger boys' trews to you,' Nerys smiled. 'They're muddy, but not quite so hard to wash.' She dried her hands and moved towards the table. 'Like some more tea, Mona?'

The young girl shook her head. 'No, thanks. I'll be going back home for my dinner as soon as I've finished by here. You have a bit of a sit down yourself; you haven't stopped this morning neither, what with the polishing and bed-making, not to talk about the cleaning of the cutlery?'

Nerys nodded. 'Aye, well I'll just fill the kettle again and then I'll drink my tea.'

She sat down just as the door leading from the stairs was pushed open unceremoniously and Howel entered the kitchen. He glanced around him and then his eyes rested on Nerys, who suddenly felt guilty because she was not busy with some chore or other.

'Good life for some!' Howel commented, seating himself opposite her. 'I see you have assumed the role of mistress of the house while Mona does all the donkey work.'

Mona looked up with her big eyes, half afraid to speak and yet smarting with the injustice of Howel's attitude towards Nerys.

'She's been hard at work all morning, Mr Llewelyn,' she said in a small voice. 'Only just put her backside on a chair before you come in by here from your bed.'

Nerys longed to smile at the baffled look on Howel's face; it seemed he could never have the satisfaction of putting her down.

'I see you have a champion,' he said at last. 'All credit to you, Mona, for your loyalty – but we can all see who has the worst job of the week!'

Nerys smarted with indignation but she did not bother to reply. In any case, Mona had the bit between her teeth now and did not hesitate to speak on her behalf.

'Oh, you're wrong, sir. The missis here has only just finished washing out the mens' trews, and *that's* the hardest job of the week – if you'll pardon me saying so.'

Howel didn't speak again. He stripped off his shirt, went to the sink in the corner and began to wash. Mona made a wry face behind his back and Nerys could not help but laugh. There was no response from Howel, but Nerys knew from the tightening of his spine that he had heard and resented their amusement.

Howel ate the breakfast she cooked for him without comment and disappeared upstairs to dress. Nerys wondered why he wasn't at work in the school; she had heard some talk of him changing his job, but knew better than to ask him any questions.

The door opened, blowing a fresh breeze into the room, and Nerys looked up to see Siona enter the kitchen – his cheeks red, his thick hair falling untidily over his forehead to give him a spurious appearance of youthfulness. He smiled at her and she smiled back – her affection for the big man had grown over the recent months.

'I've planned an outing for us, *merchi*,' he said quickly. 'I've got our Eddie to take over the boat for the rest of the day, so that we can have a picnic together – perhaps go down to the beach or to Victoria Park. I've been working you too hard and I thought it was time you had a day off.' He rushed the words out as though he was nervous and Nerys warmed to him. Siona was so anxious to keep her at the Ferry House, so thankful for all that she did that he was for ever trying to repay her.

'There's a kind thought,' Nerys said. She was about to explain that she had much to do in the house and could not possibly spare the time to go out when Howel returned to the room dressed smartly in a good suit and neat tie. He was breathtakingly handsome, his hair thick like his father's but dark and falling in waves across his brow. But his eyes met hers and they seemed filled with amusement.

'Spoiling the paid help, aren't you, dad?' he said, and though the words were spoken lightly, Nerys felt the sting of scorn in them.

'None of your business, Howel boyo!' Siona's tone was equally light, but his big shoulders were hunched aggressively.

'I'd love to go out,' Nerys said quickly. 'I'll prepare us some sandwiches; will cold mutton do, Siona?' And the boys can have some cheese and fresh bread when they come home, so they won't starve.'

Mona moved forward shyly, her hands clasped in her damp apron. 'I'll stay on a bit and see to the boys if you like,' she offered and Siona laid a hand on her thin shoulder.

'There's a good girl, and I'll see there's something

215

extra in your pay come the weekend.' He moved past Howel without another word and his footsteps could be heard heavily on the stairs.

'You seem to have some fine ideas spinning round in your head,' Howel said slowly. 'But don't count on being the missis here, will you, for I'll do all I can to put a stop to that little game.'

'I'm not playing any little games!' Nerys said angrily. 'I'm just being friendly to your father – is there anything wrong in that?'

Howel moved closer and stared down into her eyes. 'You are either very naive or very innocent – I can't decide which – but here's a warning for you: my father imagines himself in love with you!'

'That's foolishness!' Nerys drew away from him. 'I think you're just being fanciful and unduly suspicious. Siona is my friend, nothing more, and even if there was anything else it's nothing at all to do with you.'

He left the house then and Nerys sank into a chair, staring at Mona with a feeling of uneasiness growing within her. Mona read her expression and shrugged.

'One thing Mr Llewelyn is right about: his father is in love with you. I'm surprised you haven't seen it for yourself.'

'Oh, no!' Nerys rubbed one hand over her eyes. 'Well, I'll just have to let Siona know that I don't think of him in that way.'

Mona wiped her hands on her apron. 'I may be interfering with what doesn't concern me, but I'd be careful if I was you. I mean . . . poor Siona Llewelyn has been badly treated by fate this past year and if you was to make him feel a fool he'd take it badly, I know he would.'

'For a young girl, you're very wise, Mona,' Nerys smiled. 'Well, I'd best start making those sandwiches I suppose, and while I'm doing it perhaps I can think of a way of putting Siona off without hurting his feelings too much.'

'Do you have to put him off at all?' Mona asked.'I know he's a lot older and all, but he's a handsome man and you'd really be missis of this place then, wouldn't you? And he'd be good to you, mind. Look how he's got you help in the house and see how he thinks of giving you little treats and that. Could do a lot worse, couldn't you?'

Nerys remained silent, sensing the thoughts which Mona was too kind to put into words: that at her age, Nerys was lucky to have any man interested in her. She rose to her feet, surprised to learn that she was seriously thinking of accepting Siona's overtures, should he make any.

She packed the sandwiches carefully in a muslin cloth and placed a bottle of elderberry wine alongside them in the basket. She scarcely noticed what she did, so intent she was in trying to sort out her muddled thoughts. One thing she would not do today and that was burn any boats!

When Siona came downstairs, he was wearing his best waistcoat over a clean white shirt. Around his neck was tied a bright scarf and his hair was carefully brushed.

'Someone looks very handsome,' Nerys said, staring at Siona as though she had never seen him before. His eyes were deep green in his weatherbeaten face and when he smiled at her his teeth were strong and even. He could be taken for a man in his thirties, not his forties, she decided.

With Siona she would have security, she would bear children, would know motherhood – the caring for her own instead of always other people's families. Mona was quite right, she could do far worse than marry Siona Llewelyn.

Yet even as she picked up the basket and moved to the door, smiling over her shoulder at Mona, she knew that she would never agree to marry him for she did not love Siona Llewelyn. And love was the most important thing in the world. It was something she dreamed about in the night, of having someone whom she cared about and who cared for her. It meant having a man of her own to cling to when the night miseries claimed her, a true husband in every sense of the word.

As they walked to the tram-stop they chatted easily, the way friends do. Nerys liked Siona very much indeed – she could even say there was love in her heart for him, but it was not the love which blots out the sun or sends the flowers shivering in the grass; rather was it the love of a sister, or a daughter come to that.

'What are you thinking, *cariad*?' Siona asked quietly and Nerys looked quickly around, fearful that someone should overhear him calling her 'love' in the Welsh tongue.

'It's such a treat to be out.' Nerys told herself to be at ease, she was doing no wrong.

And yet it was such a strange situation; she was standing alongside Siona as though she belonged to him, as if they were a courting couple – and that's how it must appear to anyone observing them.

It was not many months since Emily's death – would the outing seem disrespectful to her memory, Nerys wondered. But she could not voice her thoughts aloud; she had no wish to make Siona as miserable and embarrassed as she was herself.

It was a relief when the tram came rocking along the line towards them. She climbed aboard and took a seat and Siona settled himself easily beside her. Nerys forced a smile as he leaned towards her, whispering in her ear.

'There's shy and quiet you are when we're out of the house, Nerys – lost your tongue, have you?'

'No, not lost my tongue at all,' she protested laughing, 'but I've heard tell that men get quickly tired of a woman whose tongue is too loose.' Now why did she have to say that? It sounded exactly as though she was fishing for compliments!

'I'd never get tired of you, Nerys, or of that lovely voice of yours. You can talk till the cows come home and I'll listen.'

How had she failed to read the admiration in his eyes before this? Nerys could scarcely believe how stupid she had been. No doubt she had filled a gap left by Siona's wife, taken her place in the home and so was on hand when he needed someone to turn to. But it was more than infatuation on his part, she was sure of that. He would soon see sense when she explained to him that it could never work.

The park was full of children and as Nerys settled herself on the grass she looked around her, thankful at least that she and Siona would not be alone. No one could point a finger or say they were misbehaving, not when they were in full view of half the population of Sweyn's Eye!

She held out the bottle of wine towards Siona and brought out the glasses, settling them down between the tussocks of grass.

'What's this then, *cariad*? A little celebration, is it?' Siona poured and wine and smiled at her over the rim of his glass.

'No, not really,' Nerys said quickly. 'I just thought we both could do with a little treat. Have a sandwich; I've cut all the bits of fat off, I know you hate to see the fat ...' Her words trailed away – there she was, leading him on again and not meaning to.

'We must talk, Nerys,' he said, putting down his glass. She felt her heart begin to beat swiftly and wanted to hold up her hands to stop this flow of words, but she was too late.

'You must know how I feel about you,' Siona said, leaning towards her. 'I'm not a man for flowery speeches and I can't spout poetry or anything like that, but there's a feeling in by here,' he thumped his

219

broad chest, 'a deep feeling for you, *cariad*, and I can't keep it in any longer.'

Nerys looked down at her hands. 'Siona, it's not the time, it's too soon after . . .' She looked up at him helplessly and he hung his head.

'I know it's not long since my Emily went, but she'd gone from me before that, see. Half the time she wouldn't bother with me – turned her face away from me, she did, and who can blame her, she being sick and all?' He paused and took in a deep breath. 'Of course we need not be married yet. I know that these things must be arranged right, but in time, Nerys . . . please say there's some hope for me in the future.'

'I'm very fond of you, Siona – more than that, I have a love for you – but I can't think of you as a husband. You were Emily's husband and that's what keeps coming into my mind.'

'It's because I'm too old for you, isn't it?' Siona said heavily. 'I'm an old fool who had the nerve to think a young girl like you would ever even look at me.'

'No, it's not that, Siona. It's just that I don't love you the way a wife should love her husband.' Where had all her fine ideas about not burning her boats gone, she asked herself in bewilderment.

He took her hand. 'Love can grow, mind, it sometimes comes stronger after the wedding.' He put his fingers to her lips. 'Don't say any more now. We shall forget I asked and just enjoy ourselves on our day off, shall we?'

He dipped into the basket and helped himself to a sandwich, but in spite of his ease of manner Nerys knew that Siona would never put aside the hope that one day she would agree to be his wife.

But he was right; they must try to enjoy their outing, for it was a rare occasion – the earlier winds had died down, the sun was shining, the birds singing and the sound of children's laughter hung upon the air.

She leaned back against the rough bark of a tree and

closed her eyes. Suddenly, frighteningly, she saw the image of Howel as he had been when he took off his shirt to wash. She saw his young slender spine, his narrow hips and broad shoulders ... and she was ashamed, for in that moment she saw the truth that the reason she could not love Siona was that she was already in love with his son.

For the rest of the day she tried to be cheerful, to make conversation with Siona, to laugh at his jokes and to enjoy herself, but a cloud of guilt and anger hung over her mind and she cursed herself for a fool. She could not have chosen more unwisely in the matter of love, for Howel merely despised her. But then she had not chosen at all; love had just presented itself to her, unasked.

Dark clouds began to race over the hills and gratefully Nerys looked up into the sky.

'We'd better get home,' she said, rising and brushing tiny pieces of grass from her skirt. 'The washing is still on the line and I don't want it getting soaked again.'

'Always so practical, aren't you, *cariad*?' Siona touched her hair briefly. 'And at the same time, so lovely.'

Nerys laughed in genuine surprise. 'Lovely, *me*? There's soft you talk sometimes, Siona Llewelyn.'

He swung the basket from the ground and firmly, she took it from him. 'I'll carry that. I won't have folks saying I'm making a slave of you, mind!'

For a moment his face fell into lines of sadness. 'Independent, just like my Emily was in her prime'

Nerys felt sympathy wash over her and she slipped her arm through his and smiled up at him. 'You're a fine man, Siona, do you know that? And I meant what I said, I do feel love for you.'

She heard the crunch of feet on gravel and looking up, came face to face with Howel. 'You're making a fool of yourself, dad.' His voice was low but harsh. 'She's half your age!'

Siona stepped back as though he had been dealt a body blow. 'Watch your mouth, son – you're not too big to have a belting, mind,' he said, the words coming through his teeth.

Howel shook his head. 'I don't want to hurt you, dad; I know how you've suffered. But for God's sake, mam's only been in her grave a matter of months and you're carrying on like this in public.'

He stopped speaking and thrust his hands into his pockets. 'All right, it's really none of my business and in any case, I'll be moving out of the Ferry House as soon as I find a place of my own, but I urge you to think, dad – just take a good look at the two of you, that's all I ask.'

Siona growled low in his throat and made a move towards his son, but Nerys quickly stepped between them.

'No, Siona, I'll not have you fighting over me, especially not with your son.' Then she turned to Howel and there was real anger in her eyes as she faced him.

'You are right about one thing – this is none of your business and I'm not asking you for any approval. Now get out of my sight before I take my shoe to you and shame you in public.'

He moved away at once, striding along the road with shoulders squared. She had bested him and forced him into silence, but she was not triumphant – indeed, she longed to put her head on Siona's shoulder and cry.

She sighed heavily. 'Come on, Siona, let's not make more of a show of ourselves than we have already. Let's get off home.'

Too agitated to wait for the tram, she began to walk and Siona fell into step beside her.

'*Duw*, there's a fine woman you are, Nerys Beynon!' His admiration was apparent in his voice. 'Never realized there was a temper behind that quiet little face of yours, and you looking as beautiful as the Queen of Sheba; standing up for me real strong and bold – makes me proud it does!'

Nerys scarcely noticed the walk home for she was lost in a cloud of gloom, her mind oppressed by the memory of Howel's tight jaw and scornful eyes. She was a fool to give him even a moment of her time; he was a bigot, an arrogant and unfeeling man.

The storm clouds which had threatened now raced across the sky, bringing a hint of rain.

'Oh, dear, the washing!' Nerys moaned and then suddenly the comedy of the situation struck her. There she was, the centre of a row between father and son, worrying about the laundry.

Quickly she gathered in the washing and bundled it into the parlour. She would start ironing later, but first she needed to make a meal for the family.

In the kitchen, Mona was sitting at the table flanked by Tom and Will. They were eating heartily and the mouthwatering smell of bacon and fried cockles filled the room.

'I thought I'd get us something as the time was going on,' Mona explained. 'Did you have a nice day out?'

Nerys smiled gratefully. 'Aye, it was fine. There's good of you to see to the boys; I'm sorry if we're a bit late.'

'Don't be sorry. I've enjoyed myself by here, looking after things in a nice warm kitchen, though my mam will be a bit worried by now so I'd better get off home.' She paused at the door. 'I've kept back a bit of ham for you and Mr Llewelyn – oh and Big Eddie's come in off the boat too; I don't think that wife of his feeds him, a real starver he is. *Duw*, that man can't half eat, mind!'

*   *   *

With the two younger boys gone to their beds and Mona left for home, the evening stretched out long

223

and empty and Nerys, unable to settle, brought out the flat-irons. Siona rose immediately and picked up his cap.

'It's me off out if there's ironing to be done,' he said apologetically. 'Can't stand the palaver of it all, it fair gets me down.'

'That's all right, you go and have a drink with the men. I'm sure you deserve it after being with me all day. And Siona, don't think any more about what Howel said. I'm sure he didn't mean any of it.'

'That's as may be, but the boy must learn his place. He's still under my roof and while here he'll show proper respect to you and me both.'

It was good to be alone in the silent house. The scent of the hot linen and the smoothing to-and-fro movement of the iron had a calming effect on Nerys and she felt some of the tension ease from her shoulders.

She placed the iron back on the hob to re-heat and unpinned her hair. It was unfashionable to have it long – most young women were cutting their hair shorter these days – but Nerys usually wore her hair in a pleat. She sat in the chair and closed her eyes and listened to the clock. It was ticking away the minutes, the hours, the days and she was not getting any younger.

Suddenly she was startled to hear the door creak open and looking up, she saw Howel framed in the doorway.

'Is dad here?' He entered the kitchen and stood looking down at her, the usual arrogance gone from his manner. 'I came to apologise.'

She rose swiftly, needing to have something to do with her hands. Thrusting the kettle on to the fire, she was so aware of his nearness that the hairs on the back of her neck seemed to rise.

'He's gone out down the public, but I'm sure he bears you no ill will, Howel,' she paused, 'and neither do I.'

He faced her then, his eyes looking into hers. 'I was a loud-mouthed idiot,' he said softly. 'I must learn to mind my own business but seeing you with him, so happy, I think the truth of the matter is that I was jealous.'

Nerys stared at him, unable to believe what he was saying. 'Why should you be jealous?' The words were a whisper.

He shrugged. 'Isn't it obvious?' He moved to take her in his arms, but she turned her face away.

'I don't believe you, Howel. The leopard doesn't change its spots so easily.' She glanced at him over her shoulder, her back turned to him as though to protect her from his words.

'Why do you think I've been so aggressive?' he asked quietly. 'It's because I didn't want to face the truth about my feelings for you.'

She wanted to believe him and her eyes searched his face, seeking desperately for any signs of his true emotions, but he was standing in the shadows and the leaping flames of the fire gave him an almost demonic appearance.

'Well, I don't know what it is you're trying to say.' She spoke edgily. 'Is it that you want to take me to your bed, or that you would like to marry me yourself? Make yourself plain, Howel Llewelyn!'

He reached out slowly and she tensed as his hands touched her shoulders, turning her to face him.

'One thing at a time, Nerys. Learn patience, there's a good girl.' He was drawing her slowly towards him and she had no will to resist. As he held her close, she could smell the fresh scent of him.

It was a strange experience, for she had never been held in this way before and she was frightened.

She tried to draw away, but he only held her closer. 'Don't be afraid of me, Nerys, I'm not an ogre.' His mouth seemed to draw her towards him and she tipped back her head and felt his fingers in her hair – wanting to laugh and to cry, and to run and hide from the new emotions that were tormenting her.

From upstairs came the sound of running footsteps and Will's voice shouting out for her: 'Will you come quickly, Nerys? Our Tom is sick.'

Nerys fell away from Howel with her hands to her face and for a long moment simply stared at him.

'I'd like to believe you care,' she said softly. 'How I would like to believe it!' Then as she turned away and went towards the stairs, a riot of new emotions raced through her and would not let her be.

CHAPTER SEVENTEEN

The spring buds were thick and fat on the pussy willow tree, the early daffodils flaunting yellow trumpets at the unfriendly wind sweeping in from the river. It was a day of lightness and breezes, but with the softness of spring unmistakably in the air. And it was Alexander's wedding day.

He sat in the parlour of the Ferry House, staring down at his highly polished boots. He had worked hard on those boots, spitting and rubbing with a soft rag and then applying Cherry Blossom boot polish in little circular movements until the surface was like glass.

The wedding had been delayed, for Sarah had fallen sick and it was some weeks before she was well enough to go to the chapel and take her vows. He smiled, for all she had been concerned about was her increasing size – worried that her frock would not fit her.

Around his neck the stiff shirt-collar felt uncomfortable and tight; his Sunday suit, a good size too small for him, constricted his breathing. There was an emptiness inside him, a sudden feeling of gloom, for it was his twin who should be going to the altar with Sarah, not him. But he felt Hector's approbation, saw again the tortured eyes, sensed the message in them that he, Alex, was to care for Hector's unborn child.

The ghosts of his loved ones seemed all around him in the early morning light – mammy with her worn but smiling eyes, and clasped to her heart the baby girl who had had so little of life. He pushed himself to his feet, knowing that it was time to leave the quiet, brooding silence of the Ferry House and make his way down to the chapel, for he was becoming thoroughly miserable and it was not sensible to dwell on the past.

Howel stood before the fire-grate in the kitchen, waiting to go with Alexander and be his man at the ceremony. He had understood his younger brother's need for a few quiet moments alone and now he smiled and moved forward to clasp Alexander to him in a rare show of affection.

'Let the past go, boy,' he said softly. 'You are doing the right thing and never doubt it.'

Sitting in Howel's gleaming car, Alex looked around him in wonder. It was a funny old world, for in a few minutes his mood had changed from the depths of gloom to a rare pitch of excitement because he was to ride to the chapel in an automobile! He recognized that there was still a great deal of the child in him yet.

'Nervous?' Howel asked solicitously. 'I'd be a jibbering idiot in your place!' He laughed and Alex glanced at him, knowing it was only a joke; he could not imagine Howel ever being afraid of anything. How he envied him!

'Your little bride looked beautiful, mind,' Howel said. 'I know you haven't been allowed to set eyes on her yet but take my word for it – she'll knock you cold when you see her!'

Alex smiled, remembering the rush of preparation which had gripped the Ferry House over the last weeks. Nerys had been as good as gold, helping to make an outfit for Sarah, and even the little mouse-like Mona had done some sewing of the little silk undergarments the like of which Alex had never seen.

Shivering, he glanced at the squat little house which nestled above the river. He would never more live beneath its roof and whenever he returned, it would be as a visitor.

Howel seemed to pick up on his train of thoughts. 'The premises in West Cross done out to your satisfaction?'

'Oh, aye, but lots more work there yet, mind – the building got run down, see,' Alex replied. 'But it's a good place, a solid place, and from there I can operate the round more easily.'

Howel smiled. 'I'm proud of you, man,' he said and the words, though few and lacking in sentimentality, were enough to bring a lump to Alex's throat.

They drove the rest of the way in silence and when the dark stone façade of the chapel came into view, Alex felt himself grow tense. For a moment, he longed to beg Howel to turn the car around; he wanted to rush home to the bedroom he had always occupied, to bury his head under the blankets as he had done when a child and to hide away from the world.

The car drew into the kerb and came to a halt, Howel drew on the brake with a sound of finality and Alex found himself stepping down calmly into the road as though there was no raging turmoil inside him.

'This is it then, brother!' Howel smiled encouragingly. 'You look a bit on the pale side, but that's natural enough for a man about to give up his freedom.' His hand rested for a moment on Alex's shoulder. 'Come on then, get inside and we'll take our place at the front of the chapel. Dad will be here with Sarah any minute now.'

Alex was grateful to Siona for stepping into the breach and agreeing to give Sarah away, since her own family refused to have anything to do with the wedding. Now he moved into the sounds of the restless congregation, aware that all eyes were swivelling towards him. He knew his family were around him, Tom and Will under the care of Nerys's firm hand and Auntie Bettyl unfamiliar in her best hat and coat. He obediently followed Howel's lead and went to the front pew, clinging to the warm dark wood before seating himself and bending his head in an attitude of reverence.

He didn't know how he could bear the waiting for Sarah to walk down the aisle. She had gone to spend the night at Big Eddie's house, taken under the wing of Bertie-No-Legs' daughter, but she hadn't wanted to leave and had clung tightly to Alex for a long moment with tears glistening on her curling lashes; he had whispered softly in her ear, telling her to be brave for soon they would be married.

But now the moment had come, for the organ was sending strident chords of music into the waiting chapel. Howel nudged him to his feet and Alex allowed himself a glance over his shoulder, taking a deep breath at the sight of Sarah, so small beside Siona's great height. She came slowly towards him, her condition not yet obvious beneath the skilfully made frock, which was straight of line with a wide sash at the hips and a great bar of blue matching the big square collar. He moved out into the aisle and then she was beside him, looking radiant, her eyes meeting his and her hand trustingly held out towards him.

'I'm doing it for both of us, Hector.' He said the words under his breath and the clasp of Sarah's hand told him she understood.

Afterwards he didn't remember the words of the service, except that they were solemn and beautiful. He made his responses in a firm but quiet voice and his heart was beating swiftly as he waited to slip the ring on to Sarah's trembling finger. She looked up at him then and nodded almost imperceptibly.

He held her shoulders lightly and kissed her mouth chastely. Then he heard the music swell again and he was walking away from the altar knowing that for good or ill Sarah was his wife.

Sarah leaned towards him and smiled. 'Don't look so downcast, boyo. I'm not going to be a millstone around your neck! I'll help you get on, mind, and build up the business; I have a good head for figures, I'll have you know.'

He put his arm around her shoulders. 'I'm just dreading the "do" down at the Mackworth Hotel,' he whispered. 'Howel would insist that he pay for a proper wedding breakfast and how could I refuse?'

'Refuse, indeed! It's going to be the best spread I've ever seen or will see again, I suppose, and I'm going to make the most of it. Come on, husband, Howel is waiting for us in that posh car of his. Hold me tightly, mind, for I've never ridden in a car before.'

As she sat close to him, her thigh pressed against his, Alex felt his blood become hot. He wanted to hold her and to crush her and to superimpose himself upon her, blotting out his brother from her senses. And yet the thought brought with it a sudden sharp feeling of guilt.

The car jolted to a stop outside the hotel and Howel led the way inside, for which Alex was grateful. He felt overawed by the splendour of the place: the potted plants in tall jardiniéres, the thick plush carpet and the air of elegance that surrounded him. This was the way the rich lived all the time, he thought, and a great surge of determination filled him that he would have all this for Sarah and for Hector's son.

Howel stood back and allowed Sarah to enter the large room, where tables were set with snowy cloths and where silver gleamed beneath multi-faceted lights. She gasped and clasped her hands together and Alex felt her joy as though it was tangible.

Flowers garlanded the tables, and Sarah was dreamy-eyed as she simply stood looking around her, hardly daring to believe that all this was for her. Howel gestured to Alex to take his place at the centre table.

'The family will all be arriving soon if the charabanc I've hired turns up on time, so get you seated in your rightful place before the chaos starts!'

Even as Howel finished speaking, the doors opened

and Nerys came timidly into the room with the younger boys in her wake. She looked around her uncertainly and Howel went forward, taking her arm and guiding her to a seat. Alex saw her flush at the gesture and it seemed she was somehow annoyed with Howel, for she pulled away sharply and turned her attention to something Will was saying.

When she glanced over her shoulder and waved a hand towards him Alex smiled in return, seeing suddenly that Nerys was a deep one. She tried to hide her feelings, but in that instant Alex knew without doubt that she was in love with Howel.

What a puzzle life was, with dad running round Nerys's skirts, eager for her approbation, and her not seeing anything or anyone but Howel Llewelyn. And there, Alex feared, lay heartache, for his brother was ambitious, wanting only the best for himself, and into that category would most certainly come a woman with wealth and breeding.

'You're very far away, Alex, what are you thinking about?' Sarah's voice was low and barely penetrated his thoughts and she had to repeat her question before Alex replied.

'Sorry, I was just wondering when dad intends coming in here. I bet my bottom shilling that he's swilling down a pint of ale in the public bar – if this place has one, that is!'

'Oh, you're not being fair to your dad – wonderful to me he was, him and Big Eddie looking after me as if I was their own kin, mind. Better to me than my own, any day.' A touch of bitterness crept into her voice and Alex leaned forward and kissed her gently.

'Forget them, my love, for I'm your family now.' He rested his hand fleetingly on her stomach. 'Me and the little rascal you've got in there!'

'Hush, Alex!' Sarah blushed richly. 'You'll have everyone talking about us if you don't behave; think we can't wait to be in bed, they will – you know what folks are like at a wedding.'

'Don't worry, no one can see under the tablecloth.' Alex smiled wickedly and rested his hand on her stomach once more. 'Starting to grow big, you are, woman – can't hide a baby, not for long you can't.'

'Well, I will even if it's only for today, so stop your nonsense before I give you a good smack around the ear!'

'Cruelty already is it, and us barely married! Hear that harsh talk from my wife, did you, Howel? Threatening to beat me already, she is!'

Howel smiled indulgently. 'Like a pair of kids, you two, but make the most of it for after today it will be nose to the grindstone again and on with your business. I expect you to make a go of it, Alex, so that I can be proud of my brother.'

The meal was served swiftly and efficiently and Alex realized with surprise that he was hungry. 'God! I could eat a horse between two shafts,' he teased as Sarah merely picked at the food. 'Come on, girl, have your fill for you won't see such sumptuousness again – at least, not until I make my first million!'

Sarah pushed his arm away. 'Anyone would think you'd been drinking ale, the way you're going on. I haven't seen you in such high spirits, not since before . . .' Her voice trailed away and Alex felt a pain as though a knife had been thrust into his stomach. He had tried to put all sorrows out of his mind, at least for today, but Sarah's unspoken words brought everything rushing back.

Seeing his face, she took his hand beneath the table. 'I'm sorry, that was stupid of me. I'm a fool for spoiling the moment.' She leaned against him and kissed his cheek, which brought a friendly jeer from the other table.

'Hey, watch that wife of yours, boyo!' Ceri was leaning forward, his eyes warm with laughter. 'I can see now how it is you beat me and Katie to the altar – couldn't wait, could you?'

'Shut up, you!' Alex replied, thankful for the interruption of his unpalatable thoughts. 'Jealous you are, man, because you're older than me and only just found a woman to take you on.'

He waved his hand to Katie, who looked very pretty with green bows in her red-gold hair. 'No offence, mind, but are you sure you know what you're doing? Firebrand is that Ceri, no pinning him down; he'll be off like a hare any time the mood takes him.'

'Sure and haven't I thought of that?' Katie said, laughing. 'Bought myself a good stout rolling-pin to keep him in order!'

Alex felt warmed. His friends and family were around him, all of them wishing him well, and he was wrong to dwell on the pains of the past; he must look to the future and live his life without guilt. He took Sarah's hand and kissed her slim white fingers. 'I love you,' he whispered and her eyes became moist.

Howel rose to his feet and called for a toast to the bride and groom. Then began the speech-making from the various men of the family, during which lewd and embarrassing allusions were made to the wedding night. Alex bore it all with good humour, for there was love and friendship in everything that was said.

But when at last the festivities were over, it was good to leave the noise of the hotel room and walk out into the spring sunshine.

'There, then, Mrs Llewelyn,' Howel said from behind the couple. 'It's time to go to your new home in West Cross.'

Sarah sighed as she climbed into the car and nestled close to Alex. 'I loved it all,' she said softly, 'the posh hotel, the wonderful food – but mostly I loved the atmosphere.' She sighed. 'You have the friendship and the love of a fine family – there's lucky you are, boys!'

234

Alex glanced at Howel as he sat in the driving seat. His profile was strong, his mouth set in a firm line and it was difficult to know what his brother was thinking. 'Thanks, for everything,' Alex said quietly and a smile illuminated Howel's face.

'It was a pleasure. I'm only too glad to help in any way I can, and that goes for the future too; if you need anything where the business is concerned, just come to me.' He grinned broadly. 'I'm always willing to put money into a certainty!'

His brother's words gave Alex a sense of accomplishment, for Howel's faith meant much more than any money he might offer.

'Here we are, then – the home of the great business tycoon!' Howel drew the car to a halt and stared at the shop with interest. 'It looks good seeing the Llewelyn name over the door. I'm proud of you, man.' Then he caught Alex's arm.

'Hey! You don't just go marching in – you have to carry your bride over the threshold. Here, give me the key and I'll open the door for you.'

It was cool inside the hallway, with a slant of pale spring sunshine throwing a jewel-like glow over the varnished and as yet uncarpeted staircase.

'Yes, you're going on to great things here, Alex.' Howel stared around him with arms folded across his chest. 'Well, I'd better not stand here talking,' he said with a smile. 'I can see your little bride is a bit heavier than she looks.'

Alex set Sarah down and she leaned against him giggling.

'I'm a good deal heavier than I used to be, that's for certain!' She glanced shyly up at Howel. 'I'm not much good at words, see, so I'll give you a kiss instead.' She reached up and kissed Howel's cheek, blushing at her own temerity.

Howel moved to the door and turned for a moment to look back at his brother. 'Good luck always be with you,' he said, then he went out and closed the door quietly behind him.

Alex stood for a moment savouring the silence of his home. He stared around, scenting the clean smell of varnish and beeswax polish and knowing that he could live in this building with ease. The house seemed to fold protective arms around him, as though welcoming him.

'Right, then,' Sarah said, 'Go and light the fire so that we can have a cup of tea, while I put my best frock away in the wardrobe.'

'Oh, aye, bossing me already, is it?' Alex smiled and ruffled her hair. 'Go on then, I'll soon have the place organized here.'

He was good at fires and had taken to lighting the fire at home of late, knowing that Nerys needed to be helped. She did a good job of caring for dad and the boys and always kept cheerful, even when she looked tired with shadows inky beneath her eyes. But sharp she could be when the moment called for it.

He crumpled some newspaper and put it behind the black-leaded bars in the grate, then placed sticks at angles like a basket to hold the coal. Usually at home he used yesterday's cinders, but here there were none, for today was the first time a fire had been lit since the house had been cleaned and repaired.

The paper set the sticks alight very quickly, for they were bone-dry. Alex watched in satisfaction, holding a blower up to the grate to draw the flames.

'There's a good husband you are!' Sarah returned to the room wearing a long wrap-over robe of pale blue which gave her a sweet, childlike appearance – almost as though she were dressed for the part of the Virgin Mary in a school nativity play.

She sat in the big armchair and curled her bare feet beneath her, smiling at him with what he recognized was an invitation.

'Come here, *cariad*,' she said softly and, throwing

236

down the paper, he knelt before her. She wound her arms around his neck and kissed his mouth and he responded warmly, feeling the heat of the fire on his back as though it reached to his loins.

'Oh, Alex,' Sarah said softly against his mouth, 'we can make a go of it, can't we?'

'Of course we can,' he said fiercely, holding her close, feeling the thrust of her breast against him with a sense of delight. She was beautiful, he loved her and she was his wife.

A loud knocking on the door startled them both and Alex moved away from Sarah almost guiltily. 'I'll see who it is,' he said breathlessly.

He moved in a dream through the passageway into the hall and blinked into the sunlight as he opened the door.

'I couldn't let your wedding day pass without bringing you a present.' The voice was low and it took Alex a few moments to realize that it was Sarah's mother, Mrs Matthews, standing on his doorstep.

'Come on in.' He tried to infuse a little warmth into his voice, but it was difficult to forget the cold way in which she had allowed her only daughter to walk out of her home.

Sarah's face lit up as her mother held a box towards her. 'Oh, mammy, I wish you could have come to my wedding!' She took the box as her mother sat on the edge of a chair and stared at her defensively.

'You know it was awkward. Charlie wouldn't agree to it and well, there's no point in going into all that – look at your present, see if you like it.'

Sarah was like a child tearing at the wrappings, anxious to see what her mother had given her. 'Oh, mammy, it's lovely!' She drew out of the box a tall china ornament of a mother holding a child, and Alex marvelled that a woman like Sarah's mother could offer such a sensitive gift.

'I'll make us all some tea, shall I?' he suggested and

brought out the cups, holding the new china awkwardly. He would never understand women, he thought, for if his mother had practically thrown him out of the house as Sarah's had done, he would have had great difficulty in ever forgiving her. Not that mam would have done such a thing; she loved her children with such a fierceness and pride that she would have died for them.

'Not for me, thanks. I can't stay.' She was drawing on her gloves, her eyes avoiding those of her daughter. 'Charlie will be wondering where I've gone, and if I'm out for too long he'll be off down the public on his own.'

She didn't turn at the door but hurried away down the street, with head bent, making for the tram-stop with all haste.

'I don't understand my mother.' Sarah's words reflected his thoughts as her hands gently smoothed the china statue. 'She takes the trouble to come all this way with a present for me, and then just vanishes from my life again.' Her eyes were moist as she looked up at Alex and his heart contracted with pity for his young, vulnerable wife. 'Mammy hasn't even said if she'll come again.' She put the statue carefully on the mantelpiece and stared up at it as though it held the secret to her mother's nature.

Alex put his hand on Sarah's shoulder and drew her to him, his cheek resting against her hair. He knew that what she most needed now was reassurance.

'She loves you, that's clear enough. It's just that your dad comes first, which is as it should be.' He tipped her face up to his. 'Don't trouble yourself about it any more, promise?'

She smiled and cupped his face in her small hands. 'We'll have love enough to fill the world, won't we, Alex?' She spoke wistfully and he closed his eyes in a moment of pain. Loving brought with it hurt, yet he was grateful for the emotions raging through him; it proved he could still feel alive and in charge of his own destiny.

'I love you so very much, my little lovely.' He bent his head, his lips seeking the warmth of her throat. She clung more tightly to him, burrowing against him like some small woodland creature.

'Let's go up to our room, Alex,' she said softly, her breath mingling with his as she reached for his lips.

Passion flared through him and though it was carnal, there was a spiritual quality to his emotions, rather as though he was standing in an arched church with choirs singing, voices rising into the rafters.

He took her hand and led her upstairs, opening the door to their bedroom with a flourish.

'Enter, my lady, and see if everything meets with your approval!' he said, anticipating her pleasure.

The wallpaper was cream and sprigged with small rosebuds, the curtains and bed-coverings in exactly the same shade of pink as the rosebuds. On the highly polished tallboy stood a vase filled with tulips and daffodils, and with a cry of delight Sarah moved into the room.

'Oh, Alex, no wonder you wouldn't let me see it – it's a lovely surprise!' She turned and looked through the window. 'And the view of the Mumbles Head with the sea lapping the rocks is so beautiful.'

She fell silent, staring at Alex with shining eyes. He moved towards her and took her in his arms.

'I would like to have bought you roses, but they were not flourishing enough and the woman in the market was asking the earth for some poor little half-grown things which wouldn't have done you justice.'

'It's all wonderful,' Sarah said softly. 'I wouldn't change anything.' She tipped back her head and kissed his mouth. 'No more talking, come with me to bed, there's a lovely boy.'

He couldn't take his eyes off her as she allowed her

robe to slip from her milky shoulders. Her breasts were full, her thickening waist detracting not a bit from her beauty. And yet Alex was aware of her pregnancy, heart-stoppingly aware.

They lay together beneath the sheets and he felt the silk of her against him. Her skin was cool to the touch and soft, much softer than he had imagined.

He wondered if she would make comparisons, for she had been loved before while he was ignorant of the physical art. She sensed his feeling and taking his hand, placed it carefully on her breast. Then she arched against him and his loins ached with desire for her.

'Take it slowly, my lovely, there's no hurry.' Sarah whispered the words, though there was no one to hear. Alex kissed her mouth tenderly as his hand, at first quiescent, began to explore her loveliness.

She was beautiful and wonderful and he didn't know how he was going to contain his love for her; his head felt as though there were pounding hooves inside it and he could scarcely breathe as her gentle fingers reached out and touched him.

He cautioned himself not to be hasty and stroked and teased her nipples, acquainting himself with all the secrets of her body. She was his first woman, his first love and an inner instinct told him that he must savour the moment.

'Oh, my love,' Sarah moaned against his lips. 'My darling, darling love, come to me!'

Alex felt as though he was grown into a man ten feet tall. He was loved and desired and here in his arms was his own sweet wife who wanted him as much as he wanted her. He would give her everything it was possible for a man to give, and he would never spend his energies on the flossies who frequented the public bars. He would be faithful for ever to his beautiful Sarah, as she would be faithful to him.

She wound her slender arms around his neck,

240

pressing herself closer as though to become one with him. And then she spoke in a husky far-away voice: 'I'm ready, my darling Hector.'

The name fell between them like a stone and the image of his twin lying torn and bleeding in the grass rose up like a nightmare before Alex's eyes. He fell over onto his back as his passion vanished like mists before the sun, his entire body bathed in pain. He was nothing in his own right, he was simply a substitute for his brother – what a fool he had been to believe that Sarah could ever love him.

Sarah sat up with her hand to her mouth, her eyes wide with horror. 'Alex?' She held out a tentative hand, but he brushed it aside.

'Don't say anything.' His voice was terse. 'You've said it all, Sarah, and don't think I blame you for I don't.'

He pushed aside the bedclothes and dressed himself swiftly, leaving the room without a backward glance at Sarah who was weeping pitiful tears into her pillow. There was a taste like sawdust in his mouth, his guts ached and there was a blinding bar of light across his line of vision.

Alex left the house and walked towards the beach, not scenting the blossoms which had begun to garland the trees, or the soft sea breeze that lifted his hair from his fevered forehead. He was only aware that he was in chains, a man imprisoned in the memories of his dead brother.

He sank on to the sand and stared at the timid waves .which approached the shore only to recede again. He was dead, as dead as Hector who was lying in *Dan y Graig* Cemetery, yet he was forced into playing out a charade of living. He closed his eyes, wishing tears would come, but there was nothing within him except empty desolation.

CHAPTER EIGHTEEN

The blossoms hung heavy and rich on the trees – pink flowering cherry and crisply white apple blossom. The sun was as warm as summer and the river flowing between the banks was imbued with a golden glow.

Nerys stood staring down into the liquid gold water, feeling alive and tinglingly aware of herself. She acknowledged that it was the thought of Howel Llewelyn which lifted her spirits, for this afternoon he would be at home and they would be together.

She knew she was playing with fire. He had not touched her, but she had received signals of his increasing interest ever since that moment in the kitchen when only the presence of Tom and Will, calling to her from the bedroom, had prevented her from going into Howel's arms.

At first it had been difficult to accept that his attitude towards her had changed from one of hostility to a warmth and a seeking to know her better. She did not know what had wrought the change and she was suspicious of it, yet she could not help but be warmed by it.

She returned to the house and the intolerable heat of the fire which was necessary for the cooking of the food. Opening the oven, she felt the top of the *bara brith*, the hot spicy cake rich with fruit and sugar and stout. Then brushing back her hair, she took up a cloth and shifted the load from the oven on to the hob. It smelled spicy, rich and mouthwatering and she stood back well-pleased with herself.

She heard the sound of running feet on the stairs and as the door burst open, she stood back with hands on hips waiting for the onslaught of the two boys. Tom swung into the kitchen, his face beaming as his nose wrinkled up in appreciation.

'Oh boy, cake!' he said and Nerys wanted to hug him to her. He was a good child and took on the responsibility for his younger brother without complaint.

'Yes, I thought you could take some with you this afternoon when you go on a picnic with Mona. I've got some dandelion pop as well, and there's meat pasties too so you should be able to make a good day of it.'

'Where's Mona taking us?' Will asked, almost falling into the room behind his brother. 'Can we go to the beach?'

'We'll see,' Nerys said cheerfully, 'but for now, go and get washed, both of you.'

She knew exactly what she was doing and she should be ashamed, for she was manoeuvring matters so that she would be left alone with Howel. Up until now they had had little chance to talk, to be together to explore each other's ways, and she wanted very much to take their relationship on to a much deeper level.

He gave her looks over the table, it was true, or brushed her hand with his and once, he had drawn near – so close that he could look into her eyes. She blushed now as she remembered her emotions, for she had longed to go into his arms, to be held close to him and to feel his mouth upon hers.

But love must be given time to grow slowly – there was no rushing matters – and yet excitement mounted within her, for today she would have time to be with Howel and to learn more about the self he kept so secret.

She wondered guiltily if she had been a little sly, for she was arranging to be alone with Howel on the very

243

day when Siona would be away from the house, gone to Sweyn's Eye on matters concerning his boat.

For once the ferry was out of action, bumping gently against the quay, smelling acrid with creosote painted on to preserve the planking of the boat from the continual wash of the water.

Not that Siona had any power or sway over her, but she owed him a great deal and she knew that he would be upset – even angry – if he found out that there were special feelings between Nerys and his eldest son.

Siona had come to look upon her as his personal property, but this was an attitude she strove to dispel; she was her own woman with her own mind, and a love that was growing ever more strong with each almost tangible sign that she received from Howel.

'We're washed and ready now, Nerys.' Will's voice broke into her thoughts and she smiled as she saw him, his little face shining, his hair slicked down damply across his forehead. He was wearing his only pair of good coarse cloth trousers which ended just above his plump knees, and a pullover of Fairisle over a shabby flannel shirt.

The boys needed new clothes and she realized with a feeling of guilt that she must speak to Siona on the matter, for she could not allow them to become ill-clothed. Emily would rise from the grave and haunt the little house if her children were neglected.

The thought made her shudder and she was pleased to see the slight figure of Mona running lightly towards the house.

'Good thing you're paying me for today!' Mona said breathlessly. 'My mam was all set to stop me coming until I said there was money in it!' She sank down into a chair, her thin chest heaving, her cheeks pink. She looked quite pretty, Nerys thought with a dart of surprise, for Mona usually seemed so mousy and colourless.

'Well, it's only fair that you get paid,' Nerys said quickly. 'I don't expect you to give up your time for nothing. Does your mam take all your wages, then?'

'There's a soft question!' Mona looked up under her eyelashes. 'If mam didn't think she could gain anything by me being out here working, she'd have me slaving in our house like a shot!'

Nerys regarded Mona carefully, seeing that her frock was old-fashioned and much patched and the colour had faded into oblivion.

'Come up to my room for a minute, Mona,' she said, smiling. 'And in the meantime, you boys start packing the food in the basket so that you can all get off out.'

Mona, surprised, nevertheless followed her meekly up the stairs and into the bedroom.

'Look, there are some things of mine which have got too small for me – do you think you could make use of them, Mona?' Nerys drew out her bag and took from it the clothes that she had brought with her when she first came to the Ferry House. Then she had been at her wits' end, without means to buy herself anything new, but the clothes were good and clean and since she had been a working woman she had been able to replenish her wardrobe.

'Oh, there's good of you!' Mona took up a frock of soft white linen embroidered with rosebuds. 'This is just the sort of thing for a nice day like this – can I wear it now?'

She was little more than a child, Nerys realized, staring at the other girl with fresh insight.

'First let me give it a going-over with the flat-iron,' Nerys offered, smiling. 'You'll feel much better when it's free of all those creases.'

'I'll iron it,' Mona said quickly, reluctant to let the frock out of her hands, and Nerys nodded.

'Right then, I'll see that the boys pack the food away tidily; you want to get out into the sunshine as soon as you can and make the most of the fine day.'

The two boys groaned when Mona spread an old sheet across the wooden table and put the irons on to heat on the hob, but she smiled good-naturedly. 'I won't be long, don't worry; we'll have plenty of time to go to the beach – and the park too, if you like.'

Nerys hid her impatience, wanting everything to be right from the moment Howel stepped through the door. She would like to have flowers on the table smelling sweetly of spring, and more, she wanted time to wash in rose-scented water and to brush out her hair and put on a fresh frock.

It was all planned like a dream, a romance out of a book, and she was sure nothing would go wrong. They would sit and talk and Howel would hold her hand; perhaps she might even allow him to kiss her. She felt the heat run through her veins at the thought of such intimacy, yet wasn't it time that she knew what love was all about?

She had witnessed love in many guises – living vicariously through the families with whom she had worked – but as for experience, she had no real knowledge of what life was about and it was time all that was changed.

Eventually Mona, glowing with delight in her new clothes, was ready to take the boys on their picnic. 'There's pretty you look, Mona,' Tom said in his grave, grown-up manner and she smiled widely.

'I feel pretty today, boyo. Come on then, let's get out into the sunshine. Tom, you carry the pop and I'll carry the basket of food.' She smiled over her shoulder at Nerys. 'I'll keep them out as long as I can and give you a bit of a break, like. It's not often you get any time to yourself, is it?'

After they had gone, the house seemed to fall into a dreaming silence disturbed only by the soft ticking of the clock and the intermittent calling of the birds.

Nerys hurriedly put away the old sheet still hot from the ironing and spread the table with a fresh white cloth. She chose the prettiest flowers from the garden – early roses in soft pink and glowing white with petals folded close, not yet ready to open. The splash of colour seemed to lend light to the room and Nerys stood back well-pleased.

But there was no time to waste. Howel had said he would be home by early afternoon and she had yet to wash in the rose-scented water she had already prepared in the great china bowl in her room.

With a last glance around the neat kitchen, at the gleaming black-leaded bars of the grate and the shimmering surface of the flame-warmed brass fender; at the mantelpiece tidied of papers and pipes and ornaments dusted and she nodded her head in satisfaction; it all looked splendid.

In her room, she removed her frock and stood in her petticoat, soaping her arms with the special rose-scented soap she had bought in the market. Excitement made her clumsy and the soap fell into the bowl with a splash, the rose-water spilling on to her bodice.

With a cluck of annoyance, Nerys took off her petticoat and bodice and stood staring at herself in the mirror. Her breasts though small were well-shaped and her waist neat above the rucked edge of her knickers. She had never paused to observe her own body before; now she felt self-conscious and vain and quickly dried her skin with a rough towel.

She heard neither footsteps on the stairs nor the opening of her bedroom door, and it was only when Howel moved into the room that she became suddenly aware of his presence. With a small scream she covered herself with the inadequate towel, her face growing flushed with chagrin. She felt disappointment bite at her; she had wanted everything to be so right, so romantic, and here she was caught at a disadvantage.

'You are very beautiful, Nerys,' Howel sounded surprised. He moved slowly towards her and she stood quite still, not knowing what to do or say. It was as though her tongue had cleaved to the roof of her mouth.

He caught the towel and pulled it away from her nerveless hands, his eyes devouring her breasts. Suddenly she came to life and found her voice: 'Go downstairs, Howel, I'll be with you in a few minutes.' But the words came out shakily, unconvincingly, and Howel ignored them. He moved closer and looked into her eyes and his own were dark, unreadable.

When his hands touched her shoulders, she felt as though a shock ran through her entire body. She stepped back a pace, frightened . . . but of what, she didn't know.

'Please, Howel.' She didn't know why she was appealing to him to leave her alone for his touch filled her with only pleasure, yet in the recesses of her mind she knew that such intimacy was to be kept only for after the wedding.

Slowly he drew her close to him, his hand holding her chin gently. He tipped her face upwards and his mouth hovered above hers for what seemed an endless length of time.

'This is wrong,' she whispered, but then her words were hushed as he kissed her. She had not imagined that such a riot of feeling existed. It was as though her passions, held in check for so long, were suddenly unleashed and her mind became a chaos of thoughts as his mouth searched hers. She was aware that her arms were around his neck, clinging to him.

He kissed her throat softly, small kisses that burned her skin. She trembled in his arms, her legs hardly able to support her. In a swift movement, he lifted her in his arms and carried her the few steps towards the bed. She struggled to sit up, her heart beating swiftly for she was suddenly fearful.

'No, Howel, no! I must dress, we must go downstairs and talk to each other. I never intended . . .' Her voice faded as he stretched out beside her, his hand gently cupping one of her breasts.

'Don't be afraid, Nerys. I wouldn't do anything to hurt you – you must know that. Don't you trust me?'

She had no idea what he meant – trust him in what way? She struggled against him as he drew her close, his hand teasing her nipple. Passion and fear warred within her; she was trembling with terror and yet the feelings he was arousing in her were so new, so precious.

He spoke to her gently, his eyes half-closed as he stroked her hair and then her shoulders, sending searing flames through her as again he caressed her breasts.

'Howel, please stop,' she whispered against his lips. 'I just know this isn't right. Please let me dress. We must talk; all this is happening too soon.'

'Be easy, there's a lovely girl,' Howel said gently. 'This is the most wonderful and natural thing in the world – there's nothing to fear, I promise.'

Then she lay still, wanting to believe him, knowing that she must some time learn the secrets of life and what better time than now, with Howel giving her love as well as passion?

Nerys closed her eyes as he removed his clothes, but behind her lids she could see his straight back, his broad shoulders and the slenderness of his waist. She had witnessed him washing of a morning and the sight of him stripped to the waist at the sink in the kitchen was all she knew of a man.

When he returned to the bed, she opened her eyes and saw that he was golden and beautiful in the sunlight washing in through the window. He gently removed her remaining clothes and like innocent children they lay together naked.

Her fear was subsiding; this new experience was so wonderful, how could it be wrong? Howel held her close, his hands smoothing her spine and the base of her neck, almost reverent in his appreciation of her. She was drugged with passion now, intoxicated by his touch, knowing that she had reached the point of no return; she must go on with this happiness which was holding her, she could not call a halt.

He moved to cover her, he was above her with his body hard against hers. She gasped a little, fear returning, but he came gently to her, speaking soothing little words of love and telling her that she was beautiful – that she was the most wonderful woman in all the world. And so the pain brought with it excitement and acceptance and she held him close, her hands caressing the silk of his shoulders as he moved, her love for him overflowing and bringing tears to her eyes.

They seemed to be together for eternity and she was one with him, moving with him, clinging to him and giving herself completely.

When they parted at last, he drew up a sheet to cover them both and then took her in his arms, holding her head upon his shoulder and kissing her hair, telling her she was his little love, his darling. And then he slept.

Carefully, she rose up on one elbow and stared at him intently, drinking in everything about him. His hair was curled damply around his face, his lashes lay dark on his fine cheekbones; she ached with love for him, for now they were joined as irrevocably as though in holy matrimony.

At last she crept from the bed and bathed herself in the rose-water from the bowl. She dressed silently and went downstairs into the kitchen, where she sat before the fire, staring round her as though seeing everything for the first time.

The colours of the flowers seemed sharper, the scents more pronounced, the fire in the grate gleamed a golden red with blue and purple flames leaping upward into the darkness of the chimney. It was as if her senses had become heightened; the world around her new and fresh.

Nerys closed her eyes and put both hands over her face. She was in love – oh, how much she was in love! She had not intended anything like this to happen, yet she could not be sorry for it had been so beautiful. Now she understood how passion and love could change the world, how a woman would fight for her man.

She realized the meaning of jealousy too, for if ever anyone tried to take Howel away from her she would kill to keep him. She smiled at such a foolish thought. He would look at no other woman, how could he now?

Hearing sounds from upstairs and feeling suddenly shy, she rose to her feet, her hands clasped together. Howel came down the stairs and into the kitchen and when he saw her uncertainty, he came to her and took her in his arms, holding her close.

'Sweet little Nerys, have I woken the sleeping princess, then?' he whispered softly. She didn't know what he meant; he was such an educated man, so clever and so handsome, yet he had given his love to her – how privileged she was!

'Come on, I'll take you out to tea at the Mackworth. Would you like that?' He took her hand and kissed her fingertips and she blushed at the remembered intimacies between them.

'Yes, that would be lovely, Howel.' The words sounded prim and prissy, absurdly formal after the passions they had shared. But he seemed to understand, for he took her hand and tucked it in his arm and together, they left the house and went outside into the spring sunshine.

*   *   *

Later, Howel left Nerys at the top of the road leading to the Ferry House and climbed into his car.

He felt sun-drenched and pleasantly tired and realized to his surprise that he had really enjoyed the time spent with her. It was not only the sweet innocence of her as he had taken her to bed which appealed to him; it was her unexpected sense of humour and the evenness of her temper. Nerys indeed was a fine, remarkable girl and would make someone a good wife.

He had intended to seduce her, he made no bones about that, but his twin motives had been first curiosity about a girl so long without a man and second and more importantly with the intention of deflecting his father from his absurd infatuation with Nerys.

Yet now he felt no triumph. Indeed, if he could put back the clock he would have left her alone, for he realized now that she was too fine to merely trifle with. She had looked at him as though he had produced a miracle, her love for him naked in her eyes. It made him feel uncomfortably aware that he had behaved like a heel.

As he drove towards the western hillside he pushed these thoughts from his mind, for he was dining with Sterling Richardson; a celebration it was really, for with the collateral put forward by Sterling, Howel had managed to make himself a decent profit. He was well on the road to a complete financial recovery and he would not forget the kindness which had made it all possible, for Sterling had not only backed him to the hilt on his investments, he had even found him a house in which to live: a fine gracious house which satisfied all Howel's longings.

Initially, his plan had been to use Sterling as a stepping-stone, but now all that was changed. They would rise to the top together or not at all.

He smiled to himself, wondering if the amorous Jenny would be at the party. It would be so easy now to put up with her teasing, her dancing first forward into his arms and then backward away from him like the tide ebbing and flowing. He knew he baffled her, which in its turn had the effect of intriguing the girl; there was no doubt that she was fast becoming infatuated with what appeared to be the unobtainable!

He drew up outside the door and pulled on the brake. To his surprise, as he looked up at the huge, gracious house, he suddenly wished he was back in the little bedroom of the Ferry House with Nerys at his side.

* * *

Nerys couldn't wait to see Howel again. He had made no arrangements, no plans, but then men were not so tidy-minded as women. He would come to her whenever he could, she was sure of it. And she was right.

'How about coming out with me to the theatre, perhaps?' he asked softly, standing on the threshold of the kitchen and smiling at her as though unaware of anyone else's presence.

Siona looked up from polishing his boots. '*Duw*, haven't set eyes on you for days, boyo – where have you been keeping yourself, then?'

Tom and Will grinned at Howel from over their supper, while Nerys felt a blush of happiness rise to her cheeks.

'No sarcasm, dad, you know I've got my own place now,' Howel said gently. 'I was telling you all about it the other day, but you didn't take much notice. Sterling Richardson arranged it for me.'

'That man seems to be meddling in our family more than a bit,' Siona said sourly, 'what with finding you a house and planning to set our Ceri up as a silversmith.'

'Don't worry, dad, he's got our best interests at heart. Now, are you coming out with me, Nerys? I've missed you,' he added softly.

'What's this then?' Siona asked in somewhat angry surprise. He put down his boots and looked from

253

Nerys to Howel, his eyebrows raised. 'How long has this been going on?'

'Nothing's been going on, dad,' Howel said evenly. 'I just think that Nerys needs a bit of a treat now and again and as no one else has thought of it, then it's obviously up to me.'

'I'd like very much to go to the theatre,' Nerys said breathlessly, 'that's if you don't need me for anything else tonight, Siona.'

'Aw, let her go, dad,' Tom put in, in his reasonable grown-up voice. 'She must get tired of sitting by here every night with us.'

'It's nothing to do with me,' Siona said at last. 'Nerys must please herself, of course.'

'I'll get my jacket,' Nerys said quickly, afraid that Siona would change his mind and raise some objection.

Out in the softness of the evening she smiled up at Howel, her eyes brilliant. 'I knew you'd come for me before too long. Been waiting days for this I have, mind – thought I'd never keep my patience.'

'I've been busy making the house presentable . . . and I lied about the theatre. I want you to see all the work I've done, so climb in.' He set the car in motion and beside him, Nerys felt a sense of excitement rise within her. Was Howel going to show her his home and then ask her to be his wife? The thought left her feeling strangely sad, for she would miss the little house by the river and the two younger Llewelyn boys who had filled her life with their mischievous affection. But, she reasoned, Mona would always be willing to look after them.

He drove the car through the roads lit by soft gaslight and then out into the broader streets of the town itself. A tram rattled by, with people imprisoned behind the windows like flies caught in amber. Nerys felt almost sorry for them, bustling away to the theatre or the music hall, passing her by without knowing that this was the happiest time of her life.

The house was tall and imposing, set in its own

grounds looking out over the sea. Nerys gasped in awe as she saw the high domed doorway and the wide heavily curtained windows and wondered if she could ever live in such a place – it was so grand.

Howel led the way inside and Nerys saw that the hallway alone was bigger than the entire ground floor of the Ferry House. The stairway stretched upwards gracefully with polished banisters and she felt herself being gently pushed towards the bedrooms. Then Howel flung open a door and inside, all was darkness. Nerys stopped short, a little frightened of the heavy silence, and then she felt Howel reach for her.

When he took her it was quickly, without the sweetness and patience he had shown before. She gasped as he came to her. All she could see was the light in his eyes and the darkness of him silhouetted against the curtained window. It was impersonal, as though she could have been anyone lying beneath him. And when it was over as suddenly as it had begun, she cried.

He lit the lamps and he seemed a stranger, his back turned on her as he rearranged his clothing. She rose from the bed, dried her eyes and stood uncertainly before him, waiting for some word of tenderness, some sign that he loved her, but there was nothing.

'I'll take you home now,' Howel said easily, as though they had done nothing more than share a cup of tea. 'I have quite a busy night ahead of me.'

Dumbly she sat beside him in the car, begging him silently to salvage something from the night, but he drove silently, intent on the road ahead. So close and yet a million miles from her!

He left her on the road near the house and drove away from her without a backward glance. She had never felt so alone, so bereft in all her life. The last thing she wanted was to walk into the warmth and light of the Ferry House, but there was nowhere else for her to go.

Siona looked at her searchingly as she entered the kitchen and the sadness in his eyes told her that he knew exactly what had happened. She turned away from him and hurried up the stairs, closing the door behind her; then she was alone with all her pain and misery and no tears to heal the hurting that was inside her.

CHAPTER NINETEEN

The sun-dappled leaves trembled in the morning breeze, forming patterns of light and shade on the worn pathway that led to Ram's Tor Farm. A band of cloud hung over the jagged cliff-top – slow to disperse in spite of the morning's warmth – and the sheep grazing on the Tor appeared shadowy, without form or colour. Alex shook his head as though to clear it and reined the horse in preparation for loading the heavy milk churns on to the cart.

'Morning, Alex. Want a hand?' Morgan Lloyd strode across the farmyard: his shirt-sleeves rolled above his elbows, his hair streaked with gold and his skin reddened with the constant exposure to sun and winds. He smiled and there was a trace of pity in his eyes as he lifted a churn and easily set it upon the swaying cart.

Alex nodded his thanks, wondering if either of them would forget the day of Hector's death, the maddened bull tearing and destroying.

'Morning, nice enough weather,' he replied, giving no indication of his thoughts. 'I should get my round finished quickly, folk rise early when the sun shines.' He forced a smile and nodded in appreciation as Morgan set a crate of eggs on the inside of the cart nearest the driving seat for safety.

'How's the business doing?' Morgan asked as he hauled forward another crate of eggs and then placed large squares of butter on the marble slab between the milk churns? 'You must be doing great things, the amount of stuff you buy from me?'

257

'Aye, business is fair enough,' Alex replied. 'I'll be back later for some sacks of spuds, as it happens.'

When the loading was finished, Morgan folded his arms across his chest. 'I understand congratulations are in order, man – you've got a son now, I hear!' He jerked his head towards the farmhouse. 'My missis has a little something for you and your wife – sentimental is Catherine about babies.'

Alex mumbled his thanks and followed Morgan, picking his way through clucking hens that pecked carelessly at the ground. He looked at Morgan's straight back, knowing that he would never fail his wife in the marriage bed; he was a man, not an apology for one.

Worriedly, Alex chewed his lip. He would never forget the humiliation of his first night as a husband – how the sound of his brother's name spoken by Sarah in passion, had turned his desire to guilt and his blood to water. Since then he had tried to be a husband; God, how he had tried! His secret thoughts and dreams brought him readily enough to passion, but it seemed that he was impotent when Sarah actually lay next to him, wanting him.

At first he'd been able to make excuses, telling her it was consideration for her condition that made him hold back, but once the child had been born he found himself uttering bumbling untruths. She had only to look at him with her soul in her eyes and the lies would stick in his throat.

If only they could have talked openly about things that hurt them, then a remedy might be found, but they were tongue-tied and each careful in case the wrong words were said.

Now Catherine Lloyd rose from her chair to welcome him into the kitchen; she was still rosy from sleep and wore a gown of fresh cotton around her slim figure. Happiness shone from her and the way she looked at her husband brought Alex near to tears.

'I've made a lace christening gown and cap for your son,' she said, moving to the dresser and taking from a drawer a delicate piece of needlework which must have involved hours of effort.

'It passed away some long evenings,' Catherine told him, reading his thoughts. 'I hope Sarah will like it.' She sounded sincere and Alex dropped his guard a little, knowing that however foolish the notion, Catherine and Morgan Lloyd would always feel a little to blame for what had happened to Hector. Somehow, to know that he was not alone in his guilt made him feel a little better.

'Thank you, there's happy Sarah will be when I give her your gift.' He moved to the door and touched his cap politely before letting himself out into the sunlit morning.

The horse pulled at the heavily laden cart, head dipping towards the ground with the effort. Alex was walking now to save the animal the extra weight, clucking in encouragement as he led the way down the rutted pathway and into Oystermouth village.

'Took your time this morning, young man!' Gladys Richardson was waiting for him on her doorstep, her gnarled hands holding out a jug to be filled with milk. 'I've not had a cup of tea yet – parched I am too. What kept you so long, Alex?'

'Stop grumbling, Gladys.' Alex dipped the long-handled measure into the churn and ladled the milk into the jug. 'Want some butter now and good fresh eggs? Come on, I've lots of things to sell before I can go back up to fetch potatoes for my shop, mind.'

'Your shop indeed – don't come the big business man with me, boyo!' Gladys prodded him playfully. 'I knew you twins when you were no more than tow-headed kids, remember?' She stopped speaking and looked up at him quickly. 'There's sorry I am, cut my tongue out I could.'

Alex fetched some eggs from the crate and counted

out a dozen. 'Nothing wrong in mentioning our Hector, mind,' he said softly. 'I wouldn't want folks to behave as though he had never been on this earth.'

'That's the spirit, boy. Come on now and help me get back inside the house. My old legs have got the bone-ache so bad that all I want to do is sit with a hot-water bottle resting on them.' She paused in the doorway. 'And tell me, how's your Sarah and her little babba? Well enough, are they?'

Amiably, Alex carried the milk and eggs into the kitchen and stowed them away on the cold shelf in the pantry. Admittedly his time was being used up, but friendliness and good service were what he was offering along with his produce, an attitude much appreciated by his customers.

By the time he got to the shop in West Cross, the sun was overhead and the butter in the cart was dimpling with moisture. He waved a hand to Sarah, who was peering at him through the window; she hurried out, her smile bright – a little too bright.

'Help me get these things inside,' he said, and though aware that his tone was terse, he was unable to help himself. He manoeuvred the churns into the back room and placed the full ones in the breeze from the open door. The empty ones he scalded with water from the kettle and laid them sideways-on so as to dry.

'Your dinner's ready,' Sarah said quickly. 'I've got some nice lamb chops and mint sauce, your favourite.'

He looked up at her without any show of emotion, but inside he was dissolving in pity. 'You're thinking of Hector again,' he said and turned away from her anguished eyes.

She came to him and put her hand on his arm. 'Alex, I'm sorry. I can't seem to do anything right and I'm trying so hard, really I am.'

'I know, girl.' He leaned his head against her hair for a moment and then moved away into the kitchen. 'You'll have to dish up the food quickly,' he said. 'I have to go up to the farm again in a minute for potatoes. You'll need to keep an eye on the shop for me until I get back.'

She placed his food on the table and sat opposite him, looking young and innocent with her hair hanging to her shoulders. 'You'll be killing yourself with all this hard work, mind – ease up a bit, there's a good boy.'

'Can you fetch me twelve sacks of spuds?' he demanded angrily, staring at her over a forkful of meat. She pursed her lips, her eyes flashing obstinately.

'You just get on with that dinner, boyo, and look out for the baby. You'll see what I can and can't do!'

Before he could say any more, she let herself out of the house and he heard the clip-clop of the horse's hooves against the roadway.

He made to rise and then sank into his chair. Let her find out for herself that the work was backbreaking – more than a man could cope with, let alone a woman who had recently given birth to a child.

He ate his meal halfheartedly, guilt tearing away at him as he told himself that Sarah would come to harm; she would strain herself lifting too much weight and then how would he live with himself? When he had finished he stood outside looking up and down the road, cursing Sarah for a fool. She had no right to take off with the horse and cart and without a word to him about her intentions.

Then he heard the faint crying of the baby and hurried upstairs into the coolness of the bedroom. The child lay in his crib, small fists waving impotently in the air, face screwed up in distress.

Alex lifted the baby and held him close. He was the spit out of Hector's mouth, even down to the tiny dimple in his chin.

'There, there, your mammy will be back soon.' As he held the baby close and spoke soothingly, the crying ceased as suddenly as it had begun.

The jangling of the shop-bell shattered the silence and carefully Alex laid the child in the crib before hurrying down into the shop to serve the customer, who was tapping the counter impatiently.

'I'll have the two dozen Welsh cakes I ordered this morning, if you please. I've not got all day to wait, either!' The woman wore an old-fashioned but expensive velvet hat and lace gloves, and was not the sort of customer he expected in his shop.

'Welsh cakes?' He looked at her as though she had gone mad and she stared at him impatiently.

'Yes, Welsh cakes. They are cooked, aren't they? I do hope so, for I'm not going back to my master and disappoint him. For his afternoon tea, the cakes are, mind.'

Alex went into the kitchen and stepped into the cool of the pantry. On the shelf was a large plate of the spicy fruit cakes which Sarah must have spent the best part of the morning baking on the huge iron griddle over the fire.

'Here they are, all ready for you. My wife has even put out an empty tin for you to carry them home in.'

'I should think so, young man, seeing as how I provided that tin! Here's the money – 1s 6d, that's correct – and it goes in that box just there usually. Tell Mrs Llewelyn I'll look forward to seeing her later on in the week, and remind her that I want six beef pies, won't you?'

Alex stood for a long moment in wonder, staring at the large amount of money in the box. Sarah must have been secretly working, cooking food for people wealthy enough to pay for it. He sighed and opening the door, looked out along the Mumbles Road. It was high time she returned; he must have been mad to allow her to make the journey up to the farm.

He heard the clip-clop of the horse's hooves and the rumble of the wheels with a feeling of relief. Then he saw the cart and Sarah riding on top like an old-time queen going into battle. Over her shoulder appeared two faces, dusty and begrimed beneath the brims of flat caps.

'Tom, Will – what on earth are you doing out here?' Alex demanded of his younger brothers as he moved forward. Peering into the cart, he saw that some of the potato sacks were empty.

'Sarah came to fetch us,' Tom said, leaping down to the ground. 'Helped her with the selling of the potatoes we did, mind – running up garden paths with our caps full of spuds and sometimes getting a halfpenny extra for our trouble!'

'What about the loading?' Alex lifted Sarah to the ground and she put her hands on his shoulders and laughed up at him.

'I gave Morgan Lloyd's labourers a pretty smile and they were falling over themselves to help me!' she said in triumph.

He took a sack on his shoulders and hauled it into the back room of the shop. 'You have some devious ways, Sarah,' he said, 'and I'm not surprised those farm workers would do anything for you. By the way, I've had some posh woman in by here asking me for Welsh cakes.'

'Oh, *Duw*, I forgot all about her!' Sarah said, hands held to her lips. 'What did you tell her?'

'I sent her off with a flea in her ear!' Alex replied in mock anger. 'Told her this wasn't a bakery and what did she think she was doing asking for you to bake six beef pies.'

'You didn't!' Sarah looked at him in consternation. 'That's Mrs Stuckey, housekeeper to the old doctor. She's been one of my best customers, and what do I care if she says she bakes the food herself?'

When she saw the smile creep into Alex's eyes, she hit out at him with her small fist. 'You rotten liar!' She started to laugh and leaned against him helplessly.

He felt moved to the core of his being. Sarah was so

soft, so lovely and he was so in love with her. If only the other thing would come right, then everything would be perfect.

'Oh, come on – stop cuddling and kissing, you two,' Tom said, removing his cap uncaring of the shower of potato dust that fell into his face. 'I'm starving and I want something to eat before my belly begins to growl out loud.'

'All right. You deserve a good feed, you two boys, for I don't know how I'd have managed without you.'

Alex shook his head. 'From now on, *merchi*, you stick to the baking and I'll stick to the farm work. You've proved your point.'

Sarah sighed. 'I suppose I'm a pig-headed woman and proud with it, but I needed to show you that I'm not going to be hanging on your coat-tails throughout our lives. I'll pull my weight and more if you'll only let me.'

She took a cold savoury pie out of the pantry and cut it into slices, handing the two boys a plate each.

'Come on, now eat your fill for there's some lovely apple tart to follow with rich soft cream to go on top – how's that, then?'

Alex sat at the head of the table, looking with gratitude towards his wife. She made him feel important in his own house and never a word about him failing her. Perhaps tonight, when Tom and Will had gone back to the Ferry House, he could hold her and touch her and be a real man. But he knew that when the moment came, terror would twist his guts and he would be useless.

Later, he took his younger brothers home to the Ferry House, both of them lying in the well of the cart replete with food and weary from their exertions.

'You'll be fit for nothing when you get to school tomorrow,' Alex said lightly, but there were only answering grunts from the two boys.

He was welcomed home like the prodigal son.

Siona clapped him on the back and ushered him to a chair.

'Cup of tea for my son, Nerys, if you please – and you boys, get you washed, you're both filthy dirty!' Siona sounded short-tempered for the moment, but then he smiled and Alex thought he must have been mistaken.

'How are Ceri and Howel keeping? Never see them these days.' Alex sat astride the chair facing into the room and saw his father shrug, his lip curling a little beneath the bristling moustache.

'Howel is gone all toffee-nosed; moved up a step from the old Ferry House, he has. Too good for the likes of us now that he's a big business man and going to run for Member of Parliament. Well, good riddance to him, I say!'

The bitterness in his father's voice surprised Alex, since Siona had always held his eldest son in the highest esteem.

'And Ceri?' Alex changed the subject quickly, noticing that Nerys had gone red to the roots of her hair and realizing there was something here he didn't quite understand. In any case it was none of his business; he had enough difficulties to handle in his own life.

'Oh, Ceri's a good 'un,' Siona said warmly. 'Out courting his lovely Katie, he is, and him set up fine in the silversmithing business. Good luck to him, I say, for he's not forsaken his roots like that other one.'

'Come on now, dad,' Alex said uneasily. 'It doesn't sound like Howel to forget his family, fair play.'

'*Chwarae teg*, indeed! That eldest son of mine doesn't know the meaning of the words "fair play",' Siona said angrily.

Nerys did not speak as she poured the tea, which ran amber into the cup with the flames of the fire reflecting through the liquid. But Alex could not help noticing that she was flushed and angry, her lips pursed together. He half-expected her to fly into a rage and berate his father, but she glanced away from Siona quickly as she handed him his cup and then disappeared upstairs.

'What's going on by here, dad?' Alex felt impelled to ask. His father shook his head and sank wearily back into his chair.

'It's that Howel. The bastard has got to Nerys – played on her sympathy, I don't doubt and got the girl to make a fool of herself.' He looked up. 'He's taken her to his bed, boy. Now I can't put it more plainly than that, can I?'

Alex could not see what all the fuss was about. After all, Nerys was a woman grown mature in years and she probably fell eagerly into the arms of a man like Howel.

But then he looked at Siona, who sat with shoulders slumped and head hanging low, and he understood. His father had hopes in that direction himself and who could blame him? He was a lusty man, some would say a handsome man . . . and come to think of it, marriage to Nerys would have been a good idea.

'Is he going to marry her?' Alex asked in a low voice, not wanting Nerys to hear. Siona looked up at him with derision in his eyes.

'Not a hope in hell!' he said. 'That poor girl doesn't know it yet, but there's talk about Howel courting this high-class lady – some kin of Sterling Richardson, I believe. More fitting to his station in life, see, boy? Too high and mighty for marrying the likes of Nerys Beynon – not that the poor girl realizes that.' He paused. 'Going to break her heart, is our Howel, but I'll be there to pick up the pieces, don't you worry!'

Alex sighed. 'This is a pretty kettle of fish, right enough.' He swallowed his tea and rose to his feet and Siona waved a hand at him.

'Do us a favour, boyo – take little Mona home to her mam's house. Don't like her walking on her own when the hour gets late. Mona!' he shouted and she came clattering down the stairs, her face flushed.

'I've finished tidying up the bedrooms. I'll start washing the linen tomorrow if it's a fine day.'

'Good girl,' Siona said absently. 'Alex is going to see you home, righto? You've done well today, Mona, and I'll not forget it when I give you your pay.'

'Only doing my job, Mr Llewelyn,' she replied, but she warmed to the praise and her smile was one of pleasure.

'Well then, dad, I'll be seeing you some time,' Alex said. 'I don't know when, mind. I'm that busy what with the round and now the shop, though I must say that Sarah works like a good 'un.'

'Aye, boyo, glad enough I am that you're doing well. Deserve it you do — and no airs and graces and forgetting yourself either!'

Alex opened the door for Mona and she stepped out into the evening air, pulling a woollen coat around her shoulders. She was a thin little thing, but her smile was friendly and he liked that.

'Your dad is in a bad mood these days,' she told him when she was seated beside him in the cart. 'At first I thought it was something I'd done, but then I realized it was nothing to do with me, thank the good lord.'

'You're a good girl, Mona,' Alex said. 'I'm sure dad appreciates you and there's no doubt Nerys blesses the day you came to the house to work, for you've taken a great load off her shoulders.'

He clucked to the horse and the animal moved along the roadway above the river unhurriedly, clip-clopping, the sounds crisp in the evening air. The sun was almost gone now, the breeze blowing in from the River Swan sharp and searching. He saw Mona draw her coat around her thin shoulders and felt pity for her.

'Cuddle up close to me, Mona, there's a good girl. We don't want you getting a chill now, do we?'

After a moment's hesitation, she tucked her arm through his and he felt the soft swell of her young

267

breast pressing against him. It was sweet and lovely and he had to remind himself that she was a young girl, innocent and untouched. Yet an unwonted passion flared through him, his muscles grew taut and sweat broke out on his brow. He felt that if he could have laid down with her in the cart and enjoyed her sweetness, somehow the act would bring him relief.

'What's wrong Alex?' Mona asked softly and the eyes looking up at him were knowing. 'Is there something you want of me?'

He looked down at her uncomprehendingly.'Mona, you're nothing but a child; you don't know what you're saying,' but he felt her arm grasp his more tightly.

'I'm as old as your wife Sarah, mind, and old enough to know what life is all about.' She tipped her face up to his and kissed his lips and he held her close to him for a long, sweet moment. Then he drew away.

'Come on, my girl, I'm taking you home,' he said swiftly, 'otherwise I'll not be responsible for my actions.'

'I think I've fallen in love with you,' Mona whispered. 'I used to watch you when you did the round with your brother; you always were the one I liked best. Hector was a fine boy, a handsome boy, but you were the most sensitive. If I could have had my pick, it would have been you any day!'

He felt warmed by her words and uplifted, for he had always fancied himself inferior to Hector, a paler version of his outgoing brother. He took her hand, grateful to her for raising his self-esteem.

When he helped her down from the cart outside the tall run-down house in the centre of the town, he allowed his hands to linger for a moment on her slim waist.

'Thank you, Mona,' he said softly. 'Perhaps we'll have a chance to talk again.' He would have let the matter rest there, but she held on to his arms.

'Will you come and take me out one day, just as a friend? I don't have many friends, Alex.'

She appeared so waif-like, so vulnerable and alone – afflictions with which he could readily identify. He smiled and kissed her cheek and spoke on an impulse: 'What if I take you to the Empire on Friday night, just as a treat; how would you like that?'

Her smile illuminated her face and Alex was surprised to see just how lovely she looked. It pleased him that he could be the cause of such happiness.

'Right, I'll pick you up at the end of Gomerian Place on Friday night then.' Feeling full of pride, as though he had done something very charitable, he climbed into the cart knowing that Mona watched him drive away.

Sarah was busy raking out the fire when he returned home and she glanced at him over her shoulders, her eyes merry as they rested on him.

'*Duw*, trust the fire to stay in good and strong just when I want to go to bed. It's always the same, isn't it? See how the coals glow even as I riddle them!'

'Here, let me.' Alex felt suddenly guilty, though he had done nothing that might be considered remotely wrong, he told himself firmly. On the other hand, he challenged himself, would he be man enough to tell Sarah of his plans for treating Mona to a night at the Empire?

'You've been a long time, love,' Sarah said. 'I've managed to keep a pot of tea hot on the hob, mind, if you want some.'

He shook his head. 'No thanks, *cariad*. I've had enough of tea at dad's house.' He swallowed. 'Got me to take Mona home into town, he did, crafty old man. Saved him a walk didn't it?'

Sarah was barely interested. 'Oh, and how is your dad? Did he mind that Tom and Will stayed over here a bit late, like?'

Alex sighed with relief. 'No, he didn't mind. Having

a grumble about our Howel, he was, and him always been dad's favourite son too.'

'What's Howel done wrong, then' Sarah asked, rubbing the dust from her fingers.

'Seems he's gone all toffee-nosed, to use dad's expression – bought himself a fancy house up on the hill with the toffs. Can't blame him really, mind; he's got to live up to his position now, just as in our way we have.' He forbore to mention his father's disgust concerning Nerys Beynon; best let sleeping dogs lie, he reckoned.

'Aye, you're right enough there, Alex.' Sarah came to him and wound her arms round his waist, leaning her head against his spine. 'Leave the old fire till the morning, the coals are mostly dead now.'

He turned and took her in his arms, kissing her mouth gently. He wanted to make love to his wife, to lay her down in their marriage bed and taste of her sweetness, yet there was no response in him to her caress.

He was ashamed, his earlier euphoria vanished as he put her away from him and went to the sink to wash his hands.

'Go on up to bed, you. I shan't be long.' He felt her hesitate and he became tense, begging her silently not to pursue the matter. She stood still where he had left her and waited for him to turn round.

'Is there some fault in me that you don't want me, Alex?' she asked, and her voice was hard with anger.

'It's not that,' he said desperately, wishing that he could explain. But how could he when he didn't know what was wrong himself?

Alex sunk into a chair with his hands over his eyes, his shoulders slumped. He was useless; he had a fine wife, a wonderful wife and yet he could not be a husband to her in the way they both wished.

He was aware that she left the room and heard the slap-slap of her slippers against the wooden stairs. He really must get them carpeted, he thought absently. Pushing himself upright, he stood looking out of the window into the darkness of his reflection. He thought he had buried the ghost of his brother, had imagined that in time everything would come right – so what was stopping him from loving Sarah now?

It was some time before he went up to bed and when he slid beneath the sheets, he knew that Sarah was wide awake in the darkness. Her back was turned to him, for which he was grateful, and when he closed his eyes it was against hot tears which burned against his lids.

CHAPTER TWENTY

The sun shone in through the window of the Ferry House, turning the coals of the fire into an ash-grey, outdoing the flames in brilliance. Motes of dust drifted like minute snowflakes trapped in a shaft of light, forever twisting and turning as though imbued with a life of their own. And Nerys sat in the drowsing silence, not seeing the summer day but miserably aware of the trouble she had brought upon herself.

It had taken days – no, weeks – to dawn on her. She allowed her hands to rest briefly on her stomach and her entire being seemed to ache with pain. How could she even begin to come to terms with the fact that she was carrying Howel's child.

Their brief love affair, if it could be honoured with such a name, had ended as suddenly as it had begun and she saw herself as nothing more than a foolish, betrayed woman. She sighed. It was an old story – that of a man taking advantage of a woman silly enough to trust him – and she had never even considered that she might fall for a baby.

She had been to see Mali Llewelyn, who worked with unmarried mothers at Tawe Lodge. Mali had been sympathetic, but her advice had been to tell the father, to allow him the opportunity to live up to his responsibilities. Nerys had not named her lover; she had held the secret of his identity to herself, not wanting to betray him, which in the circumstances was absurd.

But soon, she must make up her mind what she was

to do. Should she go to see Howel as Mali had advised, acquaint him with the fact that he was to be a father, or should she simply move right away from Sweyn's Eye?

'*Duw*, there's quiet it is, it's like a cemetery in by here!' Mona entered the kitchen, her hands dripping water. 'Nearly finished the washing now. Getting easier it is, mind, with only Siona and Ceri and the two small boys to wash for.' She seated herself at the table and rubbed her hands in her apron. 'Do your washing I would too, mind, if you'd let me.'

'I know,' Nerys smiled, 'but the least I can do to help is to wash my own things; grateful I am to have you here at all.'

Mona stared at her in silence for a moment.'What's wrong, Nerys? Something is troubling you; I can see it in your eyes, mind.'

Nerys shook her head, aware that her colour was rising. She would not insult Mona's intelligence by lying, yet how could she reveal her awful secret to anyone?

'It's nothing you could help with, Mona,' she said quickly. 'It's just a problem I must sort out on my own.'

Mona sighed. 'It's all right. I've guessed what it is by the look of you – there's a babba on the way, isn't there?'

Nerys felt her heart contract in fear. If Mona, who was nothing more than a child, could see her condition surely it must be obvious to everyone? She bit her lip and stared down at her hands, unable to reply for the sound of buzzing that was ringing in her ears. A blackness seemed to be descending upon her and she tried to lean back in her chair for support, but the world was tipping and tilting around her and the blackness would not be resisted.

When she opened her eyes, Siona and Mona were both bending over her. 'There, there, girl. You'll be all right in a minute,' Siona smiled in kindly reassurance. 'My Emily used to have fainting spells when she was in a delicate condition, so I know it's nothing to worry about.'

Nerys looked towards Mona, who inclined her head slightly. 'Had to tell him, I did – he was all for going for the doctor, see. Cat would have been out of the bag good an proper then, and it's all best kept in the family, isn't it?'

Nerys struggled to sit up and quickly, Mona fetched her a glass of water. 'Drink this. It will clear your head a bit and you'll soon be feeling as chirpy as a spring chicken.'

Tears came unbidden to Nerys's eyes. Everyone should be condemning her for a harlot, or at least for an unprincipled fool, but all she was receiving was kindness from people who were not even family.

Siona sat opposite her, his big hands reaching out to take hers. 'You must go to him,' he said grimly. 'Let our Howel know about the babba, it's only right he should be told.' He leaned forward urgently. 'He *must* know – you can surely see that, girl; give him his chance to put things right.'

Nerys nodded slowly. This was what she had wanted – other people to make her decisions – for her own mind was too full of confusion to make a sensible judgement.

'All right, I'll go up to see him this evening and tell him what's happened, see what he has to say.' Even as she spoke, her hands were trembling with fear. How could she ever look Howel in the face again?

'Righto, now it's bed with you for the rest of the day and me and the boys will see to ourselves. You'll stay for a while, won't you, Mona? Help out like with the cooking until everything is back to normal?'

Nerys got to her feet quickly. 'I'm not going to any bed, Siona. I'm not sick or anything like that. In any case, Ceri is bringing his girl to tea with us, remember?

I've got a lot of preparation still to make?' She sighed. 'And to tell the truth, I don't want to lie there awake, staring at the ceiling and wondering what's going to happen to me.'

In sudden despair, she put her hand to her face. 'It'll be the workhouse for me – up on Mount Pleasant with my hair cut in a basin crop and me wrapped in a checked pinnie, being stared at through the railings as if I was an animal in a zoo!'

'Don't be so soft, girl. Our Howel may be all sorts of things, but he'll not shirk his duty. I'll guarantee that.'

The words brought Nerys little comfort, for she did not want Howel to think of her as a duty. But Siona was simply being kind and she smiled gratefully at him. Not only was he a giant of a man with the strength of a mule, but he was also a man of fine sensibilities.

She reached out and took his hand and when his fingers curled warmly round hers, offering her support and reassurance, somehow she no longer felt so alone and afraid.

'Now then,' Mona said, putting her hands on her slim hips. 'What do you want me to do when I've finished the washing, for I mean to stay and help you out for the rest of the day.' She smiled wickedly. 'Curious I am, mind, to meet Katie Murphy. I've heard so much about her, quite a one for the men so I understand.'

Siona looked at her hard and Mona blushed. 'Well, only repeating what other folks say, I am. It seems Katie had a fine young lover who died. Then she got married, but lost her husband and the baby she was expecting. So folks say she's a jinx, unlucky in love, she is, see?'

'Gossips are usually miserable ill-informed folk, so don't ever go repeating what they say or you might end up being classed the same as them,' Siona said reasonably.

'Sorry.' Mona was not at all offended. 'But I'm still curious, for all that.' She hurried out of the kitchen before Siona could speak again and with a wry smile, he rose to his feet.

'I'd best get back to the boat. I bet there's a gaggle of customers waiting to be sculled over to the Hafod bank.' He leaned over Nerys, his eyes anxious. 'Now, don't you go worrying yourself. Everything will work out fine and your babba will be born with the Llewelyn name, that's a promise. Now, is there anything I can do for you before I go?'

Nerys touched his cheek briefly. 'There's good you are to me, Siona, and I don't deserve it.' She paused and smiled at him a little anxiously. 'You could fetch the griddle from the pantry for me and put it on the hob to warm. I'm going to make some Welsh cakes for tea.'

'Aye, I'll do that, *merchi*, for I don't want you to go lifting anything heavy, mind – not in your condition.' He manhandled the griddle from the pantry, lifting it with ease and placing it on the hob. 'Now don't go making too much of a fuss. It's rest you need, not extra work.'

He left the room then and when she was alone in the kitchen, Nerys listened to the silence, wondering what she would say to Howel if ever she plucked up the courage to go to see him. How could you begin a conversation that was bound to be a bombshell to any man? She tried to rehearse the words, but they would not come. Yet she knew Siona was right enough, Howel must be told the truth.

Nerys rose from her chair and moved towards the pantry. She must get on with the baking, otherwise there would be nothing to offer Katie Murphy for her tea. It was important that the visit be a success and Nerys intended to make every effort to please.

She placed a bag of flour on the table and set some currants and raisins in a bowl to be washed. Then she took equal portions of lard and butter, rubbing the flour and fat through her fingers with the skill born of practice. She added the fruit and a little sugar and spice and worked the mixture into a dough-like consistency before cutting out round shapes with an upturned cup.

It was difficult manoeuvring the heavy cast-iron griddle on to the fire, for it had become hot from resting on the hob. Nerys felt perspiration break out on her forehead as she sent a knob of butter spinning across the surface of the griddle.

The round flat cakes quickly cooked and browned, and the kitchen became filled with the spicy, mouth-watering smell of them. She worked swiftly, for the griddle would cool once the fire burned low beneath it.

At last, the final batch of flat round shapes was swollen, browned and cooked. Nerys grasped the handle of the griddle with a cloth and eased it back on the hob. Sinking into a chair, she looked with satisfaction at the cakes cooling in the breeze from the open door.

But there was no time to sit around, for there was still a lot of baking to be done. She built up the fire, placing the coals against the side of the oven, knowing instinctively how to bring up the correct temperature for cooking the meat and potato pasties which would sit well with the fresh green lettuce from the garden.

She was pleased to be busy, for while her hands worked over the pastry and her mind was occupied with her task, at least for a time she could forget the coming ordeal of breaking the news of the baby to Howel.

By teatime, Nerys had the entire household organized. She had insisted that Tom and Will wear their Sunday shirts and good trousers.

'But Nerys,' Will protested, 'it's too hot to wear flannel on a day like this. See how the sun still shines over the river, even though it is teatime?'

'I can't help that,' Nerys replied, unperturbed. 'We are all going to look our best when Ceri brings his lady friend home.'

Even Siona had conceded to the importance of the occasion by wearing a stiff collar and tie. '*Duw*, there's young you look, Siona,' she said, smiling, and the glint in his green eyes told her he was well-pleased.

Ceri brought Katie to the Ferry House right on time and the kitchen was immediately filled with the Irish girl's presence. She was beautiful with her hair swinging red-gold around her pale face and her large, clear eyes looked into Nerys's with complete candour.

'Sure, 'tis a banquet you've prepared for us!' she said warmly. 'Look, Ceri, see those lovely pasties and just smell the spice in the Welsh cakes. I couldn't ask for better if I was royalty. 'Tis sorry I am that I've not visited you all before this.'

Nerys felt her colour rising with pleasure at the warmth of Katie's praise. She had worked hard and it was a good feeling to be so appreciated.

'Sit down, then, and I'll make the tea,' she said quickly, smoothing down the large square collar of her dress with hands that trembled with nervousness. 'And if I were you, I'd reserve judgement on the food until you've tasted it!'

Katie was an easy guest to please and soon the kitchen bubbled with laughter and conversation. Ceri was a lucky man indeed, Nerys thought, noticing how he could not take his eyes from Katie's animated face. And yet in Katie herself, she sensed an air of reserve towards Ceri, as though she had not quite made up her mind if she loved him or not. Perhaps this was the reason why she had not come calling often at the Ferry House.

'Sure, 'tis strange we've not got to know each other before this,' Katie said. As she leaned over to talk conversationally with Nerys, it was as if she had read something of her thoughts. 'Our paths must have crossed, though, for didn't you work for Mary Sutton at one time?'

Nerys nodded. 'I looked after Stephan right up until Mary and her husband took the little boy to America.'

'Ah, but I didn't see very much of Mary in the last months before she went away,' Katie said, and Nerys thought she detected a note of sadness in the Irish girl's voice.

'Well, she was very wrapped up in her boy,' Nerys said gently. 'Stephan's eyes were bad and Mary was frantic, looking every which way for a cure for him. A hard time of it, Mary had, until Mr Sutton came back to her.'

Nerys picked up a plate of Welsh cakes and handed it to Katie, feeling as though she might have said too much. Perhaps the Irish girl did not know that Brandon Sutton and Mary had been estranged for some time.

'Sure, and aren't you a real good cook, then?' Katie said in appreciation. 'I should think I'm lucky that Ceri didn't fall for you!'

There was a fat chance of that, Nerys thought wryly. Ceri had eyes for no one but Katie and it was obvious that he adored her. A shiver ran through her – if only Howel would look at her that way, then all her problems would be solved. She swallowed hard, wondering if she should make her excuses and leave now, for she ought to be making her way up to the western slopes of the hill, to where Howel lived in his posh new house.

'And what about you? Sure you must have all the men falling over themselves, a pretty girl like you!' Katie said warmly. 'There's a sort of bloom about you – could it be you've got an admirer somewhere in the background?'

Nerys sighed. 'No such luck!' She rose from her chair and smiled her apologies. 'Excuse me but I have to go out. I'm so sorry.'

'And you say you haven't a follower – what fibs!' Katie said with a smile in her eyes. It was easier to allow her to believe what she would than to argue, Nerys reasoned, glancing at Siona as he rose to his feet.

'Well now, I've got to go and change into my working clothes and get back on the boat,' he said easily. 'Big Eddie's missis will give him hell if he doesn't get home soon! In any case, it's only tactful to leave you pair of lovebirds alone for a while, isn't it? Come on, Tom and Will; you can come out with me to the boat – but only for an hour, mind, then it's bed for you.'

Nerys pulled on her long knitted jacket, for the sunlight was fading and the air on the riverside was growing cool. As she stood uncertainly near the door, wondering how to make her departure without appearing too abrupt, Katie rose to her feet and gave her a quick hug.

'Thanks for all your trouble. You've given me a lovely welcome and sure 'tis much appreciated. Now say you'll come up and visit me soon? I'm still living with me mammy, but only until the wedding, then I'll have a place of me own and 'tis lonely I'll be – I'll need a friend.'

'I'll come,' Nerys said quickly. 'Don't you worry about that!' She needed a friend too, if only Katie knew it, she thought wryly.

Outside, she paused for a moment listening to the sounds of the river, the fussy tugs hooting as they pushed upstream, the calling of the men from a fishing boat out in the wash of the water. It had all grown so familiar to her. The Ferry House had become her home and the Llewelyns her family, but now perhaps it would all be changed.

She moved upwards along the shingle path towards the roadway, deciding she would walk down to the town and catch a tram up the gently sloping hill which rose mistily in the twilight. The air was cool, the scent of the river tangy and yet fresh with salt.

Nerys wrapped her jacket around her still slim figure, wondering when she would start to show. In spite of herself, a flame of excitement flared through her. She, Nerys Beynon, was going to have a child. It simply wasn't believable. And yet if the truth came out and she not married, she would be daubed a flossie, a fallen woman, and guilt burned within her at the terrible thought.

As she walked, she tried to imagine the forthcoming meeting with Howel. Would he shout and rave in anger or just reject her utterly, she wondered. But perhaps, just perhaps, he might take her in his arms, tell her he loved her and wanted her and that only the pressures of his business had kept him away from her.

She ached with love for him, wanting him to be with her, to talk to her, to look into her eyes. She was lonely for him.

The heaving swaying tram came towards her in the half-light and she blinked rapidly, trying to clear her head of its clutter of thoughts. Expect nothing, she told herself firmly. Ask nothing, simply tell him the truth and let Howel take the initiative.

As she settled herself in the hard, slatted seat, she was feeling the tension mount within her. Panic seized her – she must go back, run to the safety of the Ferry House and hide away from everyone.

For a moment, she considered getting off at the next stop, but then she clenched her hands together in her lap, telling herself not to be a silly, hysterical fool.

She glanced out of the window, seeing that the streets of the town were being left behind and the buildings were less numerous. Big, graceful old houses sat in leafy grounds, with long driveways leading back from the road.

Siona had given her directions very carefully, even drawing a sketch of the roadway leading to Howel's house. Nerys fumbled in the pocket of her jacket and her fingers encountered the crackling paper. She gripped it as though it was a talisman, a good-luck charm that would keep her from ill.

When she left the tram, she stood for a long while staring around her, feeling completely out of her depth. She was at the end of a long curving avenue, where the houses stared outwards to the sea with blank faces in the evening light. As she walked uneasily along beneath the pools of light from the streetlamps, everything around her seemed dead and silent except for the distant eerie howling of a dog.

She wished fervently that she had not come here and her courage failed her as she stood outside the elegant house. It was a large building compared with the Ferry House, with big windows lit warmly from within, so that Nerys felt an intruder – on the outside, lost and alone.

When finally she took a deep breath and walked up the pathway towards the door, she was trembling so much she thought she would never have the strength to reach out and ring the bell. She stood shivering, drawing her woollen jacket closer, wishing herself anywhere but on Howel's doorstep.

An old woman in a white apron and cap opened the door and stared Nerys up and down in open-mouthed surprise. 'Nerys Beynon, as I live and breathe!'

'Greenie!' Nerys said in wonder. 'You still working then? It's about time you hung up your cap and apron, now, isn't it?'

'Well, Nerys Beynon, less of your lip! What are you doing up by here, then? *Duw*, don't bother to answer a nosey old woman – come on in and let me have a decent look at you.'

Nerys found herself drawn into the warmth of the hallway that smelled of lavender polish and freshly cut roses.

'What are you doing to earn a living now that

Mary's gone to America, then?' Greenie asked, holding Nerys at arm's length, her head tilted on one side, her eyes narrowed as she tried to see better.

'I'm working at the Ferry House down by the river,' Nerys said breathlessly. 'Sort of housekeeper, I am, for Siona Llewelyn and his children.'

'Ah, that's master Howel's father, isn't it. So that's what brings you up here, then?' But she didn't wait for a reply and Nerys breathed a sigh of relief; she hadn't wanted to lie to Greenie and now there was no need.

'Well, come on into the kitchen and have a little sup of tea with me for old times' sake, is it?'

Nerys shook her head. 'No, really, Greenie I can't. I have to get back and put the boys up to bed. Another time, though.'

'Ah well,' Greenie sighed, 'I suppose you're anxious to get off back into town and I don't blame you, mind — no good being out at night alone, not safe now it isn't. Better come into the study and I'll fetch Master Howel to you. Got company he has, see, but wait you, he won't be long I'm sure.'

The study was mellow, an old room with the walls lined with books. It was a good room, where Howel probably worked at his stocks and shares; a far cry from the scrubbed whitewood kitchen table at the Ferry House, where he used to work under the old oil-lamp that sent grotesque shadows crouching in corners like beasts about to pounce.

One minute she was alone with her thoughts and the next Howel was standing beside her. His hair sprang crisply back from his face and his deep eyes were unreadable as he inclined his head in greeting.

'Nerys, is everything all right at home?' he asked quickly, concern evident in his tone.

'Oh, yes, everything is fine; nothing to worry about there.' She swallowed hard and looked down at her hands, searching desperately for a way to talk to him. He was so different, so aloof that it seemed incredible

283

that they had lain in each other's arms, kissed, caressed, become lovers.

'Well, then?' He glanced over his shoulder as a loud burst of laughter echoed across the hallway. 'My apologies if I seem impatient, but I have company, you see.'

'I shouldn't have come.' Nerys folded her jacket around her and would have left the room except that Howel was standing in her way.

'Then why did you?' He seemed genuinely puzzled as he thrust his hands into his pockets and stared at her as though perplexed.

'I wanted . . . needed to see you.' Why did the words sound so feeble? 'But now I'm sorry I bothered!'

'I'm sorry, too.' For a moment he was the old Howel as he put his hand on her shoulder and stared down at her with a glimmer of a smile in his eyes. 'Sorry that I'm not alone!' He moved away from her then and became brisk and businesslike.

'Well, Nerys, if you feel you've called at the wrong moment, please come again when it's more convenient for us to . . . enjoy each other's company. In the meantime, perhaps you would take a message back to my father for me?'

He raised his eyebrows and Nerys was unable to speak because her tongue had cleaved to the roof of the mouth with pure anger. He thought she had come here to make love with him – how *dare* he!

'I have something of an announcement to make,' he said, 'though I hope it won't make too much difference to the special relationship you and I share.'

It was as though some sixth sense told her what he was about to say and her mind was already rejecting it.

'Tell dad that I'm going to be married.' The words fell like stones into the room and Nerys felt the shock and the pain of her humiliation as though they were physical blows. She moved as though walking through sand towards the door that seemed a long way off.

'Darling, what on earth is keeping you?' The voice was English, well-modulated and filled with confidence. 'Oh, who is this?'

Howel put his arm around the girl's slim waist and hugged her. 'This is Nerys who works for my father, Jenny – nothing at all to do with you.' He kissed the tip of her nose and she laughed, pushing him away.

'Behave yourself, darling. Now what's delaying you – is it anything important?' Her frock swirled around her knees, her silk collar framed a charming face, she oozed culture and wealth and Nerys had no intention of trying to compete with her. From some inner depths she found her voice and her pride.

'Nothing important, not important at all,' she said with asperity. Afterwards she didn't remember leaving the house; all she knew was that she was walking in the darkness downhill to the Ferry House and sanctuary.

CHAPTER TWENTY-ONE

The premises where Ceri Llewelyn was to work his silver were undistinguished by any standards. The house was in Canal Street, near the skeleton of the old laundry buildings, and boasted nine rooms ranging through three floors.

'I'm disappointed,' Ceri said, staring round at the shabby peeling paintwork and the loose floorboards which would need to be replaced.

'Sure, and what did you expect then?' Katie asked, smiling. 'I think you've done very well, considering you don't have to pay Mr Sterling Richardson any rent on the house.'

'Yes, but there's so much to do before I can start up in business,' Ceri said slowly. 'I'll need to convert the outbuildings into a workshop for a start; then there'll be a great deal of renovating and decorating to be done in here before we can move in.' He rubbed his chin thoughtfully. 'I'm not sure how much money Mr Richardson intends to put into the business.'

Katie forced a smile, realizing that she was glad rather than sorry that establishing the business would take time. That would be a legitimate reason for putting off the marriage for a little while longer.

'Don't always be in so much of a rush, Ceri,' she chided gently. 'Let's take it one step at a time — now for sure, we've a lifetime ahead of us!'

Ceri put his arms around her shoulders and drew her close and Katie closed her eyes against the rush of guilt she felt. She did love Ceri, she told herself firmly, and it was unfair to vacillate between elation and painful fear at the prospect of being married to him.

He took her hand. 'Let's look at the rest of the house, *cariad*. I suppose I'm being foolish expecting it all to fall into my lap.'

The kitchen at the rear of the long building was clean and fairly bright, with tiled walls and a huge sink alongside an iron range. Katie glanced at Ceri, her hands on her hips.

'Sure, isn't this very respectable then? Better than me mammy's kitchen in Market Street! We'll be able to do a lot with this old place, given time. A few rag mats to take the chill from the floor and a good fire in the range and it will be a most cheerful place, you'll see.'

'Aye, granted it's not too bad,' Ceri agreed, turning on the tap and watching the water gush forth as though mesmerized by it. 'I suppose I wanted us to be together right now, which is why I'm disappointed that there's so much work to be done.'

Katie rested her hand on his shoulder. 'But Ceri, my love, look at the fun we'll have putting up paint and wallpaper and see how respectable we'll be – living in the same street as Doctor Soames, not to mention Mrs Benson the midwife!' She laughed wickedly. 'Come in mighty useful, too, if you're half the man your daddy is.'

He caught her in his arms and when his mouth came down on hers she felt his love, his passion and his need to possess her as he crushed her to him. She clung to him for a moment, allowing sensation to replace reason. In this at least – the forging of the bonds of the flesh – she was in tune with Ceri, but was that enough to sustain a lifetime of marriage?

'Come on,' she said, wriggling from his arms. 'A cold kitchen is no place to get amorous now, is it? Sure 'tis sorry I spoke, so I am.'

She hurried from the room and up the stairs,

287

noticing the carpet had faded into indistinctness. The master bedroom was at the front of the house, a large room furnished with a huge bed that stood beside an ornate fire-grate. Katie moved to the window and stared down at the winding ribbon of the canal; it was yellow in the sunlight, with fronds of weeds twisting and turning in the water.

'Not much needed in by here,' Ceri said. 'Just a bit of a spring-clean, a fire to air the place and fresh bedding, then the bridal suite will be ready for us!'

From behind, he put his arms around her and hugged her close, his hand straying to her breast. His mouth was warm on the back of her neck and she leaned against him, wishing that he would not pressure her into marriage, that he would just be content for now with what they already shared.

When he turned her round and kissed her mouth she responded with passion. She was a woman left alone too long, hungry for contact, needing the closeness that could only come between a man and a woman . . . but was this love?

Ceri's breathing became more ragged. He took her in his arms, lifted her on to the bed and cradled her.

'I love you so much, Katie, that it's like a fire within me,' he said softly. She wound her arms around his neck and held him tightly, closing her eyes against the sudden tears of gratitude which burned her lids. She was a miserable wretch – questioning, always questioning. Why could she not enjoy Ceri's obvious adoration of her? Had she grown too cold, too hurt ever to feel again?

Suddenly, the dust from the thick bed-sheets drifted over her and Katie sneezed violently. She sat up, pushing Ceri away as she sneezed again. Laughing, she rose to her feet and leaned against the mantelpiece.

'Sorry to spoil such a romantic moment, but sure I can't help it! Come on, let's get out of here before I sneeze my head off.'

In the street, Ceri put his arm through hers and hugged her close. 'I've heard of women having head-aches and such, but never a sneezing fit!' His eyes were bright with laughter as they looked into hers and a warmth of feeling for him swept over her.

'Has anyone ever told you what a fine man you are, Ceri Llewelyn?' she said, fumbling in her bag for a handkerchief.

'Aye, more than one lively young lady has fallen for my charms, don't you worry. Honoured you are that I picked you out, mind.'

'Oh, don't go getting too swollen-headed, my bucko, for I'll soon bring you down a peg or two when we're man and wife.' She could have bitten off her tongue as soon as the words were spoken, for it gave him the opening that he needed.

'Now, that's the point. When are we going to name the day, Katie, for I can't wait much longer?' He stopped walking and rested his hands on her shoulders, gently putting a stray wisp of red-gold hair into place. 'Let's go to your priest, tell him a date and to hell with the house being ready!'

Katie put her finger on his lips. 'Don't blaspheme in the same breath as you talk about the holy father, Ceri; 'tis not seemly.'

'Don't avoid the issue,' Ceri said soberly. 'Some-times I get the feeling you don't want to be married at all!'

'Of course I want to be married,' Katie protested. 'I want a husband and a home and children like all women do, but there's no need to rush; I keep telling you that.' She leaned against him with her head on his shoulder, regardless of the people passing them by. 'Look, why don't we just get the house in order and start up the business and then talk about fixing a date?'

He sighed heavily. 'All right, Katie, if that's what you want. Come on, let's go down into town – have tea in the Mackworth and then go on to the Empire – how does that sound?'

'Just fine,' Katie smiled in relief at her easy victory. 'Sounds like a wonderful outing, a holiday almost before we get down to the hard work of cleaning up the house. We'll start on that tomorrow, shall we? You light the fire in the range and I'll do some scrubbing. Perhaps my mammy will come and help as well – the more the merrier, right?'

'Right, but first thing tomorrow I must go into work, see Mr Richardson about what sort of money he intends to put at my disposal. It's one thing to have the buildings, but it's capital I need.'

'Sure, and aren't you talking like a proper business gentleman already, then?' Katie smiled. 'Come on, don't let's stand here any longer, people are beginning to stare.'

They walked down past the canal with its sullen yellowish face and past the Malliphant where the steam engines puffed and wheezed on the track leading to strange parts of the country. Katie realized suddenly that all she knew was Sweyn's Eye – and only a small part of it at that.

Green Hill was the side of the town where the Irish people had come to live, brought from Ireland as ballast years ago in the coal ships. And yet she still had the Irish tongue for she had grown up close to home, guarded by her mammy and daddy and taken to St Joseph's Church where she met other Irish folk.

It was true that she had visited France for a brief time, but she remembered that part of her life now through a haze of pain and sorrow. It was there that her husband Mark had gone to seek for work, where he had almost been lost to her in the arms of another woman.

Then the decision had been made for Mark and Katie to make their way back home across the Channel in order to repair the damage to their marriage. They had been in sight of the Welsh coast when the storm came, hurling huge waves against the small French barque, breaking the masts like matchwood and snatching passengers and rescuers to a grave beneath the pounding seas.

Katie could still recall the sight of her husband, crawling along the line thrown out by the rescue boat only to be dashed by an angry sea, dragged beneath the water and drowned.

'You've gone very quiet,' Ceri said softly. 'Far away are you, *cariad*?' His hand caressed her arm tenderly, as though he sensed her unhappiness. 'Come on, a penny for them!'

Katie could not lie, there was no point. 'For some reason I was remembering Mark and how he died in the sea,' she said shivering. 'Sure 'tis foolish of me to hark back to the past, for it only gives me pain.'

Ceri took her in his arms. 'And I want to take that pain away for good,' he said firmly. 'Oh, I've seen it in your eyes when I catch you unawares and I hurt for you, my lovely girl. It's natural enough to grieve for lost loved ones; don't I know that, with mam taken by the river and the baby with her, and then our Hector . . . but remembering can bring bitterness, so try to forget now, won't you?'

'Yes, I'll try. Ceri, you're such a kind person, but then I've told you that before.'

She moved away from him and caught his hand. 'Now lets stop all this maudlin nonsense and have some strawberries and cream down at the Mackworth!' She smiled up at him. 'And I'll want a box of chocolates to take into the Empire with me, sure enough!'

'You're a demanding woman, mind, and bossy too. I can see I'll have to take you in hand when we're married.'

His words rang in Katie's ears even as he led the way through the doors of the Mackworth Hotel in the

Stryd Fawr, and her heart was heavy with doubt. How could she ever give her love again when she was so afraid of having it snatched away from her?

She had heard the talk that she was a jinx on the men in her life and perhaps it was true, for long ago her lover Will Owen had died violently, a young man who had not yet matured and learned sense.

But she would not allow herself to dwell on the past. She must look now to the future, her future and Ceri's, and this time she would make sure that everything worked out happily.

*   *   *

The morning sun sent a warm glow into the room as Ceri opened his eyes and stared around him. A shaft of light fell over the bed where his young brothers lay still sleeping, Tom with his arm protectively around Will's shoulder.

Ceri put his arms behind his head and stared up at the whitewashed ceiling. Such a lot had changed in the Ferry House over the past year. Eddie married; Alex taking on a business and his dead brother's woman at the tender age of seventeen; Howel moved out to a posh new house on the hill and mam and the baby gone. Nothing remained the same. Life was like the River Swan which flowed outside the house, moving and turning ceaselessly and inexplicably.

From downstairs in the kitchen he heard the sounds of movements, where Nerys was making up the fire in order to cook the breakfast. He smiled; she was a *merchi da*, a good girl, all right.

She kept the house spotlessly clean and worked for the family from morning to night with little enough reward. And he could talk to Nerys; often they had spent an hour in the late nights talking together, though not recently he realized. And Ceri had noticed in Nerys now a quietness, a feeling of waiting as though she did not know what to do with herself. Perhaps he should get up from bed and talk to her, ask her what was on her mind, for he did not like to think of her being troubled.

Dressing quietly, he made his way downstairs on bare feet, his boots in his hand. He lifted the latch of the door that led from the stairs into the kitchen and smiled as Nerys turned a flushed face to him.

'*Bore da*,' he said and sat himself at the table, pulling on his boots.

'Good morning to you, Ceri. I didn't expect anyone to be up at this early hour.' She smiled, but there were shadows beneath her eyes and lines of strain around her mouth.

'Come on, sit by here with me and have a quiet cup of tea before you start your work, there's a good girl.'

She fetched the teapot to the table and placed it on the china stand, covering it with a knitted cosy.

'Well, what's this then? Going to preach me a sermon, are you?' There was a touch of bitterness in her voice and Ceri looked at her in surprise.

'Now that's not fair, is it? When have you ever known me to preach?' He held out his hand and covered her restless fingers. 'Out with it, what's wrong?'

She stared at him with a guarded expression in her eyes. 'You don't know?' she asked in surprise. 'I thought you above all people would have guessed what ailed me; you're usually so perceptive, Ceri.'

'Aye, but then I've been wrapped up in my own business, *cariad*; too wrapped up in it, I suppose.'

Nerys stared down at their entwined hands. 'I'm going to have a baby, Ceri.' The words fell into the silence, softly spoken but with a hint of fear behind them.

'Good God in heaven!' Ceri exclaimed, feeling shock and anger. Nerys was so gentle, so innocent even though she was older than he, but some bastard had taken advantage of her. 'I'll kill the swine, who is he?' he demanded, but she shook her head.

'I don't want to tell you about that, it would do no good. All I know is that he doesn't want me and I've too much pride to ask for anything.' She looked at him anxiously. 'But I don't want to be a burden to your family, that's what worries me. I wouldn't want to be a nuisance but there's nowhere else for me except perhaps Tawe Lodge.'

'That's foolish talk. Not one of us would see you go to the workhouse; what do you think we are, girl?' He smiled warmly. 'Siona has his faults, but my dad is a good man and he wouldn't let you be put into an institution, don't you worry! And anyway, what's another babba around the place? The Ferry House has always rung with the sound of children's voices.' He paused. 'Have you spoken to dad about all this?'

Nerys sighed. She took a long time replying and it was as though she was searching for something to say.

'Siona's a good man. He wouldn't throw me out on the streets, I know that, but I don't want to add to his burdens. He's enough to do keeping the home going without me contributing to his worries.'

'Look, we'll all chip in and help. I'm not well off, but I've earned a bit of money from the silver I pinched from the White Rock and that's yours, I insist.'

He went to the old stone outhouse and pulled out a loose brick, taking from the cavity behind a bundle of crisp white pound notes. He held the money for a long moment, knowing he was giving up a new stair carpet and the possibility of new furniture, but just now Nerys's need was greater than his own.

She was weeping when he returned to the kitchen and he put his arm around her shoulder comfortingly. 'Now you're not to worry. We'll look after you and none of us will let you suffer alone. But I wish you'd tell me who the father is – then I'd give him the greatest hiding of his life!'

Anger burned in him. How could a man – any man – lie with a woman as sweet as Nerys and then cast her aside when she was in trouble? He must be worse than the lowest animal.

Nerys clung to his hand. 'It would do no good to tell you his name. Anyway, the blame is mine too, remember. I was not forced, I went to him willingly.'

From upstairs came the scampering of feet against the boards and quickly Nerys dried her eyes on her apron. She smiled weakly at Ceri and he patted her shoulder.

'How about if I make the breakfast? I'm not working now – only got to call over to the White Rock on a bit of business – so it won't hurt me to cook some bacon and eggs.'

Nerys looked up at him wistfully. 'Would you, Ceri? The smell of cooking turns me these mornings; I suppose that's all part of having a baby, is it?'

'Aye, course it is. I remember well my mam running to the privy with her hand to her mouth.' He smiled. 'Nasty it is, but all perfectly normal.'

The two young boys burst into the room fighting and squabbling, and Ceri hushed them with a stern word of warning.

'Now boys, Nerys isn't feeling well this morning, so let's have some quiet, shall we?'

Will came to stand before Nerys, his eyes wide as he stared into her face. 'Are you going to have a babba like our mam?' he asked in a small voice.

Ceri cuffed him lightly around the ear with an apologetic glance at Nerys. 'That's the only sort of sickness they understand, see? Now mind your business, you two, and get your hands washed so that you can sit down to breakfast like civilized beings instead of hooligans!'

Will hurried over to the sink, but Tom bit his lip anxiously. 'You're not going to have a babba and then die like mam, are you?' His voice was grave, his expression showing too much adult worry for his young face. Ceri watched as Nerys held the boy close for a moment.

'Of course I'm not going to die. I'm young, mind, and as strong as a horse. Why should I think of dying?'

A look of relief washed over Tom's face. 'I don't want no more people to die and leave me,' he said in a low voice.

'Come, sit by here and have this bacon and eggs before it goes cold,' Ceri said heartily. He should have been giving his brothers more of his time, he chided himself. Guilt seared him as he realized that the only permanent person in the young boys' lives was Nerys. Dad was always out on the boat, coming in at all hours, and as for himself he had been so preoccupied with his own life that he had spared little thought for his younger brothers.

'How would you like to come down to the White Rock with me after you've eaten?' he asked as he seated himself at the table. 'Only got to see the boss for a minute and that won't take long. Perhaps we could go to Victoria Park afterwards.' He winked at Nerys. 'That's if you'll both behave like angels for Nerys when I bring you home, mind.'

He saw her gratitude and it made him ashamed. People asked so little – just a bit of kindness, that's all.

'Rest, you. Put your feet up and forget the housework. It will be here after you – isn't that what the old folk tell us?'

'Perhaps I'll go back to bed for an hour,' Nerys said softly. 'I feel as if I could sleep the clock around. There's ham and veal pie I can give the boys for tea, and I've got a pot of potatoes scrubbed ready to boil up. I suppose everything else can wait?'

'*Duw*, of course everything else can wait. Go on, off upstairs with you while I'm here to see you don't get caught up in some chore or other. And Nerys, if you ever want to talk – I've got a broad shoulder, mind.'

She stood up straight and he noticed that there was already a thickening in her waistline. Her stomach swelled gently beneath the apron but her face betrayed her condition most of all, for she was shadowed beneath the eyes and a little puffy the way his mam had been so often.

'Go on, away up those stairs and try to sleep. We'll be out for an hour or two, so you won't be disturbed.' He turned to his brothers, who were arguing over the cake of soap. 'And you two, if you're not ready in two minutes I'm going without you!'

As the door closed behind Nerys, Ceri shook back his hair, wondering again who it was could have taken advantage of her. She was normally a level-headed girl without any vanity, and he felt she must have fallen truly in love. What men could she possibly have come into contact with? She was always in the house. Suddenly the truth hit him and in spite of himself, he smiled.

'The old goat!' It must be, it had to be his father. Siona had fancied Nerys from the start, so he must have used his not inconsiderable wiles on her and she had fallen for him.

Of course, dad probably didn't know about Nerys's condition. If he did, he would do the honourable thing like a shot. And Nerys was probably afraid to tell him the truth because, as she'd said, she didn't want to add to his burdens. Perhaps it was up to him to drop the hint to dad – this was a point worth considering.

'Run up to the hut, Tom. See if dad's inside having a bite to eat,' Ceri said as he stood with his brothers on the edge of the river. 'Tell him I can't wait by here all day, I've got things to do.'

Tom made a wry face. 'Tell dad that and I'll have my backside slapped. You'll be lucky!'

He ran up the slope towards the hut where Siona was in the habit of brewing his tea when snatching a few minutes from work, and disappeared inside. Will kicked aimlessly at a stone, watching it fall into the river, sending ripples widening out in circles over the water.

His brothers were growing up into young men, Ceri thought with a pang of pain. How mam would have loved the serious, sober boys they had become.

'Can't a man have a bit of privacy then?' Siona came down the bank, his walk still that of a young man even though he must be well past his mid-forties. Ceri smiled. Well, the old man was still eager enough to take a young girl to his bed and fill her with child, all credit to him.

'Come on, you old fraud!' Ceri gripped his father's broad shoulder in an unusual display of affection. Strangely, since Howel had left the house relations between him and his father had been much warmer. 'I'm off to get my pay, man – can't hang around where money's concerned.'

Siona climbed aboard the boat and pushed off from the bank with the scull. 'Rush, rush, rush, that's all men think of today.'

'Not all, surely dad. Some men's thoughts turn lightly to love, so I hear.' He smiled. 'Getting a young girl in a certain condition too – only she's too afraid to speak of it. See my meaning, do you, dad?'

'If you're talking about Nerys, then I don't think it's any cause for humour, righto?' Siona said with a return to his usual offhand manner.

Ceri stared at his father, perplexed. 'You know about it, then? Well, I think you should know that she's very worried, dad. The girl's got serious problems and surely the answer is that you marry her?'

In silence, Siona sculled the boat towards the White Rock, his face set as though carved out of rock. Ceri sighed. 'With you, dad, I can't win,' he said bitterly. 'I don't know what it is I've ever done to you, but one thing I do know is that I can't get through to you.'

As the boat bumped the steps, Ceri saw surprise

298

alter the contours of his father's face and knew with a flash of triumph that he had caught him on the raw.

'Wait, boyo,' Siona said. 'You don't understand.' He shook his head and sank back in the seat. 'Go, you now — we can't say too much, for little pitchers have big ears. We'll talk tonight.'

'Come on, Tom and Will, don't dawdle,' Ceri said, ignoring Siona for the first time in his life. Whatever dad had to say, nothing could wipe away yet another rebuff and he had only been trying to help.

*　　*　　*

The heat in the foundry was intense. Kenny was skimming the molten lead and flames belched forth through the open doors of the furnace. Will drew back in fear, but Tom strode into the heart of the building, his eyes wide with curiosity.

'Keep back, boyo,' Kenny said as the stream of liquid lead ran from the furnace. '*Duw*, Ceri, tell them brothers of yours this is no toy we've got by here.'

'Tom, keep your distance,' Ceri ordered. 'We shouldn't even be in here so don't get too near anything, right?'

'Well, and when's the business man starting up then?' Kenny wiped the sweat from his eyes with a piece of mutton-cloth. 'And more important, when's the marriage taking place?'

'Hold your horses, Kenny,' Ceri smiled. 'The business will be starting up any day now. I've got the premises and they just need a bit of work. As for the marriage, well I don't want to go giving up my freedom too soon, now, do I?'

'Ha!' Kenny stood back from the heat. 'They all say that once they're getting a regular bit of loving, like!' He wagged his finger. 'And that's just when the little woman will put on the thumb-screws. She'll do anything to get you up the aisle, so don't say I haven't warned you.'

'Look out, Kenny!' Ceri said suddenly in alarm. 'The lead is overflowing the pot – shut the tap off, man!'

Kenny seemed to move slowly, even though there was grace and speed in his thin frame. The lead trickled on to the floor seemingly innocent, making a hissing pathway towards the shiny black of Tom's boots.

Ceri felt as though he was running through treacle, 'Get away from there, Tom! Get the hell away!'

The lead wound around the black boots, hissing through the leather like a hot knife through butter. Tom began to scream and Ceri snatched him up and ran with him to a pile of sacking. He threw him down, tearing . . . tugging at the laces, breaking them in the strength of his fear.

Tom continued to scream, tearing at what remained of the boots with frenzied hands. As Ceri slowly pulled the burned leather away, so the skin came with it; the smell was nauseating.

'Will,' Ceri said thickly, 'run and call the doctor, there's a good boy. And when you've done that, fetch dad right away.'

He cradled Tom to him helplessly, not knowing the right thing to do. It was Kenny who brought out clean muslin cloths and tied them loosely round the proud flesh that was the boy's feet.

'Jesus God!' Ceri exclaimed through clenched teeth. 'There's a curse on the Llewelyn family, for sure.'

He looked down at Tom who was silent now, his face white and shocked. 'I'll always look after you, don't you worry.'

Kenny crouched before them both, a pitying look on his face. 'You might well have to,' he whispered softly.

CHAPTER TWENTY-TWO

The late sun shone outside the windows of the Ferry House, a molten yellow glow that shot, sparkling, through the waters of the River Swan — light bouncing off the eddies of the waves diamond-like and dazzling.

Nerys stood near the upper window, listening to the soft breathing of the little boy in the bed behind her. Earlier that day Ceri had rushed into the house, his face chalk-white, his eyes anguished. Tom had been taken to the infirmary near the beach, burned by the molten lead which had flowed from the furnace in the White Rock. Now the boy was home, sleeping with the help of medicine administered by the doctor.

The door swung open downstairs and she heard Howel's voice raised in anger: 'The accident was caused by stupid carelessness on your part, Ceri. How could you be such a fool?'

Nerys hurried downstairs, anxious not to have Tom woken by the noise. Howel stood just inside the kitchen, his eyes hot with anger. Feeling pity for the guilt-ridden Ceri, Nerys stepped forward.

'Keep your voice down, Tom's asleep,' she said firmly, 'and you are not being fair. Ceri takes an interest in the boys, which is more than can be said of you.'

'Keep out of this,' Howel said tersely. 'It has nothing to do with you!'

'But it has,' Nerys said, leaning forward, anger growing within her. 'I love the boys and I it is who has to look after them.'

Howel didn't bother to answer her; he turned and

walked out of the house without another word. Nerys shrugged her shoulders and returned to Tom, tears constricting her throat.

*   *   *

Tom was beginning to mend slowly. His small feet were encased in bandages, his face sometimes twisted with pain, but he was a brave boy and never uttered a word of complaint. Indeed, it worried him that Ceri was using some of his savings to pay for the doctor and the medicines and dressings, knowing that this meant postponing his wedding to Katie Murphy.

Nerys was at her best nursing Tom, but the boy was always reluctant to trouble her. She opened the bedroom door early one morning to see him sitting up and looking much more rested, his colour normal.

'Can I have a drink of water, Nerys, please?' he asked diffidently.

'There's a soft thing to ask. You can have anything you want, my lovely.'

'But I don't want you running up and down stairs for me,' he said, his eyes flickering over her. His meaning was clear and Nerys felt her colour rise, wondering how long it would be before everyone knew of her condition.

'Don't worry about me, boyo. I'm as strong as a horse; I can fetch and carry all day and not feel tired.'

'Aye,' Tom spoke in the tones of an old man. 'That's exactly what my mam used to say.'

In the kitchen, Siona was putting out the breakfast of boiled eggs and toast, while young Will sat at the table, chin resting on his hands, waiting patiently for his food. He should have been at school, but he had begged to stay home and keep Tom company now that he was feeling a little better.

'Can I take our Tom's egg up to him, dad?' Will

asked, his eyes wide and anxious. Nerys felt like hugging the boy; his concern was so touching.

'Aye, I suppose so,' Siona agreed in his slow way. 'Why don't the both of you have breakfast together up in the bedroom – give me and Nerys a bit of peace?'

Will brightened visibly. 'Righto,' he said in an exact imitation of the way his father spoke.

Nerys smiled. 'Go on, you, I'll bring the food up on a tray – safer that way. I don't fancy cleaning up bits of toast from the stairs, mind!'

'I'll carry the tray,' Siona said at once. 'You sit down, I shan't be more than a few minutes.'

Nerys sat in the warmth of the kitchen and brushed back her hair impatiently. She felt slow and heavy in her movements and no longer could she run upstairs like a young girl. No wonder Emily Llewelyn had become sick and ill with the bearing of too many children . . . yet at least she had had the sanctity of a good marriage to protect her.

Siona returned and seated himself in the big carver chair. 'No need to worry any more, mind,' he said softly. 'It was our Ceri who gave me the idea; spoke to me, he did, just before the accident to our Tom. "Marry the girl", he said. "That's the answer to her problems".'

He ate in silence for a moment and then put down his knife. 'I realized afterwards that he thought the baby was mine; that's what most folks will think, so why not let them?'

Nerys felt a dart of fear and pain and she rose to her feet, unable to speak. She could only back away from Siona, shaking her head. Almost without seeing, she pulled on her cardigan, took up her bag and hurried from the house.

The fresh air fanned her hot cheeks and she realized that she was crying as she made her way blindly towards the river and stood listening to the soft lap of the water against the steps. Marry Siona, take the

Llewelyn name – was that the answer? She heard footsteps behind her and then gentle hands rested on her shoulders.

'I'll give you and the baby all the love in the world, *cariad*. And the boys, what would they do without you? We need you, Nerys, and that's the truth.'

Nerys rubbed her hand over her eyes. 'I can't think clearly, Siona. So much has happened so quickly and I'm confused.'

'Well, there's nothing to worry about, my little love, except your unborn baby – and the sooner he has the name that's rightfully his, the better it will be.'

Nerys turned and looked up at Siona, realizing that they had become close during the past weeks as they cared for Tom together. Big Eddie had worked the boat so that Siona could stay at home and there had been harmony in the little house.

'All right, Siona – you arrange it quickly and privately. I don't want any fuss.'

Siona's eyes glowed. 'No sooner said than done, my girl. We'll go to the little chapel up on the hill, just you and me, and get it over quickly. I'll go and see to all the arrangements right now; you go back inside and rest, and that's an order!'

She stared at him for a long moment, doubt and fear mirrored in her eyes. He touched her cheek lightly. 'It will be all right; now do as you are told and go indoors.'

There was a dreaming silence in the kitchen. The sun shone in through the open doorway and the fire burned low in the grate for the sake of coolness. Nerys could not say that she was happy but at least she felt safe and she was content.

* * *

When Siona left the table a little later, he squared his big shoulders and made his way down to the ferry-boat.

'Take me across to the Hafod bank, boyo,' he said to

Eddie, holding on to his son's shoulder as he climbed into the boat. 'I've got some business on the other side of the water and it just won't wait.'

It was rare for Siona to take a tram, for his days were spent on the water; he loved the feel of the waves slapping the planking of his boat. He knew the river in all her moods; she had been both friend and enemy to him, yet he loved her just as he loved Nerys Beynon.

He sat on the swaying tram and stared out of the window, feeling imprisoned as though in a glass cocoon. The streets seemed to flash by unnaturally swiftly and he was relieved when he reached his destination.

Siona was surprised at the size of Howel's house and for a moment, his steps faltered as he stared up at the imposing front door. But he had come here to have his say, and have it he would. Lifting the brass knocker, he let it fall loudly into place.

The old woman who opened the door looked at him in surprise as he moved inside.

'I'm Siona Llewelyn,' he said kindly. 'I'm here to see my son.' The old woman bobbed a curtsey, but her eyes were narrowed and it was clear she resented his high-handedness. 'Go fetch him,' he said more sharply, 'or do I have to search the house for him?'

'No need of that, dad. Come into the sitting room and have a drink.' Howel appeared from behind double doors, holding them open. He was wearing a good suit and a fixed smile; the big boss man, but not in Siona's eyes – not any more.

'How are things at home?' Howel asked easily. 'Sorry I haven't been over to see you all, but I've been away in London for a few days up at the stock market. Good fun it was, too, and I've made quite a killing.'

'I haven't come here to make polite conversation,' Siona said stonily. 'I'll tell you right away that it

305

sticks in my craw that Ceri has had to be the one to pay all the bills for our Tom.' He held up his hand as Howel would have spoken.

'But that's not the main reason I'm here. The truth is that I don't want you near our house again.' He briefly paused for breath before continuing: 'I know what fool trick you played on Nerys, taking advantage of her innocence – and in my book, you're no better than a rat from the sewers.'

'Now hold your horses, dad,' Howel said, his anger rising, 'Nerys is no young child but a woman full-grown – and trouble ever since she put foot in the Ferry House. She was as eager as I was for a little adventure and I didn't promise her anything believe me.'

'Oh, aye, I believe you all right. You didn't promise a thing, you just let the poor girl think you cared for her. Well, this is the situation now – that she doesn't want to see you ever again, righto? So I'll just remind you to stay away from me and mine.'

'If that's what you want then, dad, so be it, but you're only proving my point. That girl is trouble, coming between us all, can't you see it?'

'It's you who can't see straight, boyo,' Siona cried angrily. 'You put all *this*' – he swung his arm in a wide arc to encompass the room – 'all this tomfoolery before real people and real feelings. Well, from now on you're no son of mine!'

When Siona left the house he was shaking with temper, but he had had his say and meant it. If his marriage to Nerys was to be a success, then the less either of them saw of Howel, the better.

It took him some minutes to cool down and when he stared around him, looking up at the blue cloudless sky and down at the glittering arc of the sea far below, he felt better. It did not come easy to cast out a son, but Howel was turning into a stranger whom he simply didn't recognize.

He decided to walk home. On the way, he would call at the chapel and make the arrangements for the wedding. The thought cheered him and as he thrust his hands into his pockets and made his way downhill, he was smiling.

*   *   *

Tom continued to make progress. His feet were scarred and it would be some time before he could wear boots again, but at least he could walk with the aid of a stick. He was always cheerful and most of his time was spent sitting outside the door, facing the river, watching his father scull the ferry from Foxhole to the Hafod.

'Shall I fetch you a hat, Tom?' Nerys asked, noticing the pink of his face as he sat in the sun.

'Na, I'm not a cissy. I don't want to wear a hat!' Tom's face was unusually sober. 'Nerys, why hasn't Howel come to see me?'

Nerys felt the colour rise to her face. 'I'm sure he would if he could, Tom. It's probably that he's kept so busy in his new job.'

Tom pursed his lips and frowned. 'But our Ceri's trying to make a go of his business, he's decorating his house *and* working the silver and he still comes to see me!'

'I know and I'm sure Howel will come soon too, so don't you worry.' Nerys sighed, wondering if perhaps she should go up to see Howel and ask him to visit Tom; it could be that he was keeping away for fear of her embarrassing him. Well, he need not worry on that score. In just over a week she would be Mrs Siona Llewelyn and then Howel need never bother with her again.

Her thoughts were still confused and she didn't know what she felt for Howel now. Was it love, or simply a foolish girl crying for the moon? For in a way she loved Siona; he was unfailingly kind to her and what's more, he made her feel beautiful in spite of her increasing girth.

She smiled as she looked down at herself. She could still just about conceal her condition beneath a loose apron or jacket, though soon it would be obvious that she was expecting a child. But what did it matter once she was married to Siona? Folk would simply assume that they had anticipated the marriage service. Some people would look down upon her as a loose woman but there were others – those who mattered – who would always remain her friends.

As though in answer to her thoughts, Mona came up the pathway of the Ferry House trailing a bundle in her hand. Her lips were quivering and she gazed at Nerys with tear-filled eyes.

'I've had a row with me mam and I've walked out!' she said without preamble. 'Mam said I didn't earn enough to keep a bird alive and that as I was so fond of helping up by here rather than being with her in the house, I could bring my bed here. She'll calm down, mind, but what am I going to do in the meantime?'

'Sit down and have a cup of tea, that's the first thing,' Nerys said easily. 'Come on in by here, I'll put the kettle on.'

Even as she talked, she wondered where they would put Mona. The back bedroom housed the two younger boys, and Ceri too for the time being. She herself had the middle room and Siona the bigger bedroom in the front of the house.

Soon, however, she would be sharing Siona's bed and the thought brought the warm colour to her cheeks. However, she had made a pact with herself that she would be a true wife to Siona. He was a good man, he had taken on the burden of herself and her child and she would not cheat him of his marital rights. A lusty man still, he needed love and she had made up her mind to give him as much as she could.

'Well, stay here if you're prepared to sleep on the parlour couch for the time being. If you don't make it up with your mam, you can have my room later on.'

Mona forgot her own miseries and stared at Nerys anxiously. 'Have your room? Why, where are you going?' There was a note of fear in her voice and she clutched the handle of her cup.

Nerys sat down at the table and leaned her chin in her hands. 'I'm going to marry Siona,' she said flatly.

'Siona?' Mona said in surprise. 'But why marry Siona when he's not even the father?'

'Because I know he'll be good to me,' Nerys sighed. 'And didn't you tell me once that he would be a good catch?' She smiled ruefully. 'Truth to tell, I'm tired of being alone and struggling by myself. I'll be Mrs Llewelyn and my child will have a name; that's very important to me. Anyway, that's enough about me — what are you going to do? Will you sleep on the couch for tonight and then see what your mam feels in the morning? She might have got over things by then.'

'I hope so,' Mona said softly. 'There are plenty of other mouths to feed and I don't think she can do without my wages. Anyway, we'll see, but for tonight I'll be glad to sleep on the couch. Don't you worry about me; it'll be nice to have some peace and quiet away from my brothers.' She paused. 'But do you think Siona will mind me being here?'

'We'll ask him when he comes in, but I'm sure it will be all right,' Nerys assured her. 'I've told you, he's a kind man. He couldn't hurt a fly in spite of his size, he's so gentle and good.'

'Now there's a daft thing!' Mona rubbed a tear from her lashes. 'Why I want to cry, I don't know.' She put down her cup. 'Mind, Siona is no saint; he likes the ladies and always did, so my mam tells me. Selfish he can be too, like other men, but for all that I do like him very much.' She smiled. 'And it sounds as if you're more than half in love with him yourself.'

Nerys nodded slowly: 'I do love him in a way.' But not as she loved Howel! How could she express the joy and the passion he had inspired? She had felt whole and tinglingly alive when she had lain in his arms. It had been an uplifting feeling, a wondrous sensation of being among the stars.

And yet he had made a fool of her, used her and then gone off and forgotten her, making up to that Jenny woman who had money and breeding and a snobbish outlook on life. Well, if Howel was that shallow, she was better off without him.

It was later in the day when Siona came in from the ferryboat hungry for his dinner. The warm breeze had put colour into his cheeks and his eyes were as green as the seas on a cloudy day. Nerys bristled with pride in him; he was a big handsome man and he meant to take care of her, which was what she needed most of all now.

'Mona's had a row with her mammy and left home,' Nerys said as she put out a dinner of roast beef and boiled potatoes. 'Can she stay here for a while, do you think?

Siona was washing his hands at the sink. 'Aye, why not? We could do with more of her help about the place right now, but where are we to put her?'

Nerys kept her eyes on the carrots she was serving. 'I thought she could sleep in the parlour until we're wed and then, if she's still here, she can have my room.'

Siona's eyes were alight. 'Sounds like a good idea to me. Righto, that's settled then!' He put his arm around Nerys's shoulders. 'A man's a fool if he doesn't learn from his mistakes and I'll not allow you to be over-worked, that's all I'll say on the matter.'

Nerys made no reply, but she knew what he meant all right. His wife Emily had borne him many children and had worked herself into a state of decline. Siona would see that such a thing didn't happen again.

*   *   *

Mona was restless as she lay on the hard horsehair couch, wide-awake in the darkness of the night. She felt so alone. Her mother had never cared for her and had made her a drudge, sending her out to work as soon as she was old enough. And now that the other children were growing up, Mona was only useful for the money she earned. The latest row had been over money; just because Mona had wanted to keep some of her wages for herself, mam had turned spiteful, telling her that she earned little enough anyway.

But mam would get over her fit of temper in time and until she did, Mona would stay at the Ferry House with the only real friends she had ever had.

Startled by a noise from the kitchen, she sat up, her mouth dry with fear. Whoever was about the house at this time of night could be up to no good!

She pulled a shawl over her cotton nightgown and carefully opened the door. It creaked a little and she held her breath, but there was no sound except her own breathing. On bare feet, she tiptoed towards the kitchen, prepared to scream at the top of her voice should she come upon an intruder.

In the flickering light of the dying fire, she saw a figure seated in a chair, head bent in an attitude of complete dejection. This was no thief, Mona decided, as, emboldened, she went cautiously into the room.

'Good God!' Alex Llewelyn looked up at her with a startled expression on his face and Mona laughed nervously, her mouth dry, for she had always admired him.

'There's sorry I am if I frightened you, but I thought I heard a noise and I wondered who was in here.'

She saw that there were tears on Alex's cheeks; she had never seen a man cry and her being melted in sympathy for him.

'What is it, *cariad*?' Her tone was soft and she knelt before Alex feeling warm, as though she had something to give this tortured boy who was little older than she was.

'I have such a burden of guilt, Mona,' Alex whispered. 'I saw my twin brother die and it's as if I've stepped into his shoes, taking his wife as my own.'

Mona lifted her head as she heard a board creak upstairs. 'Come,' she said and, taking Alex's hand, she led him away from the door leading to the stairs and into the parlour.

Silver moonlight shone in through the window and Alex looked so pale and tired that she longed to hold him and comfort him. And why shouldn't she? It was only showing human emotion, surely?

When she put her arms around him, his head sank against her breast as though in weariness. She felt exultant; she was needed and perhaps she could offer comfort to Alex.

'Talk to me,' she whispered. 'You can say anything you want to and it will go no further, I promise.'

He looked up at her then. 'You're a lovely girl, Mona. You make me feel strong like a man should be – and that's the secret of my troubles, you see. I can't be a man to my wife.'

Mona knew instantly what he meant. She was from a household where there were many children and she knew what happened in the marriage bed well enough. She touched Alex's face tenderly and a flood of joy coursed through her, mingled with not a little fear.

'Let me help you, Alex. Let this night be one of learning about life for both of us, is it?'

She pressed her lips to his when he would have protested and slowly he lay back along the couch, his arms instinctively moving to hold her.

'I can make no promises, Mona,' he said breathlessly. 'You know that I'm married and I could never leave Sarah?'

'Hush, this night is for us. Don't talk about anyone else or think about anyone else; let us just be ourselves.' She felt as old as the hills that surrounded

312

Sweyn's Eye; she felt the strength of her power as a woman flood through her; she was wisdom and innocence and she was going to be Alex's salvation.

He touched her softly at first, his hand tentative, seeking her breast beneath the cotton nightgown. She felt a stirring within her, a fluttering of excitement and fear, for she was embarking upon something from which there could be no retreat. She put her arms around him and kissed him and then she allowed her hands to explore him, almost fearfully at first and then with growing courage.

His head was bent over her breasts and as she felt the heat of his mouth upon her, a raging torrent of emotions flooded through her body. She forgot about helping Alex, forgot about everything except the joy and torment that held her enthralled.

'Oh, Alex, love, I want you so much. I need you, Alex, for there is nobody in this world who loves me for myself.' She didn't know if he even heard her; he was breathing raggedly, his shoulders were still tense and she knew he was fearful of failing.

This thought gave her courage and it was she who guided him to her. They lay together, quiescent at first, while they both drew breath.

'You're all right, my lovely,' she whispered. 'You're a fine strong man and I've always admired you – you must know that.'

'I love you for this, Mona,' Alex replied softly. He kissed her neck and then slowly, he began to move in the rhythm of the oceans and the winds and the rains. Mona bit her lip, for she felt pain, but there was joy too because she was proving to Alex that he was whole, a man of vigour and strength.

She caressed the silkiness of his shoulders, feeling more like a mother with her child than a woman losing her innocence. She kissed his strong neck, turning his mouth towards hers, and they clung together in mutual need.

They lay side by side then, staring up at the ceiling criss-crossed with cracks which showed up in the slant of moonlight like shapes on a map. Mona heard Alex sigh in contentment and she reached out and touched his hand.

'Will you come to me again?' she asked wistfully, and he leaned up on one elbow and stared down at her.

'Of course I'll come to you again, my lovely. I'll never turn away from you now.'

She leaned against his chest, listening to his heartbeat. 'I don't ask you to give me all your love, just a little bit of it. Is that asking too much, Alex?'

He kissed her mouth. 'Don't you see, you'll always be special to me. Tonight was the first time for both of us and it's a bond that no one can ever break.'

She was warmed then and happy, for she had something which no other woman could take away.

'I'd better go before anyone catches us together,' Alex said softly, 'but meet me tomorow, Mona. I'll come to Victoria Park about six in the evening; at least we can be together and talk.' He kissed her. 'I know I've made a muddle of things, and I swore to love Sarah always and I will – but I can't let you go, Mona, not now.'

Watching him dress in silence, she knew quite clearly that she was accepting half a loaf. Yet nothing – not even the knowledge that she could never have Alex entirely to herself – could spoil the happiness that lay like a contented cat within her.

Mona sang about her work the next morning, amazed that no one could see the tremendous experience which had been hers in the night. She had been changed from a lonely, unwanted girl to a woman, and she knew in her heart that she would always love Alex whatever happened in the future.

She would have to share him, she was aware of that, for now that she had unlocked his fears and inhibitions he would be able to love his wife as a man should. And yet the knowledge that she had brought him this gift made it the more bearable.

'You're very happy.' Nerys was sitting at the table peeling potatoes, and her words intruded into Mona's mind.

'Aye, I suppose it's getting away from mam and the children and the everlasting rows that's done it.' This was a good excuse and one readily accepted by Nerys. Mona sighed and sat down, leaning her elbows on the table.

'When are you and Siona getting married, then?' She had a special reason for asking, because once she was given a bedroom of her own instead of the horsehair couch, it would be easier to be with Alex in the night.

'Well, it's going to be as soon as Siona can arrange it,' Nerys said positively. 'We're telling no one the date, simply off on our own and tying the knot. We don't want any fuss, especially with me looking like a plum pudding!'

Mona sighed softly. 'You are lucky,' she said. 'You'll be a respectably married woman soon and I envy you.' And she did, for the one thing she would never be able to have with Alex was a proper marriage, yet she was more than prepared for the sacrifice so long as she could keep the love Alex gave her.

'Don't worry,' Nerys said, and her tone was a little too bright. 'One day you'll meet a man you love and then you'll be married soon enough, I dare say.'

Mona shook her head. 'I know that life isn't that simple, Nerys. It's only a romantic dream that a girl meets a boy and then they live happily ever after. No, we must all make the most of what we can get and that's for sure.'

Nerys looked up at her in surprise. 'That's very wise of you, Mona. I wouldn't have expected so much clear common sense from such a young girl. I'd have

315

thought your head would have been full of apple blossoms and gold rings!'

Mona didn't reply. There was no need. She and Nerys were in the same boat really, both of them accepting second-best because that was all that life was prepared to offer them.

'I'd best go in and clean the parlour,' she said quietly. 'I'll fold up my blankets and put them upstairs, so that the room will be tidy if anyone calls. Then I'd better get on with the washing.' She smiled. 'And cheer up, life's not so bad, mind.'

She went into the parlour and sat on the sofa, hugging to her the memory of being in Alex's arms. She would work the day away, wishing for the hours to fly, for this evening at six o'clock she would be with her lover once more.

CHAPTER TWENTY-THREE

The chapel was empty of people. A single vase of flowers stood near the pulpit, a splash of brightness against the sombre wood of the intricately carved pews. The rain which had darkened the skies earlier had vanished now and a pale sun slanted through the window.

Nerys stood beside Siona and concentrated on the words the pastor was saying; they were beautiful words, words which would join her to Siona in marriage. And yet none of it seemed real. She could not believe that the moment had come, that now she was giving up her freedom for all time. Now there could be no miracle which would bring Howel rushing to her side, ready to declare his undying love and to set her in her rightful role as his wife and the mother of his child.

Her loose silk frock with its over-jacket of cream lace matched the small cap set neatly upon her head. The outfit was cool and comfortable and had the advantage of concealing her condition. Her slippers were soft cream pigskin, made for fashion rather than wear, but Siona had wanted her to look her best.

'It's a solemn occasion when you get married,' he had told her, unaware that his words sent shivers of apprehension through her, 'and I want my bride to look as lovely as possible, even though it's only me that will see her!'

And so they had come to the chapel, alone and unheralded, to make their vows in private – the service kept secret even from the family. It was only Big Eddie – needed to look after the two young boys and to man the ferryboat – who had any inkling of what was going on.

The pastor indicated that Siona should slip the narrow gold band on to Nerys's finger. She felt his hand cool and confident, looked into his eyes for the first time and was grateful for his strength. He leaned forward and kissed her cheek and she smiled up at him, her fingers involuntarily closing around his. He was a handsome man, a kind man and she would try to love him.

The pastor read from the scriptures in a loud solemn voice as though before a great congregation, and then music swelled from the old pipe organ and Nerys felt tears constrict her throat.

They came out into the sunshine holding hands and stood for a moment as though to gather their thoughts. Nerys had never imagined a wedding day like this one. If she had dreamed at all, it was of a young, handsome man with crisp black hair, and a crowd of well-wishers to throw petals over her as she left the church.

'We'd better get home,' Siona said almost regretfully. 'Our Eddie will be having his work cut out to man the boat and keep an eye on the boys, especially now that Tom is getting around on that stick of his.'

The tram rumbled along the track, wavering in the heat of the sunshine, and as Nerys climbed aboard she was aware of people looking at her in curiosity. She realized that she must look out of place in her silk frock and with a posy of flowers clasped in her hand. When she smiled up at Siona he inclined his head, his green eyes merry.

'We've just got married!' he announced to a woman seated next to him. 'Lovely day for a wedding, isn't it?'

The woman smiled. 'There's lovely, then, and it's lucky to see a bride in all her finery. I'm sure to have a good afternoon.' She adjusted the basket of shellfish on the pad of clean white cloth which formed a cushion for her head and beamed around her.

'What do you think, folks – we've got a little bride by here, isn't that lovely?' Heads turned and there was a murmur of congratulations and Nerys felt her colour rise in pleasure. It was as though by the approbation of strangers on the tram the ceremony had been endowed with an air of solidarity, and for the first time since she entered the church Nerys felt that she really was married.

Big Eddie was waiting to take them across the river. His broad face was smiling and glancing behind him, Nerys saw that the old planking of the boat was garlanded with white ribbons and posies of flowers.

'I know you didn't want any fuss at the wedding,' Eddie said cheerfully, 'but you didn't say anything about afterwards!' He helped Nerys into the well of the boat. 'Come on, mammy,' he joked. 'Let's get you safely home.'

The door of the Ferry House stood open. There was a silence and yet Nerys sensed the presence of other people.

As she went into the comparative shade after the bright sunshine, she could hardly see who stood before her, but a cheer rose to fill the little kitchen and spicing the air was the rich scent of roasting meat.

It seemed that the family had conspired to make the day a memorable one, and as Nerys was led to the table by a smiling Mona, she saw that it was set with a crisp white cloth and in the centre stood a vase filled with roses.

A huge pie took pride of place, the crust golden-brown, while on a large blue and white plate were layers of sliced beef still steaming from the oven. Bread there was a-plenty, crisp and fresh, with butter liquefying in its hotness.

A whole ham baked with honey and cloves lay

319

ready for the carving, and a mountain of potatoes boiled in their skins steamed in the biggest dish Nerys had ever seen. Tears came to her eyes and she brushed them aside as Tom hobbled towards her with a single rose clutched in his hand.

'Me and Will, well . . . we're glad you've married our dad,' he said quietly, and Nerys understood that while no one would ever take the place of Emily Llewelyn, she herself was being accepted and loved.

'Thank you, Tom and you, Will. I'll do my best to look after you all.' Her voice was thick with tears and she longed to hug the boys, but she knew that such a demonstration would only embarrass them.

'Good luck, stepmother!' Ceri leaned over and kissed her cheek. 'Though Katie and I should be mad at you, pipping us at the post the way you've done!'

'Take no notice,' Katie said, smiling. 'Sure, 'tis only jealousy makes him talk like that. In any case, I'm not at all sure I'll marry you after all, for haven't I let the best-looking of the Llewelyn men get away from me?' She stood on tiptoe to give Siona a congratulatory kiss. 'I wish you both all the happiness in the world, so I do.'

Nerys sat in a chair near the open door, away from the heat of the fire, and took the plate of food Mona handed her. 'Come on, girl, you must eat something – you'll need your strength later, mind!' She giggled and blushed and hurriedly moved away.

Nerys felt a cold sense of fear grip her. She had not allowed herself to think beyond the actual wedding ceremony but now, with Mona's harmless joke ringing in her ears, she knew that going to the same bed as Siona each night was a reality she must face.

She glanced across at Mona, who was talking quietly with Alex. There seemed to be an intimacy about the way they leaned towards each other, she thought, but then the moment was gone as Sarah joined the little group and laughing, put her arm around her young husband's shoulder.

'All right then, are you?' Siona crouched beside her. He had pulled away his tie and opened the collar of his shirt; he looked handsome and manly and if only she didn't love his son, she felt she could have been happy with Siona Llewelyn.

'Yes, I'm all right,' she replied. 'Surprised, mind, by all this fuss,' she went on, forcing a laugh, 'and we thought we were going to have a quiet wedding!'

'Aye, my family have a way of doing the unexpected,' Siona said soberly. 'I'm just wondering what Howel will make of all this, though it's none of his business, mind.'

Nerys didn't answer – she couldn't speak, for her throat felt thick with tears. She knew she couldn't bear to even think of Howel and what he might feel about her becoming his stepmother.

The clouds of evening darkened the Ferry House and Ceri rose to his feet. 'Don't want to break up the party, but I think it is time we were off.' He smiled at Katie and while she was busy saying goodbye to the two younger boys, he stood with Nerys in the shadowy doorway.

'How is your business shaping up?' she asked gently. 'I know you were set back, what with finding money for doctors and such for Tom, but are things under way now?'

'Aye, we've made a start on the decorating of the place Mr Richardson found for us, and I've managed to set up a little workshop in one of the outbuildings. We'll be fine – there's no need to worry about Katie and me.'

Nerys smiled. She had always got on well with Ceri; he was sensitive and thoughtful and Katie was a lucky girl. On the heels of that thought, she told herself that she must count her own blessings. She could have been cast out, a fallen woman wanted by no one, yet Siona had taken it upon himself to give her and her unborn child the Llewelyn name.

He was giving a lot more besides, for he was genuinely in love with her; he really cared, and surely that was what most women wanted from life. Abandoning her dreams of love and apple blossoms and of a fairy-tale wedding to Howel was surely a small price to pay for her security and peace of mind.

'You're far away,' Ceri said, laughing softly. 'What are you thinking about?'

'Your father,' Nerys answered honestly. 'There surely isn't a more generous man in the whole world, for there's not many would take on a woman with child by another man.'

She caught a swift look of surprise before Ceri turned away, and wondered in that instant what Ceri really thought of her. Surely he knew about Howel and her short but passionate affair with him? But perhaps not, for he was searching with his eyes for Katie, deliberately avoiding Nerys's questioning gaze.

'See you later then, dad,' he said in what seemed to Nerys to be a forced cheerfulness. 'Come on, Katie, I have to get you home.'

Katie leaned forward, her red-gold hair swinging around her face. Her skin was creamy and flawless and Nerys envied the Irish girl her beauty. Beside her, she felt frumpy and heavy-limbed, colourless and insignificant.

'Sure I've enjoyed this get-together with Ceri's family,' Katie said warmly, 'and I wish you every happiness, you and Siona both.' She kissed Nerys lightly on the cheek and as she walked down the path, turned to wave cheerfully.

It seemed that the signal had come for the party to end, for shortly after Ceri left, Alex put down his plate of untouched food and moved towards his father, resting a hand upon his shoulder.

'See you again, then, dad,' he said in his quiet way. 'I wish you all the best, mind.'

From behind him, Mona moved forward with a

smile of forced cheerfulness, glancing at Sarah and then away again quickly. She didn't speak but Sarah, as though sensing something amiss, looked directly at her.

'Were you going to say something, Mona?' she asked sharply and Mona shook back her mousy hair, suddenly appearing dull and colourless.

'No,' she said sullenly.

Alex thrust his hands into his pockets and looked down at his boots as his wife slipped her arm possessively through his.

'Come on then, Alex,' Sarah said edgily. 'We've got a baby and a home of our own to go to, mind, and Nerys must be longing to be left alone.' She glanced once more at Mona who, ignoring her, sat with shoulders hunched in the old chair near the fire-grate.

'Come on,' Sarah insisted. 'Betty-the-Milk will be weary of minding our son.'

'All right, girl!' Alex spoke impatiently. 'We'll get off when dad's ready to take us across the river!'

'Ready now, boyo,' Siona said at once. 'I'll send our Eddie in, Nerys. Give the boy a bite to eat, he must be starving by now.' He smiled. 'And when I come back the ferry will be shut for the night and opened again for no one until the morning.'

Nerys lowered her eyes. Apprehension filled her entire being, occupying her mind so that she could think of nothing to say, but Siona just laughed gently and touched her cheek, taking her lack of response as nothing more than shyness.

'Now, Tom, Will, get yourselves off to bed by the time I come back, righto?' Siona said as he moved to the door. 'Come on then, Alex, my boy. Let's get you across the river and on your way home.'

There was silence in the Ferry House after Siona had gone, closing the door on the evening air, for the two younger boys knew by experience that to be quiet and unobtrusive was to delay the moment when they had to go to their room.

Nerys began to tidy away the dishes, piling them into the deep sink in the corner of the kitchen ready for washing. Some of the food she stowed away in the coolness of the pantry: the butter and cheese on the marble slab, the bread and pies in the wooden slatted box that hung from the sloping ceiling.

For Big Eddie, she left a hearty slice of mutton and ham tart, a plate of Welsh cakes and a tankard of ale.

'*Duw*, something smells good!' Eddie himself entered the kitchen carrying with him the salt scent of the river. 'My arms are aching as though they were broken,' he said, rubbing his muscles ruefully. 'Sculling the boat with a load of people and bikes and a fish cart to boot is twice as hard as hauling coal. I don't know how our dad does it all day!'

'Come and sit by here,' Nerys said with forced cheerfulness. 'There's plenty of food in the pantry if this isn't enough.'

Eddie sat astride his chair, his thighs huge, his arms bulging as he rested his elbows on the white cloth over the table. He was the son most like Siona in appearance, Nerys thought as she handed him the tankard of ale. Yet Eddie was open and honest, lacking the mischievous charm of his father.

'Well, Nerys, did you enjoy the little surprise we planned for you?' Eddie asked, brushing crumbs of tart from his bristling moustache.

'A fine surprise it was, too!' Nerys said. 'I haven't yet had time to change out of my best frock.'

Eddie winked at her. 'Well not worth bothering now, is it? It will be bed for you once dad gets back.' He turned to his younger brothers, who were sitting still like saints, eyes wide with weariness. 'Talking about bed, how about it, you two? Not going to sit by there till dad comes home, are you?'

They moved, albeit reluctantly – Tom first, hobbling

on his stick, his face twisting a little in pain as the taut shiny skin pulled against the scars of his burns. But he walked more confidently now than he had done since the accident and Nerys smiled as he passed her, reaching out to touch his shoulder.

'*Duw*, you're almost as tall as me, boyo – eating us out of house and home, you are.'

'Aye,' Big Eddie said easily. 'Going to be tall like his brother, aren't you, Tom?'

Tom grinned sheepishly. 'And as dull, by the look,' he said, ducking as Eddie aimed a playful blow at his head.

'I'm getting tall as well!' Will was not about to be left out of the conversation; he stretched himself and teetered alongside Nerys on his bare toes, determined to impress.

'You are that,' Nerys agreed. 'Now less talk about size and more about sleep, is it?'

As the door closed behind the boys, Eddie smiled at Nerys in admiration. 'Got our Tom and Will eating out of your hands, haven't you?' he said. 'I'm glad you've married dad; he needs you and so do the young 'uns.'

'I need them too,' Nerys said at once. 'Now let's stop being maudlin like old men in their cups, and talk sensibly. Do you want another piece of tart or anything, for if you're finished, I'll start washing up the dishes.'

'Oh dear, who's a tartar, then?' Big Eddie joked, rising to his feet easily for such a huge man. 'But in spite of that sharp tongue, I'll still help with the dishes. Married life has taught me that much, anyway.'

Nerys was glad of Big Eddie's company, for his chatter kept her apprehension at bay. He washed the dishes with a thoroughness that surprised her, for she imagined him more at home lifting coal than doing housework.

'Are you happy, Eddie?' She surprised herself by

asking the question which had popped into her mind. She would not have been put out had he told her to mind her own business, but he simply glanced at her and shrugged.

'Aye, happy enough,' he said. 'I've got a good wife and a father-in-law who offers me honest pay for an honest day's work – what more could a man want?'

Nerys dried the stack of plates and put them away in the dresser absentmindedly, wondering what she asked of life. Couldn't she be content as Eddie was with a sensible compromise?

'Have another drink of ale before you go?' she asked as Big Eddie shook the water from his hands and rubbed them vigorously with a towel. Anything rather than be alone with her thoughts! She recognized the motive for her offer and wondered if Big Eddie would too, but he simply nodded his head and settled himself in the big wooden chair that Siona usually occupied.

'Dad will take good care of you,' he said softly, and she knew he had sensed her troubled feelings.

'I know,' she smiled. 'I'm a lucky girl. I've got a fine husband and a kind, caring family and I couldn't ask for more.' But she could; she wanted Howel to come even now, to declare the marriage null and void, to take her in his arms and lead her to his home where she would live in happiness for evermore.

That the idea was nothing more than a fairy-tale dream, she recognized with painful clarity. Howel had not come near the Ferry House for some time, and would not do so now.

Nerys glanced at the clock and it seemed to be ticking away the minutes remorselessly. Soon she would be Siona's wife in more than name and then there could be no turning back.

She would honour her vows, she would be a good wife and later, perhaps, she would bear Siona the child he deserved. For he was prepared to live with his son's child for ever in his sight, accepting that Howel had taken Nerys and possessed a part of her which could never be the same again. Siona was a big man in all respects, she thought, not for the first time.

'Well, girl, if I don't get back home, my wife will have the sharp edge of her tongue ready for me,' Big Eddie said, rising reluctantly from his chair. 'I've enjoyed today; it's felt like being back in the family fold again for a little while.' He smiled deprecatingly. 'A man's a child at heart, mind, Nerys – no denying that.'

She saw him to the door and watched while he walked up the sloping bank towards the roadway. It was a fair step to his home in St Thomas, but it was a fine night and Big Eddie was used to walking. She stood for a long time, watching the sky turn slowly to indigo. The heat of the day seemed to linger and even the breeze from the water was warm and balmy.

Sighing, she returned indoors and sat for a moment staring into the dying embers of the fire. Soon she would have to riddle the ashes and then set the fire ready for morning. It would be over then; she would be Mrs Siona Llewelyn and she would never be the same person as the one who sat now, holding on to her dreams until the very last shred of hope was gone.

She tucked up her frock and, kneeling on the rag mat, took up the poker. The ashes fell with the last of their splendour, scattering sparks of glowing light on to the brass fender before fading to grey. She leaned back on her heels for a moment, watching the ashes grow cold. Perhaps before the last spark died, Howel would come to her, rescue her and take her home.

'Fool!' She said the word out loud and then quickly, with sharp thrusts, pushed paper and sticks into the grate behind the black-leaded bars. The task seemed to calm her and when the fire was set, she rose and washed the dust from her hands.

Her wedding frock was streaked with coal, she

noticed, but it didn't matter; nothing seemed to matter. She stared out of the window and heard the soft wash of the river against the bank; the sound was restful and she leaned her head on her arms, closing her eyes and wishing for nothing more than sleep to claim her and take her away from reality.

She remained where she was until she heard the sound of footsteps on the gravel path. Then she sat up in her chair with a determined smile of welcome on her face.

'*Duw*, girl, I thought I'd never get home! Old Gareth turned up and nagged me into taking him across the river and I felt I couldn't refuse.' He sank into a chair. 'But I'm here now, at last, with my lovely bride!'

Nerys went to him, taking the hand he held out towards her. She looked into his eyes and saw that he understood a little of her apprehension.

'I'm not an ogre, Nerys,' he said softly, 'and I shan't force myself upon you, don't you fear, but I do have the hope in my heart that you will want to be a wife to me in more than name.'

For a moment she was tempted to take advantage of his generous spirit, to postpone the moment when she crossed the line and became his wife in deed as well as in name. But that would be cheating him. She had always known that Siona was a lusty man, he had never pretended anything different.

She smiled at him. 'I do confess to being nervous, Siona, but what bride wouldn't be? And after all, you're too much of a man to go living like a monk, now, aren't you?' She pulled at his hand. 'Come on, then – let's go to our bed, shall we?'

The way his green eyes lit up brought a tightening of her throat and she knew he would have been bitterly hurt had she spoken any differently. In any case, putting matters off would not help at all; she had taken marriage vows that day in the house of God and she meant to live up to them.

'Go on up first and get into your pretty new night-gown,' he said with a wicked smile. 'I know you women like a bit of privacy.'

She left him then and let herself through the door that led directly to the stairs. She walked on tiptoe, fearful of waking the boys. They had gone to bed late and needed to be up early in the morning.

The morning – oh, that it were here now! She closed the bedroom door and leaned against it for a moment. How silent it was with the heat of the day still trapped in the very fabric of the bedroom. The bed was large; she had made it up every morning, but never had she thought she would be sharing it with Siona.

She drew off her silk frock and hung it in the wardrobe which smelled heavily of mothballs – suddenly weary, as though all the strength and spirit had been drained from her.

Carefully she put her shoes under the window shelf and took up her nightgown of soft white cotton lawn sprigged with rosebuds. It fell sensuously round her shoulders and hips, clinging to her legs.

At that moment Siona came silently into the room. He had removed his boots, obviously with the same thought in his mind as Nerys: that the boys should not be woken.

'*Duw*, you're beautiful, *cariad*! There's a lucky man I am indeed.' He came towards her and took her in his arms and she closed her eyes, feeling the huge unfamiliar bulk of him against her with a momentary sense of panic. But Siona was gentle, stroking her hair, talking to her softly – meaningless little words which none the less soothed her.

Nerys slipped into the big bed and lay waiting while he undressed in the dark, whistling tunelessly, proof enough that he too was nervous. The thought cheered her and gave her confidence, and when he came into the bed beside her, she timidly put her arms around him.

329

'*Cariad, cariad*, my little love. I'll be so good to you, I'll look after you always.' He kissed her mouth and she was pleasantly surprised at the firmness of his lips and the sweetness of his breath mingling with hers.

'And I'll look after you, Siona, I promise you that.' She clung even closer, knowing that the time for talking was past and that her great debt of gratitude to the man who had given her his name was about to be paid.

CHAPTER TWENTY-FOUR

It was a strange new world – a world of plush offices, high finance and at the end of the day a large airy house to return to – and for much of his good fortune, he owed Sterling Richardson a debt of gratitude. Howel sat near the window, the billowing curtains bringing into the room the hot scents of late summer. He should be a happy man yet somehow he felt very much alone.

He was used to the Ferry House, the constant chatter of his young brothers, the slow humour of his father and the ever-present band of people calling to each other on the river bank waiting to be ferried across the water.

Now he wondered if it was possible or even desirable to shake off his roots, yet how could he continue to live in the old way of life when his fortunes had changed so dramatically? He was possessed of the gift for making money and he was certainly more wealthy than he had ever dreamed possible. He had made a fortune and then lost it, which was when Sterling had stepped in and backed him to the hilt, enabling him to rebuild his fortunes.

It was strange how at first he had planned simply to use Sterling as a stepping-stone and to move on whenever it suited him. However, over the months his attitudes had subtly altered and his respect for Sterling had grown, coming to a peak when the other man had carried him through his bleakest hour; now Howel was committed to his position in the Richardson empire.

Howel felt he no longer needed to prove anything.

Except for that one lapse his success on the stock-market was nothing short of phenomenal, and the money he had placed in solid gold investments had made his fortune secure.

He was accepted by the élite of the town on his own merits; he was referred to as 'that clever chap in the market', his advice was sought after and he was cultivated by every mother who wanted a rich husband for her daughter.

And then there was Jenny. She had become more possessive of late, trying to pin him down to a date for their marriage, sensing somehow that she was losing his interest.

He rose and stared out into the night sky, a feeling of restlessness gripping him. He didn't know what he wanted any more; his achievements seemed insignificant, meaningless and he didn't know why.

He heard the clanging of the doorbell with a feeling of relief and realized in that moment that he was lonely, a bird trapped in a luxurious cage. When he walked to the big double doors leading to the hallway, he was surprised to see his brother stepping into the house.

'Ceri,' he said carefully. 'Come in and have a drink.' Howel wondered that the brother with whom he had always seemed at loggerheads should come to visit him, yet he could not deny he was pleased to see him.

Ceri followed him into the drawing room, shutting the door on the curious face of the old lady who had admitted him.

'It's a long time since you came down to the Ferry House,' Ceri said slowly, 'and today, for the first time, I found out why you've been staying away.'

'I've no idea what you're talking about,' Howel said defensively. 'There is such a thing as pressure of work, you know.' He had no intention of allowing Ceri to know that dad had forbidden him to enter the Ferry House again.

'Oh aye, go on, talk like a schoolteacher, but it won't stop me from giving you a piece of my mind.'

Howel moved to the drinks cabinet and took out a bottle, pouring two generous measures of gin. 'Here, drink this, it may help calm you down,' he said easily.

Ceri stared at him in growing anger. 'Don't act the innocent. You're surely not trying to tell me you don't know what you've done?'

Howel shook his head. 'Tell me, what *have* I done?' He was growing impatient, but Ceri seemed about to get to the point, so he seated himself in an armchair and waited.

'Dad got married today,' Ceri said more slowly. 'In my ignorance, I expected you to be there. Now, of course, I see why you weren't asked.'

Howel sat upright, his hand tightening on the glass. 'What?' He couldn't believe what Ceri had just said – dad married? Then as a trickle of understanding penetrated his mind, he felt as though he'd been hit in the stomach with a sledge-hammer.

'Don't say Nerys Beynon has succeeded in making a fool of the old man?' He tried to sound casual, but there was a twisting of his nerve-ends and he found himself hoping that Ceri would laugh and deny such an absurdity.

'You're a bit of a bastard, aren't you?' Ceri said, shaking his head in disgust. 'I can't believe you've changed so much from the brother I once knew. Oh, we've never got on, I'll admit that, but I thought you had some decency about you at least.'

'Well?' Howel demanded impatiently. 'Are you going to tell me if dad has married Nerys or not?'

'Yes, he's married her and do you know why – do you?' Ceri's chin jutted forward aggressively and he looked like a man who would hit out at any moment. 'He's married her to give your child the name it deserves!' He ground out the words. 'Some of the

Llewelyn family still believe in honouring obligations, even if you don't.'

Howel walked to the window and stared out into the indigo night. Far below he could hear the wash of the sea, or was the sound the roaring in his own head? Nerys expecting his child . . . it was too momentous a concept for him to take in all at once.

He was going to be a father and it seemed that he was the last one to know about it. Suddenly furiously angry, he wanted to punch out at anything and everything. Nerys had married his father; she was out of his reach now, forbidden to him for ever, and the thought rattled him. And more, she was going to bring up his child – *his child* – in the Ferry House.

'Why didn't she come to me?' Howel said harshly. 'I didn't know about this. I should have been told, given the chance to do something about it. Oh, hell and damnation.'

Ceri made a movement behind him. 'I understand she did come to see you, to try to tell you, but she must have thought better of it. Perhaps Nerys saw something significant while she was here and she didn't want to interfere with your rich lifestyle.' He sounded bitter. 'We all knew you were running around with some fancy piece and Nerys must have seen it for herself. I don't suppose a girl like Nerys would lower her pride enough to come begging to you.'

There was a pause before Ceri continued speaking, his words pounding like blows against Howel's mind. 'Oh, when the truth first dawned on me – that the child was yours and not dad's – I was mad with Nerys for catching our father and getting him to marry her like that. But then I thought it all out and I realized it might just be the best thing all round. At least her poor little bastard will have a name.'

Howel moved swiftly and caught Ceri by the throat, his hand tightening in fury.

Ceri stood his ground. 'Aye, the truth hurts and it's guilt making you mad, isn't it, boyo?' His eyes were hot with anger. 'Go ahead and punch if you want to, but hurting me will not alter anything one bit.'

He was right and it was not Ceri's fault. Releasing him abruptly, Howel sank into a chair and rubbed at his eyes, still unable to comprehend how such events had come to pass while he remained ignorant of them. It highlighted the fact that he had become entirely estranged from his family.

'What can I do, Ceri?' He asked in a voice which was unrecognizable to his own ears.

'You're asking me for advice?' Ceri said shortly. 'There's nothing you can do now, boyo, but leave them be; keep right away, so that at least dad has a chance to make a go of things with Nerys – for he loves her, you know.'

The words rang in Howel's ears like a knell. 'But that means not seeing my own child or Nerys. Why should I cut myself off from her?'

'You seem to have been doing that quite happily for some time,' Ceri replied acidly. 'From all of us, come to that. Have you been to see if Tom's feet are any better? Do you care about any of your family any more? I doubt it. And Howel, how could you betray Nerys the way you did? She must have really been taken in by you, for she's a good girl and not some cheap flossie you picked up off the street.'

'I don't know. I suppose I was out to prove something to dad. He seemed keen on her and I imagined that all she wanted was board and bed. Was I wrong then, Ceri?'

Ceri shook his head. 'For a clever man you can be very stupid. Nerys works herself to death for us, couldn't you see that? The boys love her and children can't be fooled, they know a good woman when they see one. And to my mind you took advantage, you bastard.'

335

Howel thrust his hands into his pockets. 'She's no child; Nerys is a mature woman.' Yet even as he spoke the words he knew that he lied. Nerys might be mature in years, but in experience she had been an innocent . . . until he had come along.

'Well, I'm going. I've said my piece and that's an end to it.' Ceri was moving towards the door, but Howel held out his hand.

'Wait, how's your business shaping up?' he asked. 'I'm very interested in the silver work. In fact, if you'll let me I'd like to inject some capital into the project.'

'Well, I don't know!' Ceri said. 'You surely take the first prize for nerve. Why should I want your blood money or your interference in my business? Forget it – you and me have never been friends and now is not the time to start pretending anything different.'

Howel stared at him and sighed. Ceri was right; there was a chasm separating them which could never be bridged.

He looked out of the window, unable to shake from his mind the fact that Nerys was married to his father. What was worse was that she was expecting his child. Why hadn't she told him?

'Mr Richardson is enough backing for me,' Ceri was saying. 'I can trust him, see.' He stared intently at Howel. 'Some of his money went on doctors for our Tom, but that won't stop me, don't you worry.'

Howel felt guilt clutch at him. Ceri had selflessly given some of the little capital he had to help Tom. His younger brother had his priorities right, he'd give him that much.

Suddenly Howel was aware that he had neglected his family. He had been so wrapped up in his own problems in this new world of his, so eager to be accepted among the gentry, yet now the strides he had made were as dust for he was realizing just what he had been forfeiting during the past months.

'Well, I'm going,' Ceri said. 'I don't know why I

bothered to come here; you've not got one scrap of conscience, not about Nerys or dad or our Tom. You never think about anyone but yourself, do you?'

Howel ignored Ceri's anger. 'I'm grateful to you for putting me in the picture.' Now why did that sound like sarcasm? 'As you say, there is nothing I can do about it all now but keep away.'

Even as he paid lip service to the idea, his mind rebelled at the thought of never setting eyes upon his own child. It was unthinkable.

He led the way to the door. 'Do me a favour – tell Tom and Will to come up and see me whenever they can. They'll always be welcome here and I don't want to lose touch with the boys.'

'Perhaps you should have thought of that sooner,' Ceri said, almost sadly. 'Children get used to things all too quickly.'

When Ceri had gone, his footsteps crunching on the gravel pathway which led between tall trees towards the gate, Howel stood for a moment on the step, staring into the night sky. His sense of isolation intensified, he felt alone and lonely. Perhaps the best thing would be to marry rich, pretty, eager little Jenny and have done with it, to fill his house with a brood of babies.

But would any number of children compensate for the fact that his first-born would grow up to recognize another man as father?

Sighing softly, he returned to the brightness of the hallway and closed the door on the silent darkness.

*   *   *

Ceri was thoughtful as he moved away from the big house where his brother lived alone, and made his way to the tram-stop, surprised that he almost felt sorry for Howel – his big brother, the favoured one, the brains of the family with a future rich and secure.

Howel had everything and nothing, and Ceri counted his blessings that he himself had Katie whom he
loved more than life itself.

He felt that he must see her. It was late, but surely
she wouldn't mind him calling unexpectedly. She
would doubtless take him into her mother's parlour,
they would drink the inevitable gin that Mrs Murphy
had always to hand and he would look into the beauty
of Katie's eyes and know himself to be the luckiest
man in the world.

Soon now they would be married, for he had the
house almost ready for occupation. He had spent a
great deal of time and effort decorating the rooms
which had seen years of old brown paint, cleaning up
the walls and putting on them fresh light colours
which transformed the house into a place of warmth
and welcome. He had moved in there himself to light
fires and air the building, and all he wanted now was
for Katie to share it with him.

His workshop was fully equipped, with the
specially-constructed fireplace where the heat could
be built up with the aid of a bellows, and the large
table where he could sit and fashion the delicate silver
jewellery. Everything was taking shape.

Ceri had accepted with good grace the fact that
some of his capital had been spent on medical attention for his young brother, since Tom's accident had
essentially been his responsibility, but what had disappointed him most was the further delay to his
marriage plans. Still, that was all behind him now and
there was nothing to prevent him and Katie from
naming the day.

He strode up towards Green Hill with his hands
thrust into his pockets, oblivious to the stench from
the copper works and the intermittent shooting of
sparks that lit up the area with an unholy glow. He
had lived on the river all his life, and the river was all
that fed the multitude of tinplate, copper and lead

works with rough ore brought in from foreign countries over the seas.

Katie opened the door to him herself and seemed taken aback rather than pleased by his visit. 'I didn't expect to see you tonight, Ceri.' She didn't open the door, but stood holding it between them like a barrier.

'Sorry if I've called at an inconvenient time.' There was not a little hurt in his tone and Katie smiled at once.

'Come on in then, but you mustn't stay long for I need my beauty sleep – and sure you know that full well!'

The kitchen was silent, the fire falling low in the grate. This was nothing like the warm welcome which Ceri had anticipated and he felt somehow cheated.

'I didn't realize I had to make an appointment to see you,' he said reproachfully, standing before the fire with one hand resting on the mantelpiece. He stared at Katie and she shook back her bright hair, refusing to be provoked.

'Well, now that you've come in why not sit down and be comfortable? I'm sure I can manage to make you a brew of tea if you'd like one.'

'Aye, all right.' He sat in the old sagging armchair which was usually occupied by Mrs Murphy and watched as Katie poked the fire into a cheerful flame and set the kettle on to boil. She always eluded him, somehow; he never felt that he possessed her, not even when they lay together, and it worried him.

When she put the cup before him and settled herself in a chair opposite, he forced himself to swallow the disappointment at his lukewarm reception and smiled at her.

'Sure, and isn't that better?' she said in delight. 'You were like an old grouch when you first came in.'

'Well, I wasn't exactly welcomed with open arms, was I?' he asked softly. 'And I wanted an answer to a very important question, so I suppose I was a bit strung-up, like.'

'Oh, Ceri, important questions are to be asked in the right setting, not here in mam's kitchen with the fire dying in the grate and me wearing my oldest frock.'

'There's a silly girl!' He went to her and took her hands. 'You look lovely to me whatever you wear.' Crouching down beside her chair, he kissed her lightly.

'When are you going to allow me to set a date for our wedding, Katie? I don't like living alone!'

The words hung on the air and the silence continued for so long that Ceri thought she was not going to answer him at all.

'Oh, Ceri, can't we go on as we are for the time being?' She ended her question on a sigh and he was at once offended and frightened.

'But we've always intended to be married soon, so now that there's nothing to stand in the way of the wedding, why shouldn't we name the day?'

She looked at him with huge eyes. 'Ceri, I don't know how to say this, but I'm not sure of myself. I'd like some more time ... oh, why did you have to come here tonight?'

'You mean you don't want to marry me?' he said, raw pain choking in his throat. He saw her brush back her hair with her usual quick movements and it was clear she was searching for the right words.

'Yes, I want to marry you, Ceri, but not just yet.' She turned away, unwilling to look into his eyes. 'I still have so many old wounds that are not quite healed. Can you understand that?' she asked pleadingly.

'I only understand that you don't love me.' He heard the hollowness in his voice and saw her quick glance of alarm as he rose to his feet.

'Ceri, now don't be silly and don't take offence. You know the tragedies that have befallen me – and sure, but haven't you helped me overcome them so well?'

'So that's what I am – a sort of crutch for you. Is that all we have, then, Katie?'

340

'Don't be foolish,' she retaliated swiftly. 'We make love, we spend a lot of time going out and about together, we have great fun, so why should any of that alter?'

'In other words,' Ceri said coldly, 'you want to have your cake and eat it too – is that it? Keep me hanging on a string, but at the same time hope something better will come along! Sorry, but that doesn't happen to suit me.'

'If that's your attitude, perhaps it would be best to finish it, then,' Katie said, anger growing in her voice. 'To my mind, you're acting like a spoiled little boy who can't have his own way all the time. It seems to me that I'd be better off without you.'

'Well, now that I know how you feel, I shan't trouble you any more.' Pride was all he had left now to cover the hurt, and he drew it around him like a cloak.

'Ceri, I didn't mean that.' Her tone was suddenly gentle, pleading. 'I just wish you'd have some patience with me, that's all. To be sure I'm mixed up. I can't think clearly, all I'm asking is for some time, that's all.'

'Have time by all means,' he said in deceptively soft tones. 'Have all the time in the world.'

Ceri didn't look back as he left the house in Market Street, but his shoulders were rigid as he imagined Katie standing in the pool of light from the doorway watching him. He strode onwards with determination in every step; it might have taken him a long time to realize the situation between himself and Katie, but now that he had done so there could be no going back.

He wanted to cry, but tears were a foolish waste of time and he held his head high as he made his way down through Emerald Court and out into the Strand. He would make a success of his business, he vowed in savage determination – at least he would make something of that part of his life, even if he had to do it alone.

The night seemed to fold in around him. The lamplight splashed pools of brilliance on the cobbled roadway, the clouds lowered above his head, shutting out the stars, and it seemed that he was the only person in the world as he made his way towards Canal Street and the empty, silent house which waited for him.

CHAPTER TWENTY-FIVE

The weather was turning chill, the leaves drifting downwards and splashing the sullen waters of the river with flurries of red and gold. The breezes carried the tang of salt and autumn and the days were growing shorter now.

Within the Ferry House, Nerys had lulled herself into a state of contentment. She was a good wife to Siona as she had promised, and for his part he was tender and considerate. She was ripening now, the crisp white apron barely concealing her condition, and she found that she was changing; she was more philosophical, less prone to harking back to the past. Perhaps it was a natural offshoot of her pregnancy, but she was almost complacent as she counted the days to the birth of her child.

But sitting in the window, staring out at the river and daydreaming was not going to get the work done. She rose to her feet, picked up the empty coal-scuttle and went into the backyard.

The coal-house door was creaking in the wind, the hinges parting from the wood swollen with too much rain. Siona would have to see to that before the winter came, for the stack of logs leaning drunkenly against the wall must be kept dry in order to keep a good fire.

Nerys shovelled the glittering coal into the scuttle and coughed a little as the dust flew into her face, swept up by the wind coming in from the river. She shivered and glanced up at the sky, wondering if the day would stay fine, for it was Monday and there was washing to be done.

Siona came into the kitchen just as she was dragging the scuttle back into place and he clucked his tongue in annoyance.

'*Duw*, that's man's work. Why didn't you get one of the boys to fetch the coal before they went off to school?'

'It's all right, Siona,' she smiled as she relinquished the handle and watched him throw a pile of coal on to the fire. 'Will is so small yet and Tom's feet still give him trouble – you know that.'

He turned and took her into his arms, brushing back a stray wisp of hair and kissing her forehead.

'Look, *cariad*, I've lost one wife through too much hard work and I don't intend to lose another, righto?'

Nerys leaned against his comfortable shoulder, feeling that being loved so much was almost compensation for not having the man she really wanted. She pushed the thought from her mind, dismissing it as disloyal to her husband.

'Want something to eat, Siona?' she asked. 'It's cold out there and you need to keep warm, mind.'

He sank into a chair. 'Aye, I'll have a bit of bread and cheese, girl. The customers can wait for a while; it won't hurt them!'

She moved lightly across the kitchen, bringing the round flat cheese from the cold marble shelf in the pantry and cutting a generous portion.

'The bread's still hot from the oven – give you indigestion, it will, Siona!' She cut a chunk off the loaf with difficulty and watched as the butter melted into the warm centre of the bread.

'*Duw*, there's nothing like the smell of a fresh crust to give a man an appetite!' He caught her hand and looked up at her. 'You are happy, aren't you, *cariad*? I hope so, for I am very happy indeed.'

She was surprised. It was unlike Siona to speak of

his emotions and tears came into her eyes. She loved him, albeit in a different way from the passion and almost holy joy she had experienced in Howel's arms.

'Don't you worry, Siona. You are the best husband any woman could ask for and I can honestly say that I'm content with our life together.' She kissed his cheek and brushed back the shock of hair from his craggy, handsome face. He had wings of grey below the temples, but his moustache was still dark and gave him a look of vitality; she was a lucky girl and she must never stop believing that.

'Is Mona coming over to do the washing as usual?' Siona asked, cutting another piece of cheese and spearing it with his knife.

'Yes, she should be here any minute now. She's a good girl; I don't know what I'd do without her help and I'll need her even more when the baby comes.'

'Aye, she's a fine girl.' His shrewd eyes were twinkling. 'And I'm pretty sure our Alex thinks so too. It was a good thing when her mam took her back home, if you ask me!'

Nerys looked at him quickly. 'You don't mean . . .?' She stopped, not wanting to put into words what he seemed to be suggesting in case she was quite wrong.

'Yes, I mean that she and Alex are lovers – and I don't blame either of them. Sarah is a nice girl, a pretty girl, but since she's had that baby she doesn't seem to give Alex very much of her time.'

Nerys put her hands on her hips in mock anger. 'Oh, I see. Is that a warning to me, I wonder?'

Siona caught her and pulled her on to his knee. 'Aye, I suppose it is in a way. See, girl, a man needs a woman and that needing doesn't stop just because there's a babba in the house. To a woman, having a child is a momentous occasion, but to a man it's not so important. But then, you're a special kind of woman and you will be a wonderful mother and still be wife to me as well, I'm sure. Now, does that sound selfish, girl?'

'A little,' Nerys said softly, 'but then I know the real Siona and I'm not deceived by your words. You'll take care of me as you always took care of Emily when she bore your children.' She stopped speaking abruptly, her eyes refusing to meet Siona's as she realized what she had said. He took her face in his hands and forced her to meet his gaze.

'As far as I'm concerned, this child *is* mine,' he said firmly. 'I'll always think of it that way and so will you, righto?'

She buried her face in the warmth of his neck, hiding the hot colour which rose to her cheeks. How could she have been so insensitive? 'I don't deserve you,' she said, her voice muffled.

'And I'm a lucky old sod to have such a young and pretty wife, so hush now and get me another cup of tea, for I'm parched.'

When Siona had gone back to work, Nerys washed up the dishes and put them away and began to scrub the table. She enjoyed the task, rubbing soap into the whitened wood with the scrubbing brush and bringing it up clean and sweet-smelling. She rinsed her hands and emptied the bowl of soapy water on to the rose-bush outside the door.

'Nerys! It's me, Mona. Don't shut me out.' The girl came into the room in a flurry of excitement and Nerys stood back, seeing her with fresh insight. Mona had blossomed, there was no doubt about that.

She wore a neat woollen frock with a flat, square lace collar and her hair was cut short around her face. There was a glow about her, a sparkle in her eyes; she seemed very different from the dowdy, mousy girl who first came to work at the Ferry House. Siona must be right, Mona did have a lover.

'Why are you staring?' Mona said, smiling wickedly. 'Have I got a spot on my nose or something?'

Nerys shook her head. 'I was just thinking how

346

pretty you are. You've grown up, you're a woman now.'

'And what's that supposed to mean?' Mona was donning an apron, tying the straps briskly around her slim waist.

'Oh, I don't know – don't take any notice of me,' Nerys said quickly. 'Take the kettle of hot water for the tub and I'll put the big saucepan of water on to boil.'

'That's what I hate,' Mona said, sighing. 'The waiting around for enough water to start the wash. Do you know that in some of the big houses they have hot water coming straight from the tap? That would be heaven, wouldn't it?'

'It sounds like a dream to me,' Nerys agreed. 'Here, take the kettle and do the wash in by here; it's too cold to work outside.'

She watched as the steamy water drummed against the ridged bottom of the bath, and as Mona added cold water and tipped in a good measure of soda.

'How are you feeling?' The girl glanced meaningfully at Nerys's waistline and paused before plunging the sheets into the water, allowing them to soak for a moment.

Nerys smiled. 'I'm feeling just fine, though I must admit to being a bit slower getting around the place these days.'

'Well, that's natural enough. It don't pay to rush about anyway, not in your condition.' She placed the scrubbing-board in the water and flattened a portion of the sheet against the brass ridges, rubbing the cake of soap over the cloth with slow circular movements.

For a moment Nerys watched in silence, feeling soothed by Mona's presence and by the ritual of washing the clothes. She was slow these days – almost bovine she thought ruefully. It was as though all deep emotions were sublimated to the importance of her pregnancy.

347

She laid her hand over her stomach, feeling the child stir with a sense of contentment and of rightness. She wanted this child, wanted it with all her being, and did not regret for one moment that Howel was the father for she loved him. And yet she knew she did not . . . could not possess him. But she was safe and secure in Siona's love and no one could have all they wanted from life, she reminded herself firmly.

She glanced at Mona, who was busy rubbing hard at the sheets. The girl was prepared to accept just a small part of a man's life, the time he could take off from his wife and family, yet she seemed happy enough.

Mona looked up suddenly.

'What's all this staring about?' she asked, standing upright, her hands dripping soapy water. 'You know, don't you, about Alex and me?'

Nerys was about to make a swift denial when she saw the smile in Mona's eyes and knew that she was unashamed.

'I guessed at something.' She would not involve Siona; that might prove embarrassing. It was best to keep the matter as one of confidences between two women. 'Don't you mind that he's married? No, don't answer me, it's none of my business.'

'It's all right,' Mona said lightly.'It's a relief to talk to someone about it, to tell the truth.' She dried her hands and sat near the table, the washing forgotten. 'I love him,' she said simply, 'and in his way, I think he loves me, just a little. I'll take what I can have and make the most of it – that's the way I'm made, see?' She smiled. 'It's more difficult for us to be together now that I'm back home, mind, what with my brothers being around all the time.'

Nerys sighed. 'I suppose life is full of compromises.' She smiled across the table. 'I didn't think only a few months ago that in such a short time I would have taken a lover, fallen for a baby and got married to a man who's not the father.'

'But you seem happy enough,' Mona said softly. 'Siona is a fine, handsome man and very good to you, but much older than you, mind.'

'Yes, he's older and much wiser too,' Nerys replied, feeling defensive, 'and he's a man of great vigour, so I expect we'll have a large family.'

Mona twisted her fingers together. 'Well, in that you are lucky, for me and Alex can't afford to be caught out like that. I don't want to end up in Tawe Lodge with all them poor unmarried mothers, with hair basin-cropped and awful checked pinnies to cover their shame.'

'Surely you can't live your life like that?' Nerys said, shaking her head. 'Every woman wants a family.'

'Aye, well, not for me − not for the time being anyway, and if we're talking about living my life I can only hope that things change. Perhaps I'll meet a rich merchant and fall in love with him instead of Alex, who knows?' She laughed. 'Anyway, I'd better get on. There's a lovely breeze blowing outside and I should be able to get all the washing dried if I get a move on.'

She took a pot of boiling water from the fire and poured it into the bath in steaming gushes. 'That'll warm it up a bit.'

Nerys sighed reluctantly. 'I must get on with the cleaning; there's a lot to be done and me by here like a fool gossiping! I'll go and make the beds clean and fresh and sweep around, get out of your way. Later we'll have a nice bit of cold ham and some fried potatoes.'

Upstairs, Nerys stood in the window looking out at the river flowing swiftly down towards the sea. There was a tug pushing and hooting its way upstream and she could see the ferry-boat over at the Hafod bank taking passengers aboard. He worked hard, did her husband; he was a good man, an honest man and she was very fortunate.

There were some who would say she was lucky

beyond deserving, for she had come to the Ferry House without a penny to her name, with no future and no prospects. To marry the owner of the ferry-boat, who though not wealthy made a comfortable living, was an excellent stroke of luck for any woman.

She sighed and turned from the window, moving across the room to the chest where the clean linen was stored. Taking out the sheets for the double bed she shared with Siona, she sent them billowing like sails to come to rest neatly in place. Then she smoothed out the creases and plumped up the pillows, changing the white cases deftly and efficiently, for in the days when she looked after a variety of children in different nurseries, she had made many beds.

Tom and Will now enjoyed the splendour of having a room each. The boys took great pride in tidiness and there was little to do except some dusting and putting away the clothes. Nerys took up the rag mats and swept the linoleum with careful strokes of the brush, for her bulk got in the way these days.

She replaced the burnt-out candle in Tom's room, sighing as she saw that he had been reading in bed in spite of her protests that he would ruin his eyesight. He was a fine brave boy, still in pain sometimes from the scars on his feet, but good-humoured always and growing big and handsome very much like his eldest brother.

'Nerys!' Mona's voice calling up the stairs startled her and Nerys put down the candle-holder abruptly. 'I've got a fresh cup of tea; come and have it while it's still hot.'

Nerys took up the brush and the dusting cloths and went downstairs. The freshly-washed sheets were flapping wetly on the line, sending sprays of dampness over the garden.

'You've done well,' Nerys said, smiling. 'Or is it that I'm getting slower at my chores?'

'A bit of both, I dare say!' Mona was flushed with

exertion, the pink of her cheeks seeming to run down into the neckline of her frock. 'Phew! I'm not sorry to sit down, mind.'

'Well, I've done upstairs. I'll just have to do a bit of polishing in the parlour and then I think I'll have a rest this afternoon – perhaps take a walk into town or something.'

'That's the way, get out of the house for a while. You can see too much of the same four walls, mind,' Mona said reflectively.

'What are you going to do this afternoon?' Nerys asked, hopeful of having company, but the colour in Mona's cheeks deepened. 'Perhaps you'd better not answer that,' she added quickly.

'I think Siona's coming up the bank,' Mona said, deftly changing the subject. 'Looks as though he's starving for his dinner by the way he's hurrying.'

Nerys went into the pantry and brought out the ham. 'Here,' she said to Mona, 'cut some of this for us and I'll fry up yesterday's potatoes.'

Siona entered the kitchen with a crashing of boots on the stone floor and Nerys glanced over her shoulder at him in surprise.

'That bastard son of mine, he's got some gall!' Siona's eyes were glittering, green like fronds of grass in a stream. 'Asking me how you were keeping, mind! I nearly threw him over the side. *Duw*, it's bad enough that I've got to put up with him in my boat without him rubbing salt into the wound.' He began to cough, seeming to have difficulty drawing his breath, and Nerys moved towards him quickly.

'Now sit down and stop carrying on like that; it's not good for you.' She was aware that her pulse was rapid and her mouth dry. Howel had actually asked after her, so didn't that mean he must care a little?

Guilt washed over her then and she returned to her cooking, bending over the pan, turning the potatoes

351

with a quick gesture of the fork as though to exorcise her feelings.

She put Siona's dinner on the table and touched his hand. 'Look, love, I'm your wife and nothing is going to alter that. I'm right out of Howel's reach; he'll never have the cheek to come here and I certainly wouldn't go to him, so forget him – he's not important.'

'All right, girl, I'll be sensible, but the very sight of him makes me feel I'd like to strangle him.'

'Hush, Siona, he's your son, your own flesh and blood. I don't like to hear you speak that way.'

'Aye, Cain and Abel were of the same blood too, but it didn't prevent a murder, did it?' Siona picked up his knife and fork and began to eat and miserably Nerys sat opposite him.

'Mona!' she called, for the girl had gone out into the garden supposedly testing the sheets for dryness. 'Your dinner's on the table.' She smiled as Mona entered the room and sat down, glad to be able to have a third party present.

'Washing drying well, isn't it?' she said and Mona nodded, eating her dinner in silence and obviously discomfited by what she had overheard. Nerys smiled at her.

'Not much privacy for anyone round here, is there? Live in each other's pockets, we do, and it's a good thing that we get on so well together.'

A shadow darkened the doorway and Nerys saw Mona's face light up in pleasure.

'Hello there!' Alex made his way into the kitchen, eyes only for Mona who seemed to be glowing. 'Can a man ask for a bite to eat, 'cos I'm starving.'

'Sit down, boyo, what are you doing over here? Finished your milk round in the Mumbles already, have you?' Siona asked amiably.

'I should say! Good God, dad, by dinner-time I've been working a full day. Up before the dawn, I am, mind.'

'Sit down, Alex,' Nerys said. 'What do you fancy — some bread and a bit of cheese, is it?'

'Sounds lovely.' Alex smiled as Nerys rose to her feet and fetched more butter from the pantry. 'Hope I'm not putting you out, mind.'

Nerys smiled warmly in return, meeting Alex's eyes. 'You know better than to even think of that,' she said softly, 'though I wouldn't say no to you cutting the bread if you've a mind to — fresh, it is, and tearing beneath the knife.'

Mona leaned back in her chair, her task of doing the rest of the washing forgotten. She looked up at Alex as though he was ten feet tall, watching as he deftly sliced the bread. He met her eye briefly and winked.

'How's the shop doing, Alex?' Nerys asked quickly. 'I expect it's running well with you in charge.'

Alex sat down. 'It's just wonderful. Business is building up very nicely now that people are getting to know me. Situated well, we are, half-way between Mumbles and Swansea.' He paused to savour the fresh bread.

'And how is our Ceri managing his silver-smithy?' he asked amiably. 'I should think he'd have plenty of customers if he keeps his goods cheap enough. Should get himself a market stall; people are always looking out for pretty gifts. And another idea, he should make christening cups and teething rings, that sort of thing; there's always someone willing to spend money where babies are concerned.'

'You should see him, talk it over with him,' Nerys said approvingly. 'Sounds like very good advice to me.'

'Aye, I might just do that,' Alex said, taking a watch from his waistcoat pocket. 'I've got a bit of time to spare.' He glanced at Mona and she immediately rose from her chair.

'Well, I'm going to call it a day,' she announced. 'The water's gone cold and in any case I've done most of the bedding, so what's left can wait.'

Nerys felt Siona's knee pressing against her and she was afraid to look at him because she knew she would see his amusement in his eyes. He was very broad-minded, but then he was a man. No one seemed to be giving a thought to the pain it would cause to Sarah if she found out.

'Here, let me do that.' Alex carried the ridge-bottomed bath outside with ease, and Nerys heard the wash of water running down the yard.

'You don't mind if I go now, do you?' Mona asked, her eyebrows lifting.

Nerys shook her head. 'Go, you, you've done a day's work in one morning. I'll see you tomorrow, shall I?'

'Try to keep me away.' Mona drew off her enveloping apron and hung it behind the door, flattening down the lace collar of her dress. She looked neat and slim and full of freshness, and Nerys envied her for the time she would be able to spend with her lover.

Siona laughed aloud once the door had closed behind his son. '*Duw*, he's a chip off the old block, all right,' he said wickedly. 'Mind, I'm a reformed character now,' he added quickly. 'Know when I'm well-off, I do!'

'I should think so,' Nerys said in mock indignation. She rose and began to clear the table, feeling restless and strangely lonely.

'I'm going down into town this afternoon,' she said softly, 'I did ask Mona to come with me, but now I see why she wasn't the least bit interested.'

Siona leaned back in his chair. 'I could always take time off, mind, if you need a bit of company.'

'No, indeed, I wouldn't hear of it. You have your work to do and I won't have you feeling you must nursemaid me.' She smiled. 'I'll go on my own, I'm a big girl now.' She indicated the roundness of her figure ruefully. 'A very big girl.'

Siona rose and took her in his arms, holding her gently to him. 'You are lovely,' he said positively.

'There are roses in your cheeks and a clear look in your eyes and I love you.'

She leaned against his ruggedness, as always feeling protected by him. 'You're good for me – know that, Siona?' she said, cupping his face with her hands.

She had only just begun to learn about this man who was her husband; love of a kind was growing between them and she was grateful for it.

Later, as she walked down into the heart of Sweyn's Eye, her shawl drawn round her both as a protection from the cold and as a means of concealing her condition, she felt released. It was good to be out of the house. Mona was right; it didn't do to be confined within the same four walls, however comfortable.

She heard the cries of a cockle-woman who, basket upon her head, was walking straight-backed along the Strand. She passed the fish market near the docks and heard the fussy hooting of tugs taking a ship out on the tide.

'Nerys!' The voice behind her made her freeze into stillness. She could neither answer nor turn her head until a hand resting on her shoulder released her.

'Don't touch me!' she said quickly as she looked into Howel's face. 'You have no right.'

'I have every right!' His eyes were glittering. 'You are carrying my child; the thought has eaten at me day and night since I knew. Why didn't you come and tell me Nerys, at least give me a chance to learn the truth from your own lips?'

'I did come,' she said flatly. 'Perhaps you don't remember. You were rather taken up with some high-born young lady at the time and my presence was simply a nuisance, so I went away.'

'But I didn't know about the baby,' Howel said, as though talking to a backward child. 'It was your place to tell me.'

She turned away. 'My place? Oh yes, I know my place all right and it isn't in your big house among your rich friends. Leave me alone Howel. I'm married to a man big enough to take on the responsibility for me and the baby; your father is worth ten of your sort any day.'

Nerys became aware of someone at her side. She glanced up quickly and her mouth became dry as she saw Siona standing close to her.

'I'm glad I came after you and was just in time to hear your remarks,' he said, putting an arm around her shoulder. 'Otherwise I might have thought this meeting was arranged.'

'Well, then, you would have misjudged me, Siona,' Nerys answered, feeling cold and unhappy, aware that people were glancing at them in curiosity.

'Look, Howel, just go away and leave us alone,' she said, needing to ward off any anger which might spring up between father and son. She took Siona's arm and all might have been well, but Howel would not let the matter rest.

'But you are carrying *my* child,' he insisted. 'I have a right to say how that child will be brought up. I can give the baby advantages that you cannot – the benefit of a good education, for example.'

Siona would have moved forward – his face was dark with anger, his green eyes afire – but Nerys held her hand against his broad chest.

'You have no rights in law,' she said coolly to Howel. 'I happen to know that a child born in wedlock is considered the husband's offspring.' She watched as he stepped back a pace; it was clear he knew she spoke the truth.

'But morally . . .' he began, only to stop speaking as she leaned towards him, her eyes cold.

'Don't you dare to talk about "morally", you are the last one to use such an argument. Goodbye, Howel. Don't come near me again, do you understand, or I'll have the law on you and a man in your position can well do without such a scandal.'

She held her head high as she walked along the street with her arm through Siona's, but inside there was no sense of triumph only a cold pain.

'*Duw*, I didn't realize you were so clever,' Siona said in admiration. 'How did you know all that stuff about the law?'

'Oh, I learned about it from my employer Mary Sutton. She bore a child and was not certain of the father.' She glanced quickly at Siona. 'But a good woman was Mary and her husband realized it himself in the end.'

'Well, anyway, I'm proud of you,' Siona said, 'and grateful that you were loyal to me. I don't deserve it.'

'Of course you deserve it,' Nerys assured him. 'I'm your wife. I owe you everything, Siona, and don't you forget it!'

Her words were bravely spoken, but in her mind she kept seeing Howel's face and the pain in his eyes. In that moment all she longed to do was to crawl into her bed and cry tears of bitterness, for she felt she would never see him again.

CHAPTER TWENTY-SIX

The sun was mellow; the breeze which had drifted the leaves from the trees in the early morning had died away and the day was one of autumnal beauty.

Alex reached out and took Mona's hand and she turned to him, her eyes soft as they looked into his. The town was left behind now, for he had led her to the train that wound its way along the Mumbles road towards Ram's Tor.

As the train had sped past West Cross, he had not even glanced out of the window to where his shop stood busy and successful – with Sarah, his wife, serving the customers and trying to keep the baby happy at the same time. He should not feel guilty, he told himself, for he worked from sunrise to sunset most days with very little time to himself.

'We shouldn't be so brazen, mind,' Mona said, 'walking about the cliffs hand in hand for all to see.'

Alex knew she spoke wisely, but if wisdom came into his reasoning he would not have laid with her, would never have tasted the sweet wine of being a man. He was grateful to Mona and he enjoyed being with her, for he felt whole in her presence and for him that was enough.

'Let's walk down to the beach then, shall we?' he suggested. 'There we can be private among the dunes.'

'Oh, aye, I know what's on your mind, boyo!' Mona said, smiling up at him. 'Wicked you are, Alex, but a real man, mind.'

Alex felt warmed. This was what he wanted to hear,

for he had feared himself impotent as he had lain night after night beside his wife, unable to make love to her.

He held Mona's hand tightly as she negotiated the steep path leading down to the small sheltered curve of Limeslade Beach. The sun lay in warm pools amid the craggy grey of the rocks and the pebbles chattered like a gaggle of old women as the waves, small and harmless, receded from the land.

He found a niche for them among the sun-warmed rocks and put down his coat for Mona to lie upon. She was sweet and golden in the sunlight, her eyes welcoming, and he knew with a sharp sense of pain that she loved him.

'Come on, *cariad*, don't just stand there staring at me.' She held up her thin arms and he crouched down beside her, wondering at her need for him. She was so young and yet so womanly, asking nothing from him except that he be with her whenever he could.

'Why are you so good to me?' He stretched out beside her, easing himself into a more comfortable position on the rocks. Her hand reached towards him and her warm, soft fingers curled trustingly in his.

'Now, I don't have to tell you the answer to that, do I? You know that I love you, Alex. I think I've loved you since I first set eyes on you, and that was a long time before I came to the Ferry House to do the washing!'

'You're too good to throw away your life for me.' He turned and buried his face in the warmth of her neck, she smelled sweet and clean, with the scent of soap and starch emanating from her. Somehow, although she was not the beauty his wife was, Mona stirred his senses so that he was always eager for her.

'What have I thrown away?' Mona asked, brushing his hair with her lips. 'There's nothing to give up, good boy, no one in my life who is half so important to me as you.'

This was what appealed to him most – her unstinting love and trust, her need for him, her unashamed delight in his love-making. She had been innocent when he had first taken her, virginal and sweet, and she was all his.

'Will you ever give me up, I wonder?' she said wistfully.'I mean, if Sarah was to find out about us and put you on the spot, would you turn your back on me?'

Alex leaned up on one elbow and stared down at her. 'I can't imagine my life without you, Mona, and I mean that.' He sighed. 'I don't want to hurt Sarah, so all I can hope is that she never does find out about you.'

Mona turned to face him, her hand resting on his cheek. 'Are we very wicked, Alex? Will we burn in hellfires like the preacher tells us?'

'We are not wicked,' Alex said softly. 'We are two people who have need of each other and that can't be a sin.'

She wound her arms around his shoulders and Alex felt the sweet press of her breasts against him. He felt the fires begin in his belly as tenderly he folded her in his arms and held her close.

Her mouth was soft, her lips parting under his. She loved him and wanted him and he felt like a man grown into a giant, willing and able to bring delight to the woman moaning and straining against him.

He took his time and felt the autumn sun warm on his bare back, adding to his pleasure and joy, for taking Mona as his woman was a delight, a happiness that exploded into thousands of fragments as she cried out his name.

They lay for a time in happy silence, hands clinging and pulses slowing to a normal beat. After a while, Mona rose and ran naked into the sea like a nymph, with her hair clinging wet and fine to her skull.

He put his arms behind his head and must have

slept, for when he opened them once more she was fully dressed and watching over him so protectively that he felt his throat constrict with tears.

He wished that now they could go home together and sit beside the fire and talk, for with Mona he could converse as he never could with Sarah. But soon, he must take Mona to her house near the river where she lived with her large family and leave her there while he returned to his wife.

'You won't fall in love with someone else, will you, Mona?' He was wrong to ask it of her and yet she was his; he could not bear to think of another man even touching her hand.

'There's a daft question!' She hugged his arm to her. 'I love you, there's no room for anyone else.'

She made him feel humble and yet at the same time he glowed with the pride of his possession of her. He, Alexander Llewelyn, had turned her from a girl into a fulfilled woman.

'Let's get back then,' he said the words on a sigh. 'Our little bit of heaven is over for today.' He smiled, a little embarrassed by his expression of sentimentality, but Mona's eyes sparkled and he knew he had said the right thing.

The field of Ram's Tor Farm stretched out to the cliff-top and back into the hillside and Alex could see men working on the land. He shuddered, remembering as he always did when he came this way, the manner in which his twin had died. Sensing his feeling, Mona hugged his arm closer to her side as if to comfort him.

The road cut between the cliffs wound down to where the Mumbles train waited like a red snake to take people into the town. He would ride with Mona part of the way instead of walking, Alex decided, for today he was late and Sarah would be justifiably angry with him.

'You'll be all right if I get off at West Cross, won't

you, love?' he said, helping her up the high step and into the body of the train. She nodded, seating herself near the window and brushing down her hair self-consciously, now aware that she looked dishevelled.

'Of course I'll be all right,' she whispered. 'Anyway, there's some of your customers aboard, so it will look as if we've met casual-like if you get off before me.'

Alex didn't care about being seen with Mona. No one could know of the intimacy they shared and after all, she did work for his father so what was more natural than sitting next to each other if they happened to meet on the train?

'When will I see you again?' Mona asked softly, her head bent. 'I don't want to nag, but if I know when we're to meet I can think about it and plan and look forward to it, see?'

On a wash of gratitude, he surreptitiously squeezed her hand. 'I'll take you out tomorrow night. We'll go out of town, up to Morriston perhaps, and I'll treat you to supper in some nice hotel.' He saw her eyes glow and whispered wickedly, 'How would you like to make love in a real bed like we used to when you stayed at the Ferry House?'

'Hush.' She glanced round her quickly and, assured that no one was watching, smiled up at him.

'That would be lovely,' she mouthed the words. 'I can't wait! Shall I meet you near the Rising Sun as usual?'

He nodded and swung himself to his feet, for the train was drawing to a stop. 'See you soon.'

He alighted from the train and stood watching as it snaked its way along the line into the town. He felt lost for a moment, as though part of him was slipping away, then he turned and made his way across the Mumbles road and towards his home.

The shop was busy and in the back room the baby

was crying. He was immediately absorbed into the business of serving his customers, leaving Sarah free to attend her child.

The boy was so like Hector, even down to the gestures of his chubby fists, that it tugged at Alex's heart to watch him. It was as though his brother had been reincarnated and was watching through the baby's eyes.

He was relieved when it was time to put up the shutters; he threw the bolts into place and leaned against the door for a moment, drawing his breath. It was cool in the darkened shop and he could tell by the amount of money in the drawer that it had been a good day. That meant Sarah had been busy, with little time to rest.

He walked purposefully into the kitchen, where she was standing over the range cooking a meal. The baby was in his pram sleeping and Alex suddenly felt the weight of his responsibilities press in on him.

'Sit down, love,' he said to Sarah. 'I'll cook the supper.' She obeyed instantly and he saw the dark shadows around her eyes with a feeling of guilt. 'I'm sorry I've left so much of the work to you, but I'll be here all day tomorrow – after I've finished the round, I mean.'

'Don't worry, I've been managing,' Sarah said quickly. 'The only trouble is that the baby's teething and he's a bit cross, but I feel better now that you're here.'

She sank into a chair and he saw with surprise how thin she had become. She had always been a bonny girl full of health and vitality, but now she appeared drained, low in spirits as much as in body, and he was suddenly anxious.

'Are you all right, Sarah? Not sickening for something, are you? You're very pale.'

'I'm tired, Alex, and worried. Perhaps this is not the time to talk about it, but I want you in my bed. You are my husband and I'm lonely for you.' It seemed that now the floodgates were open, she could not stop her flow of words. 'I'm a woman, Alex, young and strong. I don't want to live my life as a nun!'

He was taken unawares, for he had not thought of Sarah as having needs and desires. He had imagined that she would always be hankering after Hector, her lover and the father of her baby, seeing Alex only as a substitute.

He rose to his feet, embarrassed by her beseeching eyes. 'I don't like to talk about such things,' he said softly. 'I don't want to hurt you, Sarah, and yet . . .' He shrugged, unable to say that with her he was impotent.

'Well,' he paused, trying to think of the right thing to say, 'as you said, this really isn't the right time to talk. There are accounts to be done and the shelves to be filled out and a dozen and one things. We'll discuss it later. Shall we?'

When she replied, her voice was tight and hard. 'Later I shall be in bed alone and falling asleep with weariness. What am I working for, Alex, tell me that. Is it just to keep up a pretence of being a happy married woman?'

He put his hand lightly on her shoulder. 'Sarah, I wish I could explain to you how I feel, but the words stick in my throat.'

'I know.' She was soft suddenly, her eyes moist, her anger dissipated. 'It's the ghost of Hector, he is always there between us. But it's time to bury the dead, Alex, and to think of the living – for the living it is who continue to feel pain.'

She took her baby in her arms and made for the door. He wanted to call her back, to reassure her that everything was going to be all right, but was it? Not even he could guarantee that.

He took out the books, laid them on the table and stared down at the figures, but they swam together before his eyes and it was not weariness but tears that blinded him, and he didn't know if they were for Sarah, Mona or himself.

* * *

Sarah stood in the entrance of the shop, hugging her son close to her breast. She had opened up early in response to an urgent knocking on the door, and tried her best to smile at the customer who stood with basket in hand waiting to enter.

'You're an early bird, Mrs Gethin. Run out of tea or sugar, have you?'

'*Duw*, run out of everything if you ask me,' the woman replied. 'I don't know what we'd all do without you and your shop.' She brushed past Sarah and frowned at the dimness of the room. Sarah put the baby down and opened the shutters with a sigh of resignation.

'I want a few goods, it's true,' the woman said, leaning against the counter, 'but really I'm here for your benefit.'

'Oh, aye; what is it then, Mrs Gethin? Are you paying me some of the money you owe me?' Sarah asked, tongue in cheek.

'No, girl, it's much more important than that.' She leaned forward confidingly. 'There's something you should know about your husband!'

Sarah felt her scalp prickle. She knew that Mrs Gethin was about to say something unpleasant and there seemed to be no way of stopping her, but she had to try.

'I'm sure there's nothing you can tell me about Alex that I don't already know.' She spoke with a cheerfulness she was far from feeling, but her words were greeted with a derisory sniff.

'Carrying on, he is!' Mrs Gethin's mouth twisted as though in distaste. 'And with that young girl Mona who helps out at the Ferry House. Don't worry, *merchi*, the wife is always the last one to know.'

'I don't believe a word of it,' Sarah said indignantly. 'Now can I get you anything, Mrs Gethin, for I'm much too busy to stand around listening to silly gossip.'

'Oh, gossip it might be but it's not silly – don't you fool yourself, my girl!' Mrs Gethin lifted her basket and walked away in a huff. 'Only trying to help out, I am, see and you too hoity-toity to listen. Well, on your own head be it.'

The shop door shut with a bang and Sarah stood for a long moment staring at the cord on the blind, watching it swing to and fro as though it was mesmerizing her. The woman had spoken the truth and Sarah knew it. Of course Alex was unfaithful, that explained a great deal.

It was the crying of the baby that brought her to her senses and she picked him up and held him close. She did not weep for she was beyond tears, but she needed to talk to someone. Perhaps advice from someone older and wiser than herself would help to ease the ache in her heart.

Nerys Beynon would listen sympathetically. She had lived in the Ferry House and must know Alex pretty well. Maybe she would be able to tell Sarah what she must do to save her marriage.

She would shut up the shop, she decided, go into Sweyn's Eye and take the tram to the riverside. She was sure that Nerys would welcome her; she would be fair and wise and would do her best to help.

Sarah could not find it in her heart to blame Alex entirely, for she realized a little of the difficulties he faced. He had a business on his hands, a thriving business, and it made for a great deal of work.

But what was worse, he had his brother's death on his conscience and that was where the thorn dug into the flesh.

She washed the baby and dressed him warmly, for

the day was blustery and cold with nearly all the trees stripped bare of their leaves.

On the swaying Mumbles train, which in reality was more like a tram, the baby fell asleep and with a feeling of love, Sarah hugged him closer. He was everything to her, the only being in the whole world who loved her. But no, she felt that Alex loved her too, except that he could not show it.

The river flowed swiftly between the banks, the wind whipping up waves which drove their way towards the sea and the docklands. Sarah shuddered for she was afraid of the river. She felt the child grow heavier in her arms as she walked along the bank to the Ferry House. Feeling a little timid about approaching Nerys, yet determination sustained her as she walked up to the half-opened door and knocked hard.

'*Duw*, there's a fright you gave me! Why, Sarah, come in. There's nothing wrong with Alex, is there?'

'No, it's nothing like that. This is just a little visit, that's all, a chance for me to get out of the house for a bit,' Sarah said, smiling.

Nerys was flourishing and it was clear to see now that her pregnancy was pretty much advanced. She looked content and happy and smiled warmly as she beckoned Sarah inside.

'That baby of yours must weigh a ton!' Nerys smiled. 'Have a nice cup of tea to revive you – and there's fresh Welsh cakes in the tin.'

With a sigh of relief, Sarah sank into a chair, allowing Nerys to take the baby and settle him in the corner of the sofa, where he snuggled down sleepy and content. She took the cup of tea but waved away the cakes; she was much too strung-up and nervous to eat.

'Well, I must say that baby is taking it out of you,' Nerys said in concern. 'You're so thin!'

'It isn't the baby.' Sarah felt she might just as well

367

leap in with the truth straight away, before her courage deserted her. 'It's Alex; he's going out with another woman.'

She saw the colour rise to Nerys's cheeks and knew that Alex's affair was no secret. 'Please, Nerys, don't feel you have to say anything about that; it's not the real cause of the problem, you see.'

'Well, then.' Nerys seated herself opposite Sarah and leaned forward, chin on her hands. 'Tell me about it, if it will help.'

'I wouldn't mind so much about Mona . . .' Sarah began. 'Well, perhaps that's not true; I do mind a lot, but what's worse is that Alex has no desire to come to my bed and it's not right or natural. Am I so hideous then that he turns his back on me?'

Nerys frowned.'Has he not slept with you at all since your marriage?' she asked and by the bright spots in her cheeks, Sarah knew that she was embarrassed.

'Not once,' Sarah answered truthfully. 'I think he feels something for me, yet he cannot or will not make me his wife in anything but name.'

Nerys sighed and leaned back in her chair, running her hand over the swell of her stomach almost absentmindedly. The gesture was a familiar one, reminding Sarah of the time when she was carrying her own child and felt him move beneath her heart. She had been happy then, and Alex's abstinence from marital relations with her was only respect and consideration on his part for her condition. But now she was over the birth and she wanted more than her husband seemed prepared to give.

'I know Alex pretty well,' Nerys said softly. 'He loved Hector deeply, more deeply than anyone who is not a twin can understand. They had a language without words, those two, and they were like two halves of the same fruit.'

She paused and stared at Sarah. 'You know what I think? Alex is afraid to take you as his wife for fear of being disloyal, taking what is rightfully his brother's.'

Sarah sighed. 'I do understand that, it's what I've thought myself, but how can I persuade him out of that way of thinking?'

Nerys shook her head. 'I'm not sure, but if I were you I would dress up and be beautiful for him, seduce him deliberately as though he was a lover. Try to make him forget everything except that you are a woman and he's a man. Look, shall I keep the baby here tonight so that you can be alone with Alex? Would that help?'

'No, thank you all the same,' Sarah said. 'I can put Teddy in the back bedroom; he goes off to sleep early anyway, he'd be no problem.' She smiled, beginning to warm to Nerys's idea.

'What if I get in some bottles of ale and make a special meal for Alex – might that do some good, do you think?'

'Well, it can't do any harm, can it?' Nerys bit her lip. 'But don't pin too much on being successful straight away. Alex must see that you are your own woman, a personality in your own right and not simply a wife – anyone's wife. Do you know what I mean?'

Sarah nodded. 'Yes, I think I do.' She bit her nail thoughtfully. 'I've been swamped with work and with caring for the baby, not to say downcast at Alex's neglect of me. I suppose it might look as though I was being reproachful to him always.'

'Well, don't stay indoors thinking too much about your life. Go out when you can and make friends; don't always be there when he expects you. Perhaps he takes you for granted and feels you'll always be at his beck and call.'

'Aye, I'm just like a doormat,' Sarah said ruefully. 'I think you're right, Nerys. I must show some spirit. I've

369

lost my gift of laughter and I must be a misery to live with.'

'Now you're being too hard on yourself,' Nerys smiled. 'But I would say this – don't go straight home but buy yourself a nice frock, something new to wear. That will make you feel much better.' She took in a deep breath. 'Now, how about a fresh pot of tea and some cakes? All this advice-giving has made me hungry!'

By the time Sarah left the Ferry House she felt much better and her hope was high that she could win Alex over, make him forget that she had been his brother's woman. She would be patient but persistent; she had used her womanly wiles once, she reminded herself. Had they deserted her for ever just because she was a mother?

*   *   *

Before she left the town, Sarah went into the large Emporium in the *Stryd Fawr* and, ignoring the disdainful looks of the superior shop assistant, chose for herself a new dress of finest rust-coloured wool with a white collar of heavy lace. She knew it would suit her slimness and accentuate the neatness of her waist. While in town, she decided to have her hair cut and took a deep breath at her own daring; she was spending far more money than she should.

She wondered if Alex would be home from his milk round and if he was, would he worry because she was out? But when she returned to the shop in West Cross it was to find the place silent and the stable at the back standing open and empty. A stab of jealousy gripped her. Was he with Mona, lying with her in some sweet field of coarse autumn grass?

'Forget her!' she told herself and put her baby into his bed, where he promptly fell asleep.

Sarah washed her hair until it squeaked clean and when it was dry, looked at herself in the mirror. The cut made her face seem fine-boned, almost elfin, and well-pleased, she brushed it vigorously until it shone. She tried on her dress before the wardrobe mirror, seeing a different woman from the Sarah she had been earlier that morning.

When she heard the downstairs door open, she knew Alex had come home. There was no food prepared for him, but somehow that didn't seem to matter. She walked slowly down the stairs feeling almost faint with nerves, but there was no sign of it as she entered the kitchen where he was standing before the fire.

'*Duw*, there's smart you're looking, girl!' he said quickly. 'Good god, you've cut your hair and damn fine it looks too!' There was a warmth in his eyes that made her heart beat swiftly with hope. She went to him, put her arms around him and looked up into his face.

'And there's a strong man you've become – just look at the muscles on you!' She tilted back her head. 'Are you coming a-courting me, then? It's about time you did, mind.'

She forgot about the meal she had been going to prepare and taking his hand, led him upstairs and into the large cool bedroom which had real carpet on the floor and good lined curtains against the windows.

Pulling him down beside her, she pressed her lips against his cheek. 'I love you, Alex, I love you so much it hurts.' She took his face between her hands and kissed him and his mouth was warm and passionate against hers.

She slipped out of her dress and stood before him, her hands held out invitingly. 'I want you to come to me, Alex, to love me the way you should.'

He half rose to his feet, his hand on his belt, and for a moment she thought she had won. Then he turned away and sank on the bed.

'I can't *cariad*, I just can't.' His tone was muffled by the pounding in her ears and she moved forward and swung him round to face her.

'You can't take me in our marriage bed, but you can make love to that flossie Mona in field or hedge, or on the beach or anywhere else the mood takes you!' She saw the shock in his eyes with grim satisfaction.

'Do you think I'm dull then, so stupid that I can't put two and two together? You're the talk of the place, the pair of you, and I'm not going to stand for it another day – do you hear me?'

She picked up her dress with savage fingers, pain and jealousy mingled in her mind like a poison. 'As far as I'm concerned, you just made your choice and you've chosen her. Well, have Mona – let that slut slave for you every hour of the day the way I've done, and good luck to her!'

Alex reached out and caught her to him, his face close to hers, anger burning in his eyes.

'Don't talk that way. I won't have it, do you hear? Mona is no slut, understand that!'

'That's right, stick up for her! I hate you, Alex. I could stick a knife into you right now!'

She beat out at him, catching him a hefty blow across the face and he grasped her wrists and pressed her down on the bed.

'You bitch!' He twisted her arm above her head and she kicked out at him with her feet, almost crying in her fury.

'Let me up, you no-good-ram!' She ground the words through her teeth. 'You are only fit for lying with whores!'

His mouth was upon hers then, but not with any tenderness; he was ripping at her petticoat, his eyes dark with anger.

'I'll show you, you vixen!' He pushed her clothes aside and then he was upon her like a madman, thrusting and punishing.

Slowly her anger changed to passion. He was here with her, only she wanted tenderness not anger. She clung to him, kissing him and murmuring his name, 'Let it be beautiful, Alex, let it be loving.'

He paused and looked down at her as though seeing her for the first time. Then he moaned and held her close . . . kissing her mouth, her throat, her breasts . . . gentle now in his passion.

'My love,' she said softly, 'you've come to me, at last.'

CHAPTER TWENTY-SEVEN

The sounds of Market Street penetrated to the upper room of Murphy's fresh-fish shop where Katie lay on her bed with hands behind her head, lethargically contemplating her future. Had she been too hard on Ceri, she wondered – letting him go off the way he had done, believing that she didn't really love him. And *did* she? The question raced around her mind and seemingly there was no answer to it. All she knew was that she didn't want to be married to him, not yet at least.

She sat up and moved towards the window, staring down into the busy street. An autumn wind was blowing the leaves along the cobbled roadway and the shawls of the old women were whipped into a life of their own as they fluttered like birds around bent shoulders.

The younger women wore coats which reached to calf-length, and the more fashionable had hats pulled well down over their ears. It was a street which had been familiar to her since childhood for she had spent most of her life there. Perhaps that was the trouble; maybe she needed to get away. Far away so that she could think more clearly about her future.

'Katie!' Her mother's voice rang loudly up the stairs. 'Come down and help me, girl, for sure there's such a crowd in the shop that I can't manage on my own.'

Reluctantly, Katie left the window and the privacy of her room for the bustle of the fish shop. She hated handling the cold fresh fish, hated seeing the bulging eyes that stared at her as though in reproach, and most of all hated the smell which clung to her clothes.

'Serve Mali, she's been waiting quite a while,' Mrs Murphy whispered, and with a smile of welcome Katie went forward.

'Sure 'tis nice to see an old friend,' she said softly. 'Glad to see you're still coming over here yourself and not sending one of your maids!'

'That'll be the day,' Mali said quickly. 'How else would I keep up with all my friends if I didn't come shopping myself? Hoping for a chat, I was, but I can see you've got your hands full by here.'

'Well, go through into the kitchen,' Katie offered, opening the door. 'I'll be with you as soon as the crowd thins out a bit.'

Katie served efficiently, but with only half her mind on the task. She was thanking providence for sending Mali along just at this moment when she needed someone sensible to talk to.

'Two pieces of cod, wasn't it, Mrs Benson?' she said and deftly cut down the centre of the fish, then with a flick of the knife drew the flesh from the bones. 'There we are, they should fry up a treat now that I've boned them.'

She went back into the kitchen and, grimacing across to where Mali sat waiting for her, washed her hands thoroughly with carbolic soap.

'Sure 'tis good to see you, Mali.' Katie sat down opposite her and leaned forward in her chair. 'Are you still working up at Tawe Lodge with the unmarried mothers then?' She saw Mali nod and hurried on anxiously, 'I'm glad you came today of all days, for to be sure I could do with some advice and you've always been fair and sensible.'

'Well,' Mali said dubiously, 'if I can help, I will – you know that – but I'm no oracle, mind.'

'Sure, I'm not saying you are,' Katie replied, 'but I just want someone from outside the situation to give me an opinion. It's about Ceri. I don't know if I love him or not, but one thing is certain; I don't want to be married to him, not yet anyway. What am I to do, Mali?'

Mali bit her lip and was silent for a long time, considering what Katie had said. Eventually, she shook her head.

'All I can say is that I couldn't wait to be Sterling's wife. I wanted to be with him so badly that it was hurting me all the time, like a pain that wouldn't go away. I *had* to have him.'

'Well, I don't think my feelings are that intense,' Katie said softly, 'but then you have only loved one man and I have been mistress and wife before I met Ceri – wicked I am, sure enough.'

'You do yourself an injustice,' Mali said sternly. 'Anyone would think you were a flossie, to hear you go on.'

'Sometimes I feel like one, for sure I've lain with Ceri, led him on to believe I loved him and would marry him, when all the time my head was telling me it wasn't right.'

Mali sighed softly. 'Why don't you get right away from Sweyn's Eye for a while? You could get in touch with Rhian Grey; she's in Yorkshire now, as you know, and I'm sure she'd have you to stay – at least for a while, until you can sort your feelings out.'

'Rhian left Sweyn's Eye such a long time ago. I shouldn't think she'd want me landing on her doorstep,' Katie said, shaking her head.

'Nonsense. She'd be delighted to see someone from home. Sterling has kept in touch with Mansel Jack ever since he worked here on the munitions. Good friends, they are.' She paused for a moment, chewing her nail thoughtfully. 'What if I ask Sterling to get in touch with Mansel Jack and sound him out, then I'll bring you the address and you can think about writing to Rhian?' She put her arms around Katie's waist. 'But for now, forget all your worries and come out to town with me. I want a new pair of shoes and a silk blouse. I'll leave my shopping bag here and send over for it later – is that all right?'

Mrs Murphy raised her eyebrows heavenward when she saw that Katie was going out. 'Sure and the girl don't think of her old mammy any more, leaving me on my own with a shop full of people – what's the world coming to, I ask you!'

'Don't go on,' Katie said, smiling. 'Daddy and the boys will be back shortly and you'll have plenty of help then.'

It was cold out in the street and Katie drew her woollen hat down over her bright hair. 'Remember when we were children Mali? Everything seemed so easy then; we laughed and played and never thought of falling in love.'

'Oh, I did,' Mali said. 'From the time our mam was buried in *Dan y Graig* cemetery and I came upon the posh funeral of Mr Richardson and saw Sterling in the graveyard, I dreamed every night of him, even though I thought then that I hated him for being a boss and giving my father the push from his job.'

'You've been very lucky, Mali,' Katie said softly, 'and you've deserved it all, for sure you're a good and generous girl.'

'Huh! No longer a girl, mind, but thanks for the kindness.' She tucked her arm in Katie's and smiled warmly. 'We'll do a bit of shopping and then how's about us having a nice meal in the Emporium tea-rooms?'

'Sure that sounds lovely,' Katie said, lifting her head high. She would put her troubles behind her and enjoy the day and later, she would think about going away from Sweyn's Eye and from Ceri Llewelyn.

*   *   *

377

It was little over a week later when the letter came from Rhian asking Katie to go and stay with her in Yorkshire, and during that time Katie had seen or heard nothing of Ceri.

She sat on the bed listening to the sounds of the street outside her window, wondering how she could bear to leave all that was familiar to her even for a short time. She could imagine her mammy's response to such a move; Mrs Murphy would be tearful and angry in turns, but at last she would give her blessing, for she had seen her only daughter through many sorrows and only wanted what was best for her.

Katie let her mind dwell on how Ceri would react to her plans. She knew that she owed it to him to speak frankly, to tell him she was going away, but he had not come near her since they had quarrelled and she had missed him . . . but not enough to convince her that she should marry him. Yet the prospect of seeing him, of perhaps being in his arms again, disturbed her. She was acting like a silly girl, she told herself, a foolish child not knowing what she cried for.

Downstairs, her mother was sitting in the kitchen with the inevitable bottle of gin at her side. She glanced up with raised eyebrows and it was clear she was curious about the letter.

'Well?' she said softly. 'Are you going to tell me what's happening then, for sure my nose has been twitching with unasked questions this past week!'

Katie sat beside her mother and held out the letter. 'It's from Rhian, Rhian Grey as she was before she married. She's invited me to come and stay with her in Yorkshire – and I think, mammy, that I should accept.'

'And what about that fine boy of yours, that sweet Ceri Llewelyn? Is it finished between you, then?'

Katie hung her head. 'I don't honestly know, mammy, but I must get away – right away – try to sort myself out'.

Mrs Murphy sighed. 'You'll lose him. He's a handsome boy with good prospects; some other girl will snap him up while your back is turned, you'll see, Katie.'

'I shall have to take that risk,' Katie said soberly, 'but I'll go to see him, try to explain – perhaps he'll have enough patience to wait for me.'

'Patience? Where their feelings are involved men have no patience – haven't you learned that yet, Katie?'

Katie shook back her hair, 'Well, I must go, mammy. That's all there is to be said on the matter.'

'So be it.' Mrs Murphy hugged her daughter and there were tears in her eyes that trembled on sparse lashes. 'Just be a good girl and don't stay away too long.'

Katie returned to her room and taking a pad out of her drawer, began to write to Rhian.

* * *

Mona was unhappy. She had not seen Alex for many days and she grieved for the closeness there had been between them. He was not sick, she knew that, for he still continued his milk round and served in his shop in West Cross. She had walked there more than once to wait outside his house, hoping for a glimpse of him. And she would go again, for the pain that was in her would not let her rest.

She bent now over the wash-tub in the kitchen of the Ferry House, rubbing away at the coarse trousers which were stained with mud. She was sure that Tom and Will must spend most of their lives on their backsides on the slippery banks of the River Swan, for their clothes were always so hard to get clean.

'Want to stop for a rest now?' Nerys was behind her suddenly, holding out a cup of tea.

'Aye, I've just finished these trousers. Get them on

the line I will, to blow in the wind, then I'll have a little bit of a sit-down.'

As Mona pegged the clothes to the line that stretched across the yard, she heard the sound of a masculine voice from the kitchen and her pulse beat fast. Could it be Alex come to see her?

But once inside, she saw it was Ceri sitting near the table, not Alex, and her spirits dropped. Her feelings must have been apparent, for Ceri smiled at her.

'Hey, I'm not that bad-looking, am I?' he appealed to Nerys. '*Duw*, here's me coming to offer the girl a bit of work at my house, and her looking as though I'm the last person on earth that she wants to see!'

'Sorry,' Mona said quickly. 'I was far away. What's this work you're offering me, then?'

'I want you to come over to Canal Street and do a bit of cleaning for me, just like you do here. If you've got time, that is?'

'Oh, yes, I've got time,' Mona said, forcing herself to smile. 'I could do with the extra money too, for my youngest brother needs a new winter coat. But what about Katie, won't she be doing the cleaning?' She saw Ceri frown.

'The least said about that subject, the better!' He rose to his feet. 'Look, I'll leave you the key. Perhaps you could get over there this afternoon and tidy up, like. I've made a right mess of the place, I'm afraid.'

'Don't worry,' Mona said, feeling a sudden affinity to Ceri, who had obviously quarrelled with Katie. 'I'll get the house tidy for you in no time.'

'There's a good girl, I knew I could depend on you. A right hard little worker you are, in spite of being only a half-pint in size!' He smiled and ruffled her hair and Mona touched his hand in what she hoped was an understanding gesture.

When Ceri had gone, Mona sat drinking her tea in silence and it was Nerys who spoke first.

'Poor Ceri, it looks as if things have gone wrong for

380

him and Katie. He didn't say much but then he didn't have to; his attitude gave away the fact that there's been a rift of some sort. What a pity – I thought they were so well suited to each other.'

Mona shrugged, not wanting to delve too deeply for she was still smarting herself.

Suddenly feeling decisive, she rose to her feet. 'I shall have to call in at my house before I go up to Ceri's,' she said. 'I've got to collect some cleaning things if I'm to tackle the mess he said he's made.'

'That's all right,' Nerys said gently. 'Go, you – most of the jobs are finished round here anyway, and this afternoon I'm going to put my feet up and rest. Siona's made me promise.'

'And quite right too!' Mona drew on her coat and pulled the belt tightly around her slim figure. Her mind was not really on what she was saying, for she had decided to give it one last try; she would go down to West Cross and talk to Alex, try to make some sense of what was happening. He owed her an explanation and she was going to see that she got it.

She caught the Mumbles train from Rutland Street and sat on the seat, staring out at the sweep of the coast to her left. Far over the bay she could see the craggy rocks of Mumbles Head jutting into the sea, and beyond that the dim violet shape of the hills of the Devon coast.

Although it was cold, a mellow sun was shining, bathing the sea in a golden glow. Mona felt tears burn her lids for the times when she had shared the splendour of the same view safe in Alex's arms.

She alighted from the train at Black Pill Station and walked along the sea-front towards West Cross, trying to compose herself for she was trembling. What would she say to Alex? Would she even speak or would she rush straight into his arms?

Her fear was that he would reject her out of hand, refuse to even acknowledge all that had passed between them. But the overriding urge within her was to see him, whatever the outcome.

The shop stood a little way back from the road, with boxes of vegetables spilling from the doorway on to the pavement.

She stood for a long time trying to summon enough courage to face Alex, knowing he was back from his round for the cart lay drunkenly at the side of the building while the horse grazed in the field nearby. Slowly she moved forward and, for a moment, was blinded by the dimness of the shop which smelled of coffee grounds and the earthy scent of potatoes.

When her eyes became accustomed to the gloom, she saw that Alex's wife was standing quite still on the other side of the counter watching her. Sarah came round and closed the shop door, turning round the 'Closed' sign and slipping home the bolt.

'You'd better come out to the back room,' she said without preamble. 'There's a lot to be sorted out between us.'

So she knew . . . Sarah was aware of the other woman in Alex's life. The thought sent shock waves running through Mona's body as, trembling, she followed Sarah into the neat kitchen.

'I have to tell you that it's finished between you and my husband,' Sarah said calmly, almost pityingly. 'He's my husband now in every way.' She emphasized the last words, so that Mona could not misunderstand.

'Well, he's been my man for many a month and nothing can alter that!' Mona retaliated.

'No, nothing can alter that,' Sarah agreed, 'but it's over now, finished, and I don't want you around Alex any more – do you understand?'

'Surely it's up to him to tell me that himself?' Mona demanded, becoming angry in the face of Sarah's certainty that Alex would not want to see her. 'He's a man, a real man and he won't be dictated to by you or anyone else.'

'Nonsense!' Sarah said, 'He's a coward in the way most men are cowards when it comes to facing up to unpleasant situations. Why do you think you haven't seen him for days? Do you honestly believe I've had him chained indoors?'

'I don't care what you say, or what arguments you use. Nothing will convince me it's over unless Alex tells me so himself,' Mona said in a low voice.

Sarah sighed. 'All right, have it your own way.' She went to the door leading to the stairs and called out.

'Alex, will you come down here, there's a good man? There's someone here to see you.' She turned to Mona. 'He's been having a nap; indeed I was going to join him once I closed the shop for the dinner hour.'

'Liar!' Mona said, stung into speech. 'I know he hasn't slept with you since your marriage, he told me so himself.'

'Oh yes, that was the case,' Sarah said calmly, 'up until the time he thought he was going to lose me.' She smiled. 'Since then we've made up for lost time and I don't think he'd have the energy for another woman these days.'

Mona wanted to strike out at the smiling face; she wanted to lash and hurt as she was being hurt. She almost took a step forward, but Alex came into the kitchen, his shirt unbuttoned to the waist.

'Good god, Mona!' he said in astonishment. 'What on earth do you think you are doing here in my house?'

'I came to talk to you, to ask for an explanation as to why I haven't seen you, but your wife has told me quite plainly that she keeps you happy in bed these days and so you don't need me any longer.' She could not keep the bitterness from her voice. 'Is that true, Alex?'

'I'm sorry, Mona, I didn't want to hurt you.' He rubbed his hand through his hair, glancing from his wife to Mona with a lost expression on his face.

383

'Tell her, Alex,' Sarah said softly, insistently. 'Tell her it's over; it's the kindest way in the long run.'

'Sarah's right. It's over between us, Mona, and I'm sorry if I led you to think that anything permanent could come of our affair.'

'I love you, Alex,' Mona said and to her own ears, her voice was a whine. Quickly, she pulled herself together; she would not allow Sarah to see her beaten. 'But if you say it's over, then I have to accept your decision.'

She turned to Sarah, the desire to hurt undeniable. 'Alex had me many times. We lay together and made love long before he came to your bed. Remember that, Miss Smug, and don't be too sure he won't do it again!'

She had the satisfaction of seeing a fleeting shadow of doubt pass over Sarah's face before she turned away, but Sarah swiftly hit back.

'And you remember that I am his legal wife, that we are married before God and in the eyes of the people of Sweyn's Eye. You, Mona, are nothing more or less than a fancy piece.' She stared at Mona with hard, angry eyes. 'I am at his hearth and in his bed now, so you'd better go.'

'Yes, I'll go,' Mona spoke softly. 'But I'll leave you wondering, always wondering which woman occupies the most important place of all, that place in his heart . . . for I had him first, mind.'

She turned and opened the bolts of the door with studied calm, letting herself out into the cool of the day with a feeling of having struck the last blow. It was unkind of her, unfair perhaps, but Sarah in her smugness had asked for it.

Walking across the road to the beach, she sat on the coarse grass which grew in the dunes. There she put her hands over her face and let the bitter tears flow unchecked.

Later, she rose and made her way to Black Pill to

catch the train back to the heart of the town. She bought cleaning materials in one of the shops on the *Stryd Fawr*, deciding she would not return home but would go straight to Ceri's house and begin the cleaning. That at least would take her mind off her humiliation and heartache.

Canal Street lay along the banks of the yellow waters of the canal. The old, twisted wreck of the burned-out laundry had been taken down, leaving a patch of coarse grass and weeds. It was next to this land that Ceri's house stood – tall and, like the rest of the buildings in the street, in need of a coat of paint.

She let herself in with the key Ceri had given her and the musty smell of stale bread and cooking fat assailed her as she moved down the long dark passageway.

He had not exaggerated. The kitchen was like a battlefield, with a burnt-out pan standing on the edge of the range and a sink full of dirty dishes. The stone floor badly needed scrubbing, coated as it was with grease, and the windows could scarcely let in any light for the dust that clung to them.

Mona took off her coat and hung it on the back of the door, then she rolled up her sleeves with determined stabs of her fingers. It was as though there was not a minute to waste as she built up the fire, stoking it well with coals, and filled the kettle with water from the tap over the big stone sink.

She tackled the dust and dirt of Ceri's kitchen as though it was a personal affront, keeping her mind doggedly on her task and refusing to think about Alex. With the dishes washed and the burnt pan scoured until it shone, she stood back with a feeling of achievement, waiting for the kettle to boil so that she could wash the floor.

Still Mona did not pause to think or feel; she didn't wish to dwell on the scene in Alex's house, with Sarah ordering him to tell her it was all over between

385

them, for it was all too painful and humiliating. But in spite of herself, her eyes kept filling with tears.

She knelt on a pad of newspapers and scrubbed at the stone floor until the grey slate gleamed almost blue in the afternoon light. Her arms ached and her back felt broken in two, but it seemed as if she was driven into punishing herself with more and more effort.

She tackled the parlour next, then the long, dark passageway between the rooms, and by then the scent of lavender polish hung heavy upon the air. At last, exhausted, she sank into a chair and with her head on the freshly scrubbed table, she fell asleep.

It was dark when she opened her eyes and Ceri was in the room, lighting the oil-lamp, placing it beside her and taking her hands in his.

'Mona, what's this? I didn't want you to kill yourself to do all the work in one day, mind.'

Suddenly she was crying. She looked up at Ceri and held out her arms to him for comfort.

'Please, help me,' she begged through her tears. 'I'm so unhappy that I want to die!'

'Now, now, you mustn't go talking like that. Nothing's so bad that it can't be got over.'

'It's Alex,' Mona stammered, her head against Ceri's shoulder. 'I thought he cared for me, but he doesn't want me any more and I'm so alone without him.'

'It's all right,' Ceri smoothed her hair. 'You cry it all out and then you'll feel better, believe me.' He put his arm around her shoulder. 'I've gone through the mill myself; I know the humiliation of being unwanted by the one you love.'

He was kind, so very kind and as he kissed away her tears, Mona clung to him and found comfort in the strength of his arms. He sat in the big arm-chair and drew her on to his lap; then bending his head, he kissed her mouth.

'Oh, Ceri, let me stay with you for a while. I'm so afraid of being alone,' she said in a whisper.

'Don't worry,' he said softly. 'Come on, now; be a brave girl, dry your eyes and then I'll make you a nice hot sweet cup of tea and tuck you up into my bed. You'll be safe under my roof, I promise you.'

Mona clung more tightly to him, drawing his head down so that she could reach his lips.

'I don't know that I want to be safe, Ceri,' she said, looking up into his eyes that were strangely shadowed in the lamplight. 'I want the comfort of a strong pair of arms around me – is that wicked?'

'No, not wicked, just human.' He kissed her lightly and then with more passion. 'We want to comfort each other, Mona. I don't think anyone could blame us for that.' He stood up, then lifted her easily and made for the stairs, kicking the door shut behind him with a click of finality.

* * *

From outside the window Katie had witnessed the scene, a drama with no words. It seemed to her then that her journey to tell Ceri that she was going away for a while was wasted, for he had soon found consolation in another woman's arms – a much younger woman who clung to him as though she was drowning in his embrace.

Well, Katie thought wryly, she could go away to Yorkshire with a clear conscience for Ceri was no longer in need of her. What her own needs were, she was still not sure, but it was clear now that one phase of her life was over and the time had come when she must look to a new beginning.

CHAPTER TWENTY-EIGHT

The winter darkness hung around the Ferry House like a shroud, the gloom pierced only by the oil-lamp which shone from one of the ice-covered windows. In her bed beside Siona, Nerys lay awake, staring at the nimbus of light – the flame that flickered from the wick trapped behind the tall chimney of the lamp, smoking and spluttering as the oil burned low.

She was uneasy as she lay listening to Siona's soft breathing beside her, yet she could not say why. She stared down at him and as always was amazed by the way he slept – so soft, so silent, almost as though he had merely closed his eyes for a moment. Nerys was glad he was resting easy, for of late he had been coughing badly; and no wonder, the way he was always outside however cold the weather.

Slipping from under the bedclothes, she leaned towards the table, her hand moved the chimney of the lamp as she blew out the last flickering flame. In the darkness, she crouched against her husband for warmth and he in his sleep caught her hand and held it.

Tears came to her eyes; he was a good man, such a good man and he deserved all her love. Yet her innermost being cried out for his son, although Howel Llewelyn might just as well be a million miles away so far removed from her was he.

The pearly grey and the pinkness of the dawn were streaking the windows when she felt her first pain, and now she understood her sleeplessness and feelings of unease.

The pain grew, circling her body like a band of silk thread pulled tighter and tighter until she thought something must snap. She lay still, hardly breathing until the contraction subsided and then she gently shook Siona's shoulder. He was awake at once.

'What is it, *cariad*? Have you started in labour then?' He sat up and rubbed his hand through his thick hair so that it stood up on end, and Nerys could not help but smile at him.

'Yes, I've started. I think you'd better get dressed and go for Mrs Benson.' She held his hand. 'But first, Siona, see if the fire's still in and build it up, for we'll need hot water, mind.'

He pulled his flannel shirt over his head and smiled at her. 'You're talking to me now, girl, Siona Llewelyn – and I've been present at so many confinements that I've lost count! Hush your chatter now, save your strength and I'll be back before you know it!'

On his way out he must have roused the boys, for Tom came into the bedroom and sat at the edge of the bed. He was grave-faced, a sober boy, matured beyond his years by pain. Although he was well again now and most days could walk without effort, he remained quiet and serious always as though his youth had been dissipated on the day of the accident in the foundry.

'I've seen to the fire. Our dad just caught it and now I've built it up. Are you all right, Nerys? Do you want a cup of tea or something?'

In the doorway Will stood watching, his nightshirt fluttering around thin white legs. He was younger than Tom in every way and still had the round innocence of childhood in his face.

'Yes, there's a good idea, now,' Nerys said quickly, feeling the pain begin to rise within her. 'Go on, Will – get the tea-cups ready and you, Tom, watch out when you pour on the boiling water, mind.'

Will disappeared at once but Tom, sensing her agitation, took her hand and smoothed it softly.

389

'I know it hurts, so don't be afraid to show,' he said gently. 'The nurse always told our mam to relax and go with it, not to fight against it.'

Nerys bent her head, turning so that her face was against the pillow. Surely the pains should start slowly, not in full flood as hers seemed to be?

She heard Tom go out of the room and sighed in relief. It was enough to bear the distress without trying to disguise her feelings from the boys. She heard them talking softly downstairs, heard the familiar rattle of tea-cups in saucers and as the pain receded, she felt better at once. By the time Tom entered the room with a tray in his hand, she was able to smile.

'There's lovely boys, you are,' she said gently. 'Put the tray down near me on the table and then I can help myself. Wait, Tom.' She slid out of bed and moved slowly to the trunk in the corner of the room. 'I'll get out the baby clothes and you can warm them for me on the line above the mantelpiece.'

Her fingers trembled as she touched the small garments – the nightgown whitened by much use and the undercoat with its maze of straps and ribbons for covering the baby's feet.

She and Siona had decided that there were enough tiny clothes in the house without buying more, yet now that the moment had come Nerys wished that her child could at least start life with something new to wear.

'Get back into bed, Nerys,' Tom said, taking the clothes from her hands. 'Your waters could break at any time, mind.'

Nerys longed to reach out and ruffle Tom's hair, but that was a caress offered to a child and Tom was not a child . . . not any more.

'All right, let me lean on you then and I'll get back into bed. You're quite right, mind.'

'What if I put brown paper under the sheets like the nurse does, Nerys – saves the mattress, see?'

She smiled. 'I think you know more about all this than I do, boyo, so go on ahead and do what you think fit and I will watch and learn from you.'

He shrugged. 'Well, I remember mammy having our Will, though no one knew I stood in the passageway until he was born. And when we had our little sister, I understood more about birthing then for I was grown-up.'

Nerys shivered a little in the chill of the room and looked longingly towards the bed.

'I won't be a minute,' Tom said quickly. 'You just hang on there and I'll be back before you know it.'

She heard him hurry downstairs with the uneven gait that was his legacy from his burns and her eyes filled with tears. He was a fine boy, was Tom, and he reminded her so much of Howel that it was painful to look into his eyes.

Tom reappeared almost immediately and tucked the brown paper beneath the sheets with deft efficiency, smoothing out the creases with hands that were growing stronger, the hands of a young man.

'Righto,' he said in exactly the way his father uttered the word. 'Into bed with you, then, and I'll cover you over.'

'Good, just in time!' Nerys gasped, 'For I feel another pain coming on.' She lay under the sheets and tried to tell herself that she must go with the pain, but it seemed her body was battling with her will and winning.

She couldn't help moaning a little and covered her mouth with her hand, for she didn't want to upset or frighten Tom.

As the pain rose to a crescendo, she felt her fingers gripped and she clung to the young boy's hand, encouraged by his presence. At last the wave was subsiding and as she rubbed the sweat from her eyes, she saw Tom smiling at her.

'I can hear dad outside. The nurse will be with him

391

and you'll be all right now.' At the door he turned. 'You haven't had your tea yet. Go on, drink it, it's good for you.'

Mrs Benson was getting old now and she came into the room slowly, tying her apron around her ample waist. But her eyes were keen and she exuded an aura of strength and purpose; Nerys immediately felt safe.

'Here, Siona,' the nurse said briskly, 'fetch me a big bowl from the kitchen and some strips of linen, though why I am telling you all this when you've birthed almost as many babies as I have, I don't know!'

Alone with Nerys, she made clucking noises, soothing even as her experienced hands moved deftly beneath the sheets.

'There's a good girl, then; coming along nicely, you are. Young and strong, see, that's the way mothers ought to be.'

Nerys wondered if Mrs Benson was alluding to the fact that the last woman she had attended in the Ferry House was Emily, who had been much too old for childbirth, but the nurse did not pursue the matter.

'Ah, I can see there's a pain coming. Let me put my hand on your stomach and I can gauge the strength of it. That's right, good girl, don't fight it. Take a deep breath, now; there, that wasn't so bad, was it? We'll soon have you delivered, you're a mother who doesn't believe in hanging about by the looks of it!' She smiled and pulled the sheets back in place. 'But your legs and feet are cold and we can't have that, can we?'

Nerys watched as Mrs Benson moved towards the chest of drawers and rummaged inside as though well used to the house, as indeed she was. She drew out a pair of Siona's wool socks and grunted with satisfaction.

'Let's just get these on you, that's right. Now you'll be warm enough when I have to take the blankets away, see?'

It was as though she was being taken over, Nerys thought – like a little child who was to be tended and cared for as though she had no will of her own. She was a little fearful of Mrs Benson and respectful too, for the well-being of her baby was in this woman's hands.

Siona returned to the room carrying a bowl and with strips of clean linen hanging over his arm. He handed them to the nurse and then sat beside Nerys and smiled at her encouragingly.

'Tell me when the pain is coming and I'll rub your back for you, *cariad*. It sometimes helps to ease it a bit.'

'He's right, mind,' Mrs Benson said cheerfully. 'Got a good man by there, you have, Nerys – and don't ever forget it!'

The time between the pains grew shorter and Nerys found she was greatly comforted by Siona's presence. He dried the perspiration from her forehead and sat with her until Mrs Benson told him to start fetching the water up from the kitchen.

The hours seemed to run into each other as Nerys endeavoured to bring forth her child. She clutched at Siona's strong forearm as the urge to bear down became irresistible. She heard herself growl deep in her throat and then there was a blessed relief from pain.

In the sudden, breathtaking silence came a sharp cry. Nerys opened her eyes and saw the midwife holding the baby aloft.

'You've got a fine son,' Mrs Benson said in her strong voice, 'and he's a nine-pounder, if I'm any judge.'

She worked quickly and efficiently and then with the baby wrapped in a broad strip of linen, she placed him in Nerys's arms.

'There, mother, wasn't he worth all the effort, then?' She leaned over the bed, her eyes misty, and smiled in

393

satisfaction. 'I do like to see a normal healthy birth. You're a natural mother, mind, and should have a few more before you get too old.'

Nerys scarcely heard her, for she was staring in awe at the petal-pink face, the pursed mouth, the eyes open and looking up at her as though in recognition. And he was Howel's son to the last eyelash.

As if in a dream, she heard Mrs Benson's voice in the background. 'Come on, Siona. Help me tidy up and call down the stairs to those boys of yours; they can be making us all a hot, strong cup of tea.'

Nerys had been holding her baby close and only reluctantly allowed the nurse to take him away to be washed. Mrs Benson worked quickly with the ease of long practice and dressed the crying baby with deft fingers.

'There, now,' she said. 'He's all washed and gowned and his hair slicked down – a little civilized being instead of a naked scrap of humanity!'

And he did look different, Nerys thought as she stared down at her son with tears in her eyes, knowing she would never forget that first moment when she had held him to her wrapped only in a piece of linen. He had seemed part of her then but now, already, he was a separate being.

'He's a fine boy,' Siona said, holding out his finger and allowing the baby's tiny hand to cling to his. 'What shall we call him?' he sat beside her gingerly, afraid of disturbing her.

Nerys looked up at him. 'If we had had a girl, I would have liked her to be named Emily.' She saw the smile in Siona's green eyes with a sense of pleasure. 'Now that I discover it's a boy, I wondered if you'd like him to be called Emlyn?'

'Emlyn,' Siona said thoughtfully. 'There's a fine name for a boy. Yes, I like the ring of it; it sounds sturdy and strong.'

'Hello, Emlyn,' Nerys whispered softly, her lips against the fine mop of dark hair. 'Hello, my little son.'

Siona rose from the bed. 'Shall I bring Tom and Will in to meet the new arrival?' he asked and from where she was busy packing her bag, Mrs Benson spoke up quickly.

'Fetch them by all means, then perhaps we'll have that cup of tea! I'm parched after all that work, mind, and so I expect is the little mother.'

Siona left the room swiftly, like a small boy scolded, and Nerys smiled as the nurse winked at her.

'Got to keep these men on their toes, see, girl, or go all sentimental they will at times like this.' She paused near the bed. 'I'll come in to see you for several days yet, watch that you don't get any fevers or anything like that. And remember on the third day the milk will come in, but you must put the boy to suckle before that – let him get the idea, see?'

'But I won't know what to do,' Nerys said worriedly. Mrs Benson laughed, putting her hands on her plump hips and leaning forward, her chins wobbling.

'Bless you, *merchi*, you don't have to do anything. The milk comes in, you put the nipple in the baby's mouth and he sucks – that's all there is to it! Supply and demand, see. The more that little rascal demands, the more you will supply; it comes naturally and I don't hold with these modern nurses who make a big song-and-dance about it.'

She drew on her coat. 'Now, you just drink lots of water or tea, whatever you like, and leave nature to do the rest. See you in the morning.'

Nerys lay back against the pillows with her son tucked into the bed beside her. The crib was made up all ready for him, but she wanted to hold him just a little longer.

She was feeling drowsy by the time Tom and Will crept into the room, but she smiled up at them and beckoned them both forward.

'He's so tiny,' Will whispered. 'See his little hands – they're like butterflies' wings.'

Tom put a cup down on the table. 'The nurse said you must have lots to drink and dad's gone to ferry her back across the river, so I'm in charge.'

Nerys nodded as though it was the most natural thing in the world for a boy of his age to care for her. 'That tea is just what I need, Tom.' She edged away from the baby and sat up, feeling a soreness that she had not expected. Tom noticed her wincing and took up the cup, holding it towards her.

'My mother used to say that it takes a day to birth a baby and two weeks to get over the pain of it,' he told her.

Nerys looked at him gratefully. He was a perceptive boy and wise beyond his years; she had grown to love both children since she came to live at the Ferry House, but in many ways Tom was special, like the brother she had never had.

'You should put the baby in his own bed and try to get some sleep,' Tom said, frowning. 'Shall I take him?'

For a moment Nerys hesitated. She wanted her son close to her, but Tom was right – she did feel unutterably weary.

'All right, then,' she said at last. 'If you two will pull the crib nearer my bed, I'll promise to try to sleep.'

When Tom had gently settled the baby beneath the blankets, Nerys sighed and relinquished the cup to Will's eager hands.

'Thank you both for being such a help,' she said warmly, her tongue already feeling thick in her mouth. She heard the boys creep from the room and snuggled beneath the blankets, feeling so drowsy that she could hardly keep her eyes open. She heard the sound of rain pattering on the windows, heard the wind singing in the bare branches of the trees and then she slept.

As the days passed, Nerys grew stronger, but she was glad that Mona was coming to work as usual in spite of the extra hours she put in cleaning up at Ceri's house in Canal Street.

'How do you get it all done?' Nerys asked, holding Emlyn to her breast where he suckled eagerly. Either the midwife had been right or else Nerys had been exceptionally lucky, but feeding did come easily to her.

Mona had just finished cooking the dinner and was serving Nerys with a big bowl of potato and mutton stew.

'Oh, working for Ceri's easy now that I've got the place straight!' Mona did not look directly at Nerys, but placed a plate of crusty bread on the table beside the stew. 'He's a man alone and a bit untidy, but the work is easy compared with down by here in the Ferry House.'

Nerys wondered at the blush which came to Mona's cheeks; could there be something between Mona and Ceri now that her romance with Alex was ended? But it was not polite to ask questions.

'Put the baby in the crib for me, Mona, there's a good girl,' Nerys asked. 'I can tuck into that lovely *cawl* then; I've just realized I'm starving.'

Mona took the baby eagerly and held him close. 'I'd love a babba of my own,' she said softly. 'Oh, look at him, he's smiling at me.'

'I doubt it,' Nerys said, amused. 'The nurse tells me it's just wind!' She tasted the stew, which was as delicious as it smelled.

'You're a good cook, Mona,' she said in appreciation, 'and a good worker too. You'll make somebody a fine wife one of these days!'

'I sometimes wonder,' Mona said, tucking the baby in the crib. 'My life seems to be spent cleaning in some other woman's house.'

'I know exactly how you feel,' Nerys sympathized.

'Remember, I looked after other people's children for years. Like you, I didn't have a house of my own until I married Siona.' She smiled. 'And you're a lot younger than me, mind – you've a lifetime before you, so don't take second-best.'

'Like you did, you mean,' Mona said, then clapped her hand to her mouth. 'Sorry, I shouldn't have said that, I've spoken out of turn.'

Nerys replacd the bowl on the tray and lay back against the pillow, feeling suddenly drained. It was true that in marrying Siona she had accepted a compromise, knowing that Howel had simply enjoyed a short fling with her and had no intention of making any sort of permanent relationship.

'But I'm lucky for all that,' she said softly. 'Siona is a good man and kind to me, and I truly believe he loves me.'

Mona sank on to the bed and stared at Nerys, a small baby gown clutched in her hand. 'And I'd settle for that,' she said in a whisper. 'The man I love is married, and now that he and Sarah are happy together he doesn't want to risk anything, so it's me out of the picture!' She glanced down at the tiny garment.

'See, Ceri and me – well, we've brought each other comfort. I think he'll ask me to be his wife before much longer.'

'But is it really over between him and Katie Murphy?' Nerys asked in surprise and Mona nodded.

'Oh yes, she's gone away to Yorkshire now. Left Sweyn's Eye – at least for the time being – so it's final, they're finished all right.' She sighed. 'Ceri needs me and I need him – we're like two lost souls clinging together.'

Mona rose to her feet. 'But this isn't going to get the work done, is it?' She glanced out of the window. 'It's too wet to do washing, so I've scrubbed the kitchen floor and polished all the brass.' She sighed. 'I'll be going up to Ceri's soon, but first I've one more job to do.' At the door she turned to look at Nerys, smiling easily now as though no hurtful confidences had been exchanged. 'The mangle roller is splintering, so I'm going to sew some strips of flannel around it – give it a bit of a longer life, see?'

When she was alone, Nerys leaned over and looked into the crib, drinking in the beloved sleeping face of her son. Mona was right; life was full of make-do and compromise and she had not come out of it so badly. As she lay back against the pillows and stared at the rain rolling down the windows, unaccountably there were tears on her cheeks, running into her mouth salt and bitter.

* * *

It seemed no time at all before she was up and about again, feeling nothing more than a slight tiredness. The nurse had stopped calling, seeing no reason to visit a perfectly healthy mother and baby, and Nerys was proud of the way she had recovered from the birth.

She enjoyed her son, treasuring the moments when she held him to her breast, feeling with joy the force of her milk flowing to her child. His small hands would grasp at her – delicate, long fingers pressing into her flesh – and her love for him was boundless.

Siona was a good father, never once reminding her that the child was not his but the offspring of the son he had rejected in anger. He held the boy often and Nerys could not but wonder if he always saw Howel, as she did every time she looked into the infant's face.

'You should take Emlyn out and give him a taste of fresh air,' Siona said, holding the child gently in his arms.

'But it's still so cold,' Nerys protested. 'Spring is a

399

long way off yet. I'll take him out when the weather improves.'

'Wrap him up warmly and put him in the shawl Welsh-fashion – bound close to you like that, he'll not feel the cold,' Siona insisted.

'All right, I suppose you do know more about children than I do,' she conceded, smiling.

So in the afternoons, Nerys made it her habit to walk along the river bank with the baby bound to her by the shawl of good thick flannel. He seemed to like the outings and looked around him with wide eyes. People stopped her often, fussing over the baby and exclaiming on his sharpness, and it warmed Nerys's heart whenever her son received praise.

It was almost inevitable that one day she would come face to face with Howel, but when it happened she was lost, unable to think or move as he came towards her and drew back the shawl, staring into the wide eyes of his son.

'What have you named him?' Howel's voice was quiet and Nerys wondered if she imagined the slight tremble in it.

'We decided on Emlyn, for it was the nearest name to Emily that we could think of for a boy.' She felt as though she was shaking from head to foot, and would have walked away but Howel caught her arm and drew her to a wooden bench at the side of the road.

'Let me see him, just for a few minutes,' he urged and she sighed softly, feeling that he had the moral right to hold his own son in his arms.

He held the baby gently, staring in wonder at the features so like his own. 'I want him,' he said so softly that Nerys thought she had not heard him. 'I must have him, Nerys. He's my son, my firstborn.'

'Give him back,' she said deliberately, keeping the panic from her voice. 'Look, he's shivering with cold and he needs to be close to me.' As she wrapped him carefully against her breast, his small hands clutched at her.

'He's hungry,' she said abruptly. 'I must take him home to feed him.' She stepped from Howel and then paused. 'You can't have him,' she said, 'not *ever*. Legally he is Siona's child, so don't forget that, will you?'

'Look, Nerys, please let me see him from time to time. I must see him; I have feelings too, you know.'

'Feelings? You don't know the meaning of the word. You are quite ruthless; you would separate me from my baby if you thought you could get away with it. Leave me alone, Howel, I am begging you just to leave me alone.'

'I'm sorry, I was foolish,' he said hastily. 'Of course I can't take him, he is dependant on you for his very life, I do realize that. But say you will come here again, this time next week and just show him to me — is that asking very much?'

'I'll think about it,' Nerys said more gently, 'but don't depend on anything, will you, Howel?'

She had only walked a few paces when he called to her: 'Nerys, I can give him so much . . . a good education, a fine home. Not now when he's tiny, of course, but keep your options open. Be a sensible girl, think of what's best for our son.'

She spun round to face him. 'Oh yes, you can give him everything, but can you give him the love that Siona gives him? Who do you think holds him close when he cries in the night? Siona, of course.' She paused and took a deep breath, then rushed on, 'Siona it was who comforted me in my labour and Siona who first held Emlyn in his arms. He is the true father in every way that counts. You can't buy ties like that, Howel — they can only be forged through love and trust.'

In spite of herself she began to cry and he came to

401

her and held her close, careful not to harm the baby who lay between them. He tipped up her face and brushed away her tears with his finger-tips.

'I love you, Nerys.' He spoke almost in surprise and then his mouth was gentle upon hers. 'I love you, do you understand?'

She pushed him away. 'Perhaps you do but even if it's true, your declaration has come too late. I'm married to Siona; because of him I have the respectability of being Mrs Llewelyn and I wouldn't hurt him for the world. The best thing you can do is just to keep away from me, Howel, for you'll only cause more heartache.'

Nerys moved swiftly away then, heading towards the river feeling suddenly cold and weary. She felt Howel's lips on hers and knew at last how tender he could be. But it made no difference for as she had told him, it was too late.

In the warmth of the Ferry House, she laid Emlyn in his crib and put away the shawl. She decided that she would not go out again for a while, because she feared that Howel would be waiting for her and did not know if she would have the strength of mind to resist his appeals to see his son.

'He has no right!' Nerys spoke the words out loud in an effort to convince herself, but still she felt within her heart that Howel had every right. For at the moment when she had lain with him and conceived of his child, she had surrendered her independence of spirit.

The truth was that she had never thought of herself as anything but Howel's woman, and not even her marriage to Siona solemnized in chapel could change this conviction.

Sitting down, she put her arms on the scrubbed whiteness of the table, smelling the soap and the fresh clean scent of the wood. She would like the relief of tears, but her eyes were dry.

How long she remained so, she didn't afterwards remember; she only roused herself when the baby began to cry.

As she lifted him to her breast, she saw his eyes bright with tears and was reminded painfully of the appeal in Howel's dark eyes as he had begged her to bring their son to him. Although she knew she must put him out of her mind, think of her husband who loved and trusted her, yet there was a tiny flame of happiness within her as she remembered Howel's words of love.

CHAPTER TWENTY-NINE

Christmas Eve came to Sweyn's Eye with a fall of fresh snow that lay in white drifts along the river banks and covered the hills with a cloak of pristine beauty. It crunched underfoot with a dry crispness and Nerys, glancing through the window, was happy to see Tom and Will enjoying the winter weather, building a snowman in the yard and throwing white flurries of snow at each other's heads.

Siona was seated in his chair near the fire. His colour was unnaturally high and as he began to cough, Nerys went to his side.

'You are not going out on the ferry-boat, mind, not in this weather. Folks will just have to put up with it.' He did not argue and that alone was enough to frighten her, for Siona worked the ferry whatever the conditions. When Nerys rested her hand on his shoulder, he turned and his lips brushed her fingers. With a surge of emotion, she put her arms around him and held him close, his head against her breast.

'*Duw*, you're burning up, my love! You must have a fever.' She looked down into his green eyes. 'Come on, Siona, let me tuck you up into a nice comfortable bed and I'll mix you up one of my herbal remedies – soon have you feeling fine again.'

'Righto, *cariad*,' he said, 'perhaps a spell in bed will do me a bit of good.' He grimaced. 'I've got such a head on me you'd think I'd been drinking ale all night in the bar at Maggie Dick's.'

She went upstairs with him and waited while he

undressed, tucking him into the blankets as though he was a child. 'Now rest easy, mind, and don't go worrying about the boat or anything. Just think of yourself for once.'

He caught her hand and held it tightly. 'You are a dutiful wife, Nerys, and I know I shouldn't ask for more, but I do have the hope deep within me that one day you will love me as I love you.'

'Hush, now,' she said quickly, 'and stop fretting.' She moved to the door. 'No one could ask for a better husband than you, Siona, and that's the truth.'

She hurried downstairs and paused to look down at Emlyn, who was fast asleep in his crib. He was a good contented baby with the fine, strong features of the Llewelyn men; he looked as much like Siona as he did his natural father and the thought pleased her. If there was any way in which she could have made the baby Siona's child, she would have done it eagerly, for Siona *was* Emlyn's father in every respect except one.

Pushing the uneasy thoughts from her mind she moved over to the mantelpiece where, high up above the fire, she had hung to dry the herbs she had collected in the summer. She took down some leaves of bugloss, crushing the dryness between her fingers, and dropped them into a bowl along with a few elder roots. She ground them patiently into a powder before adding some honey and hot water. Carefully, she strained the mixture and filled a jug with the liquid.

'We'll soon have you right, my boy,' she said to herself as she climbed the stairs.

Siona obediently took the drink, grimacing a little at the taste. '*Duw*, there's foul stuff – it tastes so awful it must do me some good!'

He was still very hot and his eyes were red-rimmed. Nerys felt a dart of fear as she sat beside him and took his hand in hers. She sat with him until he fell asleep and then she left the room quietly, looking back at him, worried at his high colour.

The boys came in from the yard and Will was pinched with the cold. He held out his hands to Nerys and she took them and began to rub some warmth back into the cramped fingers.

'You boys should have come indoors before this,' she said in concern. 'We've got your dad bad as it is, and I don't want you boys going down with a chill or anything.'

'What's the matter with dad?' Tom asked in his sober, adult way. Nerys smiled reassuringly. 'It's just a little fever, but I want him to stay in bed for a day or two. He needs looking after, which is difficult – him being as stubborn as a mule!'

'Will he get up with us to open the presents tomorrow?' Will asked earnestly and Nerys smiled.

'Well now, who says you're going to have presents, boy *bach*?' She patted his cheek. 'Father Christmas comes only to good boys, so why don't you get out the cloth and lay the table for me?'

'Father Christmas!' Will snorted in derision. 'What do you think I am, a silly baby?'

As he moved to the drawer and took out the cloth, Nerys smiled to herself. Will was a good-natured boy, always ready to help, and she felt a stirring of excitement as she thought of the gift she had bought him.

Will adored looking up at the stars. He spent hours studying the night skies and she had known at once what she wanted to get for him. It had taken her a great deal of walking and much patience, but at last she had managed to buy him a telescope from the pawn-shop. It was dented and the brass had needed cleaning, but it was in good working order.

Tom had been more easy to please. He was artistic and fond of drawing patterns on paper, so she had bought him a box of paints, a set of pencils and rulers and a large pad.

'You're far away, Nerys.' Tom was standing looking at her with a smile on his face. 'A penny for them!'

406

She patted his cheek. 'Not worth a penny. Come on, let's get our tea before Emlyn wakes up for his feed.'

Later, when the boys were in bed, she filled their stockings with fruit and nuts and some new coins that shimmered brightly in the light from the fire. She had small gifts wrapped in bright paper – a pair of gloves for Will, a scarf for Tom – and these she put at the top of the stockings so that they jutted out invitingly.

For Siona she had knitted a thick woollen waistcoat in a shade of green that matched his eyes, labouring over the intricate pattern in the daytime while he was out on the boat. She smiled now as she placed the parcel beside the stockings and it suddenly occurred to her that this was her first Christmas spent as a married woman and a mother.

Nerys tiptoed upstairs and settled Emlyn into the crib which Tom and Will had carried to the bedroom earlier. She had bought the baby a small brown teddy bear and though he was far too young to appreciate it, she had been unwilling to leave him out of the festivities.

She kissed his soft cheek and undressed silently in the darkness, not wanting to disturb Siona. But he was awake beside her and his skin was hot to the touch.

'Siona,' she whispered, 'shall I get you some more medicine?' She leaned up on one elbow and rested her hand on his forehead, feeling with concern the heat emanating from him.

She lit the lamp and poured him some of the mixture she had made earlier. His eyes were unseeing as she held the cup to his lips. She made sure he took all the medicine and then she dampened a cloth and began to sponge his face and body with water from the jug on the dressing table. Nerys was used to fevers for she had nursed children through colds and chills often enough, but Siona seemed to be gasping for breath and sponging him with water was not helping. Fearfully, she stood for a moment wondering what to do.

Downstairs the fire was still alight. For once, she had not bothered to riddle down the ashes in preparation for the morning. She boiled a kettle of water and then took a bowl and towel back upstairs with her. She propped Siona up against the pillows with difficulty, for he was a heavy man to move, then held the steaming bowl to his face and covered his head with the towel, gently draping it around his face. After a few minutes, his breathing seemed easier.

She spent the night tending Siona, forcing medicine between his dry lips and keeping up a constant supply of steaming water. Light was streaking the sky when Siona at last responded. His green eyes were focusing on her, the glazed look was gone and she clasped him in her arms, relief bringing the tears that burned her lids.

'Oh, Siona!' she whispered. 'What would I do without you?' She held him close and he patted her shoulder, his voice stronger when he spoke.

'*Duw*, there's a fuss. I'm all right now, my lovely, thanks to you.' He kissed her cheek and for a long moment, they clung together in silence.

* * *

Christmas Day passed quietly. Nerys took the children to chapel for the morning service with strict instructions to Siona to stay in bed, but when she returned he was sitting in his chair, a little weary but looking much more like his old self.

'Can we open the presents now, Nerys?' Will asked excitedly and as soon as she nodded her approval, he began to tear the paper from the parcels.

Siona caught her hand. 'Thank you,' he said over the sound of the boys' excited chatter. 'You were wonderful to me through the night; I don't think I'd be sitting here now if it wasn't for your nursing.'

She kissed him lightly. 'I realized something last

night,' she said softly. 'I couldn't face life without you at my side.' She moved away from him then and her tone was brisk when she spoke again: 'Still an invalid, you are, mind; shouldn't be out of bed at all and as soon as we've had dinner, it's back upstairs with you!'

'All right, *merchi*,' he said smiling. 'I know when I'm licked.' He dipped his hand into his pocket and drew out a small box. 'This is your present, from the boys and me.' His smile widened. 'You thought we'd forgotten, didn't you?'

She opened the box and saw, nestling against the silk lining, a pendant of gold set with two matching opals. The green in them reminded her of Siona's eyes when he looked into the sun and she gasped with pleasure.

'Oh, Siona, it's lovely,' she said. 'Come on, then,' and she knelt before him. 'Fasten it up for me.'

He did as he was bid and then drew her against him, his arms around her warm and protective. She clung to him, wondering at the happiness she felt and the sense of belonging that wrapped itself around her like a comforting blanket.

This was a Christmas Nerys would remember for as long as she lived.

* * *

Seated at Sterling Richardson's table, Howel stared into Jenny's cool eyes and wondered if he would have preferred to spend Christmas alone. How he had ever imagined there could be a serious relationship between them, he could not think. Jenny was lovely and she had breeding, but she couldn't hold a candle to the girl who had borne him a son.

Nerys had blossomed, there was no other word for it. He had caught a glimpse of her earlier that morning, taking the boys to chapel, and she had radiated warmth and love and a kind of inner peace which gave her great beauty. And jealousy had burned within him.

'Come along, Howel,' Jenny said archly, 'let's leave this old married couple together and have a walk around the grounds.'

He rose and followed her into the hallway, shrugging himself into his overcoat. It was just as well if he began to let her down lightly, he thought, for she was a nice girl and he didn't want to hurt her.

The snow was crisp beneath his feet and Jenny took the opportunity to cling to his arm. He frowned and expelled his breath, which clung like mist on the cold air.

'Do I sense a change in you?' she asked, her voice nervous and high-pitched. Howel glanced down at her, searching for the right words to say.

'Yes, I think you're right. I have changed in more ways than one,' he said at last. And it was true; the hard-headed ambitious man he had once been was not completely vanished, but the rough edges had been fined down by the events of the last few months.

'I can't think that you could have changed too much,' Jenny said, clinging closer to him. 'After all, you're not a young lad who sways like a leaf in the wind, are you?'

He sighed heavily. This was going to be more difficult than he had first anticipated. 'I suppose not,' he agreed, 'but a man does sometimes have second thoughts.'

'Well, I hope you are referring to your business and not your social life,' she said with forced lightness.

'Jenny,' he began, 'just don't push too hard, I . . .' He didn't finish his sentence because she put a small gloved hand over his mouth.

'Don't say anything now, just let's enjoy ourselves. It is Christmas, after all, and I haven't thanked you for your lovely gift.'

He had bought her a bracelet, a plain circle of gold,

and he had not really given it much thought, but Jenny seemed to set great store by it, taking it as a token of affection rather than the polite gesture it really was.

She swung herself round into his arms and smiled up into his eyes. 'Hold me and give me a Christmas kiss, won't you?' Jenny said lightly. And even as he held her close, Howel was wishing himself back in the warmth and homeliness of the Ferry House near the river.

CHAPTER THIRTY

Sweyn's Eye was held in the grip of a harsh winter. Ice patches formed on the roadways, nestled between cobbles like milk solidified and patterned windows with a marvellous tracery of glittering silver.

The Canal too, was ridged with ice; near the banks, rushes were trapped within an opaque grave. And on the perimeters of the River Swan the bravest of the children skated and played, cheeks flushed and rosy, thick scarves flying like banners.

Inside the house on Canal Street, Mona hauled the scuttle from the coal-house, her face flushed by the biting whip of the wind. She intended building up the fire so that Ceri would feel welcomed home by the cheerful blaze. He had left earlier that morning with a case full of silver ornaments, making for the offices of Sterling Richardson.

Ceri had been edgy and nervous, knowing that the meeting was one of great importance, for upon its outcome would rest the future prospects of his business.

Mona busied herself with the preparations for the cleaning of the brasses, wanting to have the place spotless when Ceri returned. She felt the need to impress him with her efficiency, although in fact he was forever praising her efforts to make him comfortable.

She took a bowl from the pantry shelf and put into it half a pound of soft soap, pressing it down with the back of a spoon. Carefully she added two tablespoons of turpentine, two of paraffin and lastly, half a pound of rotten-stone. As she mixed the pungent smelling ingredients together she sighed, her thoughts drifting to the moment when she had opened her eyes to the morning and found herself in Ceri's bed.

She had been a little dazed with sleep at first and had stared at the figure beside her, expecting to see Alex's thin frame. She had almost reached out and spoken his name, but then it was Ceri who was turning to face her. It had been something of a shock, when he had smiled at her and then held out his arms, as though knowing how strange and ill-at-ease she was feeling, she had gone into them gratefully.

They both knew that they were consoling each other, and yet was that such a bad basis for a relationship? Unrequited love was a painful thing to bear alone and as Ceri had laughingly told her, the one certain cure for a lost love was a new love.

She rubbed at the brass fender with unwarranted fervour; the flush in her cheeks was not entirely due to her efforts, for she felt slightly uneasy at the thought that she had gone from one brother's arms to another's so quickly. Wasn't there something in the Bible about it being a sin to lie with brothers? But perhaps that was only if she had been married to one.

She put away the polish mixture, scraping the residue into a tin for use another day. Ceri was not a rich man – not yet at least – and she would do all in her power to save him money.

Hearing the sharp crunching of steps cracking the ice outside the door, she turned and tried to read Ceri's face. He smiled in triumph, his eyes gleaming and without a word, Mona went to him and hugged him.

'They were most impressed!' He swung off his topcoat and hung it with his scarf on the hall stand. 'Got quite excited they did, Sterling Richardson and his board of directors. A ready market for my stuff in

413

London, that's what they said.' He paused for breath before continuing excitedly. 'I'm to take on an assistant immediately, a few assistants if necessary and to hell with the expense!' He hugged her close. 'This is only the start, Mona. We'll go a long way, you and me.'

She buried her face in his neck, warmed by his enthusiasm and happy to be included in his plans. And she could walk beside Ceri, go anywhere with him with her head high, for he was a single man and not beholden to anyone.

'Let me cook you some food,' Mona said, releasing herself from his arms. 'You've been out ages, you must be starved.'

'Aye, I am hungry. Throw some bacon in the pan, love, while I go and see to the fire in the workshop.' At the door he paused. 'Tonight we must celebrate. I'm going to take you for supper to the Mackworth Hotel in the *Stryd Fawr* – would you like that?'

'I'd love it,' Mona said in quiet triumph, knowing he wanted to be seen with her, would be proud to have her at his side. But her happiness faded almost at once, for she would have to go home to fetch some clothes. There she would come face to face with her mother, who would be angry at her staying out all night again. But then wasn't her mam always angry at her for one thing or another? She decided not to dwell on the unpleasant prospect of mam's disapproval; she would cross that bridge when she came to it.

They ate together, with Ceri talking almost nonstop about his plans for the future. 'I'm going to make a good quantity of silver teething-rings,' he said. 'It seems the rich like their children to cut teeth on precious metal, not on bone rings like ordinary children!'

He crunched a piece of toast with relish and Mona could see that he was dreaming of future success. It was wonderful to think that she would be involved in it all, sharing his joys, yet a part of her knew she would give everything up to be with Alex again. And Ceri – was he wishing that it was Katie sitting opposite him?

'I'll have to go home later,' she said. 'I must get out my best wool frock for tonight.' She looked at Ceri anxiously. 'My mam might just give me my marching orders this time; she's already told me I'm more out of the house than in it these days, what with staying at the Ferry House to help Nerys. So now that I've stayed the whole night by here with you again, she'll probably go mad.'

Ceri leaned forward earnestly. 'Why don't you and me get married? It would solve everything, wouldn't it?'

Mona stared at him, her eyes wide, her pulse suddenly pounding the blood through her veins.

'Do you mean that, Ceri? You're not joking with me, are you? You don't have to marry me just because we've . . . well, been together, mind.'

'I know I don't have to do anything,' Ceri agreed, 'but we seem to suit each other very well don't we? You're a damned hard worker too, and have shown more interest in what I'm trying to achieve than anyone else ever has. I think it would work out fine.'

She looked down at her hands shyly, trying to imagine it; Mrs Ceri Llewelyn, with a ring on her finger all proper-like. And Alex knowing that if he didn't want her, then another man did.

'I'll marry you, Ceri, and very honoured I am too!' She looked up at him. 'It will be in church and with a ring on my finger all proper, won't it?'

'Yes, if that's what you want.' He leaned forward and took her hand. 'That's settled then!' He put down his cup. 'Now I'd better get some work done.'

He paused at the door. 'Look, if you need some money to buy clothes or something, I have some I can spare.'

She shook her head. 'No thank you, Ceri, but ever since I began working at the Ferry House I've put by what little money my mammy didn't take from me, so I'm all right.'

He returned to the room and kissed the top of her head. 'You're a good girl, Mona, and I just know we'll be fine together – you'll see.'

When she was alone in the kitchen, Mona sat for a long time looking at the littered table. She had committed herself to marriage with Ceri now and she was glad. She would go home, fetch her few things and move in with him. Perhaps here in the house on Canal Street she would find the sense of belonging which so far had eluded her.

Quickly she washed the dishes and tidied the kitchen; before she left she made sure the fire was well banked up; it would not do to let the house grow cold.

She was not prepared for the cutting wind that drove in from the sea, or for the crunch of ice beneath her feet which made walking hazardous. She almost turned back, but the thought of going out to supper with Ceri was a spur and cautiously she made her way to the tram-stop.

It was from the window of the swaying tram that she saw them – Alex and Sarah arm-in-arm, hugged close together against the wind and smiling into each other's eyes. Any last flickering hope she might have harboured that she meant anything to Alex vanished; it was clear as daylight that he adored his wife.

As she watched them stop and look into the warmth of a lighted shop, where the display was of baby clothes, frilled cribs and soft toys, she felt a choking sensation in her throat. When the tram moved away, she whispered softly, 'Goodbye, Alex.'

Mona alighted from the tram as it jerked to a halt and made her way to her mother's house. It was situated in a mean cobbled street hidden behind a large brewery, and smelled always of ale. She had

416

been thinking of the coming meeting with trepidation, but now, after seeing Alex and his wife together, she felt a hard and angry knot inside her.

It seemed that a shell had formed around her and she felt that nothing ever again could hurt her so much as Alex had done. In any case, she had always been an unpaid servant for her mother; even before the days when she was old enough to go out to work, she had acted as nursemaid to the younger children, and the time had come when she must be herself.

'And where in God's name have you been?' The words were hurled at her like hard stones, but Mona no longer felt intimidated by her mother.

'You're fast earning the reputation of a slut for yourself, do you know that?' Her mother's voice droned on, but Mona ignored her and hurried up the stairs to the room she shared with her younger brother. She took out her clothes from the wardrobe and folded them carefully before tying them up in a brownpaper parcel.

'Mona, where are your wages? I need them to buy food,' her mother called from the foot of the stairs. 'Come down here at once and speak to me, girl. Stop being so sullen and difficult – always were a moody devil, you!'

Mona sighed, dipped into her bag and took out some shillings. She returned to the kitchen and put the money down on the table.

'That's all I can give you, mam, and it's the last you'll get from me. I'm moving out.' She wasn't angry, just indifferent to the icy stare her mother gave her.

'What do you mean, moving out. Are you staying up at the Ferry House to help Mrs Llewelyn, is that it? If it is, I'll have you know that I need you here with me.'

'No, mam,' Mona said gently. 'I'm moving out for good.' She walked slowly to the door. 'I'm getting married, mam – respectably married, see – and don't worry for you won't miss me.' She paused. 'I suppose

417

you may miss the money I bring in, but you'll just have to put up with that. I'm sorry.'

'Married, indeed? Do you think I believe that for a minute, you hard bitch? Well, don't you try to come back here when you're tired of chasing around after men.' Her mother's face was pinched with disapproval. 'Oh, I know you haven't been up to any good these past months; I've heard the rumours that you've been seen about with a married man. I've had to put up with all the nasty gossip – and us a family that always had a good name.'

'Well, in that case, you'll be glad to be rid of me.' Mona didn't feel hurt. She must be past feeling pain, she decided as she opened the door. 'I'm going now, mam.'

Outside in the frosty street, she watched her breath hang in puffs on the cold air and wondered why it had taken her so long to take the final step and leave home. She suddenly felt free, free of her past and everything in it. From now on she would look to the future and make out of it the best life she could.

* * *

Ceri felt the sweat run into his eyes as he put down the pincers and the silver ring he had been fashioning. It was one of a pair of wedding rings and he was making them for his marriage to Mona.

He would show them to her when she returned home from her trip to the market, and he tried to imagine how her young face would light up with happiness. She put such store by something as simple and yet symbolic as a ring – a lost soul, was Mona, a little bit like himself.

When the rings had cooled, he would clean them up with a mixture of powdered ammonia, chalk and methylated spirit to bring out the clean glow of the silver. But that would have to wait, for now he had

418

another meeting with Mr Richardson. He buttoned up his overcoat and pulled on his scarf, for the wind outside was enough to freeze a man to death.

Ceri didn't bother with the tram, but walked down towards the Hafod and the site of the lead works. This was the place his mother had always feared and dreaded, yet out of it had come a great deal of good and at least now he had hopes for a creative and comfortable future, thanks to Sterling Richardson.

Of course, there had been that awful accident when Tom was burned by the lead, but the boy had got over it now and was almost as good as new. A sudden thought struck him; why not train Tom in the art of silversmithing? It would make a good career and had the advantage of being a job which could be done sitting down if necessary – and anyway, Tom had always been artistic. Pleased with this idea, he decided he would call at the Ferry House later and put the proposition to dad, and of course to Tom himself.

Sterling was seated behind the desk in his big airy office. A cheerful fire burned in the grate and there was a homely smell of lavender polish in the air.

Duw, there was a lovely way to spend your days, he thought, unbuttoning his coat.

Sterling rose to his feet. 'Come in, Ceri, and don't be fooled by all this. I'm often out on the road or up to my eyes in paper work, but now you've caught me at a good time!' He smiled. 'I'll just order us a hot drink; you look frozen.'

Ceri was seated in a chair, staring round him at the paintings on the wall and the plushly carpeted floor, when suddenly Howel appeared in the doorway.

'Have you been down to the Ferry House recently?' he asked and surprised, Ceri shook his head. 'Not for a few days, but as it happens I'm going there later. Why, what's it to you?'

'I suppose we're still enemies, Ceri, and that's fine by me, but do you know how dad is?'

419

'Dad – why, is he sick or something?' Ceri asked, concerned. He stared at Howel, who was pacing the floor.

'He's not been working the boat for some days – in bed sick, so Big Eddie tells me. I'll have to go down there myself and find out, I suppose.'

'Do you think that's wise?' Ceri could not keep the hostility out of his voice. 'You surely know you would not be welcomed there?'

Howel thumped his fist against his palm in frustration. 'I'm not only concerned about dad, I want to see the child. I feel I have the right; he's my son, after all!'

'It has damn-all to do with you!' Ceri said angrily. 'Nerys is married to dad and the baby is his as far as anyone else is concerned. Why not let sleeping dogs lie? After all, you've got Jenny. She'd be much more suitable as a wife for a man in your position, I'd have thought. You're no longer one of us, Howel, can't you see that?'

But it was as if Howel had not heard him. 'I'll have to talk to Nerys, make her understand that I have to see the boy.' He looked up at Ceri. 'You know the funny thing? I've fallen in love with Nerys, isn't that ironic?'

Ceri could not believe he was having this conversation with the hard-headed Howel and felt a little at a loss. 'I've had to learn that we can't always have what we want in this life,' he said gruffly.

'A bloody philosopher now is it?' Howel retorted, anger in his eyes. 'You're so smug it's no wonder that Katie Murphy walked out on you.'

'Mind your own damn business!' Ceri replied. 'It seems you hear far too much for your own good.'

Sterling returned to the room just then and seated himself behind the desk. 'Please excuse us, Howel, there's a good chap.' If he had heard the angry exchange between the brothers, he was not showing

420

it. 'Let's get down to business.' He drew a folder from the desk drawer and consulted the figures before him as Howel left the room, closing the door behind him.

'By my reckoning, you'll have to employ quite a few silversmiths within a period of about six months,' he said, and Ceri felt his pulse quicken with excitement.

'But my workshop is so small,' he protested. 'I don't have the equipment to cope with more than about three workers.'

'You farm the work out,' Sterling replied. 'That way you have no overheads. The men you employ will need to have their own workshops; they will work under your direction and the stuff you buy from them must be cheap so that you make a profit when you sell to us.'

'What's to stop any ambitious silversmith going over my head and selling direct either to you or to London?' Ceri asked quickly.

'A good question,' Sterling smiled easily. 'First, I myself will take out a contract to buy solely from you. As for anyone trying to go direct to London, they would simply not have the contacts. I don't think you can see yet how large this business could become.' He paused. 'When you're making a good profit on the silver, you must go into gold. There's plenty of demand for watch-chains and that sort of thing in both gold and silver. You could end up owning a big concern, if you handle your end properly.'

'I'll do the work,' Ceri said quickly. 'I'll also continue to make jewellery to my own designs. You might know about the financial side of things, sir, but I know that my customers want something that's just a bit different and it will be my trade mark to make the unusual.'

'You've got a point there,' Sterling conceded. 'Yes, you're right, you stick by your guns. As you say, you know that side of it better than I do. Now, I won't keep you long; just study these figures and then we can talk about money.'

By the time Ceri left the office, his head was ringing.

He was a little apprehensive about Sterling's plans to forge ahead quite so ambitiously, he had to admit. His own idea had been to 'make haste slowly', to build up a reputation for himself as a reliable and skilled craftsman. But he could see that by doing things Sterling's way, the profits would roll in much more quickly – and profits were what most concerned men like Sterling Richardson, for he was a business man through and through.

Still, he was lucky that Sterling wanted to back him. He stood a much better chance than if he were on his own, and most men would give their right arm to be in his position. And yet he felt as though something of the joy of creation had gone out of his life; he had security but little adventure, and the business was not entirely his own any more.

Mona was in before him – he could tell by the succulent smell of roast meat coming from the kitchen.

'Hey, have you forgotten that we're going down to the Mackworth tonight?' he asked as he went to warm himself before the cheerful blaze of fire. She glanced at him, her face flushed and her hair tangled around her face; she really was quite pretty, he thought in surprise.

'No fear.' She drew the meat tin out of the oven and placed it on the hob. 'I haven't forgotten anything, so don't think you're getting out of it! This meat is for tomorrow's dinner, all right?'

'Good. Well, I've got a few things to sort out in the workshop, then I'll have a wash and brush-up ready for our little jaunt.'

'Fine. While you're in there, I'll be able to bathe first. I know how long you men take to prettify yourselves.' She laughed up at him and playfully, he slapped her hand.

'Not so much of the cheek you, lady!' Ceri told her as he left and went into the workshop. The fire was burning low, but he didn't need it now. He sat at his bench and taking up the wedding rings, began to polish them. Tonight, he would propose properly to Mona, offer her the ring and settle himself to a good steady future. Both he and Mona had made mistakes, both had been hurt and let down and they understood each other.

He put the rings into a leather pouch and, raking down the fire, closed the door on the workshop and hurried back across the freezing yard into the kitchen.

Mona was just rising out of the tin bath, a slender girl but with shapely hips and firm young breasts. She was so different from Katie, who was womanly and mature, yet Mona was just as beautiful.

She caught the look in his eye and after a moment, held out her arms to him. He set her down on the soft rug in front of the fire and kissed her slender throat. She held him close, her eyes closed as her body arched towards him.

'You are lovely, Mona,' he whispered, though why he kept his voice low he didn't know, for there was no one to hear him.

He caressed her body that glistened with water, and saw that her nipples were delicate and pink against alabaster skin. She seemed virginal and although he knew that he was not the only man to possess her, that seemed not to matter.

The first few times they lay together they had been blind with hurt and need, seeking solace from each other in the darkness of the night, but now he wanted to savour the sweetness and enjoy her for herself alone.

'Do you think you could learn to love me – just a little?' she asked, her eyes large and luminous. He kissed her lids and tasted the salt of her tears and his heart moved within him.

'We could both learn to love – just give it time, *cariad*,' he said gently. She raised herself up and kissed his mouth and he responded eagerly.

The firelight flickered over them, warming ... exciting ... and as Ceri touched the young breasts, he was roused as never before, for now he was the strong one. Mona needed his approbation, sought his praise as he had sought kind words from Katie. But he would forget her, put Katie right out of his mind.

'Love me,' Mona whispered, her slender arms winding around him so that her breasts jutted against him. 'Love me, Ceri, please!'

Later they laughed together, taking it in turns to bathe each other, and Ceri felt as though Mona had brought him to the realization that he was a young, strong man. In her presence he felt renewed, revered almost, since her respect for him was obvious.

He took her to the Mackworth Hotel, enjoying her naive excitement at being in such a glamorous place. The lamplight shimmered on the glasses from which they drank sparkling wine, and Mona had about her the glow of a woman who is loved.

'I've got something for you,' he told her, putting his hand in his pocket and taking out the pouch containing the rings. He tipped them on to the cloth, where they lay in two pools of brightness.

'One for you and one for me,' he said gently. 'I'm asking you formally to be my wife, Mona.'

'Oh, Ceri!' Her eyes glowed as they met his. 'I accept and I'll be true and faithful to you always.'

He took her hand. 'With this ring, I thee wed,' he said, kissing her fingers. 'That is my pledge to you now, but I will arrange the real wedding as quickly as possible. I don't see any point in waiting.'

Her fingers curled within his. 'We'll learn to love, won't we, Ceri? Already I feel you are a very special person. I think I'm half-way in love with you now, if the truth be told.'

'We shall have a new beginning together,' he replied. 'Come on, I'm going to take you home, for I feel the blood singing in my veins whenever I look at you and I want to take you to bed!'

'Ceri, there's shameless you are! Hush, someone might hear you.' But she laughed and her eyes sparkled and he could see that she wanted him too.

They hurried home through the icy streets and once inside the house, he took her in his arms. 'Come on to bed,' he said softly. 'Isn't it good to know that we won't be alone in the darkness of the night?'

'It is very good,' she said, slipping her hand in his. Then he led the way upstairs and in the silent moonlit room they loved each other and afterwards she cried in his arms. He asked no questions, he simply held her close.

In the morning there was a letter lying on the mat and he picked it up, his pulse racing as he recognized the handwriting. It was from Katie. He stared down at the envelope for a long, agonizing time and then, slowly, he tore the letter in tiny pieces and holding open the door, scattered them to the winds.

CHAPTER THIRTY-ONE

A heavy fall of snow cast an eerie, silent whiteness over the streets of Sweyn's Eye, transforming the dingy courts and cobbled roadways into a place of beauty. On the river bank the snow drifted into shapes and curves around the grounded boats, as though they were works of art carved by a giant hand. But in spite of the extreme weather conditions, the ferry-boat still ploughed its way across the river, with Siona recovered enough to take the early morning workers to the White Rock copper and lead works.

In his office in the White Rock buildings, Howel stood staring out at the men who stamped along the yard with booted feet slipping in the snow. He thought of the times his mother had condemned the works as an evil force, draining the workers of strength – the lead, she always claimed, tainted the blood. She was probably right, for he had seen in many of the men the pallor and the thinning of the frame which heralded the onset of an incurable sickness.

Howel moved from the window impatiently. He had spent a sleepless night considering the proposition put to him by the local Liberal Party; they wanted him to accept nomination as their candidate to stand for election as Sweyn's Eye's Member of Parliament in the next election. If he accepted and was subsequently elected, it would mean moving to London or at least buying a house there, and he found himself reluctant to sever all his old ties.

Once more he recalled how his ambition had been to use Sterling Richardson and then to move on, but now he no longer wanted that. He respected Sterling, was grateful to him and hoped to honour his agreement to stay in business with him.

And then too there was the problem of Nerys and his son. He wanted them both so badly that it was becoming an obsession. How many times had he cursed himself for throwing happiness away so lightly?

He took a deep breath and came to a decision. Today he would visit the Ferry House. He would risk his father's anger and Nerys's scorn, knowing that he had deserved both. But he had to set things straight, to somehow make his peace.

He resolved that he would speak with Nerys and ask her to give him the boy to raise when he was old enough to leave his mother, impressing on her that in his care Emlyn could have every advantage. And yet he could not deny that he wanted Nerys herself as much as he wanted his son.

The decision made, he took out a folder of figures and tried to read them, but they might as well have been written in a foreign language for all the sense they made. Snapping the folder shut, he rose to his feet. He could no longer sit in the office; he would go out into the cold crisp air and hope that it would help to clear his mind.

'Oh, Howel, I was hoping for a word with you.' Sterling stood in the doorway blocking his exit and Howel assumed a smile, concealing his impatience to be away.

'Certainly, what can I do for you?' He stood back a pace to let Sterling inside and then closed the door, expecting the matter to be one of business.

'I have an invitation for you from my wife.' Sterling smiled and shrugged. 'It's more like a royal command, actually – she wants you to come up to supper with us.' He scratched his eyebrow. 'The lovely Jenny is invited too. I think the girl is feeling more than a little neglected, not that it's any of my business of course.'

Howel nodded. 'I'll be there – indeed I am delighted to accept. It's about time I ate a civilized meal and enjoyed the company of beautiful women.'

'Good!' Sterling moved over to the desk. 'I'm very pleased with the jewellery and ornaments your brother has been making. He's more than a craftsman, he's an artist and he could go far with the right handling.'

'I do realize that,' Howel said evenly, betraying to Sterling nothing of the conflict between Ceri and himself, which was family business after all. 'I'm just off to the Ferry House now, as it happens,' he added.

'Oh well, don't let me stop you.' Sterling moved to the door. 'Give your young brother Tom my regards, will you? I still feel bad about the accident.'

'Well, don't,' Howel said quickly. 'Just because it happened in your works does not make it your responsibility.' It had been Ceri's fault, plain and simple, he thought bitterly.

'Anyway,' Sterling said, 'I can tell Mali to expect you tonight?' He smiled meaningfully. 'I am sure she will be delighted you're coming and so will Jenny – she's been like a little lost soul because she hasn't seen anything of you for some time.' He paused. 'I know she's a spoiled madam and a little tease, but she is genuinely fond of you . . .'

'Right then, see you later,' Howel agreed, deliberately not commenting on the subject of Jenny's affections.

As he left the works, he pulled up his collar against the coldness of the wind which raced in with the flow of the river from the sea. It was early for visiting and as he didn't want his father to know of his call, he skirted the river bank and moved up to the road out of sight of the ferry-boat. He would approach the house from the rear so that he would not be seen.

Snow was still falling in small flurries. Howel looked up at the sky, which was grey and heavy with no sign of lightness breaking through the clouds. There was plenty more snow up there and the town would be lucky not to be completely cut off from the surrounding villages.

He thought of Alex making his calls out in West Cross and wondered if the road through the rocks to Ram's Tor would be blocked. It seemed an age since he had been with his family, mainly through his own actions but partly because of Siona's attitude over Nerys. And who could blame the old man? It was a basic instinct to keep hold of what was yours.

Howel wondered if he would still have anything in common with his family. It was true that his brothers were not without drive and ambition. Alex, for one, was carving a comfortable niche in society for himself; his business was successful in a moderate way, thanks to his and Sarah's hard work.

And Ceri . . . Howel had the grace to realize that his brother would some day be wealthy, but only if he had the right sort of help for he was an artist without the hard-headedness that a man needed in business.

Howel recognized that he himself was very comfortably situated, now. He had not set out primarily to make money, but to assuage his ambition to make a mark on life. But what did it amount to now, when all he wanted was to hold his son in his arms?

He slipped a little on the bank behind the house and put out a hand to steady himself. The wall was rough and cold to his touch and he was reminded of his childhood when he would come in from the snow, his hands tingling painfully, and his mother would rub warmth into them with her gentle touch. What a lot had happened to him since those far-off days!

Nerys was alone in the kitchen, where the fire glowed in the grate and the brasses gleamed. She had made changes, for a good carpet had replaced the rag

429

mats on the floor and comfortable armchairs had been substituted for the old wooden ones.

She had his son to her breast and as he saw her staring down at Emlyn with all the love of motherhood in her eyes, he felt a constriction in his throat. She must have felt the coldness from the door, for she looked up and then quickly covered herself, her face flaming with colour.

'Howel! What are you doing here? You know your father would go mad if he saw you?'

'We have to talk,' he said, closing the door and leaning against it as though to bar her exit.

'We have nothing to talk about.' She wrapped the boy in a shawl and put him down in the crib, standing with hands on her hips as though daring him to touch the child.

Slowly, he moved forward. 'I'm not here to hurt anybody,' he said softly, persuasively. 'I only want to ask you to let me do what I can for my son. Can't you see you are depriving him of the finest advantages in life? He could go to the best schools, grow up to be a gentleman.'

'Oh yes, you would take him away and make what you call a gentleman of him, but what about love, Howel? Would that fine lady you are courting love him as I do? And what of the children you and she would have together? Can't you see that Emlyn would be pushed into the background? If not, you are a fool!'

He moved to touch Nerys's shoulder, to put her aside so that he could look down into the crib at his son. But then she was in his arms, he was kissing her as though he would never let her go and a blinding pain caught him as he realized how very much he loved her. He must always have loved her, ever since that first time they had been together.

'My lovely,' he murmured. 'My beautiful Nerys, why have I let you slip away from me? I've been so blind and stupid!'

He held her close and kissed her eyelids, her throat, and once again tasted the sweetness of her mouth. She was so soft in his arms, so dear to him, how *could* he have been so blind for so long?

She pushed him away fiercely. 'Howel, this is wrong and foolish. Please go, you'll only cause trouble if you stay.'

'But you love me, you can't deny it?' He would have reached for her again, but she lifted her hands as though warding him off.

'I don't know how I feel, but it makes no difference. Anyway, nothing can be changed now so go away, Howel.'

'I love you,' he said softly. 'I love you, Nerys, and I was a fool not to have seen it before.'

Her shoulders drooped. 'Well, even if you mean it – if you are not just saying the words so as to get near your son, it's too late. I'm married to Siona, I'm his wife and nothing will change that.' She stared up at him with determination in every line of her features.

'Howel, if you really do love me then walk out of that door now and leave me alone, I beg of you.'

He let out his breath on a long sigh, closing his eyes, knowing he was beaten. She was right; the only decent thing for him to do was to get out of her life and stay out. And yet he had to make one other request.

'Perhaps you will allow me to see Emlyn sometimes?' He moved to the crib and without touching his son, stared down at him, drinking in every detail of the tiny boy's face as though to impress the delicate features on his mind.

'I'll go away, Nerys,' he said, 'to London. I'll get right out of your life and give you peace of mind. But I can't give up my child entirely.'

She put her hands over her face to hide her tears, but he saw them trickle over her fingers and the pain within him was almost unbearable. He should go without another word, yet how could he give up everything without a fight? 'I'll be back,' he said softly.

He held his head high and walked stiff-backed up the bank and on to the road, hoping that the redness around his eyes would be attributed to the keen wind blowing in off the river.

* * *

Nerys sat for a long time, simply staring down at her hands. She had thought her acceptance of life without Howel was complete but now, hearing him say that he loved her, she felt confused and disturbed.

She was forced into movement at last by the crying of her son. She picked him up and held him close and with his soft hair beneath her chin, she felt near to tears. Her life was such a muddle.

By the time Siona came in for his dinner, she was more composed. 'Sit down by the fire, love,' she said in concern. 'Look, your poor hands are blue with the cold. And oh, Siona, you really shouldn't be working again, not in this weather.'

'I'm all right,' Siona said gently.'Just fetch me a hot cup of tea and I'll soon start to thaw out.' He bent over, his shoulders hunched towards the fire.

'Is there ice on the river?' Nerys poured the tea quickly and placed it on the table, where Siona took it and cradled it in his big hands as though to warm them.

'Aye, there's ice all right, but mostly at the edges of the water. One big piece damn nearly struck the boat this morning, mind, but I managed to push it away with the scull.'

Nerys felt a sense of fear that made her hands tremble. 'Oh, *cariad*, why not finish work for the day? Let the people walk down into town and cross the bridge to get to the White Rock!'

'I'd not be very popular if I did that!' Siona protested. 'Take the men almost an hour, it would, especially the older ones. Anyway, I won't be going out now until the next shift comes off work, for there are not many passengers about; most sensible folk are staying in their homes. By the way, what did Howel want?'

The casual way Siona brought his son into the conversation startled Nerys and she sat down quickly, her hands clasped in her lap.

'I was hoping you wouldn't have seen him,' she admitted, slowly, trying to read his mood from the expression in his green eyes.

'Aye, and so was he,' Siona said calmly. 'Well, what did he have to say for himself this time?'

'He just wanted to see the baby,' Nerys told him. 'I asked him to go, Siona, not to come here any more – and he won't, I promise.'

He leaned back in his chair and stared at her for a long moment in silence and she felt as if he could read her very thoughts.

'You are a good woman, Nerys, and a fine wife. I'm proud of your strength of character – that's something I've always admired. But I won't have you feeling guilty, mind. You've done nothing wrong; you didn't ask him to come here and when he did, you sent him away.'

He leaned forward, his eyes clouded. 'Saw him go I did – head held high, mind, shoulders squared – and I wanted to thrash him within an inch of his life!'

'Please, Siona, don't talk about it,' Nerys said quickly. 'He's gone and he won't come back – that's all that matters, isn't it?'

'Aye, I suppose so, girl, but folks can't help their feelings – only human nature to have feelings and nothing to be ashamed about, mind. That's my last word on the subject. Now, woman, fetch my *cawl* for I'm starving!'

Nerys ladled hot meaty soup into a bowl and brought it to him. 'I'll cut you a nice thick slice of bread,' she offered, forcing a smile. 'It won't take a minute, I wasn't expecting you back just yet.'

'No, well, I wanted to see if you were all right after Howel's visit if the truth be known.' He glanced up at her. 'I don't like to think of you upset or anything.'

She put the bread on the table and placed her arms around his shoulders, kissing his forehead lightly. 'You're a fine man, Siona Llewleyn, have I ever told you that?'

'Well, maybe, but I don't mind you saying it again,' he smiled. 'Now go away and let a man get on with his dinner, there's a good girl.'

* * *

Howel stood at the window for a long time, staring out into the snowy landscape without really seeing it, mulling over the events of the past hour. Dad was a big man in every way and he had done the right thing by Nerys, giving her and the baby the Llewelyn name. But now, by his very selflessness, dad had bound Nerys even more closely to him and she would remain with him to the bitter end.

Howel was moved by Nerys's loyalty to Siona. Come to think of it, there had been a great deal more than loyalty in her eyes when she spoke of him – there had been love.

He returned to his desk and attempted to work, but the figures kept blurring before his eyes. He would have to do the decent thing and assure Nerys that he would leave her alone in the future, but he hoped he would be allowed to visit the Ferry House from time to time, to see his brothers and of course his son.

When Sterling came into the office wearing his coat and hat and ready to leave, Howel was still sitting staring at the same page of figures.

'See you later then? Don't forget, we'll be expecting you.' Sterling moved closer into the room, frowning a little. 'Is anything wrong, Howel? You look a little worried.'

434

'No, it's nothing that talking about will help but thank you, Sterling. I shall be glad of company tonight.'

And yet later, when he entered the brightly-lit hallway of Sterling's home, he knew at once that he should not have come. The small talk seemed trivial in the light of the events of the afternoon and even the deliciously cooked food seemed to stick in his throat. All he could think of was the look in Nerys's eyes when she had spoken about dad – the warmth there which he had never seen before.

Jenny seemed to be her usual brilliant self; her eyes shone with mischief and her skin radiated good health. And yet when he thought of Nerys with her shadowed eyes and pale, drawn little face, he knew there was no one who could hold a candle to her.

'Jenny, we must talk,' he whispered and she smiled up at him, taking his arm, so sure of herself that he almost felt sorry for her.

'I mean to take Howel to see the new winter roses in the conservatory,' she said coquettishly. 'Don't make a face at me, Sterling, I'm determined that tonight you are not going to talk about work!'

When they were alone, Howel put his hands on her shoulders and looked down at her pityingly. 'I'm saying goodbye to you, Jenny,' he said. 'Whatever there was between us is over, I'm sorry.'

She stared at him as though she did not believe him, but after a moment she realized he was deadly serious and drew away from him, dignity and pride warring with tears of pain and humiliation.

'Very well, there's no more to say, then.' She turned from him and moved elegantly back towards the sounds of laughter from the drawing room. 'Goodbye, Howel, my love,' she whispered.

CHAPTER THIRTY-TWO

The ice and snow continued to grip Sweyn's Eye with
deathly fingers, keeping people within the warmth and
protection of their houses. A biting north-easterly wind
swept the waves against the twin piers of the docks,
booming and rushing between the wooden struts as
though to destroy them. The ferry-boat lay against the
flight of wooden steps, buffeted by the rushing river as
though it was nothing more substantial than a cork
from a bottle. And today it would not be taken out, for
the family were celebrating Siona's birthday.

Within the Ferry House there was an air of peace and
tranquillity. A bright fire burned in the grate and the
two boys sat quietly on the rag mat in the glow of the
flames. Tom and Will were both absent from school,
suffering with winter colds which Nerys feared might
turn to fevers if neglected. Tom was playing with a
piece of wire, twisting it into various intricate shapes,
while Will lay on his stomach engrossed in the book he
was reading.

Nerys boiled the kettle and poured hot water on to
the jug filled with sliced lemons, adding a little honey
to sweeten the drink. She had carefully stored the
precious lemons since summer, keeping them in a cool
cloth beneath the pantry shelf, knowing she might have
to use them for just such an eventuality as this.

Siona came into the house on a blast of cold wind,
carrying an armful of logs. He set them down beside the
fire and carefully criss-crossed some of the pieces of
wood in a nest over the flames. Then he added the coal

436

in large chunks of gleaming blackness, finally filling in the gaps with the small duff which would keep the fire burning for hours.

'*Duw*, something smells good!' he said, looking up from his task as Nerys handed him the first cupful of lemon water.

'Wash your hands before you drink and remember – you're cheating, mind, for you haven't got a cold!'

Smiling she turned to the boys. 'Tom, here's yours; it's a bit full so be careful. Will, pay attention now and don't spill it; it's very hot.'

Nerys took a little of the lemon water for herself and sat beside the crib, looking down at the baby while she drank. He was a good child and even when awake did not often cry for attention.

She leaned over him, loving him with all her being, grateful to Howel for at least he had given her a beautiful son.

'What does "institution" mean, Nerys?' Will asked, looking up from the book he was reading. 'It says by here that the boy was wicked and was put into an institution for his sins.'

'Oh, I suppose it means the workhouse, Will.' Nerys smiled at him. 'You know, just like Tawe Lodge up on the hill.' She leaned forward. 'And what wickedness did the boy in the story do to be given such punishment?'

'He stole a loaf of bread to give to his starving sister!' Will's eyes were wide; he was not much younger in years than Tom, Nerys mused, but so much younger in his ways.

'Well, that seems a little harsh,' Nerys said and Siona, who was drinking deeply from his cup and coughing a little at the sharpness of the drink, looked over his shoulder.

'You don't want to believe all the nonsense written in those books, mind,' he said gruffly. 'They're meant as a sort of warning to you not to do wrong, that's all.'

Nerys subsided in her chair, only half listening to the conversation going on around her. She had forced herself not to think too deeply about the events of the past days, hoping that by now Siona would have forgotten Howel's visit and put the whole thing out of his mind. She wanted nothing to spoil the harmony of life in the Ferry House, but her husband's silences and brooding looks told her that he was still troubled.

She glanced now at Siona who looked well and strong, his shoulders straight as he sat in his chair. He had recovered fully from his sickness, but there was a sadness that lingered in his green eyes.

Yet sitting opposite him in the warmth of the kitchen, it was difficult to believe Siona had any cause to worry at all. He was a fine, handsome man and still had the strength of muscle, the feeling of energy which had always characterized him. She wondered what was going on in his mind – did he think she still pined for Howel? And *did* she? She could not have explained her feelings even to herself; all she knew was that when she was with Siona at their own fireside, she was happy.

He sensed her look and his eyes, green and warm, met hers. She smiled and fingered the opal pendant that she had worn since he gave it to her for Christmas.

'A penny for them,' Siona offered, leaning forward with his face very close to hers.

'My thoughts are worth more than a penny, I'll have you know,' she replied. 'I was day-dreaming, remembering how handsome you look in the summer sun and wishing this cold winter was over.'

'Aye, winter is a time of darkness when all ills are magnified,' Siona said. 'But remember, it is a time also of new beginnings when the seeds are stirring beneath the ground, so there's no need to be downhearted, righto?'

'How about some more lemon?' Nerys asked quickly, afraid he would see her tears. Could she begin anew; could she ever put her past mistakes behind her; would Howel let her?

438

The baby began to cry and she lifted him, putting him to her breast unselfconscious of the presence of the boys, for they were well used to the sight of a baby suckling. As she looked into her son's face and saw the green glint of his eyes, she knew she held in her arms as much happiness as anyone deserved.

A knocking on the door startled her. She draped a shawl over her shoulder to conceal her breast and Siona moved quickly from his chair, for it was too cold to keep folks on the doorstep.

'Ceri and Mona, there's good to see you – come on inside,' Siona said heartily. 'What on earth brings you two out on a day like this?'

Ceri shook the snow from his coat. 'Your birthday, of course, dad. Didn't think we'd forget, did you?' He seated himself next to his father. 'I wanted to see you,' he was saying quietly, 'to assure myself that you're all right, but I needn't have worried – you're obviously fighting fit again!'

'*Duw*, a little fever doesn't bother me. I'm the same as I always was, good for years yet.' Siona smiled. 'But you shouldn't have come out in this weather, birthday or not. You and Mona will take sick next and then a fine pickle you'll be in!'

'Siona's right,' Nerys said. 'Take off your damp coat, Mona, and while you're at it, put the kettle on for some tea, if you don't mind.'

Mona smiled. 'Mind? Of course I don't mind; part of this household, I am, don't forget!'

As the two women sat close together and talked quietly, Mona looked shyly at Nerys and twisted a piece of hair between her fingers.

'You don't think I'm awful going to live with Ceri, do you?' she asked softly. 'I mean, I was Alex's girl first and loved him fine, I did, even though he was married. But Ceri is good to me, he gives me comfort; is it wrong of me to accept what's kindly offered?'

'Wrong? I don't think wrong comes into it. You do

439

what you want to do and forget other people's opinions.'

'I know,' said Mona, 'but what you think is important to me, for I can talk to you as I can to no one else.'

'Well, then, I think that you and Ceri look content with each other; you have a certain closeness . . . I feel you will find happiness together, but that's up to you – I'm no prophet, mind,' Nerys laughed.

'Aye, we were lucky to find each other.' Mona glanced across the room at Ceri and seeing the look, he winked at her.

She winked back and then smiled as she caught Siona's eye on her. 'He looks well again now,' she said to Nerys.

'Yes, Siona's been over the fever for ages now – strong man, is my husband, and not one for lying in his bed.' She saw Mona's smug look and realized that there was a world of pride in her voice when she spoke of Siona.

'Don't give me that "told you so" look,' she said. 'It's just that I'm learning a bit of sense at last.'

'Well, I should think so,' Mona agreed, her eyes full of laughter. 'That's a fine man you've got there, and there's half the town of Sweyn's Eye willing to take him on if you don't want him.'

A loud thumping at the door startled Nerys. It swung open, letting in a gust of cold air and Big Eddie stood on the threshold, his face grimed with dust.

'I've brought you a bag of coal off the cart,' he said. 'I'll just shove it in the shed for you – it's a sort of birthday present, dad, but I'll want something to eat for my troubles, mind!'

Nerys put the baby into the crib and made a wry face at Mona. 'It looks as if you and me will be rather busy, doesn't it? I thought I was going to have a quiet day!'

Eddie's booming voice seemed to fill the kitchen as he took up a sheet of newspaper and placed it carefully on one of the armchairs to protect the covers from coal-dust before sitting down.

'Come on, Nerys girl, I could eat a scabby horse between two carts!' he said grinning. '*Duw*, have I been away from this house so long that you've forgotten about my appetite, then?'

'Don't keep on, Eddie,' Nerys chided in mock reproof. 'I'll get out the ham and make a big mound of sandwiches – will that do you?'

'Do me fine, girl,' Eddie said. 'And remember, there's plenty more coal where that came from.' He was grinning. 'Now that I'm partner with Berti-No-Legs, I can pay back a little of what I owe my family.'

'Oh, that's wonderful news,' Nerys said, kissing Eddie's cheek. 'I'm sure you deserve it, you working so hard on the coal round.'

'*Duw*,' Siona said hoarsely, 'I'm proud of you, boy. Always knew you'd make good, I did, mind.' He coughed to hide his embarrassment. 'It's like a madhouse in by here. I'd forgotten what it's like having a big family around – used to a bit of peace now, I am.'

Nerys held the hard pat of frozen butter to the fire and watched it begin to melt. She felt strangely happy, feeling for once that she was the hub of the house, that she really belonged.

It was no surprise to her when a few moments later, Alex arrived; it was obvious that the brothers had planned the whole thing. Snow clung like a cloak around Alex's shoulders and clutched in his arms was a huge box which he set down on the table with a sigh of relief.

'*Daro!*' he exclaimed. 'There's a job I've had getting up here from West Cross.' He took off his coat and shook off the snow which fell melting to the ground. 'Been a tram derailed, see, up on the Neath road; nothing can get past that way.'

His brows were edged with snow and he brushed it away as it began to melt like tears running down his face. 'I knew I wouldn't see you at the Hafod bank, dad, guessed you'd have the day off, so I went into town and round the long way.'

Nerys moved to stand near the table at Mona's side and felt the girl grow tense. She saw that Mona's face was flushed as she looked at Alex and it was clear that she still felt something for him, though their affair had been over a long time ago.

Ceri must have understood a little of what Mona was feeling, for he put his arm around her waist and she smiled up at him gratefully as he nuzzled his lips against her cheek.

'Come on, Alex,' Nerys said warmly. 'Grab a bite to eat while you can, for I swear Big Eddie is going to demolish the lot!'

As she handed round the food, Nerys couldn't help thinking that the only one of Siona's sons who wasn't in the house this morning was Howel . . .

Alex was busy taking groceries out of a box, storing them away in the pantry – butter, cheese, even potatoes without a word about payment.

'Funny birthday present, dad,' he said, 'but I haven't got time to go shopping and food is always welcome, isn't it?' Nerys felt her vision blur. They were good boys, these Llewelyns, all of them proud of their father, and she wondered if his recent sickness had made Siona's sons more aware of how dear he was to them.

Ceri of course was always a little cooler than the rest of the boys; there was still a barrier between him and his father caused by long-standing differences, mainly over Howel. She pushed the thought away quickly, not wanting to trouble her mind with problems . . . not today, on Siona's birthday.

Then she saw him move towards Ceri and rest a hand on his shoulder and the two men smiled, a conciliatory smile which said much more than words could ever do.

Nerys tried to guess how Siona must be feeling about Howel's absence. Did he wonder, as she did, if Howel would suddenly come to the Ferry House and shatter the mood of celebration? But she saw in his face only love and gratitude, and knew then that he was happy with his family around him and that he chose not to think about his eldest son.

When they were alone, she decided, they would talk, really talk. She wanted to tell him that she would be loyal to him always, that she cared for him very much indeed, even if her emotions were thrown into confusion whenever she thought too much about Howel.

There was a sudden silence, as happens sometimes when a crowd of people come together. Nerys looked at Siona and, meeting her eyes, he smiled and there was such a wealth of love and pride in him as to make her feel small and humble.

She was about to speak, to move forward with the plate of sandwiches, but she was stopped dead in her tracks.

The noise that shook the Ferry House was like a crack of thunder, crashing over the chimneys, reverberating through the kitchen so that the very walls seemed to tremble.

'Christ!' Siona said, rising to his feeet. 'Sounds as though there's been an accident on the river.'

He rushed to the door and even from where she stood behind him, Nerys could see the thick smoke billowing towards the banks.

'My God, it looks as if there's been a collision. See, the *Trusty* is holed by a huge piece of ice, crippled she is! *Duw*, her boilers have gone up too, by the look of it.'

'Good God!' Alex exclaimed softly, fearfully. 'Howel is going out on the *Trusty* today, I was only talking to him about it last night.'

Siona pulled on his coat and scarf. 'Eddie, Ceri and

you too, Alex, come with me. There'll be injured to fetch out of the river and we must move fast; the water's freezing.

Nerys grasped his arm. She was shaking with fear, frightened that Howel might be on the wrecked tug and at the same time fearful that Siona and the boys might come to harm.

'Please don't go, Siona,' she begged, her voice trembling. 'Let someone else help in the rescue.' She clung to him tightly, her knuckles gleaming white, but slowly he uncurled her fingers and kissed them gently.

'I've got to go, love. The river has been my life, those men out there are my mates and my son might just be with them. I can't stand by and do nothing – you must see that, lovely girl.'

He pointed to the rushing, freezing water. 'Look, *cariad*, some of the other tugs are already going over to the *Trusty* to fetch off the injured. I've got to be there too.' He turned to his younger sons. 'You, Tom and Will, look after Nerys and the baby, mind!'

He kissed her cheek and without another word, hurried away. Then he was alongside his sons, struggling to launch the ferry-boat in the swirling icy river.

Nerys stared after them as they pushed out into the wash of the water and she had never been so frightened in all her life.

'Come on,' Mona said. 'Let's get the kettle on to boil. I'll stir up the flames. Will, you get the tea-pot ready, the biggest one you can find.'

Nerys scarcely heard her; she was drawing on her boots, lacing them up with sudden determination.

'Get me the first-aid box, Tom, and some blankets – there's a good boy.' She turned to Mona. 'Keep an eye on the baby for me; I might be needed down on the bank – at least I can look after the ones who are not too badly injured.'

444

Mona didn't argue. 'Right, then. Wrap up warm, mind, and don't worry about the youngsters. They'll be all right by here with me.'

Nerys had not realized how cold it would be beside the river, for the wind whipped against the waves and sent sprays of icy water against the snow-bound bank.

The men began to gather, old men who had no work and the young boys who should have been at school. A patch of ground was cleared of snow and a fire lit, the acrid smoke rearing up into the air on the crackling sound of sticks catching alight.

The river was alive with activity as tugs and rowboats intercrossed each other with seeming lack of direction, while above the crippled vessel a pall of smoke hung in the air.

'Oh, Siona!' Nerys breathed and strained to see the figures which were being put into boats and brought across from the burning, crippled tug. But she could not identify anyone, for the smoke was too thick and black.

After what seemed an eternity, the first of the walking injured were being put ashore and Nerys, recognizing one of them, moved forward eagerly.

'Gareth Owen, are you all right?' she asked, wrapping a blanket round the shaken foreman of the lead works. 'Were you on board the *Trusty*?'

'Aye, girl, a contingent of us from the works were out, see, on business. Didn't reckon on this lot, though.' He rubbed his wet face. 'Luckily I'm not too badly hurt – a bit of a cut on my arm but no burns, thank God!' He sat down heavily on the ground and one of the old men handed him a tot of brandy.

'Gareth, was Howel on the tug?' Nerys asked, her mouth dry with fear as she waited for a reply. Gareth shook his head.

'Yes, he was, love, but I don't know what happened to him. The accident was so sudden, there was just this terrific noise and confusion and then I was in the water.'

Nerys bit her lip, watching as some of the injured were being taken down the river straight to hospital. She moved as near the water's edge as she dared and stared out at the maze of river craft, straining her eyes as she tried to distinguish the ferry-boat from the confusion of vessels.

Her breath caught in her throat as she saw a huddle of men crouched in the well of the overcrowded ferry-boat which was pulling across the river, struggling towards the shore. She could see that Siona was sculling furiously, having difficulty in avoiding debris that was being tossed down river from the stricken ship.

Nerys tried to identify the passengers, but could not. She cried out, her hand to her mouth as a huge piece of jagged ice hit the ferry-boat broadside. The boat rocked uncontrollably for a moment, like a toy on the belligerent waves. Then she screamed as she saw Siona lose control, his scull floating away uselessly in the strong current.

For a moment, nothing seemed to happen and then the boat was pounded again by the ice. Like a slow, huge monster, the boat turned over and the men were washed into the freezing water.

Nerys thought she cried out, but no sound came from her lips. She would have run into the river, but restraining arms held her back.

Ceri was the first to surface. He was dragged out of the river and he crawled shivering towards the fire, a streak of blood across his forehead. Behind him were some of the crew brought in from the *Trusty*; they were smoke-blackened but otherwise appeared to be unhurt.

Nerys moved forward, galvanized into life as Big Eddie staggered up the bank with Alex in his arms. Eddie lowered his brother to the ground and then, satisfied that the boy was unhurt, he turned and lumbered back towards the river.

'Dad!' he called frantically, but his voice was lost in the noise and confusion.

'Oh, God, let Siona be safe,' Nerys murmured, wrapping a blanket around Alex's shivering body. He opened his eyes and looked up at her. 'Dad, where's dad? Is he all right?' he whispered, but Nerys could only shake her head.

She stared at the river, at the dark icy water, and willed Siona to rise from its depths. She remembered how she had met him, how she had almost drowned and Siona it was who had saved her. A hard knot of pain lay like a stone within her and she feared for the life of the man who had given her love and comfort.

'Siona, please come back to me,' she said, unaware that she was speaking out loud.

As if in answer to her pleas, a figure rose from the river, water cascading from him as he staggered forward bent double under the weight of the man lying limply on his shoulder. Nerys moved as though in a dream, watching the men fall to the ground, one of them lying still against the frozen earth as trembling, she moved nearer.

She fell to her knees, fear cold within her. Howel was still and lifeless; his face looked frozen as though carved out of stone.

'Siona!' she cried, crawling over the hard snow, not feeling the cold or the cut of the ice against her knees. She was uttering his name over and over again as though, by saying it aloud, it would make him safe.

Siona lay face up, his green eyes clear as a morning stream. He reached out to her, his big chest heaving as he gasped for air.

'Oh, Siona, thank God you're safe!' She put her cheek against his. 'I love you so much,' she said softly as he lay before her with water in his hair. 'Only when I thought you were gone from me did I realize that you mean everything to me.'

They clung together for a long moment and she felt his heart beat against hers as though it was within her own body.

'Howel!' He struggled to sit up and turned to look . . . seeing the silent form being covered with a blanket, he closed his eyes in pain.

'You did all you could, dad,' Ceri was suddenly beside him, slipping an arm beneath his shoulders and helping him to his feet. 'You risked your life for our Howel, dad, and I'm proud of you. No man could have done more!'

Ceri turned away, his eyes brimming with tears, and called out to his brothers to help him fetch Howel home. Big Eddie and Alex responded instantly and the blanket-covered figure was laid reverently on a makeshift stretcher.

Nerys turned to Siona and put her shoulder beneath his. He looked down at her with tears in his eyes and, swallowing her own, she looked into his face.

'Don't grieve, Siona,' she said shakily. 'In the end, in spite of everything,. you did all you could to save Howel. Remember what you said to me about winter being a time of ills, but also a time for new beginnings? It will be true for us, I promise.'

She leaned her head against his shoulder. 'I know it's wicked, but all I wanted was for you to come out of the water safe and sound. I couldn't think about anyone else.'

He drew her to him and they clung together in silence. Feeling tears on her cheek Nerys could not tell if they were Siona's or her own. All she knew was that her heart was aching with thankfulness that this man, her love, was here in her arms.

They walked together towards the welcoming light from the doorway of the Ferry House, clinging tightly to each other. Behind them the river moved ceaselessly down to the sea.

Nerys glanced back at the darkness of the water, sighing raggedly. The river was sometimes cruel and it had taken many lives. But today the river had relented, had given back her husband, the man she loved most in all the world . . . and even as she wept, she knew that these were tears of gratitude.

THE END